K.D. Richards is a native of the Washington, DC, area, who now lives outside Toronto with her husband and two sons. You can find her at kdrichardsbooks.com

A true Renaissance woman, **Deborah Fletcher Mello** finds joy in crafting unique story lines and memorable characters. She's received accolades from several publications, including *Publishers Weekly*, *Library Journal* and *RT Book Reviews*. Born and raised in Connecticut, Deborah now considers home to be wherever the moment moves her.

SHIELDING HER SON

K.D. RICHARDS

COLTON'S SECRET SABOTAGE

DEBORAH FLETCHER MELLO

MILLS & BOON

First Published in Great Britain 2022
by Mills & Boon, an imprint of HarperCollins*Publishers* Ltd
1 London Bridge Street, London, SE1 9GF

www.harpercollins.co.uk

HarperCollins*Publishers*
1st Floor, Watermarque Building,
Ringsend Road, Dublin 4, Ireland

Shielding Her Son © 2022 Kia Dennis
Colton's Secret Sabotage © 2022 Harlequin Enterprises ULC

Special thanks and acknowledgement are given to Deborah Fletcher Mello
for her contribution to *The Coltons of Colorado* series.

ISBN: 978-0-263-30351-3

0722

MIX
Paper from
responsible sources
FSC™ C007454

This book is produced from independently certified FSC™
paper to ensure responsible forest management.

For more information visit: www.harpercollins.co.uk/green

Printed and Bound in Spain using 100% Renewable electricity at
CPI Black Print, Barcelona

SHIELDING
HER SON

K.D. RICHARDS

To Justin

Chapter One

"Just a little farther," Erika Powell encouraged, shoot-ing a glance over her shoulder. Daisy Hargrove, the town librarian and the closest thing Erika had to a best friend, followed several paces behind Erika.

"Ugh. You said that half a mile ago. My legs are ready to give out." Daisy rubbed her back through her designer fleece, emphasizing her point.

Erika ignored her friend's complaints. Daisy had been all for adding hiking to their regular exercise routine when Erika had suggested it in April, but as summer gave way to autumn and then a new year, her enthusiasm for the great outdoors had waned.

In fairness, they'd never walked this far or this long before, but a restlessness had settled over Erika sev-eral days ago that she hadn't been able to shake. She'd hoped a nice long hike might help settle her nerves, but it hadn't worked. Marching ahead anyway, she traversed the packed dirt path that cut through the twenty-seven acre plot of land she'd purchased two years earlier.

"I thought you wanted to lose ten pounds before spring," Erika reminded her friend.

"I do," Daisy huffed. "But I didn't plan to lose them all in one day." She stopped, hunching over with her hands on her knees.

Erika did a one-eighty, marching in place so her heart rate wouldn't slow and she could see her friend. Daisy's alabaster skin was flushed pink and a bead of sweat trickled from under the wool cap she wore despite the frosty January air. She and Daisy put truth to the saying "opposites attract" in almost every way. Daisy was twenty-nine, petite with a blond bob, and eyes as blue as a cloudless sky. A stark contrast to Erika's five-foot-ten slim, muscled frame and brown skin. And those were just the physical differences. Daisy was gregarious and outgoing, but preferred to fill her down time indoors reading, a sought-after characteristic in a town librarian. Erika would much rather spend what little free time she had—after caring for her ten-year-old son, Marcus, and converting the large farmhouse they lived in into a bed-and-breakfast—exploring out among nature.

"Come on. The bluff is just up ahead, and the view is so worth it," Erika cajoled. "This is one place that's definitely going to be on the list of tours I offer my guests."

Erika couldn't stop a tiny thrill of excitement coursing through her when she thought about the B&B. Her B&B. Years of scrimping and saving, first to purchase the seven-bedroom, four-bathroom farmhouse just east of downtown Carling Lake were finally going to pay off.

Daisy started walking again. "I haven't seen Sam's guys working on the house lately. How are the renovations going?"

Erika felt her lips twist into a frown.

Daisy's brows rose. "Uh-oh. That face. What happened?"

Erika blew out a heavy sigh. As excited about the B&B as she was, the renovations were another story.

"Sam's guys haven't shown up to work on the house for a few days now. And Sam hasn't been answering my calls."

Daisy waved away her hand. "Oh, well, you know contractors. Sam's pretty reliable, though. I wouldn't worry."

"All I do is worry lately. Starting the B&B is like having another child." Erika kicked a rock on the dirt path. It rolled ahead of her. "The B&B's location, on the Carling Mountain, surrounded by nature, literally steps away from the lake, is idyllic. And I'm hoping it leads some customers to choose Carling Mountain B&B over Ellis Hanes's place in town."

Daisy made a face as if she'd smelled something foul. "Is Ellis still giving you a hard time?"

"Is grass green?" Erika rolled her eyes and kicked the rock again, this time harder, sending it skittering into the tall brush along the sides of the trail. "He's been telling anyone who'll listen that my property isn't zoned for a B&B."

Daisy snorted. "Now I know that's a lie. You and I went through the town records ourselves."

To save attorney's fees, Erika had done her own research into area zoning, local business regulations, variances and licenses. The former library had been of little help. But Daisy's arrival a year ago had been a big boost to the fact-finding effort. Daisy had thrown herself into helping Erika with her research, calling the county and state authorities and facilitating interlibrary loan requests from other area libraries.

"The Dellosas ran their B&B out of your farmhouse for twenty-eight years," Daisy said with a shake of her head. "The family that bought it from them used it as a private residence, but that wouldn't change the zoning."

Erika exhaled. "I know. I even had Warren McClaine look into it and he said the same thing." Warren McClaine, like his father and grandfather, was the sole attorney with a practice in town. "I think Hanes was only trying to get a rise out of me."

"Sounds like something that weasel would do. Don't worry." Daisy patted Erika's shoulder. "Nobody listens to Ellis Hanes."

"You haven't lived in Carling Lake that long." Word of mouth was important to any business in a small town and plenty of people in Carling Lake not only listened to Ellis Hanes, they were swayed by his opinion. The Hanes family was one of the town's oldest and most distinguished families. The Carling Lake community was supportive, but there was still the small-town hierarchy to deal with. Their hotel and B&B bookended the town on either end and employed a significant number of residents. Although she'd lived in Carling Lake for ten years, to many residents, she was still a newcomer. An outsider.

Not that she minded. A bit of distance between her and her neighbors suited her just fine. She'd come to Carling Lake looking for a fresh start. A place where nobody would recognize her or ask too many questions about her past, and she'd found that. She was friendly with everyone, but only had a handful of people she'd call friends. And even they didn't really know who she was.

And she planned to keep it that way. It was the only way she knew to keep Marcus safe.

"Are we there yet?" Daisy's whine snapped Erika out of her morass. She chuckled.

Daisy was one of the handful of people Erika counted as friends. During the hours spent at the library researching zoning and hospitality regulations, she and Daisy had hit it off. Or to be more exact, Daisy had decided they were going to be friends, and Erika would soon learn there wasn't much that Daisy wanted that Daisy didn't get. If Erika were being honest with herself, she'd needed a friend. A real friend, not one of Marcus's friend's mothers, who'd engage in polite small talk while the kids had a playdate, but someone that was hers and hers alone.

She'd shared more about her life before Carling Lake with Daisy than with anyone else in the world. Not enough for Daisy to put the pieces together and figure out who she really was, but she hadn't wanted to outright lie to her only friend in town. *Obfuscate* was a better word to describe it. If Daisy noticed Erika's evasions, she never mentioned it.

"Just around this bend," Erika said, leading the way to one of her favorite spots.

She inhaled, taking in the smell of pine and wet grass, which was as invigorating as a cup of hot coffee in the morning. Birds called to each other and some distance away she heard the faint sound of a branch snapping under the footstep of an animal far larger than a bird. A black squirrel scampered across the well-worn dirt path in front of her. A crow circled overhead. The forest burst with life and, aside from being with Marcus, there was nowhere Erika would rather be.

The path curved, and a gully came into view, feet away. Whatever water had created the deep ravine had ceased to flow long before she'd purchased the property. But the rope bridge someone had strewn from one side of the gully to the other remained, for which Erika was grateful. If it hadn't been there, she may have never seen the view from the bluff on the other side. As far as she was concerned, it was as close to heaven on earth as she was likely to find.

Daisy huffed her way to Erika's side. "Okay, what is it you dragged me all the way up here to see?"

"This." Erika spread her arms wide, feeling as if she could almost wrap them around the forest.

One of Daisy's eyebrows rose in a sharp arc. "A dried-out gully?"

"No. Not the gully. The view. Come." Erika moved toward the rope bridge. "It's better on the other side."

Daisy eyed the wood slats with undisguised suspicion. "Are you sure that thing is safe?"

"Of course." Erika threw the words over her shoulder as she started across. "I come out here a couple of times a week."

The bridge swayed in answer as the wooden boards creaked under her feet.

Erika glanced back, looking to make sure Daisy was following, but a sharp cracking sound had her head snapping back around.

The walkway in front of her fell away.

Instinctively, she reached out for the rope beside her, but her hands only skimmed it before it disappeared. Her legs scissored, desperate to find solid ground. A scream tore from her throat.

And then she was falling, her slim form cutting through the air like a knife.

She felt the impact of her body meeting the gully's floor, but what she'd remember when she finally regained consciousness was the searing flash of pain that ricocheted through her skull just before the darkness descended.

Chapter Two

James West wrapped his hands around his second cup of coffee for the morning. Tucking his scarf into the collar of his fleece, he stepped onto the back porch of the small, rented cabin and drew in a deep breath. As he had the past five mornings since arriving in Carling Lake, he'd driven into town before the sun rose over the mountains and had breakfast at the diner, but he'd grown fond of lingering over a second cup of joe and watching nature greet a new day.

It was a morning routine that he thought he could get used to, even if he wasn't thrilled by the reason he was in Carling Lake. He'd known working for his family's security and private investigation firm was only a temporary career move when he'd taken the job after leaving the military. But his current assignment, essentially spying on Erika Powell, the single mom who owned the farmhouse next door to his rental, left an unpleasant taste in his mouth. That he'd felt an instant attraction to Erika the moment he'd laid eyes on her. Well, that potentially posed a different problem.

He leaned against the porch railing and watched the sun finish climbing over the mountains. A flash of something moved in the trees beyond the yard. A woman bolted out of the woods.

James recognized her as Daisy Hargrove, the town librarian and, based on the frequency of her visits to Erika's house, a friend of his neighbor. He also recognized the expression on her face. Fear.

The woman started for Erika's house but pivoted his way when she caught sight of him. James set his coffee down and hopped over the porch railing, meeting the woman in the middle of the backyard.

"Help me, please," she rasped, her breathing labored from running.

James reached out a hand, steadying her while scanning the tree line for threats. "Come on, let's get you inside." He wasn't sure what was going on, but she was frightened and, if there was a threat, they were both sitting ducks out in the open like this.

The woman gripped his arm, stopping him from leading her inside. "No. We have to help Erika. The bridge over the ravine fell while she was on it. She's hurt. I couldn't get cell service, but she's not moving. She didn't answer me when I called out to her."

James had come across the ravine and the rope bridge the woman was referring to on one of his hikes through the forest. The drop was at least six or seven feet onto packed ground below.

James stepped away from the woman and toward the trees. "Call an ambulance. You can use the landline in my cabin. Then stay here so you can direct the EMTs to the gully."

He plunged into the woods at a run.

The gully was approximately a ten-minute hike from the cabin, but at a run, he made it in less than half that time.

The posts that had anchored the bridge on either

side of the ravine still stood, but there was no bridge between them.

James's gaze swept down and he sucked in a sharp breath. Erika lay sprawled on the ground below.

"Erika," he shouted, hoping for a response but not expecting one. His pulse raced. She remained deathly still and unresponsive.

James navigated down the side of the ravine as quickly as he could without tumbling down himself. Her body was angled away from him, but he didn't see any sign of her breathing.

He reached beneath her coat collar and pressed two fingers to her neck.

Relief flooded through him when he found a weak but steady beat there.

"Erika, can you hear me? Come on, open your eyes now."

Still no response.

He took stock of her potential injuries. Her light brown skin was sallow and blood matted the hair at her temple, the splatter on the rock next to her head revealing the cause.

He pulled his scarf from around his neck and pressed it to her wound. "Help is on the way."

He hoped he wasn't lying to her. An impact hard enough to draw blood and cause unconsciousness wasn't good. She needed medical attention now. His cell was in his back pocket, but he struggled to get service in the cabin, so it did not surprise him when he, like Daisy, failed to get a signal.

The end of the rope from the bridge caught his eye. He slanted toward it, careful not to touch it. Only a small part of the thick rope's edge was frayed. Most of the end was even.

As if a sharp blade of some sort had cut almost all of the way through it.

The sound of footsteps and voices drew James's attention to the top of the ravine.

"Here. She's down here," James called up the hill.

A man came into view, his bright orange skullcap marking him as an EMT.

James shifted his gaze back to Erika. "Hang in there. You're going to be alright. Help is here now."

Stepping back so the EMTs could take over, he studied the fallen bridge more closely. One end of the broken piece looked slightly frayed, but most of the fibers had smooth ends as if they had been sliced through as opposed to fraying over time.

James's senses buzzed, a feeling he'd learned not to ignore after four tours in Afghanistan. There was a chance, a good one if his gut was correct, that Erika's fall wasn't merely an accident.

He took several pictures with his phone and then hurried to help the EMTs carry the backboard Erika now rested on.

At the top of the ravine, the EMT strapped the backboard to a gurney and rushed to get back to the trail where James assumed they'd parked the ambulance. A question bothered him as he jogged behind the EMTs, anxious to get back to his place and follow them to the county hospital.

Had it just been Erika's bad fortune to be the person crossing the bridge when it gave out or had someone rigged it intending for her to fall?

Chapter Three

Erika's eyelids felt like lead, but she forced them open to find harsh fluorescent overhead lighting beating down on her. She pressed them closed and groaned again.

A rustling sound came from her right, and Daisy's gardenia-scented perfume wafted under her nose. "Erika? You're in the hospital. You're going to be alright but you took a nasty fall."

The memory of walking onto the bridge and the feeling of abject panic when she no longer felt the wooden slats beneath her feet came rushing back. The monitor next to her bed beeped faster.

"Everything is going to be okay." Sheriff Lance Webb's voice prompted Erika to open her eyes again.

A nurse pushed through the room door. "Ah, you're awake. Dr. Blackwell will be glad to hear it." The nurse pulled the blood pressure cuff from the hook on the wall and wrapped it around Erika's arm. "How's your head?" The nurse tapped Erika's stats into the tablet she'd entered the room with.

"Like the Penn State marching band is on the field."

The nurse chuckled and tucked her tablet back under her arm. "How about I get you some ibuprofen for that?"

"Yes, please. Thank you."

Erika turned back to Daisy and Lance once the nurse left. "How long have I been unconscious?"

"You regained consciousness not long after they got you to the hospital," Lance answered. At six foot three, trim, well-muscled with a roguish smile, the town sheriff cut an impressive figure that had earned him a spot as one of the town's most eligible bachelors. Lance's famous grin was nowhere to be seen at the moment, though. "The doctor gave you a sedative, so you'd rest. You've been out for a few hours."

"A few hours?" Panic sparked in her chest. "What time is it? I have to meet Marcus when school lets out."

"Don't worry about that, honey," Daisy said, covering Erika's hand with her own.

"Clarke has already agreed to get Marcus from school this afternoon when he picks up Devin," Lance said. "Marcus and Devin can have a sleepover tonight and Bridges will drop them both off at school tomorrow."

Deputy Clarke Bridges and his husband, Steve Sanchez, were parents to Marcus's best friend Devin and often helped her out with Marcus—picking up, dropping off or babysitting when needed.

"The school won't let you take Marcus unless I give them permission." Erika angled her body to reach for the phone on the bedside table. A sharp pain slammed through her head and she fell back against the pillows.

"Don't move," Lance barked out. "I called the school and explained what happened. It wasn't a problem. The doctor wants to observe you overnight."

She may have spent more time with Daisy over the last year, but Lance held the mantle of being the first friend she'd made after moving to Carling Lake.

Lance had been a deputy then and somewhat new

to Carling Lake himself. His recent election as Carling Lake's first Black sheriff hadn't pleased everyone in town. There'd been a spike of vandalism and a rumored illegal gambling ring had led to some rumblings about his stewardship. She knew Lance was under a great deal of stress at the moment and regretted adding to his burden.

"I don't want to stay in the hospital overnight. Marcus will worry." It had been just the two of them for all of Marcus's life. Even though he was only ten, he was fiercely protective of her, and she of him.

Daisy reached for her hand and squeezed. "Marcus is fine. You can call him later."

"The doctors don't think you have a concussion, but you took a nasty fall. You should rest. And not worry." The voice was deep, gravelly and unfamiliar.

Erika shifted her gaze to the other side of the room where the comment had come from. Her new neighbor leaned against the windowsill. She had no idea why he was there. "I…ah, I mean, Mr.…."

The nurse chose that moment to return, which gave Erika a moment to regain her composure and study the man up close while she downed her pain pill. Not for the first time this week, she noted how incredibly good-looking her new neighbor was.

Where Lance radiated calm, competent authority, James West was breathtakingly imposing. Tall, broad-shouldered, with a neatly trimmed beard and a shaved head revealing smooth dark brown skin, the man exuded a rugged attractiveness. She'd seen him jogging through town in workout shorts and a tee a couple of times in the week since he'd arrived and knew that his clothing hid a well-toned body.

The nurse retreated from the room again.

Daisy shot a bright smile at the man on the other side of the bed and picked up the conversation where they'd left off. "I had to go back to your house to call for an ambulance. James saw me and ran to help you while I called."

So it was James already. Apparently, Daisy had wasted no time getting friendly with the new guy. Erika flushed with guilt the moment the thought floated through her mind. Daisy was her friend and Erika wasn't looking for a relationship, certainly not with a man just passing through town. No matter how chivalrous or handsome he was.

"All I did was stay with you until the EMTs got there," James said, straightening and moving closer to the bed.

It wasn't nothing, especially since she'd been less than welcoming once she found out that he hadn't rented the cabin for a few days like most tourists. James West would be her neighbor for at least a month. She didn't know why that put her on edge. It was really no concern of hers who stayed in the cabin. Yet, the moment she'd seen him arrive in his shiny black SUV, her defenses had gone up. Unjustifiably, it appeared.

"Thank you for coming to my aid, Mr. West."

"Please call me James. And no thanks are necessary. I'm just happy I was around to help."

"Erika, if you're up to it, I'd like to ask you a few questions," Lance said, taking a small notebook out of the interior pocket of his black jacket.

"I'm up for it." She gave a slight nod and was grateful when it didn't set off another jackhammer in her head.

"How often do you go to the bluff?" Lance held a pen over the notebook at the ready.

"Once, maybe twice a week. The walk is good exercise, and the view of the mountains is the best in Carling Lake. It helps me think. Plan."

She usually went to the bluff by herself, but she was shaken by the thought that Daisy, or someone else, could have stepped onto that bridge and been hurt. Or, God forbid, Marcus might have wandered out there by himself.

"Okay, and I assume you didn't notice any damage to the bridge on your prior visits," Lance continued his questioning, keeping her thoughts from spiraling toward the worst-case scenarios.

"No. I look regularly. Marcus isn't allowed to go that far from the house without me, but it's not unusual to find a tourist who has ventured off the public hiking trail even though I've posted private-property signs."

"Before today, when was the last time you made an inspection?"

She bit her bottom lip, thinking. "I walked to the bluff Friday afternoon before picking Marcus up from school."

She'd gone to the bluff to cool off after running into Ellis. The rival B&B owner had intercepted her as she was coming out of the hardware store and suggested she'd regret it if she persisted in attempting to open her B&B. Ten years ago, she'd promised herself that she'd never again allow herself to be bullied by anyone, and their exchange had ended with harsh words, something that was becoming quite a regular occurrence on the rare occasion they spoke to each other at all.

Lance glanced up from taking notes. "Friday, four days ago—" his eyes narrowed "—and you didn't notice any damage then."

Had she looked for damage then? The walk to the

bluff was her attempt to settle and regroup before she had to collect Marcus and go into Mom mode.

She tried to remember whether she'd looked at the cables and anchors? She couldn't recall. "To be honest, I'm not sure I looked. I was there because I was upset."

Lance's brow knitted together. "Upset? Why?"

Erika rolled her eyes. "Ellis Hanes felt the need to tell me, yet again, why I should give up on the B&B now before I lose my shirt. And I told him, yet again, where he could stick his faux concern. We made a bit of a scene in front of Laureano's hardware."

James's mouth twitched, a sexy almost-smile turning his lips up and adding a twinkle to his eye.

Whoa. She must have hit her head harder than the doctors thought.

"How am I just now hearing about this?" Lance asked with a chuckle, bringing her back to the conversation.

Erika shifted her gaze from James's face to Lance's. "Because you've been busy dealing with the vandalism cases and that underground gambling ring that's got everyone in town talking."

"And making eyes at that new waitress at Mahoney's Grill," Daisy interjected.

Lance shot Daisy a quelling look. Daisy winked.

"Excuse me," James's deep voice rumbled through the room. "Being new to town, I'm not familiar with names. Who is Ellis Hanes?"

"A giant tool, and Erika's nemesis," Daisy spat.

Erika slapped her friend's hand lightly. "He's not my nemesis." She looked at James. "Ellis owns the Carling Lake Hotel and the Carling Lake B&B. He's not happy I'm set to become the competition."

"Even though the town gets more than enough tourism to support an additional B&B." Daisy frowned. "As it is, during the tourist season, all the hotels within a fifteen-mile radius are booked solid."

"Yes, but that allows Ellis to jack up the prices of his rooms to ridiculous levels," Lance said.

"I see." James massaged the dark stubble covering his square jaw. He focused on a spot on the wall and a groove cut a line through his forehead as if he were thinking deeply.

Lance cleared his throat. "Getting back to my question. You can't say for sure there was no damage to the bridge last Friday?"

"Not for sure," Erika said. Lance shot a glance across the room at James. She looked from one man to the other. "What was that look?"

"Nothing for you to worry about." Lance closed his notebook and slid it back into the inner pocket of his coat. "I should have a preliminary report for your insurance company by next week."

Her insurance premium was already set to increase significantly when the B&B officially opened. Reporting the bridge's collapse meant her premium would skyrocket. An expense she neither needed nor could afford. Still, she wasn't going to let Lance blow her off.

"Are you thinking my fall wasn't an accident?" She pushed herself up straighter in the bed.

"I don't want you to worry. My office is going to investigate." Lance shot another conspicuous look at James. But her neighbor's eyes were locked in on her face.

"I told the sheriff that the rope looked like it had been cut. At least partially," James said.

Lance hissed a swear and pinned James with a glare. James held the sheriff's gaze. "She has a right to know."

Erika couldn't focus on the disagreement between the men. The room had shrunk rapidly until it felt as if there wasn't enough air left in the room to inhale a breath. A voice she hadn't heard in years whispered through her mind.

If you ever try to leave me, I'll find you and I'll kill you.

It had been a long time since she'd thought of the man who'd regularly uttered those words.

But even if the bridge had been tampered with, Ronald couldn't have done it.

Ronald was dead. She was sure of that.

"Erika, you okay?" Daisy asked, pulling the men's attention from each other and focusing it on her.

"I'm fine," Erika said, looking from Daisy to Lance. "Really, Lance, I'm okay. The idea that this might have been something other than an accident threw me for a minute, that's all."

"We don't know it wasn't an accident," Lance snapped. "That snowstorm last week had extremely high winds. It's possible something clipped the bridge. As I said, we'll know more once we investigate."

James's brow arched into a dubious expression.

Erika offered a wan smile.

"You're probably right. That storm was massive. And I promise I won't worry until I know there's something to worry about." It was a lie, but one of many she'd told her friends since they'd met.

"I need to get going." Lance moved toward the door. "Can I give you a lift, Daisy?"

"No. I'm going to stay the night here with Erika," Daisy said, pulling her chair closer to the bed.

"Daisy, no. There's no reason for you to spend the night in an uncomfortable chair."

"I want to. I don't want you to be alone in the hospital."

Erika waved her off. "I can't ask you to do that. Not when I need another favor from you. Do you think you can pick me up tomorrow morning when I'm discharged?"

Daisy's nose crinkled. "Oh, I'm scheduled to open the library tomorrow, but I'm sure I can get someone to cover my shift." But the tone of her voice contradicted her words.

Like most local government agencies, there was never enough money in the library's coffers, and Daisy had complained more than once that she did the work of three full-time librarians.

Erika felt a stab of guilt for adding to her friend's load. "Don't worry about it. I can call a cab."

Daisy's bob shook. "No way—"

"I can give you a ride," James cut Daisy off.

Erika didn't hide her surprise. "I can't ask you to do that."

"Really, it's not a problem." James smiled, revealing a dimple in each cheek and confirming her earlier thoughts.

Definitely sexy.

"I come into town every morning for breakfast. I can swing by after and pick you up."

There was no reason to decline, except that she didn't like relying on others. Especially strangers. But he was her neighbor, and he had rushed to her aid. And it was only a ride.

"If it's not too much trouble."

"No trouble at all," James said.

Daisy, then Lance, gave her a gingerly hug before heading for the hospital room door.

James followed them, turning back before crossing into the hall. "I'll be here by nine."

At the answering nod, he let the door snap shut softly behind him.

Erika reclined on the uncomfortable hospital pillows. Her headache was slowly receding, making clear-headed thought possible. She'd moved to Carling Lake when Marcus was still a baby. It had taken years for her to feel safe, to trust, but she'd gotten there. Now an old familiar fear lurked.

Had her past finally come back to haunt her?

Chapter Four

Sketching usually helped James clear his head and relax, but tonight his mind wouldn't slow down. He laid the charcoal pencil next to his half-finished drawing and rolled his shoulders. The sketch he'd been working on for the last several days, a farmhouse perched on a slight incline overlooking a vast lake, had called out to him from the moment he'd seen it. The sketch was a far cry from the gritty cityscapes he usually drew. The hip avant-garde New York gallery that had recently sold two of his pieces and had been gently pressuring him for more would probably laugh in his face if he presented them with this piece. But then he already knew he'd never sell this sketch. Gift it, maybe.

James's gaze wandered to the window. Erika's farmhouse was dark and serene. He'd checked that all the doors were locked, and the windows secured when he'd returned from the hospital. But he couldn't shake the feeling that there was more to Erika's fall than a simple accident.

His phone rang, pulling him from his musings. He said, heading for the kitchen.

"How's it going?" Ryan asked without preamble.

"I'm working on it," James answered evenly, grabbing a beer from the fridge.

Although he was six years James's junior, Ryan helmed West Security and Investigations, the security firm that their father had started two decades ago. That made his younger brother his boss, at least for the time being.

"You've been there for five days already. Are you making any progress?" Ryan asked impatiently.

"I'm handling it," James snapped. He took a long gulp from the bottle and reminded himself Ryan idled on impatient.

If Ryan had noticed the irritation in James's tone, he ignored it. "Handle it faster. We've got other cases."

Several weeks ago, West had been hired by the executors of Roger Overholt's estate to find his estranged daughter-in-law, Erika Overholt, a task that was usually straightforward. In this case, it had taken weeks to track down the woman they were pretty sure was Erika Overholt, although she now went by the name Erika Powell. Roger had decreed that all his heirs must be notified about the terms of the will simultaneously. Erika Overholt's disappearing act left billions in limbo.

"When you assigned me this case, you said you thought I was the best man for it. I do things my way, in my time." James set his glass on the counter and looked out the window of the sink at the expanse of his and Erika's lawns heading back toward the forest. The moon was high and round, casting shadows over both backyards.

"You are the best man for the job. You love nature. Fresh air. Hiking. All that outdoorsy stuff. You fit right in."

"Right. So let me fit in. You know I can't simply walk up to Erika Powell and ask if she's really Erika

Overholt. And before you say it, I will not break into the woman's house."

Breaking and entering was more their other brother, Shawn's style. He was so good at it; most people never even knew he'd been inside their homes.

But it wasn't James's style. He didn't want to break the law or invade Erika's privacy unless there was no other choice. The trouble was he hadn't worked out how to get the information he needed. But he wasn't about to share that with Ryan.

A shadow at the tree line behind Erika's house caught his attention. James leaned forward, not sure what he was looking at, although his gut reaction said that it wasn't anything good.

"James? Are you still there?" Ryan asked.

"No," he said, ending the call.

It was lucky that he hadn't turned on the overhead lights when he'd moved into the kitchen. He stood in the darkness, watching for movement, or changes in the depth or composition of the shadows. Several minutes passed, but he was used to waiting.

Finally, the shadow moved. A man. In dark clothing. The man slid between the oak trees bordering the property. From where James stood, it was clear Erika's house was the man's target.

But what exactly was he planning to do?

It was possible word had gotten out that the house was empty and an easy target for a burglar. But something told him this man's intent wasn't burglary.

James slipped out the front door of the cabin and rounded the side of the house. Whoever was in the woods was good, keeping to the shadows. But James was better.

It seemed like hours, but the man finally stepped out

of the trees. He moved fast now that he was out in the open backyard. He bounded for the house like a heat-seeking missile.

James moved just as fast, tackling the intruder in the middle of the yard. They hit the frozen ground hard and rolled. Something shiny flew out of the intruder's hand and sailed across the lawn.

James noted the man's pale skin and dirty blond hair before he aimed a blow at his face. The man recovered quickly, rearing up and nearly flipping James. Off balance, James took a punch to his side and another to his nose. Even with a gloved hand, there was plenty of power behind the punches.

Blood spurted from James's nose and his ears rang. He'd had his nose broken once before and was pretty sure the damage had fallen short of a break, but that knowledge did nothing to temper the pain at the moment. Taking advantage of James's shift in focus, the man lurched to his feet and fled back toward the trees.

James pressed his sleeve to his nose and took off after the man. Ignoring the branches whipping him in the face, he followed the sound of footsteps and labored breathing a short way into the woods. The thud of heavy footsteps grew fainter as the man increased the distance between them. He obviously knew where he was going, a claim James couldn't make.

James slowed. He didn't know the woods well enough to go tramping through them in the dark. Instead, he headed back to his cabin, going over the attack.

It was too much of a stretch to believe the attempted break-in was completely separate from Erika's fall.

He'd staunched his bloody nose by the time Lance

Webb and another deputy arrived. He switched on the outside lights and met them on the front porch.

"Mr. West, this is Deputy Clarke Bridges." Webb gestured to the short stout man next to him. "You called in a B&E?"

"Attempted. And not here. I caught a man trying to break into Erika's farmhouse. We tussled in the backyard there but he got by me."

Webb cocked his head, openly assessing the injuries to James's face.

He'd cleaned up as much as he could. His nose wasn't broken, but he'd be breathing out of one nostril for a day or two and the swelling wasn't pretty.

"I hope you gave as good as you got." Bridges smirked.

An open question, as far as James could tell.

"I chased the guy into the trees there but didn't get very far. Figured it wasn't the wisest course of action to go chasing through the woods after dark."

"Can't argue with you there," Webb said. "I want to take a look at the scene and then I'll be back to take your statement."

Webb and Bridges descended the porch stairs and headed for Erika's house.

James retreated into the cabin, started a pot of coffee and watched the lawmen work through his kitchen window. The beams of their flashlights cut wide swaths of light through the darkness as the men searched for evidence.

After returning from the hospital last night, he'd run a background check on Sheriff Lance Webb. The thirty-nine-year-old had served on the Atlanta police force for nine years, earning his detective shield. He'd racked up several commendations, so James didn't doubt the man was competent. And he seemed to care for Erika, enough so that James wondered whether the two had something going other than friendship.

Not that it was any of his concern, he thought, rubbing at the prickling jealousy rising in his chest.

Webb turned, his eyes locking on James through the window. Webb started for the cabin and James let him in through the back door.

"Have a seat." James motioned to the kitchen table. He'd packed away his drawing materials while he waited for the sheriff to arrive, so the walnut wood was now bare. "I'll get us some coffee, then you can ask your questions."

"I'd appreciate that." Webb pulled the wool hat from his head and tucked it into his coat pocket. "It's colder than a mother-in-law's kiss out there."

"I wouldn't know about that. Never married." James poured two mugs of coffee and carried them to the table.

Webb took the cup with a tired smile of thanks. "It's just something to say. My former mother-in-law is one of the loveliest ladies I know. I'm just sorry she didn't rub off on her daughter."

James eyed the sheriff over the rim of his coffee mug.

As if realizing he'd plunged into territory he didn't want to tread, Webb straightened, set his mug aside and pulled a notebook from his coat pocket. "Okay, let's start from the beginning."

James took the sheriff through the events of the evening, from when he first noticed a figure in the shadows to their fight in Erika's yard and the intruder's escape into the woods. He left out that he'd been sketching before spotting the intruder.

Although he'd recently sold a couple of pieces, he generally kept his hobby to himself. A part of him, he could admit, remained insecure about his talent despite the sales. More than just insecurity. His drawings reflected how he felt about and saw the world.

He'd brought three of his finished pieces with him and they hung on the walls of the cabin now. The only indication that they were his work was the tiny signature in the bottom left corner.

"So you see this guy skulking around and you thought the best course of action was to confront him rather than call the sheriff's office?" Webb asked, his expression pinched.

"Yes." James smiled, raising his mug to his lips.

"And how did that work out for you?" Webb said, motioning to James's face.

Point taken. He had a bloody nose, and he'd let the intruder get away. But if he'd waited for the sheriff, the man would have made it inside Erika's house. It was empty, but he still could have done damage. And there was no guarantee Webb would have arrived in time to catch the man, even if James had called before approaching him.

"We found a can of kerosene in Erika's yard," Lance said.

James felt his brow furrow. "That must have been what fell out of the guy's hand when I tackled him." Which also confirmed he'd done the right thing confronting the guy before calling for help. Erika's home could have been engulfed by the time Webb and the fire department arrived.

"We'll run it for prints, but I'm not holding out hope. It's twelve degrees out there and I'm assuming the guy had on gloves." Sheriff Webb's eyebrows went up in question.

James nodded.

Webb scratched a note on his pad, then looked across the table again. "I checked you out."

James let the corner of his mouth quirk up. "Did you like what you found?"

"You're cocky, but I guess you have a right to be. You've got an impressive military record."

James took another sip of his coffee. The impressive military career had come at a cost—it always did. But experience had taught him it wasn't a cost society wanted to think about or face, so he said nothing.

"What I want to know is what brings you to Carling Lake?" Webb asked.

So the sheriff's snooping hadn't led to West Security and Investigations. James wasn't surprised. He had only been working for West for a few months and New York State didn't require him to have his own private investigator's license as long as a licensed private investigator supervised him. Finding a licensed PI in his family had never been a problem so he hadn't seen a reason to spend the time or money getting a license of his own. That would come in handy since the last thing he needed was the good sheriff telling Erika her new neighbor was a gumshoe.

"Just taking some downtime while I figure out my next move. Carling Lake seemed a good spot for that."

Webb nodded. "We have our fair share of tourists coming to town looking for a little R&R and to commune with nature. Some even end up setting down roots."

"I don't know about roots, but the rest, relaxation and nature sound good to me."

"Hmm."

James set his mug on the table with a thunk. "Something you want to say to me, Sheriff?"

"Don't get yourself all worked up. I was just thinking that since you're close, you might be inclined to keep an eye on Erika and Marcus. I'm not at all comfortable with today's incidents."

"Incidents, plural? I thought you were chalking Erika's fall up to an accident."

Webb frowned. "I never said that. I looked at that rope. The cut was clean just like you said. But I'm not jumping to any conclusions."

"Not jumping to any conclusions but not taking any chances, either?"

"Erika and Marcus are important to me." Webb's words elicited another stab of jealousy that James ignored. "You have a particular skill set that can be useful as their neighbor."

James's eyebrows arched. "Erika doesn't seem like a woman who'd appreciate having someone hovering over her."

"I'm not asking you to be Kevin Costner to her Whitney Houston," Webb said, eliciting a smile from James at the dated movie reference. "Just keep an eye out for them when they're home."

Since he was already doing that, there was no harm in agreeing to Webb's request.

"I'll need you to come down to the station and sign your statement. I'll call when it's ready," Webb said, rising from his seat.

James watched as Webb and Bridges got into separate cars and took off down the gravel drive.

Keep an eye out for them. Webb's voice resounded in James's head.

He planned to do more than that. Whether Erika's last name turned out to be Overholt or something else, he was going to make sure she and her son were safe.

Chapter Five

The dream was familiar, although it had been more than five years since she had it last.

Erika sat in the passenger's seat of her husband's sporty red Porsche. Roland wore a tuxedo, the bow at his neck undone. The gold beaded gown and strappy heels she had on cost more than all the clothes she'd ever owned before meeting Roland Overholt.

Roland was drunk, a state that had become common for him, and driving too fast and erratically. It was a miracle they'd made it as far as they had without getting into an accident, but it was late and thankfully the roads weren't heavily traveled.

They'd just left a party celebrating the opening of a new division of Overholt Industries. Roland had gone into the night, exuberant. He'd expected his father to appoint him to run the new division, a first step toward succeeding the old man when he retired. But Roger had passed over and humiliated both his sons by announcing his choice of one of the other senior Overholt executives for the position. Insult meet injury.

Roland dealt with the situation the way he dealt with everything, by hitting the open bar and downing whiskey until his father pulled him aside and demanded he leave.

So they'd left because Roland always did what his father told him to do. And Erika always did what Roland told her to do. She had begged Roland to pull over and let her drive, but he was lost in his head. Ranting and raving about his father underestimating him. Never believing in him. How a new division of Overholt Industries should be run by an actual Overholt.

The sound of a car horn pulled her attention from her husband's tirade. It all happened in seconds, but it felt as if they were moving in slow motion. They'd veered into the oncoming lanes. Blindingly white headlights shone through the windshield.

She looked back at Roland. His eyes had grown wide. He wrenched the steering wheel to the right but panicked, overcorrected. The Porsche sailed over the blacktop, then over the grassy patch that ran along the side of the road. The thick trunk of the tree barreled toward them and Erika heard the crunching sound of metal, tasted blood in her mouth before the world went black.

Erika started awake. She pressed a trembling hand to her chest, felt her racing heartbeat.

"Everything okay in here?" A nurse rushed into the room.

"Yes. Just a bad dream." Erika tried to smile, hoping it would soften the worried expression on the nurse's face. Her heartbeat was already slowing, and after taking her blood pressure, the nurse deemed her well enough to be left alone again.

Erika padded into the bathroom and got into the shower.

She was more than well enough to be left alone. She was thriving, and she was doing so using her smarts and grit despite all the times Roland had told her she wouldn't survive without him. She'd done more than survive.

Ten years after the car accident that took Roland's life, it was almost as if Erika Overholt was herself a dream. That the woman she was now had ever believed Roland when he'd said she was nothing without him was almost laughable. He'd tried his best to make her nothing. He'd belittled her and undermined her confidence at every turn. Nothing she'd done was good enough. *Why did you let the gardeners plant gardenias? Are you trying to embarrass me in front of the entire neighborhood? Why did you have this room painted that color? I feel like I live in a bordello. Why did you buy that dress? Everyone will think I married a streetwalker.* There was nothing too small to escape his criticism. Piece by piece, he chipped away at her. He hadn't seen her as her own person. Everything she did reflected on him. And nothing was never good enough for Roland Overholt.

They'd been married five years at the time of the accident, and the happiest moment in her marriage was when the doctor told her Roland hadn't made it.

For the briefest of moments, she'd been relieved.

Then the doctor had given her another piece of news that had sent fear like she'd never known before coursing through her. She was pregnant.

She'd been released from the hospital only to find Roger Overholt and his attorney in her home. None of the Overholts had bothered to visit her in the hospital, and she hadn't expected Roger's sudden appearance to portend good things.

She'd been right.

It turned out she and Roland didn't own the house they'd been living in. She'd naively allowed Roland to handle all their financial affairs. The house, the cars, the bank accounts. None of it was Roland's, which meant none of it was hers.

All she'd get was a hundred thousand dollars from a life insurance policy that Roger couldn't cut her out of per California law. It wasn't nothing, but for a woman who'd spent the past five years married to the millionaire son of a billionaire, it may as well have been.

Her father-in-law gave her five hours to pack her bags under the watchful eye of his attorney and left.

That night, lying sleepless in her hotel room, unsure where to go or how she'd feed the life growing inside her, she'd let herself consider, just for a moment, whether she should have let Roger know about his grandchild. The Overholt bloodline meant everything to Roger and even though he treated his two sons like dirt, that was better than he treated everyone else, as long as they submitted to his will. When they didn't, Roger made sure they paid for it. The one Overholt who'd slipped through Roger's grasp, his daughter, Daisy, had been cut off and banished from the family. Erika hadn't ever even met the woman, only hearing about her during one of Roland's drunken rants.

Erika thought back to all the times that Roland had belittled her in front of his family. How Roger had looked on, almost with pride, as if his son bullying his wife was something to be proud of. If Roger had known she was carrying an Overholt, he'd have made sure that he had control over the baby's entire life. Roger would do his best to turn her child into him.

She'd vowed then and there she wouldn't allow it. And she hadn't.

She pushed thoughts of Roger Overholt from her mind as she dressed. The Overholts weren't part of her and Marcus's lives, and they never would be.

At just past nine o'clock, Dr. Lucas Blackwell, the attending physician who'd seen her when she'd been admitted to the hospital yesterday, bustled into the room with a tablet in one hand and his stethoscope looped around his neck. "Well, aren't you an early riser? How are you feeling this morning, Ms. Powell?" He set the tablet on the bed next to her and with practiced efficiency grabbed the blood pressure cuff from the wall mount at the head of the bed and wrapped it around Erika's right arm.

"I feel fine. Ready to go home," Erika answered, forcing a smile.

They both fell silent while he worked.

"On a scale from one to ten, ten being the worst, how would you rate the pain?" he asked as he took his stethoscope from his ears and pulled the cuff from her arm.

"Two." Erika ignored the repeated pounding in her head that marked her answer as a lie.

Dr. Blackwell glanced up from the tablet he was using to record her vitals, his expression reflecting his skepticism.

He held her gaze, letting the silence stretch between them.

"Okay, it's more like a six. But a manageable six," she tacked on quickly.

The doctor nodded and went back to making notes. "I'll have the nurse bring you something for the pain when she brings in your discharge papers. It's just extra strength acetaminophen, but it will also help with the body aches."

The combined headache and body soreness was probably closer to an eight, but there was no way she was going to admit it. She had no intention of spending another night in the hospital. She'd spoken to Marcus on the phone last night. The fear and concern she heard in his voice had twisted her heart. She'd tried to assure him she was fine and that staying overnight at the hospital was only a precaution, but the best thing she could do for both of them was to get home.

Dr. Blackwell poked and prodded a bit more before announcing she was free to go, provided she took it easy for the next few days. Erika readily agreed, and he left to print her discharge papers.

She eased off the bed and went to the small closet in the room. The black coat she'd been wearing when she'd fallen hung inside next to her shirt. She had hope that a good scrubbing would get the bloodstains out of the coat, but her shirt was a lost cause. The EMTs had cut it off on the way to the hospital and only the pieces remained. Someone, one of the nurses no doubt, had left a scrub top in the closet and she'd put it and her dirt encrusted jeans on after her shower.

She grabbed her coat, tossed the shirt in the garbage and hobbled back to the bed.

Lance's questions about the bridge's maintenance and her fall had been running through her head since he'd left the day before. She knew Lance said he'd look into her fall, but she wanted to take a look at the bridge rigging for herself. Her brain pounded at the thought of the walk to the bluff.

Maybe not right away. But in a few days, when the headache had subsided, she'd take a walk out to the bluff. She was responsible for the maintenance of her property after all, and if the bridge collapse wasn't an act of nature…

She wouldn't let herself go there yet. She and Marcus had been safe in Carling Lake for the last eight years, and there was no reason to think that they weren't so any longer.

But if the Overholts had found them?

They'd run again. And this time she'd make sure they'd never be found.

Chapter Six

A knock on the room's door jerked her out of her thoughts.

James West's broad frame nearly filled the doorway. She wasn't a small woman at five foot ten, but Ronald had been several inches taller than her, and even all these years after his death, physically imposing men usually initiated her defenses. But there was something about James West, a gentleness in his eyes, that kept her walls from immediately going up.

"Sorry, I didn't mean to startle you," James said, coming farther into the room.

"No apology necessary. I was just…lost in thought."

"How are you feeling?" he asked, flashing a smile that made her heart race. Thank goodness she was no longer on a machine, or he'd know exactly how his presence affected her.

"I'll live. Right now I just want to get home and see my son."

"I spoke to Sheriff Webb this morning. He said his deputy will drop Marcus off at school and pick him up this afternoon and bring him home."

Erika narrowed her eyes. "Why'd you have to speak to Lance this morning?"

James's smile fell away. "There was a situation at

your house last night. The sheriff came out, everything is okay, but I called him this morning to follow up."

She was about to demand details when the nurse returned with her discharge papers and the pain medication Dr. Blackwell had ordered. An orderly followed, pushing a wheelchair. The nurse reminded her to take it easy until her headache went away before exiting the room again. James helped her into her coat, and the orderly pushed her through the winding hallways, James marching dutifully at her side, to the front entrance of the hospital.

They made their way slowly to the shiny black and chrome SUV Erika had seen parked in front of the small cabin next to her property for the last several days.

James took great care, settling her into the passenger seat before he climbed behind the wheel and pointed the vehicle toward home.

Erika waited until they'd turned onto the two-lane highway leading away from the hospital and back to Carling Lake before reiterating the question she'd asked back in her hospital room. "What kind of situation was there at my house last night?"

James glanced at her quickly before turning his attention back to the road ahead. "There was someone skulking around your backyard. Don't worry, I intercepted him before he made it inside."

"Is that what happened to your eye? It looks painful."

James nodded. "It's not as bad as it looks."

"Did Lance arrest the guy?" Carling Lake had its fair share of crime from pickpocketing the tourists to a growing opioid drug problem just like everywhere else in the country.

"I'm sorry. He got away."

A ripple of unease moved through her sore body.

First, the bridge collapsing and then someone trying to break into her house. Had she been found? Had Roger Overholt found her and Marcus?

The once familiar swell of panic rose in her throat, but she pushed it back down.

Don't overreact.

Erika Overholt had ceased to exist ten years ago. Erika Powell had hidden her trail well, using part of the life insurance payout to purchase a black market identity. She and Marcus were safe. Her father-in-law had been quick to kick her to the curb after Roland's death but if he knew he had a grandson, another Overholt heir, she was sure he'd stop at nothing to get Marcus under his thumb. Just as his two sons had been for their entire lives.

"You okay over there?" James eyed her from the driver's seat.

"Yes," she said, pulling herself back into the present. The pain medicine the doctor had given her had kicked in. Her headache was gone and her limbs no longer felt like lead. "Thank you for watching out for the house last night."

"Not a problem. I just wish I'd caught him."

"Well, I'm sure Lance is on top of it."

She tried not to be too conspicuous as she studied the man driving her home. His sleek black leather jacket was completely inadequate for the cold that wafted off the lake, but it certainly gave off a dangerous, sexy vibe. Jeans hugged his strong thighs, upping the sexy to nearly off-the-chart levels. Even his purplish black eye was doing it for her.

Erika bit her bottom lip and looked away before he realized she'd been ogling him.

She couldn't help the very feminine reaction she

found herself having to his presence, but knew she couldn't, wouldn't, let it go anywhere. He was just passing through. She knew some of the young singles who lived in and around Carling Lake were happy to engage in temporary flings with the tourists and she didn't judge. To each their own. But casual dating had never worked for her.

Lately, dating of any fashion hadn't been working for her. It wouldn't be fair. She'd never be able to be completely honest with a partner, so what kind of relationship could she really ever have? None. She'd reconciled herself to that fact long ago. It didn't mean she wanted to live her life alone, just that she didn't have any other choice. But if she did?

Maybe she'd have given James West a chance. She could do worse than a man who'd ferry a neighbor he barely knew home from the hospital.

Yeah, why would he do that? a voice in the back of her head intoned.

After years of being careful about who she let get close to her and Marcus, she couldn't stop the little slivers of suspicion that crept into her mind anytime she met a new person. But she pushed the doubt away. What was the point of having created a new life if she couldn't trust a little? Romance may not be in the cards, but surely a ride from a neighbor wasn't dangerous. At least not to anything except her libido.

"Have you lived in Carling Lake long?" James asked. They were stopped at a traffic light, and he'd caught her ogling him like a teenaged schoolgirl.

She cleared her throat and focused her gaze out the front window of the SUV. "About eight years now." The signal changed, and he put the car in gear.

"And you have a son? How old is he?"

She smiled at the thought of her son. "Marcus. He's ten going on thirty. Do you have kids?"

"No. I haven't really stayed in one place long enough to find a woman I'd like to be a mother to my kids."

The knowledge that he wasn't forever tied to another woman in that way made her slightly giddy, although she knew she had no right to be.

"But you live in New York now?" she asked, with the intention of putting her thoughts back on neutral ground. At his questioning look, she added, "Your license plate."

He nodded. "Born and raised New Yorker, actually. I enlisted in the Marines when I was twenty but I've been out of the service for a few months now."

Something about the way he said it made her think that he wasn't exactly happy about his separation from the military but he didn't give her the chance to inquire further. "How about you? Are you from Carling Lake?"

"No," she answered without elaboration. "Where'd you serve?"

He shot a glance across the car that let her know he hadn't missed the shift back to his life as the topic. "Mostly Afghanistan, although I've seen quite a bit of the world."

"That must have been nice. Seeing the world, that is."

"It had its moments. You don't travel much?"

She laughed. "Try not at all. Between work and Marcus, I don't have a lot of free time or money for travel."

"I can understand that. My father raised four sons pretty much on his own. There wasn't a lot of money for traveling then, either. You mentioned you're about to open your home as a B&B. Running a B&B, is that what you did before you moved to Carling Lake?"

She narrowed her eyes at him, suspicion creating a knot in her belly.

Was it her imagination, or was he fishing for information about her past?

"No. I pretty much just went from one job to another before I moved here."

"A jack-of-all-trades. That will probably come in handy for an innkeeper," he said with a smile.

"I hope so," she said, forcing herself to relax. He was just making conversation. A nice guy doing the neighborly thing, giving her a ride home. "I'm actually a staff writer for the *Carling Lake Weekly*. At least I am for another few weeks. Once the B&B opens, I'll be running it full-time."

"You really do have a lot on your plate. Mom. Journalist. Businesswoman."

Erika felt her body warm at the admiration in the glance James shot her from the other side of the car. "So you've been in Carling Lake for almost a week now. How do you like it?" she asked, hoping to turn the conversation in a direction that would stop the butterflies fluttering in her stomach.

This is what comes of not having been on a date in longer than you can remember, she admonished herself. *You get all fluttery around the first good-looking guy to swing through town.*

"It's nice. Much quieter than New York City but quiet is more my speed, anyway."

"Have you taken advantage of any of the town's amenities? We've got great hiking trails and there are several things you can do at the lake, fishing, paddleboat, even a booze cruise. There's a lot to do besides jog, although I can't say I mind the view."

She couldn't believe she'd actually said that. Her

mouth had obviously been moving faster than her brain. The doctor said she didn't have a concussion, but she had to wonder if he'd gotten it wrong. At least then she'd have an excuse for flirting with a man she hardly knew.

James's lips curved into a smile. "Happy to be of service."

She faced forward and prayed she wouldn't die of embarrassment. Maybe a fling was in order—not with James West of course, but clearly the lack of male companionship was causing her to lose the ability to talk to a man.

James turned the SUV onto the private road that her B&B and his cabin shared.

A familiar white F-150 was parked in the wide driveway in front of the B&B.

James frowned at the truck. "Expecting company?"

"It's okay. That's my contractor. I'm glad to see him here. He's been MIA the last few days."

Samuel Hogan was one of the most sought after contractors in Carling Lake, although that was admittedly not a difficult distinction to earn in a small town. Erika had been ecstatic when his bid for the part of the renovations she wasn't equipped to DIY had come in under her budget.

Unfortunately, their business relationship had gone downhill in the last several weeks. Hogan was two weeks late getting started with the work, and it was taking much more time than he'd originally told her it would take to finish. Even now, he was the only truck parked in the driveway, signaling the crew of five guys that had been working on the house last week weren't there with him.

She'd been conservative in her budgeting and scheduling, but if Hogan didn't step things up, the renovations wouldn't be finished in time for her to petition for the certificate of occupancy she'd need to open for the start of the tourist season.

Sam Hogan rounded the side of the house as James helped Erika from the SUV. He carried a large, battered toolbox in one hand, held the keys to his truck in the other and sported a deer-in-the-headlights expression when he caught sight of Erika and James approaching.

"Mr. Hogan. Sam. I'm glad to see you," Erika said, rounding the front of the SUV and stopping next to Sam's truck.

Sam gave her a tight smile and hoisted the toolbox into the back of his truck. "Ms. Powell, I heard about your fall. Glad to see you're feeling better."

"Thank you, Sam. I'm glad to see you. There's still a lot that needs to get done before the B&B will be approved for occupancy," Erika continued, trying to keep her tone cordial. "I hope you aren't leaving."

Sam ran his hands through his thinning hair. "I'm sorry, Erika. I'm not going to be able to finish your job. Not on your schedule, anyway."

Erika fought to keep her cool. "Not just my schedule. The schedule we agreed upon in the contract we both signed."

Sam dropped his gaze and shifted from foot to foot. "I'm sorry, but you see, I got a line on this job. It's a big one and well…it's just with things being so tight and all, I just can't say no. This could be the job that rockets my company to the next level."

"I can't see how it could be good for your company when people hear how you've abandoned a client mid-project." James crossed his arms over his chest and eyed Sam.

Sam's gaze swung up and locked onto James, his

eyes narrowing. "I don't remember anyone asking for your opinion. Who are you, anyway?"

"You'd better hope I'm not a potential customer," James answered.

Sam swallowed hard.

Erika drew in a deep breath and held her hands up in a stop motion. "Sam, this is unacceptable. We have a contract. You're already behind schedule. I can't afford any more delays."

"And I can't afford not to take this other job. All of your big projects are done. It'll take me four or five months but I can get back to your job after I've finished this one. Or if you want to look for another contractor, I'm willing to take what you've already paid me and void the rest of the contract. You could probably even go with a handyman for what's left. Whichever works for you."

"What works for me is for you to hold up your end of our deal." Erika fought against frustration to keep herself from yelling at the contractor. "What is this other job, anyway? I don't know of any big projects taking place in Carling Lake right now."

It was quite the opposite. For the last two or three years, the town had been suffering from a decline in tourist dollars that had left the city coffers lighter than in past years. The last several city council member meetings had been focused on reinvigorating the flow of tourists to the town.

"It came up kind of sudden." Sam was back to shifting his feet.

Erika got the feeling that she was not going to like whatever he was about to say.

"Ellis Hanes is looking to renovate a wing of the hotel. He wants the project done in time for the tourist season." Sam's face turned the color of a ripe tomato. At least he had enough character to be ashamed of leaving her in the lurch.

Of course, Ellis was behind this. Another attempt to run her out of business before she even got started.

"Look, this isn't just about me. A renovated hotel will help with bringing in more tourists. The whole town will benefit."

"My B&B will bring in more tourists as well, also benefiting the town," Erika gritted out.

Sam wrenched open the truck's driver's side door. "I'm sorry, Erika. My decision is made." He hopped into the truck and started the engine. Sam wound his window down until he could hang an arm out and pat the side of the door. "Let me know what you decide about the work here. Like I said, either way is fine with me."

Sam threw the truck in reverse and roared off without giving her the chance to respond. "What am I going to do? If I don't get these renovations done soon, there's no way I'll have my occupancy permit in time for my spring and summer bookings."

"Maybe I could help."

"You have your contractor's license?"

"No, but my father taught all his sons to be handy, and I've been helping my brother Ryan renovate the house he bought for his family. As long as your contractor wasn't lying about the big projects being done, I can probably handle it."

It was better for a lot of reasons if she kept her distance from him and he from her. "I couldn't ask you to do that. I mean, you said you were here for rest and relaxation. Becoming my handyman is hardly a restful vacation."

He cocked his head. "That's a matter of perspective." He gave her another one of his brilliant smiles.

"Thank you, but no. I appreciate the ride from the hospital." She turned and headed for the house.

"Here, let me help you."

Erika held up a hand to stop him from moving any closer. "No, really. I've got it from here. Enjoy your vacation, Mr. West."

Chapter Seven

"There's something strange going on here." James spoke to Ryan using the hands-free setting in the SUV as he made the short drive from his cabin into downtown Carling Lake for the second time that day.

On his way out, he'd seen Erika dragging her trash bin to the edge of her property. He'd been about to rush over to help when a preteen boy sprinted down the porch steps and took the bins from her hands. Good. At least someone was looking out for the stubborn woman. Erika may not have a concussion, but a head wound was nothing to take lightly. She should have been resting.

You're here to do a job, not play nursemaid.

That might be true, but it didn't stop the protective impulses that seemed to flare whenever Erika got within his eyesight. Maybe it was just compensatory guilt because he felt bad about lying to her, about why he was actually in Carling Lake. But the fluttering he'd felt as she sat beside him in the SUV on the way home from the hospital whispered that guilt wasn't the emotion that was stirring his loins.

"Weird how?" Ryan's concerned voice pulled James out of his head.

"Yesterday morning a bridge gave out while Erika was on it. Then while she was in the hospital someone tried to break into her house." James filled in a few more details for Ryan.

"I'll admit the lady had a tough day, but it sounds like the local sheriff is on top of it. I don't see how it affects the job you're there to do," Ryan said.

"You don't think it's fishy that we're hired to find Erika Overholt and then she just happens to fall from a bridge and almost have her home broken into?"

James just couldn't shake the feeling that something about this case was wrong. If Erika Powell really was Erika Overholt, she'd gone to extremes to hide her identity. Why?

West's research into the Overholt family had turned up not-so-veiled insinuations by the family members that Erika may have had something to do with her husband's accident, but the police reports were unequivocal. Erika's husband's car had slid off the road during a heavy rainstorm and slammed into a tree, killing him. The toxicology report had put his blood alcohol level at well above the legal limit. The Overholts may not agree, but it was a miracle that Erika hadn't also been killed that night.

So why all the subterfuge on Erika's part?

"I just don't understand why all the secrecy. If the woman I'm watching is Erika Overholt, she's been hiding who she is for years. And now the executors of Overholt's will are asking us to keep secrets. None of it sits right with me."

"According to Overholt's attorney, the will specifically requires that the grandson and daughter-in-law be found and their identities confirmed before they are told of any behests. Actually, all the heirs have to be told about their inheritance at the same time and place. Apparently, Overholt was controlling and eccentric until his last breath."

"And beyond," James sighed.

"We've been hired to do a job."

"And asking questions is part of that job." His statement elicited a groan from the other end of the line. "Look, I'm going to do what you sent me up here to do but it can't hurt if I poke around."

Ryan was right that they'd been hired simply to find Erika Overholt and her son. Once they did, the attorneys for Roger Overholt's estate would take it from there. If Erika didn't want the inheritance, wanted to continue to live under the radar as Erika Powell, she could. He wasn't doing anything wrong.

Then why didn't it feel right?

"Whatever, man. Just don't let your poking around interfere with the case. The attorney for the executor of Overholt's will is expecting results soon. It's already taken us longer to find this woman than we'd hoped."

Over the last two months, West Security and Investigations had run down several leads that had only led to dead ends. Erika Overholt had disappeared off the map—not easy to do in this day and age. James wasn't even totally sure how Ryan had finally been able to track her down. His brother was good at what he did, he'd give him that.

"I thought I'd figured out a way into the house but it turned out to be a dead end."

"How so?" Ryan asked.

"Erika's converting her house into a B&B. Her contractor quit on her unexpectedly. I offered to help out, but she shut me down cold."

"That's too bad," Ryan said, sounding disappointed.

"If there's anything that can prove Erika Powell's identity, it's in there."

"I'll figure something out."

"I have faith in you." Ryan fell silent for a moment. "How's the second part of your mission coming?"

"I don't know if I'd call it a mission."

"I would. In your downtime, you're supposed to be camping and fishing and whatever else you outdoorsy types do in the woods. And most importantly, figuring out what your next steps are going to be after the military."

"I plan to do all that *outdoorsy* stuff as soon as I've finished this job. As for the rest of it…"

"Look, you know you can work for the firm as long as you like. Hell, you're entitled to a fourth of the business."

James West Sr. had left the business to all four of his sons in equal shares when he'd retired. At the time, James had had no intention of leaving the military and his next oldest brother, Brandon, had just embarked on a promising legal career. They'd both sold their interest in the family business to their two youngest brothers.

"No. You and Shawn have done a great job turning West into a first-class security and investigations firm. You deserve to own and run the business. I may not be sure what I want my post–Marine Corps life to be but I don't think private investigations and personal security is for me."

"Well, just know that whatever you decide, you've got my support."

"Thanks, man."

They ended the call as James pulled into the parking lot next to the Lakeside Diner. The lunch rush had subsided and the diner's only other customer was a sole male sitting at the counter. James selected a table against the wall and sat so he could see the entrance.

A server with the name Kelly embroidered on her uniform bounded over to his table. She flashed a sultry smile and poured water into his glass from the pitcher she carried. "Welcome to the Lakeside Diner. What can I get you, something special today?" The tone of her voice made it clear she was talking about more than lunch, but just in case he'd missed it, Kelly shot him a wink.

The door to the diner opened and James made eye contact with the sheriff. He turned back to Kelly, purposely keeping his expression bland. "Burger and fries, please," he said, nestling the laminated menu back between the salt and pepper shakers on the table.

Kelly's smile dimmed. She scratched his order on her pad and turned away from the table.

"I'll have whatever he's having." Lance slid into the chair on the opposite side of the table.

Kelly poured Lance a glass of water before leaving to put in their order.

"Make yourself comfortable," James said.

"Don't mind if I do," Lance smiled. "This isn't New York City. You want to eat alone, you don't come to the diner."

"I have no problem with company," James countered.

"I talked to Erika last night. Thank you for making sure she got home alright."

"It's not a problem. Despite what you might have heard, we New Yorkers can be neighborly, too."

Lance chuckled. "You know I haven't always been the sheriff. Before I moved to Carling Lake, I did an eight-year stint as an officer in the Atlanta Police Department."

"Atlanta. That's a long way from Carling Lake."

"That was the point." Lance's expression hardened for the briefest of moments before it evened out. "We got a print off the kerosene can we found at Erika's last night."

"That was quick."

"We run prints in-house. The fingerprint came back to a Brian Whitmer. I recognized the name. He's one of several regulars who show up at the start of the tourist season to take on seasonal work for the businesses in town. So far no one knows where he is."

"He's probably gone by now."

Lance sighed. "Yeah, I figured that. I put out an all-points bulletin but with no fixed address and no description of a vehicle, it may take some time to run him to ground."

"Anything on the rope from the bridge yet?" James asked.

Lance shook his head. "That I had to send to the county lab. It may be a few days. If we're lucky."

"Here you are. Two burgers with fries." Kelly returned and set a plate in front of each of them.

"Thanks."

"Thank you," James seconded.

Lance must have been as starved as James because he dug in the minute Kelly walked away from the table. James followed suit.

"Carling Lake doesn't get many marine snipers passing through town," Lance said after he'd finished half the food on his plate.

"Former sniper," James said, washing a handful of fries down with a sip of water.

Lance wiped ketchup from his mouth. "Why'd you leave the service?"

James cocked an eyebrow. "You don't already know?"

"I only checked your criminal record to make sure Erika and Marcus weren't in any danger with you next door. The rest of the story is yours to tell."

James took a long sip of water, eyeing Lance over the rim of the mug.

"Or not." Lance shrugged.

James waited several more beats before speaking. "There was a suicide bomber on my last tour in Afghanistan about a year ago. I was a good distance away, which probably saved my life, but a piece of shrapnel still found me. Tore through my hand, damaging tendons."

"I'm sorry to hear that, truly." Lance's voice rang with sincerity.

"Thanks. With lots of therapy, I've got what the doctors call *normal function* back."

"But normal function isn't enough for a sniper."

"No, it is not."

"It's probably enough for a sheriff's deputy."

James felt the corner of his mouth creep upward. "Are you making an offer?"

"One of my deputies just got engaged and is moving to North Carolina in the coming weeks to be with his fiancée. I'll be looking for another deputy."

"Do you make job offers to every tourist who comes to town?"

"Just the special ones." Lance grinned. "What have you been doing since you left the service? I mean job-wise."

He didn't want to lie, but he couldn't tell the truth, either. "A little bit of this. A little bit of that."

"Okay, but you're what? Thirty-six, thirty-seven. You can't do *a little bit of this and a little bit of that* for the next twenty years."

"You sound like my brother," James deadpanned.

"So what are your plans?"

James glared across the table. "I'm still working on that."

"Lots of vets go into law enforcement," Lance said pointedly.

James arched an eyebrow. "I don't think it's for me."

"Because of your hand?"

James stayed silent.

They ate in silence for several minutes.

Lance swallowed the last bite of his burger. "Do you have anywhere to be?"

James shot Lance a questioning look. "Not particularly."

"Good. Come on. You can leave your car here. I'll drive." Lance rose, dropped enough money to cover the entire bill on the table and headed for the exit.

James considered for a moment. He wasn't sure getting too friendly with the sheriff was a good idea. Lance was bound to be upset if he learned James had been lying since his first moments in town. But he was curious about what the sheriff had in mind. He pushed up from the table and followed Lance out of the diner.

James closed the door on the passenger side of the sheriff's cruiser as Lance started the engine.

Lance filled him in on the people, sights and scenery they passed as he drove.

James wasn't sure why, but he mentally cataloged each turn, drawing a map of the town in his head as they drove.

Fifteen minutes after leaving the diner, Lance hit his left-turn signal and coasted into the parking lot of a single-story cinder block building on the outskirts of town.

Lance parked, climbed out of the car and headed for the building without a word.

James followed, almost missing the small sign to the right of the door. Precision Gun Range.

A short man, not much more than a foot taller than the glass case he stood behind, with a beer belly and only a handful of gray strands failing miserably at covering the bald spot at the top of his head, looked up as they entered.

The man broke into a wide smile at the sight of Lance. "Been a while, Sheriff. Come to let me show you up again?"

"Not today, Ari. My friend here and I want to get some target practice in."

Ari's gaze shifted to James. Up close, James could see that the man was at least twenty years older than he and Lance, but the light in his eyes was bright. "Who is your friend, and does he know how to shoot?"

James slanted the older man a look, but Lance only chuckled. "I'll say he does. Ari Levy meet Master Sergeant James West, US Marine Corps."

James reached across the glass case and shook Ari's hand. The older man gave him a thorough once-over.

"Guess I don't have to worry about you accidentally shooting yourself in the foot, then."

"No, sir, you don't," James said, finding the older man growing on him despite his surly personality.

"James was a sniper," Lance added.

"Good for you." The older man didn't appear impressed. "Well then, can I load you up?"

"Yes, please. This was a last-minute idea so we'll need the works. Ammo, ear and eye protection, and a gun for my friend."

"You got a preference?" Ari asked, collecting the items they'd need and setting them on the counter.

"That a SIG?" James jerked his chin at the gun on Lance's hip.

"P226," Lance said, reciting the model of the gun.

Ari reached into the glass case and extracted a gun in a holster that looked exactly like the one Lance wore. "Slow day, so I won't charge you for the space. Send the bill to the sheriff's department?"

"You can send it to the department but make it to my attention," Lance answered. "This one is on me."

"Gotcha." Ari made an air gun with his finger. "Lanes are ready to go. Have fun, boys."

James and Lance gathered their equipment and James followed the sheriff through a heavy metal door. The smell of gunpowder filled James's nose the moment he crossed the threshold.

"Your friend is a character." James sat his gear on the counter in the lane closest to the door. Lance took the next lane.

"Don't let him fool you. Ari might not be a marine sharpshooter but he's a damn good shot."

Lance disappeared behind the divider separating them. James put on his safety goggles and ear protection and loaded his gun with target ammo. He could hear Lance on the other side of the divider going through the same routine.

James took a deep breath, pulling the trigger as he exhaled. His shot missed the mark wildly, leaving a hole in the white space next to the dark silhouette on the paper. He adjusted and took another shot. Better. But his hand was already trembling.

This time he'd hit the target, but nowhere near the

bull's-eye. The sound of his blood thundered in his ears. He could feel his body tensing with swelling anxiety.

He took another deep breath, clenched his right hand more firmly with his left in an attempt to stop the trembling and emptied the clip.

Each shot was better than the one before, and all of them had hit the target in an area that would have been debilitating to an actual person, but nowhere near as good as he'd once been. Beads of sweat collected on his forehead by the time he'd empty the clip, as much from frustration as from the exertion of trying to hold his hand steady.

He ejected the empty magazine and set the gun on the counter.

Lance stepped around the divider and removed his earmuffs. "You're not that bad. Not bad at all."

James also removed his earmuffs. "Not bad isn't good."

"You'd more than pass the firearms test."

"Law enforcement isn't for me."

Lance pulled the protective glasses from his eyes. "Look, I barely know you so maybe I'm overstepping my bounds here but I have friends who have left the military and found the transition…difficult." Lance placed a hand on James's shoulder. "If you want to talk, I'm a good listener and even better at keeping what I hear to myself."

James waited for Lance to return to his lane, then dropped his protection goggles back over his eyes. He still didn't think law enforcement was for him, but the people of Carling Lake were definitely growing on him.

Chapter Eight

The third contractor of the morning was politely laughing Erika off the phone when the banging at her front door started. She peeked around the wall separating the kitchen from the foyer and through the side windows, and saw Daisy standing on her porch.

"The best I could do for you is to have someone out there in late May," the contractor on the other end of the phone line said as Erika opened the door to let Daisy in.

"Thanks anyway," Erika replied before ending the call.

"I bought you dinner for tonight and some staples that should keep you for a few days. What are you doing out of bed?" Daisy breezed through the front door and into the kitchen, a casserole dish in her hands and a recyclable shopping bag hanging from her arm.

"Thank you, but you didn't have to do that. I'm fine. I rested all day yesterday. And most of the morning. Steven Sanchez offered to take Marcus to school for the rest of this week."

Erika made a mental note to thank Devin's fathers for everything they'd done for her over the last several days and followed Daisy into the kitchen. "I have to find a contractor to finish the work on the house."

"Ugh." Daisy made a face. "I heard Sam left you in

the lurch." She put the casserole in the refrigerator and set the grocery bag on the island counter. "I thought he had more integrity than that."

So had Erika. She'd known Sam for the last eight years, ever since she'd moved to Carling Lake, and she'd heard nothing but great things about him and his work. He'd done the heavy lifting on renovating the kitchen three years ago when she'd purchased the house. "Ellis has a lot of influence and deeper pockets than I do. No one wants to run afoul of him."

Daisy slammed a loaf of bread onto the counter. "That doesn't excuse Sam. He had a contract with you and he should have kept his word and done the job he'd agreed to do."

Erika grabbed a jar of peanut butter and a box of ready-made pancake mix and walked to the pantry. "I'm not disagreeing with you but I can't make him do the work so I have to find someone who will."

"Any luck?"

Erika's gaze traveled to the window. She'd glimpsed James this morning out on his porch. She'd spent the night feeling guilty for how dismissive she'd been of his offer to help with the renovations. He was only being nice, neighborly. Which had instantly aroused her suspicions. But maybe she was letting her general mistrust of people cloud her judgment. "No."

Daisy braced herself against the counter. "Okay, give," she said with interest in her eyes.

"Give what?" Erika worked to wipe whatever Daisy had seen in her expression from her face.

"Why did you just shoot a longing look out the window at your gorgeous neighbor's cabin?"

Erika rolled her eyes. "I didn't shoot a longing look anywhere." Daisy stared. "I may have glanced out the window." Daisy continued staring through narrowed eyes. "Okay, James was here when Sam quit and he offered to help me finish the renovations."

"That's awfully nice of him," Daisy said, eyebrows wagging suggestively.

"What are you, twelve? Come on." Erika gave her friend a good-natured shoulder bump. "He's a complete stranger. I said no."

"Why? You need help. He can help. How much do you need to know about the man who's installing a toilet for you?"

When Daisy laid it out that way, it did seem like she might be being a bit overcautious.

Erika pushed away from the counter and grabbed the electric teapot, filling it with water before setting it to boil.

"And maybe he'd be willing to do a little renovation on your love life." Daisy slid out of the way when Erika went to shoulder bump her again. "Come on. I've lived here for a year and you haven't gone out on one date in that time. I wouldn't be surprised to learn you haven't been on a date since you moved to Carling Lake."

"Now that's not true. I have been on a date in the last eight years."

A few years after she'd moved to Carling Lake, she'd briefly dated a man who was also new to the area. Unfortunately, he found the mountain air and small town did not work with his city sensibilities and had moved back to the West Coast after a few months.

"Okay, but how long ago was that?" Daisy didn't wait for Erika to answer. "From the way James was looking at you in the hospital, he'd totally go for it. There is definitely chemistry between the two of you."

"There is no chemistry. And he's a tourist." *Liar.*

She recalled the butterflies in her stomach when he'd driven her home. She was attracted to James West. Erika reached into the cabinet for two teacups.

"Which makes him perfect for your purposes. You can ease back into the dating game, no pressure, no long-term expectations. Just some good old-fashioned adult fun." Daisy wiggled her eyebrows.

"Daisy!"

But now that Daisy had placed the idea in her head, she wondered if that was why James had offered to help her with her house? He had to have some reason for making the offer, right? Had he assumed the small-town single mom would be open to a fling?

"What? I'm talking about dinner, maybe dancing." Daisy tried for an innocent expression and failed. "What did you think I was talking about?" Daisy couldn't keep the laughter out of her voice and Erika found herself laughing along with her friend.

"Look, I am not interested in a man at this point in my life," Erika said, carrying her tea to the kitchen table and sitting.

Daisy followed with her own cup. "Remember a couple of days ago when you and I were at the coffee shop in town and James jogged by. Your eyes nearly popped out of your head."

"It's February in New York and he was out jogging in a sleeveless T-shirt and shorts. Anybody would have stared. I was merely concerned that the man was going to get hypothermia," Daisy said, fanning herself dramatically.

"That man is too hot to ever have to worry about hypothermia."

"Ah, you are incorrigible. Okay, I will admit, he's

hot. I shamelessly ogled all those rippling muscles as he jogged past. Are you happy now?"

"Thrilled!" Daisy said, clapping.

"This changes nothing. I'm not getting involved with a tourist."

"But you should let him help you with the renovations." Daisy held up a hand when Erika opened her mouth to protest. "It's the only way you'll get done in time to file the occupancy papers and get the permit before March, and you know it."

"I have a few more contractors to call. Maybe one of them has had a job fall through or is in a slow period."

Daisy's expression was doubtful.

Erika glanced at her watch. "Hey, I don't mean to rush you out but I want to stop by the *Weekly* before I pick up Marcus."

"Do you not understand the words *take it easy*?"

She knew her friend was just watching out for her, but Daisy's tone still grated. "I do, but I also have a job to do. And it's not like checking in and going through my email is taxing work."

At the front door, Daisy pulled her into a hug. "Call if you need anything." Letting go, Daisy bounded out the door and down the porch steps before turning back. "And think about letting your hot neighbor help you with your renovations. All your renovations," her friend said, laughing as she hopped into her car and drove away.

Thirty minutes later, Erika walked into the lobby of the *Carling Lake Weekly* and was unsurprised to find the reception desk empty. She worked as a part-time reporter. The *Weekly*'s other two employees were the owners Aaron and Margaret Sutton. Everyone in town knew to go right up to the second floor if they had business at the *Weekly*.

Erika moved through the lobby, casting only a passing glance at the framed front pages decorating the walls. Beyond the lobby area was the large room that housed the printers. The *Weekly* was one of the only local newspapers that still maintained its own printing facilities. The Suttons supplemented the income the *Weekly* brought in by handling the printing for several of the surrounding towns' weekly newspapers as well.

The second floor was set up bullpen-style. The three employee desks sat in a loose circle about six feet apart from one another. There was a conference room in one corner of the room and a small break room in the other.

Aaron looked up from the bulky computer screen on his desk as Erika walked into the bullpen. "What are you doing here?"

"I work here." Erika quirked an eyebrow. "Unless you're trying to tell me something?"

When she'd pulled into Carling Lake eight years ago with a two-year-old in tow and relatively few references, she'd expected to have to pick up a job waitressing or manning the cash register at a fast-food joint to make ends meet. She would have been fine with that. It wouldn't have been the first time. Since leaving the Overholts two years prior, she'd not stayed in one place longer than six months. That had made it very difficult to develop a solid résumé. She'd also been too afraid that working in journalism might lead to the Overholts one day accidentally discovering where she was and that she had a son who, with each passing year, looked more and more like his father.

The only job available when she'd gone to town had been the receptionist position at the *Weekly*. She'd accepted the position. It paid a lot more than waitressing and allowed her to save toward the down payment she needed to buy the B&B and start a new dream.

From the moment she'd started working at the *Weekly*, Aaron, Margaret and their son, Francis, had taken her and Marcus into their family. Soon enough, she was feeling the itch to get back on a beat. It took over a year to convince herself that none of the Overholts would be caught dead reading a small-town paper. She'd approached Aaron about creating a part-time staff reporter position and, despite the fact that she couldn't tell him about her degree in journalism, he'd given her a chance.

"You know what I mean. Lance called Margaret and told her about your fall yesterday, although she'd already heard it through the town grapevine. We would have come by to see you but the sheriff put out the word you needed rest."

"I know. I got Margaret's voice mail and the flowers she sent were at the house when I woke up this morning."

"Why aren't you at home resting?"

"I rested all day yesterday and this morning. I need to do something."

Aaron screwed up his face. "I don't like it."

"I'm just here to check my email. See if I got any response from the federal government on my FOIA request." Erika took a seat at her desk and booted up her computer.

The Freedom of Information Act was a federal law every journalism student became intimately familiar with. Many a big story had come from combing through information the law compelled the government to turn over to an intrepid journalist.

"That could have waited another day or two," he said, surliness tinging his tone.

"But I couldn't have." She ignored Aaron's frown and scrolled through her emails.

As a twenty-something journalism student, she'd imagined a career as an investigative reporter in a big city at a nationally recognized newspaper. Then during her junior year, her mother had gotten sick. Her illness had been unexpected and had claimed her mother's life quickly. When she met Ronald, she'd been alone and deeply depressed, on her way to failing out of school. Roland had seemed like a bright light at the end of an endlessly dark tunnel. And he had been until Ronald went to work for his father's company.

She shook off those memories. That was all in the past. She enjoyed her job at the *Carling Lake Weekly*. It may not have been the *LA Times*, but she was honored to work with the Suttons and proud of how they kept the community informed of important news.

But over the years, she'd found herself entertaining the dream of running a bed-and-breakfast. Maybe it was the influence of living in a tourist town. Or maybe more than just her name had changed when she left LA. Maybe her dreams had, too. Whatever it was, she was looking forward to becoming a business owner.

There was no response to her FOIA request, but she did find an email from a familiar sender. The source had first contacted her several weeks earlier via an email with an attached letter showing the town of Carling Lake had been awarded a three-hundred-thousand-dollar grant from the feds for the restoration of city hall. Whatever message the sender was trying to convey, she hadn't gotten it.

The restoration of the historic city hall building was a

constant topic at council meetings. After several years, the town had finally allocated the funds for the renovations. She had covered many of those council meetings and she couldn't remember hearing anything about the town applying for or winning a grant. She'd followed up with Susan Garraus, the treasurer, and Ellis Hanes, who served as town mayor, but they'd both claimed to know nothing about the grant. She called the federal office that had supposedly awarded the grant, but the contact person hadn't returned any of her more than a half dozen calls inquiring about the money. Hence, her as yet unanswered FOIA request.

Her reporter instincts had tingled, but without more, there was nothing for her to pursue.

Erika clicked on the new email from the source. Unlike the first email, this one included a message in addition to an attachment.

WHERE IS THE MONEY?

She opened the attached document. It was another letter, only this time the government was demanding the town provide evidence that the three-hundred-thousand-dollar grant had been used as outlined in the grant application.

Where's the money?

That was the three-hundred-thousand-dollar question. The government clearly believed it had sent the money to Carling Lake. So where was it?

Her instincts were tingling again. There was something to this, she was sure. She just had to sniff out the story.

"What are you looking at so intensely?" Aaron asked from his desk.

"Another email about the grant."

"The one that Ellis and Susan say doesn't exist."

"One and the same. Only according to this demand letter I'm looking at, the government not only thinks the money exists, they think Carling Lake has it."

Aaron stood and came around the desks. He read the letter over her shoulder. "It definitely looks like they do. And you haven't heard anything about your FOIA request."

Erika shook her head. "Only that they received it and there are responsive documents."

Aaron rubbed his chin. "I have a few reporter friends in DC. I'll call them and see if they have any contacts at the office they're willing to share with me."

"Thanks. I'm going to visit Susan again. Maybe she's turned up something since we last spoke."

Aaron's eyebrow arched. "Rest. Lance specifically said the doctor mentioned you needed rest."

Erika glanced at the clock on her computer screen. She logged out of the system and grabbed her purse, dropping a kiss on the older man's cheek as she slid past. "I've got to pick up Marcus. I'll see you later."

As EXPECTED, THE parents waiting outside Carling Lake Elementary for their kids to come running out of the school building at the sound of the dismissal bell had heard about her fall. Erika accepted the words of concern, demurred on offers of help and deflected attempts to pry the story out of her of how she'd fallen. Undoubtedly, whatever the gossip mill had dreamed up was far more entertaining than the truth, anyway.

The school bell finally rang. Erika's heart swelled to nearly bursting when she caught sight of Marcus running across the playground with his arms outstretched.

Marcus bowled into her, pushing her back into the fencing surrounding the playground yard and making her sore muscles tighten. Not that she minded a bit. Hugs from her nearly eleven-year-old son were coming fewer and further between as the years ticked by and she savored every one he willingly gave.

"How was your day? Are you still okay?" Marcus leaned back, but kept his arms around her waist. His big brown eyes emanated concern.

Her heart twisted at the worry etched on her son's face. Marcus had barely left her side the evening before, bustling about the house, making sure she was comfortable. He'd made them dinner, two peanut butter and jelly sandwiches and a salad, which had mostly just been lettuce, but he was proud of himself, so she happily ate it. He'd even let her have control over the television remote. Her son was turning into a kind, caring, self-sufficient young man and she couldn't have been prouder.

"I'm fine. You don't have to worry about me." They stood partially blocking one of the exits, parents and kids streaming around them, but Erika ignored the looks.

"I know you said you were fine, but I was still a little worried about you being on your own all day." Marcus looked up at her sheepishly.

"Now you know how I feel whenever you're out of my sight." She dropped a kiss on his forehead.

"Mooomm!" Marcus stepped from her arms, scanning the playground to see if any of his friends had seen him get a kiss from his mother.

"Come on," she said, smiling and pulling him back to her side. "I thought we could stop by Moulton's and get a couple of cones before heading home."

"Definitely!" Marcus bounced up and down with excitement. Like her, Marcus ascribed to the idea that ice cream wasn't just for the summer months.

Moulton's ice-cream parlor was only a short walk from the school. Erika left the car in its parking space and they strolled through Carling Lake's downtown area, a series of interconnecting streets that were home to a variety of shops designed to serve the needs of both the full-time residents and the tourists. A secondhand bookstore, antique and souvenir shop, and clothing store with kitschy T-shirts in its window stood side by side with the post office, a bank and the local pharmacy.

Moulton's, a town and tourist favorite, was housed in a redbrick building with an old-time awning over the door. The shop had been in operation for forty-two years according to the plaque by the register, but the building itself had stood for more than one hundred years, serving as the town's first police station. From housing prisoners to fifteen of the best flavors of homemade ice cream Erika had ever tasted—an upgrade in her humble opinion.

The shop wasn't busy. Although it was Erika's contention that ice cream never went out of season, one which Moulton's apparently agreed with since it was open all year, not everyone enjoyed ice cream in the cool temperatures of February. More for her and Marcus, who never turned down sweets.

It was a sunny day, so she and Marcus took their ice cream—raspberry crumble for Erika and blueberry blues for Marcus—to the park a half block away.

Between licks, Marcus told her about what he'd done in school that day. Unlike some parents, she never had to pull a description of his day from her son. Maybe it was because they were all each other had, but she was lucky that they were close.

Although Marcus had only paused long enough for Erika to get in a few "uh-huhs" and "that sounds fun," he still somehow managed to finish his ice-cream cone before she did. The appearance of a couple of guys he recognized from school on the basketball courts may have been a motivating factor. Marcus quickly abandoned her to eat her cone alone.

She didn't mind. She loved how independent her son was, often reminding herself that his intelligence and self-sufficiency must be a sign that she wasn't screwing him up too much in those difficult times when she doubted herself as a mother.

She was finishing the last bite of her cone and readying to signal to Marcus that it was time for them to head home when a familiar and unwelcome voice came from behind her.

"Heard you've been having a bit of trouble the last couple of days. Really sad to hear that."

Erika took a deep breath and counted to ten before turning to face Ellis. She immediately regretted it when she saw the Cheshire cat grin he wore. The rage she'd felt when Sam Hogan had admitted that he was walking off her job to take on Ellis's returned with a vengeance. She fought the urge to slap the grin off Ellis's face.

If she could have separated his character and personality from his looks, she might have found him attractive. She knew his olive-colored skin resulted from the tanning salon off Route 127 rather than any time spent outdoors and his blond hair was cut a little too long and his highlights a little too well placed to be natural. He had coal-gray eyes that many of the women in town found irresistible, which he didn't mind using to his greatest advantage. In his late forties, he was a confirmed bachelor but prolific dater. From what she'd heard, he was generous with his girlfriends until he tired of them, which didn't take long, at which point he unceremoniously moved on.

"Hard to believe since you're the source of one of my problems."

Ellis waved away her accusation. "Ah, come on now, Erika. It's just business. Sam Hogan is the best contractor for miles and I always get the best."

Erika let her gaze travel over the impeccably cut suit and coat he wore down to the loafers, probably Italian or some other ridiculously expensive kind. Ellis's entire look screamed that he had money and wanted everyone to know it. Too bad money couldn't buy integrity.

"And you suddenly had to renovate your hotel this close to the beginning of the tourist season?"

"I moved when the numbers dictated. The way I see it, you should thank me. I taught you a valuable lesson. If you want to go head to head with me in business, you better toughen up."

She shoved her hands in her pockets to keep him from seeing that they shook with anger. She wasn't a violent person by nature, but she detested Ellis. "I don't want to have anything to do with you at all."

His eyes narrowed and his lips thinned. "That's too bad. I was going to say that I'm sure I could find a job for you at one of my properties when your B&B tanks. But of course you'd have to work on your attitude."

She stepped toward him, getting into his space. "My attitude is just fine but if you don't like it, feel free to leave me and my attitude alone."

Ellis's sneer deepened. He opened his mouth to retort, but stopped when a deep voice spoke behind Erika. "Is there a problem here?"

Chapter Nine

The slightly paunchy, sandy-haired man looked James up and down derisively. "Best you mind your own business. I'm talking to the lady."

James stepped closer to Erika. "Not if she doesn't want to talk to you."

Lance had just dropped James back at his car when his gaze had landed on Erika talking to a man in the park across from the diner. Based on Erika's body language, the conversation was not one she welcomed. Without considering whether she'd appreciate his intervention, and more than a little frustrated by the target practice session, he'd stalked across the street.

The man's back straightened, his chest puffing out. "Look, I don't know who you think you are but this isn't any of your business."

James dropped his gaze to Erika's face. "Is he bothering you?"

Erika's scowl deepened. "This is Ellis Hanes." Ah, now the animosity made sense. James's dislike for the man grew exponentially. "He was just sharing his unsolicited opinion that my business doesn't stand a chance and I should just give up. And I was about to explain that it will be a cold day in—"

"Got it," James said, fighting the smile that wanted

to break out. A strong woman would never not be sexy. He turned back to Hanes. "You heard the woman. She doesn't want to talk to you."

"Who the blazes are you?" Ellis asked, indignation ringing in his tone.

"James West. Erika's neighbor."

"Well, neighbor. I'm the mayor of this town and this conversation doesn't concern you. We need to talk." Hanes reached out a hand to grab Erika.

Erika recoiled.

James slid in front of her, blocking Hanes and simultaneously stepping into his space. "I don't care if you're the President of the United States. The lady doesn't want to speak to you so it's in your best interest to walk away right now." James only had a few inches on Hanes, but it was enough to allow him to look down on the man.

"Or what?" Hanes's gaze was hard, but there was a tremor in his voice that signaled he knew he'd gone too far.

James leaned forward slightly, crowding Hanes even further, and lowered his voice to just above a whisper. "Leave."

Hanes took a step back, his eyes darting from Erika to James. They'd attracted the attention of a couple leaving the diner on the other side of the street. The man and woman gawked at them as if they were watching a movie unfold. They'd managed not to attract the attention of Marcus and his friends yet, but that luck would not hold if Hanes continued to press the issue.

Undoubtedly sensing he'd lost this round, Hanes took several more steps backward. "We'll continue this conversation later, Erika." Turning on his heel, Hanes stalked away.

Something about the incident didn't sit well with

James. It wasn't unheard of for a less-than-ethical businessperson to attempt to keep others out of their market, but an aura of desperation hung around Hanes. And desperate people did stupid, sometimes dangerous, things.

Ellis Hanes was one man James planned to keep an eye on.

James turned to Erika, ready to apologize for jumping in where he hadn't been invited and take his licks for doing so.

"Thank you," she said before he uttered a single sound. "Ellis can be a pain and I was hoping not to create a scene in front of Marcus."

"You're welcome."

As if his mother saying his name had summoned him, Marcus jogged up to them. "Hey, Mom." Marcus eyed James with naked curiosity. "Aren't you the guy renting the cabin next to our house?"

"Marcus! Manners!" Erika admonished.

Marcus dropped his head for a moment before raising his gaze to James's and thrusting out his right hand. "I'm Marcus Powell. Pleased to meet you."

"James West. And yes, I am renting the cabin next to your house."

Marcus's eyes lit up. "Cool. Do you play basketball?" Marcus jerked his head to the now-empty court. "My friends had to leave, but we don't have to go home yet, do we, Mom?" Marcus looked to Erika for approval.

"Just a little while longer. We need to get home."

Marcus shifted his gaze back to James. "Cool, so you want to come?"

His jeans and black leather boots weren't exactly regulation attire, but the way Marcus was looking at him made it impossible to say no to the kid. "Sure. It's been a while since I've been on a basketball court though so go easy on me."

The rapid shift in mood was a little disconcerting. A minute ago, he'd been running off a belligerent Ellis Hanes and now he was engaged in a pickup game with a ten-year-old.

Marcus was quick on his feet, and it was easy to see that he had talent.

"You're pretty good," James said after Marcus got around him for a third time.

"Thanks." Marcus bounced the ball from one hand to the other before passing it to James. "I want to try out for the school team next year so I've been practicing."

"It's paying off."

James took a shot. Pain ricocheted up his arm, but the ball made it into the basket.

"You're not so bad, either, for an older guy."

James flexed his fingers before pressing his hand to his heart. "Ouch." He glanced at Erika, who watched them play from a picnic table close to the basketball court.

"You know what I mean." Marcus shot the ball. It bounced off the backboard and into the basket. "My friend Devin is going to try out for the team, too, and sometimes we play two on two with his fathers. They're your age but they can never play a full forty-minute game without getting tired."

James bit back his laughter. "Well, it's not as easy when you're our age."

Marcus stepped up to the foul line. "I guess so. I like playing with them, though. My mother doesn't know anything about basketball and I don't have anyone else to practice with. My dad died before I was born and no siblings." Marcus took a shot. It bounced off the rim.

James chased it down, thinking about what Marcus had just said. The plight of the only child wasn't something that he was familiar with, not with three younger brothers always underfoot, but he was more interested in the comment about Marcus's father. Ronald Overholt died in a car accident almost eleven years ago. The timing was right.

He passed the ball back to Marcus. "I'm sorry about your father. Did he play basketball, too?"

"Um… I don't know," Marcus said distractedly, passing the ball back and forth from hand to hand behind his back.

"Your mom never told you anything about him?" The moment the words left his mouth, James felt like a jerk. He was pumping a child for information on his late father. If he had any doubt that he wasn't cut out for investigative work, the wave of contempt he felt for himself put it to rest.

Marcus pressed the basketball to his chest and eyed James with suspicion. "Not much. She doesn't like to talk about him."

James could feel Marcus closing off, and the loss felt like a punch to the gut. "Here, can I show you a little trick that will help you with your free throws?"

He had Marcus widen his stance just a bit and showed him how to loosen his wrist more and let it fall forward more naturally as he took the shot. The awkwardness from moments earlier faded away as the ball sailed through the air and into the basket.

"Wow, thanks," Marcus said with a smile that sent a bolt of pride sailing through James's chest.

"Not bad for an old dude, huh?" He gave Marcus's shoulder a pat. "I may not be much of a ballplayer but my brother Brandon was all-state in high school. I paid attention."

"Is he coming to visit you soon?" Marcus's grin was wide.

"Alright, alright. Why don't you practice a bit more while I take my old bones over and talk to your mom."

James walked toward Erika, an unfamiliar feeling rising inside. Marcus was caring, intelligent and quick-witted—a great kid. James hadn't had a lot of contact with kids. Ryan and his wife had just had their first child, and while James knew her three uncles would spoil her as rotten as her parents allowed, she was still an infant.

He sat on the bench next to Erika, pressing his hand against his thigh. All the bouncing and shooting had aggravated his injury. The palm of his hand felt as if it was vibrating.

"Thank you for doing that."

"No problem. He's good and, more importantly, he's a terrific kid."

"He is." She smiled.

"He mentioned his father passed away. I'm sorry."

Erika stiffened. "Thank you." A beat of silence hung between them. "What's wrong with your hand?"

So she'd noticed. He gave his standard answer. "Damaged tendon."

"Is that why you left the military?"

Silence stretched between them for a long moment before he answered. "Yes."

"What happened?"

He thought about evading, shutting down the line of conversation as he normally did whenever anyone but Ryan or one of the other guys he'd served with brought up his time in the military. But he surprised himself when he realized he wanted Erika to know.

"A suicide bomber." The words made his lungs constrict. He beat back the images that threatened to deluge him and forced himself to continue. "A piece of shrapnel tore through my palm. Can't have a marine sniper who can't shoot straight so I took a medical discharge."

There must be something in the water in Carling Lake. In the span of two hours, he'd shared his story with more people than he had in the last six months.

Erika covered his hand with hers. "I'm sorry."

"Thanks, but there are a lot of guys who have it harder than I do." And a lot of guys who didn't make it home. He had no right to complain or wallow.

"That doesn't change your loss," Erika said as if she'd read his mind.

He wasn't so sure she was right, but he didn't want to discuss it, either. "That's part of why I'm in Carling Lake. To take some time and figure out what I want to do with the rest of my life."

Erika's mouth turned up into a smile. "How's it going?"

"So far, not good. I went to the shooting range with the sheriff earlier today. He seems to think I could pass the firearms test to become a sheriff's deputy but I'm not sure law enforcement is for me."

"What is for you?"

He thought about the call from the gallery owner and the dozens of drawings he had in his apartment before pushing the thought away. Becoming a professional artist was an even more fantastical idea than joining the Carling Lake sheriff's department.

"I have no clue," he answered honestly.

"I was in a similar place when I first came to Carling Lake."

He arched an eyebrow. "How so?" He watched as she wrestled with whatever she was about to say. If she was really Erika Overholt, she'd spent years keeping that secret. He couldn't believe she would just blurt out the truth to a virtual stranger in the park.

"I married Marcus's father when I was twenty-one. My mother had just died, and I was alone. I met my husband, and he seemed like my knight in shining armor. By the time I realized he was anything but, I felt trapped. I got married right out of college. Never had a real profession. My husband was not nice. He made sure I was completely dependent on him. Then he died, and I found out I was pregnant. And that's a whole different level of terror. But eventually Marcus and I landed in Carling Lake, and I don't know, one day at a time I figured things out. I'm sure you will, too."

Erika shook her head, and he got the feeling she was shaking away the painful memories.

His gut twisted with the instinct to protect this woman and her son. And to show the man who was supposed to have protected them, who'd been lucky enough to have had Erika in his bed every night, just what he thought of him.

Which was something he was definitely not supposed to be thinking or feeling. Yet with each passing day, Erika filled more and more of his thoughts. The floral fragrance of her perfume. The kindness in her smile. The way her cheeks flushed when she was irritated or angry.

"We should get going," Erika said, pulling him from his thoughts. She rose and walked toward the basketball court.

Marcus trotted over to meet her, then looked past her at James. "See ya later, James. Maybe we can play again?"

He waved at the boy. "Anytime." It shocked him to realize just how much he meant it. Wrong or right, he was falling for Erika and her son.

Chapter Ten

"I understand. If your schedule opens up…" Erika heard the dial tone before she ended her statement "…please let me know."

She set her phone down on the table and crossed off the last name on the list of contractors she'd written up when she'd gotten home from the hospital earlier that day. There was no one within a thirty-mile radius who could take on her job immediately.

She glanced out of the kitchen window at James's cabin. Well, almost no one.

On the drive home after her run-in with Ellis, she'd vowed that her B&B would be up and running by the start of the tourist season as planned.

Buying the house and turning it into a B&B had become her dream not long after she'd moved to Carling Lake. It had taken years to earn the money for the down payment on the house and several more to save enough for the renovations that would be needed to turn it into a B&B.

She'd come home and, after throwing together a quick dinner, then getting Marcus started on his homework, redoubled her efforts to find a contractor by expanding her search window.

Her determination had yielded no results. Every

business owner in Carling Lake and the surrounding tourist-oriented towns were sprucing up for the tourist season. Any contractor worth their salt, and some who weren't—she knew because in desperation she'd called them, too—had been booked months ago.

She could handle some of the work herself. Two of the guest rooms and a bathroom upstairs needed painting, but the rooms also needed their hardwood floors refinished and she wanted to install a new vanity and toilet in the bathroom. Those were renovations she didn't trust herself to do, at least not well. And she couldn't afford for them not to be done well.

First impressions mattered. She didn't want the B&B to get a reputation for being rundown or shabby. Everything had to be perfect when she opened the doors to her first guests.

And she'd do everything in her power to make it happen, even trusting the very attractive stranger renting the cabin next door.

She glanced out the window a second time, but again just saw the side of the cabin. She had to admit James West looked like he knew his way around a power tool.

She looked out again. *So what's the plan then, Erika?*

"Why do you keep looking out the window?" She turned to find Marcus looking at her quizzically from across the table, where he worked on his homework.

She took a deep breath before answering. "Because I need to go talk to our neighbor. To ask him a favor."

Marcus cocked his head to the side. "So go ask. You always tell me that if I need help, I should just ask and that most people like to help."

She had said that, but she'd been thinking more along the lines of help with algebra and sentence diagrams, not letting a stranger into their lives.

As the years passed in Carling Lake, she'd let her guard down somewhat, befriending Lance and Daisy. But she'd remained on guard, mostly. She could not let Roger Overholt know he had a grandson. There was no way the billionaire philanthropist and businessman would allow them to live in peace. He'd want to have complete control over Marcus, his heir, just like he'd controlled Ronald. And he'd do anything to get it. She wouldn't allow it.

But Marcus didn't know any of that. By the time he'd been born, she'd had her Erika Powell identity in place and had given him her last name. He didn't know he was an Overholt. Didn't know they were essentially hiding from his birth father's family. And she didn't want him to know. She couldn't give him the material things Roger Overholt could, but she'd worked hard to give him a normal childhood free from the fear and terror she'd felt living as an Overholt, and that was priceless.

"You're right," Erika said, standing. "I'm going to talk to him. I'll just be a minute. You keep working on that algebra." She left the house, crossed the two front yards and knocked on the cabin door before she allowed herself to overanalyze the situation further.

She wasn't inviting James into her and Marcus's lives. She was taking him up on his offer to do work on the house. He'd be working for her, nothing more. If he was still wanted the job, that was. She had been pretty rude when he'd extended the offer. He may not be willing to help her out now.

All these thoughts ran through her brain in the seconds between her knocking and James opening the door.

And then all thought fled. James stood in the doorway in a form-fitting sleeveless T-shirt that clung to his sweaty chest. On his right biceps was a tattoo of an eagle and the letters *USMC*. His dark mesh shorts revealed equally muscled calves and thighs.

"Erika? Everything okay?"

"Yes. Great. I'm…good." She shook her head. *Get it together! He's just a man.* But it had been a while since she'd been with a man. Especially one who looked like the one standing in front of her. No. Scratch that. She'd never been with a man who looked like James West.

James's forehead crinkled with concern. "Erika, you're starting to worry me here. Are you sure you're okay?"

"Does your offer to help with the work on the house still stand?" she blurted out. Her mind had obviously decided to forcibly take the reins from her libido.

"Oh…sure. Yes, of course it still stands." Despite his words, she couldn't help but note the look of surprise on his face.

"If you've changed your mind, I understand. I wasn't very gracious about your offer earlier and I apologize for that."

He smiled, and a ripple of sexual awareness traveled through her. There had been men after Ronald, but it had been a while since her last relationship, and James West was incredibly sexy.

Her pulse kicked into high gear.

"One thing you should know about me," James said, seemingly oblivious to her reaction to him, "is I don't say things I don't mean. I'm ready and willing to help in any way I can."

She felt her shoulders fall and realized how much tension she'd been carrying in them. "Great. Thank you. I know we still need to work out payment but I'm kind of in a time crunch."

He waved a hand, dismissing her statement. "There's

no need to pay me. You'd be giving me something to do with myself. How about I get started tomorrow morning?"

She would pay him, but tomorrow was soon enough to fight that battle if need be. "Great. Wonderful. See you tomorrow. If you come over around seven, you can have breakfast with me and Marcus before you get started," Erika said, already walking backward toward her house.

"I'm looking forward to it." His smile grew, and she turned away, physically fighting the urge to run back into her house.

She'd done it. She'd asked for help, and he'd agreed. Now she just hoped she wouldn't regret it.

Chapter Eleven

"Reed Johnson is a marine. Do you know him?" Marcus pushed his frameless glasses up the bridge of his nose and stared across the table at James expectantly.

"I can't say I do. There are a lot of marines," James answered the latest in the barrage of questions Marcus had asked about the Marine Corps and the military. From all appearances, Marcus and Erika had been up and at 'em for quite some time. The house had smelled of freshly brewed coffee and pancake batter already sizzled on the stove when James arrived promptly at seven o'clock.

Marcus nodded his head knowingly. "Charlie Mulhern is a sailor. That means he's in the Navy."

"I can't say I've met him either I'm afraid." James sipped his coffee, amused and flattered by the young boy's enthusiasm.

Erika headed for the table with a serving plate loaded with pancakes. "There are a lot of people in the military. You can't expect Mr. West to know them all."

He sent Erika a grateful smile. He wasn't used to being around children, especially not ones as inquisitive as Marcus.

He could already tell Erika would be an excellent B&B owner and hostess. She manned the six-burner stove like a professional chef, preparing three different kinds of pancakes—banana-nut, strawberry and a rainbow-sprinkle for him and Marcus to pass judgment on as possible breakfast offerings for future B&B guests. He wasn't sold on strawberry, but the other two definitely earned his stamp of approval.

Marcus ate with gusto, reminding him of how often his father had complained about the massive amounts of food he and his three brothers consumed as teens.

Erika joined them at the table, and they all tucked into breakfast.

Marcus polished off four large pancakes before he spoke again. "Do you like fishing?"

"I haven't done it in a long time but, yes, I do," James answered, bringing his coffee cup to his lips.

"Mom and I are going next Saturday. Do you want to come with us?"

He did. It amazed him, but he was finding that the more time he spent with Erika and Marcus, the more time he wanted to spend with them. A dicey situation, given that he didn't know how Erika would feel about him by next week.

Erika swallowed the bite of pancake in her mouth hurriedly. "I'm sure James has other plans for his weekend. We wouldn't want to impose."

Marcus's face fell.

He hated to disappoint Marcus, but inserting himself into their lives too far risked even greater disappointment later.

"I'm not sure I'll be free next weekend, but can I have a rain check?"

"Sure, whatever," Marcus responded sullenly.

"It's almost time for school. Go finish getting ready. And don't forget to brush your teeth," Erika called after him as he headed through the door at the rear of the kitchen.

"Sorry about that. Let me show you around the house while Marcus is getting ready for school." Erika motioned toward a long hallway to the right of the foyer.

She raised her hands and gestured. "Well, this is the kitchen. As you can see, there's not much to do here. I had it renovated when we moved in four years ago because, well, because we needed to eat." She pointed to the door Marcus had disappeared behind. "Through that door are my and Marcus's bedrooms and a small private sitting room. You don't have to worry about that area."

Erika turned and began walking back toward the entrance hall. With its massive, curved staircase including intricately carved wood railings, it would make quite the impression.

"You probably noticed the large sitting room when you came in. Then there's what used to be the small sitting room. I've turned it into a library for guests who want a little quiet area." She led him down a long hallway and into a room with several four-top round tables. "Here's the dining room where I'll be serving a buffet breakfast."

"The banana-nut pancakes get my vote," James said, stepping into the room after her.

Erika turned, bumping into him and stumbling.

He reached out and steadied her.

"Sorry, I…didn't see you," she said breathlessly. The desire in her eyes kicked his heartbeat up a notch.

Erika stepped back out of his arms, and he fought the need to pull her to him again. "I was just going to say I don't know why I'm showing you all this. The work that needs to be done is on the second floor."

He moved aside and Erika moved past him, out of

the room and back toward the front of the house. He let out a deep breath meant to steady his raging libido, and followed her upstairs.

"There's a third floor I hope to open up to guests one day." Erika pointed upward as they reached the second-floor landing. "But for now I just have the rooms on this floor available."

Erika opened the door on the left. They stepped into a sunbathed room with medium-brown wood wainscoting and matching wood framing the windows. "All the bedrooms are pretty much the same. The upper walls need a fresh coat of paint but I don't want to touch the wainscoting or window trim. The floors do need refinishing though."

"And how many rooms are there?" he asked, taking stock of the project. Painting was tedious work but not difficult. Refinishing the floors would be the biggest lift, but he'd helped Ryan refinish the floors in his new house, so he knew the process.

"Four bedrooms and two bathrooms up here." Erika led the way out of the room. She opened another door farther down the hall. "This is the first bathroom. It's dated but everything works so I'm not touching it for now."

James took a quick look around the bathroom and agreed with Erika's assessment. She took him to the door at the end of the hall. "This is the second bathroom."

She opened the door, and he saw right away why she'd been so distressed when Sam Hogan had walked out on her. The bathroom had no vanity or toilet and the light fixture that should have been hanging over the medicine chest sat in the tub.

"It looks worse than it is. The old vanity and toilet

were pink with gold flecks. Way too 1960s for the feel I want. Sam was just helping me give the space a more contemporary look. I've ordered the vanity and toilet already but I don't know the first thing about installing them."

"I can help with that." He'd never actually installed a vanity or toilet, but how hard could it be. With the help of the internet, he was sure he could figure it out.

She closed the door and led him back down the front staircase. "You really think you can handle all this?" Erika chewed her bottom lip.

James was suddenly hit with the urge to promise her anything that would wipe that worried expression off her face.

"Yes. I've refinished floors and anyone can paint walls. I've never installed a vanity or toilet before but I've seen the actors in the commercials do it." His attempt at a joke did nothing to wipe the skepticism from her eyes. "Honestly, I've got this. You said you already ordered the vanity?"

Erika nodded. "From Laureano's hardware store. It should be in any day now."

"Then I'm sure there's someone there who can help me if I get into trouble. I'll be fine."

She watched him for a moment longer, then gave a small smile. "Okay. You're right. I've learned plenty about renovations and the clerk at the hardware store has been very helpful." Her smile widened, and his heart flip-flopped in his chest.

"So I need to drop Marcus off and then I'll be back to help." She led him back to the kitchen, using the rear staircase, and cleared away the remains of breakfast.

He'd been hoping to have time today to search the house for some proof that she really was Erika Overholt. "If you have other things to get done, I'm sure I'll be fine working by myself."

Erika glanced at him over her shoulder. "I won't be much help but I'm free today after I take Marcus to school." She carried an empty plate and cup to the dishwasher.

And she probably wanted to make sure he knew what he was doing and wasn't going to ruin her chances of getting the B&B open in time. Smart.

He followed her, handing over his dishes.

"I was thinking you could work each day while Marcus goes to school but it's kind of a madhouse around here when he gets home," she said as she rinsed the syrup off his plate before putting it in the dishwasher next to her own. "Getting dinner together and doing homework. I think it would be better for Marcus's studies if there were no renovation distractions. I think we can still get everything done with that work schedule. Don't you?"

"I don't see why not. If we need to, we can always put in longer hours as we near your deadline for submitting the occupancy paperwork."

Marcus appeared in the kitchen doorway. "Mom. I'm ready. Let's go!"

Erika rolled her eyes. "I'm being summoned. Everything we need should be in the basement. Far right corner. The prior owners left an old electric sander. I figured you could use that, but it's too heavy for me to haul up the stairs. Would you mind?"

"Not a problem."

"Great. Back in twenty."

The back door to the house slammed closed as he made his way downstairs. Twenty minutes wasn't a lot of time to search a house of this size, but if there was proof of Erika's real identity in the house, he'd be most likely to find it in the private quarters. Maybe he'd get lucky and be done with this assignment today, after all.

He headed back through the kitchen to the door that Erika indicated led to her private quarters. It opened onto a nice-sized living space with a comfortable looking sectional sofa situated in front of a television. A desk was pushed into one corner of the room; a laptop and a stack of papers sitting on top. He noted several paintings of Carling Lake gracing the sunny yellow walls, clearly not done by a professional but they were very good, nonetheless. Two large windows looked out over the backyard and the trees beyond. A short hallway led to three closed doors. The overall feel of the space was lived in and cozy.

He went to the desk first. It wasn't a very imaginative place to hide anything but then many people weren't all that imaginative when attempting to hide things. The most common hiding places were behind photos, the underside of drawers, behind the toilet or even inside of one, and the oldie but not so goodie under the mattress.

He checked all the usual spots in the living room and bathroom before moving on to the bedroom. Marcus's room was a blue with glow-in-the-dark star and planet stickers pressed onto the ceiling and walls. A pair of Captain America pajamas were strewn across the unmade twin bed. Toys, books and a single shoe sat atop the dresser and a second laptop was on the desk in this room.

He did a quick search of the room, including looking between the mattress and box spring, but he was fairly confident that Erika wouldn't hide anything that could identify her as Erika Overholt in here. It would be far too easy for Marcus to accidentally come across it.

Instinct and experience told him that he'd most likely find proof of Erika's true identity in her bedroom. That was if there was any evidence in the house at all. There was always the chance that she'd rented a safety deposit box at a bank or that there was no proof to be found whatsoever.

Time was dwindling.

He crossed the hall to Erika's bedroom and opened the door. The walls in this room were a soft gray and a gray-and-white rug took up most of the floor. The room was larger than Marcus's but the dark wood king-sized four-poster bed, matching vanity and dresser took up a lot of the extra space. An off-white duvet covered the mattress and a bevy of pillows rested against the headboard. The smell of lilacs lingered in the air, triggering an image of Erika in his mind. He could imagine her here, getting dressed for the day or propped up against the pillows, reading before turning in for the night.

He shook his head, dispelling the distracting images and thoughts and got to work.

As he'd done in the living room, he checked behind the paintings of Carling Lake and the mirror on the vanity before lifting the mattress. Nothing. The single drawer in her night table also revealed nothing of interest.

He wasn't surprised. If Erika Powell really was Erika Overholt, she'd been hiding that fact for a very long time. She wasn't likely to leave evidence of her real identity someplace he'd easily find it. The bedroom had a single narrow walk-in closet on the wall opposite the bed. The folding door was off its track and he fought the urge to put it to rights. Dresses hung next to a row of skirts followed by a handful of blouses. Several pairs of slacks pulled up the rear of the most organized closet he'd ever seen. Jeans and sweaters, all neatly folded, were stacked on the shelf above. Below the hanging clothes was a tidy row of shoes—heels, flats, low-slung booties and knee-length boots. Erika obviously had a thing for shoes.

Going through Erika's closet felt weirdly intimate and guilt stabbed at him as he did. Would she hate him if she found out he'd invaded her space? He couldn't blame her if she did. Just another sign that he was not cut out to be a private investigator. He searched the pockets, the interior of the shoes and behind the stacked clothing, careful to put everything back just as it had been. If there was anything there, Erika had hidden it exceptionally well.

He closed the closet door, making sure to leave it slightly askew as he'd found it.

He was out of time. Erika would be back at any moment and, if he didn't want her to ask questions about what he'd been doing while she was gone, he needed to get that sander upstairs.

HE FOUND THE sander just where Erika said it would be in the basement. Thankfully, it was a newish lighter-weight model than the huge drum sanders of the past. He carried it up the two flights of stairs and was only slightly winded when he set it down in the bedroom.

He turned to head back downstairs for the rest of the tools when footsteps sounded below.

He glanced out of the bedroom window. The driveway where she parked her van was still empty.

Whoever was in the house, it wasn't Erika.

His nine-millimeter was locked up in his cabin—he hadn't expected to need it to sand floors. That was a mistake he wouldn't make again.

He snuck down the curved staircase, hoping the creaky wood wouldn't give away his position. Whoever was in the house must have seen Erika drive away and assumed it was empty. An assumption the intruder would come to regret.

In the foyer, James stilled, listening for any sounds. Silence reigned for long enough that he'd just about concluded he'd imagined footsteps when a rustling sound came from the direction of the kitchen.

Definitely not imagined.

He moved into the kitchen, keeping his eyes and ears peeled for any movement or sound. The room was empty. He headed for the door to Erika's private residence. He could hear someone moving around on the other side of the door.

Without a weapon, his best bet was the element of surprise.

James flung the door open, charging into the room, his eyes scanning the space quickly.

And landing on Erika, who stood in front of a desk, steps from the door, a sheath of paper in her hands. She shrank back, her mouth open, ready to scream.

He stopped, just missing barreling into her.

They stared at each other for a moment, and then Erika's face hardened. "What do you think you're doing?"

"I heard footsteps down here and you'd left," he explained quickly. "I thought your would-be burglar might be making a second attempt."

She shook the papers in her hand. "Marcus left his homework. I came back for it."

He held his hands up in surrender. "I'm sorry. I may have over—"

The sound of a thud overhead had him stopping mid-apology. Erika's eyes went to the ceiling, letting him know she'd heard it, too.

"Did Marcus come inside with you?" he asked in a whisper.

She shook her head. "I left him in the car around back."

The sound of footsteps thundering down the front staircase sent him bolting back toward the door. "Lock yourself in the car with Marcus, and don't get out for any reason," he called over his shoulder.

He caught a flash of a man dressed in all black dashing through the front door of the house as he ran through the kitchen for the foyer. He hit the porch at a full sprint in time to see the intruder duck into the woods on the other side of Erika's long driveway.

He didn't bother to chase the guy this time. He turned back to the house as Erika stepped out onto the porch with a rifle at the ready.

"He got away?" Erika's face was ashen, but she held the rifle in steady hands.

He nodded and climbed the porch steps, his frustration with himself flaring over having lost the intruder for a second time. "Marcus okay?"

"Locked in his room. I figured he'd be safer there than in the car and I wanted to be ready if our visitor circled back." She patted the barrel of the rifle.

"Let's give Marcus the all clear and call Sheriff Webb." He reached to open the screen door.

Erika grabbed his hand to stop him. Warmth spread through him at her touch.

"We can't call Lance."

"Someone is obviously targeting you."

Erika stepped closer. "Listen to me. No one can know about this, do you understand? No one."

Chapter Twelve

"I don't understand. I thought you and the sheriff were friends," James said.

Lance was as close a friend as Erika had in Carling Lake, but he didn't—couldn't—know everything about her. The current string of events had the potential to force Lance to look more deeply into her background than she was comfortable with.

"We are. And Lance would do everything he could to find the guy. But I can't afford to have people think my B&B is unsafe."

"There might be more at stake than the B&B's reputation. Assuming this is the same person who tried to break in the night you were in the hospital, they seem determined to keep trying until they get whatever it is they are after."

She could see the wisdom in what James was saying, but she needed time to think. There was a slim chance the events of the last two days meant Roger Overholt had discovered she'd given birth to his grandson, but she suspected the source of her recent troubles might lie closer to home.

"I don't think so."

James sent her a penetrating look. "Is there something you're not telling me?"

If he only knew. But he couldn't know, not if she wanted to ensure she and Marcus would continue to be safe. She had to keep reminding herself. She couldn't even be sure the recent incidents had anything to do with who she'd been.

She set the shotgun across the table on the porch. "I don't have any evidence but I think Ellis Hanes might be behind the break-ins."

"The guy who stole your contractor from you."

"Yes."

James looked as if he were considering it. "I'm not discounting the possibility that Hanes is trying to sabotage your B&B. Corporate espionage isn't exactly new, but your theory wouldn't explain the first attempted break-in. That happened before your contractor walked off the job."

"Ellis still could have sent him."

"Okay, let's say this Hanes guy is behind the break-ins and the bridge. That's all the more reason to report this to the sheriff's department."

"We didn't even get a good look at the man. Lance will come out and take our statements and nothing will come of it except that people will hear about another incident—" she used air quotes "—at my B&B."

"Erika—"

"Just stop, okay. You don't get it. Calling Lance would be a waste of time. Ellis Hanes and his family are revered in this town. Nobody will take my side against his even if they do believe me. I'm on my own here," she said, her voice breaking as the raw truth of that statement hit her. She lowered her head, fighting the tears and wariness. The weight of not only the last several days but the last ten years, years spent concerned that Roger Overholt would show up out of the blue or that someone would discover her real identity.

James stepped forward, reached down and hooked her chin with his forefinger, lifting it until her eyes met his. "You're not on your own. You have me."

His words rumbled through her. The same physical awareness she'd felt when he'd given her a ride home from the hospital and given him a tour of the B&B earlier in the day flooded her body.

He moved his hands to her upper arms, rubbing them softly.

She stepped closer, stepping into his embrace when his arms encircled her waist. His hard muscled body pressed against her softer form.

James's eyes never left hers, and the look on his face was intense and intoxicating, beckoning her to lean in and taste his full lips. The butterflies in her stomach kicked up another notch. He lowered his head slowly, giving her a chance to back away.

She knew it was a bad idea, but she wanted him to kiss her more than she had wanted anything in a very long time.

Before she could talk herself out of it, she raised her head and met his kiss.

He caressed her lips with a firm, slightly demanding kiss that sent a surge of excitement through her. She deepened the kiss, felt his surprise at her aggressiveness before he let her take the lead.

She might have completely lost herself in his embrace, but the sounds from inside the house yanked her back into reality.

She placed a hand on his chest and stepped back. "We can't. Marcus might see and you're only here for a short time."

Disappointment spread across his face, but was quickly replaced by acceptance. "I understand."

"I just think it's better if we keep things…" *Casual* wasn't the right word. That implied that she was open to more kissing, maybe even more than kissing. Was she? She let her gaze travel over the man in front of her. No, she wasn't a casual fling kind of woman. And she had a son to think about. "Professional. It's best that we keep things friendly, but professional."

"Friendly but professional," James said the words as if they were foreign to him. And the intensity of his stare hadn't eased since she'd broken off the kiss.

"Yes."

"If that's what you want."

"I should get Marcus to school." She grabbed the rifle from the table and turned to go into the house.

"I guess I should get back to work."

She felt his solid presence as he fell into step behind her.

Friendly but professional. It wasn't what she wanted, but it was what was best.

She had to keep telling herself that. And maybe, eventually, she'd even believe it.

Chapter Thirteen

Erika had kept her distance from James in the two days since their smoldering kiss. She'd held up her part of their deal and continued to make breakfast, but she'd allowed Marcus to dominate the conversation with his unceasing questions about the military and what it was like to live in New York City.

She'd liked the kiss a lot. It had awakened feelings she hadn't even thought about in a decade. Despite her intention to keep James at arm's length, she found herself thinking about him often. There was something in the way he looked at her. As if she were the most interesting woman in the world and he couldn't take his eyes off her. But there were too many complications to pursue those feelings. James would go back to his life eventually and it wouldn't be fair to him or Marcus to pull him too close when whatever they could have would be based on lies.

She'd hoped to have time to help with the renovation, but she'd mostly kept to the private residence space she and Marcus shared, focusing on her work for the *Weekly*.

That was where she now sat, at the small desk she'd crammed into a corner of the living room, putting the finishing touches on a story about Moulton's new flavor to kick off the tourist season, she'd been tapping every resource she had in an effort to get to the bottom of the mystery of the missing grant money. Unfortunately, she hadn't turned up anything except a renewed resolve for answers. Which was why she had decided that she needed to pay another visit to the treasurer's office.

Susan Garraus had been less than helpful when Erika had brought the first letter granting Carling Lake the money to the town treasurer's attention. She'd claimed to have heard nothing about it at all, but something about her denials hadn't rung completely true to Erika's ears. But without any proof that Susan wasn't being honest, there'd been nothing Erika could do.

Maybe now, with this apparent demand letter from the government, Susan would be more forthcoming.

Erika glanced at her watch. It was 2:12 p.m. The middle school let out at four o'clock. That left plenty of time to talk to Susan before she had to pick up Marcus. She grabbed her purse, pulled the door open and stepped into the kitchen. She stopped short when she caught sight of James at the island, a fresh pot of coffee in the machine.

"There's enough for two if you want a cup," he said before taking a sip from the mug in his hands.

"Thanks. I'm good. I was on my way out, actually."

"Where are you headed?"

"I need to pop into the town treasurer's office to check into something for a story I'm working on. I shouldn't be too long."

"I'll go with you." James took a big gulp from the mug, then set it in the sink.

"No. I don't think that is a good idea." She took a step toward the back door.

"The hardware store called. The vanity is in. I can

pick it up while you do whatever you need to do. It doesn't make sense for us to drive separate cars."

His statement was logical, but she felt like being in the car with him would be too awkward.

"We should talk about the kiss. It obviously made you uncomfortable—"

"No, we shouldn't and it didn't." Her gaze slid from his.

"Really? Because you've barely spoken to me or looked at me in the last two days and you don't even want to take a five-minute ride into town with me."

"Fine. You're right. You can come with me to pick up the vanity."

She turned her back to him and went to the van. He slid into the passenger seat as she started the car.

They rode in silence, his statement about their kiss replaying on a loop through her mind until she pulled into a parking space outside of city hall.

She put the van in park, cut the engine and turned in her seat to face James. "The kiss… Our kiss. It didn't make me uncomfortable. At least not the way you're probably thinking. It's just… I haven't been kissed like that in a very long time. It was nice." That was the understatement of the decade. "Very nice, but it can't happen again. I just don't have room in my life for… complications. I have Marcus to consider and the B&B renovation. You're not going to be in town that long, and there's this person breaking into my house—" She felt herself babbling.

"I get it. I do," James interrupted. "Look, I get that things are complicated right now." He hesitated and for a moment his face darkened and she got the sense he was about to share a secret with her. But then his expression softened. "I don't want to make things harder for you but I can't deny there's something between us."

"James—"

"Wait, hear me out. I told you that I'm in Carling Lake to figure out what comes next in my life. That means taking stock and being honest with myself and what I want. You and I are bound to be…complicated." The shadow passed over his face again before clearing just as quickly. He reached across the console for her hand. "But that doesn't mean it's not worth a shot."

She felt herself weakening.

"I can't talk about this right now. I need to get to the treasurer's office." Erika exited the van. James did the same and fell into step beside her. She stopped and turned to him. "The hardware store is that way." She pointed over her shoulder.

"I know. I figured I'd go with you and then we could both walk over to get the vanity."

"Why? I mean I can handle this on my own."

"I'm sure you can, but I've always wanted to see a journalist in action."

"James—"

The look on his face brooked no nonsense. "We're wasting time."

The tension in Erika's body only heightened once she was inside the Carling Lake treasurer's office.

Carling Lake town treasurer, Susan Garraus, stood at the counter in the front office. Her eyes flicked to James and a slow coquettish smile slid across her face.

A flicker of jealousy rose in Erika's chest, watching Susan check out James. Susan was about ten years older than Erika's thirty-seven, but she was still an attractive woman. Shiny brown hair fell in waves to her shoulders and while her designer glasses definitely contributed to a librarian-ish aura, the look veered more toward sexy librarian than frumpy librarian.

Susan's gaze turned to Erika and her expression hardened, her lips puckering as if she'd just bitten into something extremely sour.

"Hi, Susan. I'm hoping you can help me out. You might recall our conversation a few weeks ago about an award of a grant by the federal—"

"I recall," Susan cut her off. "And as I told you then, there is no grant."

Erika kept her smile. "I received another letter." She pulled a copy of the attachments from both the emails from her purse and laid them on the desk facing Susan. "This one looks like a demand from the government asking Carling Lake to show that the grant money is being used as specified in its application. Carling Lake may not have applied for the grant or received any money, but it sure seems like the federal government thinks it did. I'm sure you can see how that's a problem that the citizens of Carling Lake deserve to know how their elected officials are handling it." She reached back into her purse and pulled out a small notebook.

These days most reporters recorded their interviews using their phones but New York required all parties to a conversation to consent to a recording. Consent Erika doubted Susan would give her. Interviewees were more forthcoming when she used pen and paper, anyway. There was something about the old-school method that people found less intimidating.

Susan's eyes narrowed to slits. "It's not a problem because there is no grant. I don't know who's sending you these letters or what they are filling your head with but it's all fake."

"The letters are addressed to this office." Erika

pointed to the salutation. "Are you saying you've never seen them before?"

"I'm telling you, I know nothing. About. A grant."

Susan's persistent denials only intensified the feeling in Erika's gut that she was lying. She glanced over at James, who hadn't said a word since they'd entered, but whose face reflected disbelief as well. "Have you spoken to anyone in the federal government to find out what's going on?"

"I don't have to answer that," Susan sneered.

"So the treasurer's office is not at all concerned that it might be on the hook for three hundred thousand dollars no one seems to know anything about?"

Susan's face turned red, but she simply stared across the counter at Erika.

"Is that a no comment from the treasurer's office, then?"

Susan pursed her mouth and turned away, disappearing into a rear office without another word.

"That went well," James said as he followed her from the office.

"About as well as every conversation I've had with Susan over the last couple of weeks has gone. The thing is I'm sure she knows something about this grant money." They exited the building and turned toward the hardware store.

"I have to agree with you there," James said. "She was definitely nervous about something. What is the story with the grant?"

She quickly filled him in. "I've tapped into every source I have. My boss even has a few calls out to his own sources but so far, nothing."

"I know a couple of vets who work for the feds now. I can't promise anything but I can see if either of them

knows anyone who works for the office that distrib-
uted the grant."

James's offer was another chink in her armor. "That
would be amazing. Thank you."

She was lost in thought as they piled back into the
van and headed to pick up the bathroom vanity at the
hardware store. That James was going out of his way
to help her even though they'd just met touched her. It
had been a long time since she'd had someone step up
for her. Of course, there were Lance and Daisy but it
was different with James.

*Different because your feelings for him are much
more than friendly.* Okay, she was willing to admit it
to herself. She was attracted to James West. What did
it matter? Feelings or no feelings, she wasn't wrong
about not needing additional complications in her life
at the moment. Between starting a new business, the
attacks on the B&B, her work for the paper and raising
Marcus on her own, she had more than enough to keep
her busy. And once James figured out his next steps,
he'd leave Carling Lake, and her and Marcus, behind.

She snuck a sidelong glance at him as she drove. The
most logical decision was to keep things professional.
Even if that left her just the tiniest bit crestfallen.

Chapter Fourteen

"It's gorgeous. I love it. Thank you so much, Taria."
Erika threw her arms around Taria Sanders, part-time
clerk at Laureano's hardware and full-time waitress at
Mahoney's Grill. The other woman stiffened, and after
giving Erika's back a perfunctory pat, stepped out of
the embrace quickly.

"Sorry."

"No problem." Taria waived the apology away but
the expression on her face left no doubt that the hug had
made her uncomfortable.

Taria had largely kept to herself since she'd come
to town several months earlier. Erika couldn't say she
knew the woman well but she'd been a tremendous help
when it had come to tracking down the semicircular
light cherrywood antique vanity Erika had fallen in love
with when she'd seen it in an architectural magazine.
Erika doubted very much seventy-two-year-old Vincent
Laureano, owner of Laureano's hardware, would have
searched through the dozens of web pages Taria had to
find the manufacturer.

"You paid in advance so you're all set. Let me just
go find someone to help you get this into your car."

"That's what I'm here for." James smiled.

Taria blinked. "Okay, well I'll just wrap it back up and push this to the back door. You can load from there."

The vanity was already on a pushcart but Erika had had Taria remove the foam padding wrapped around it so she could inspect it before she officially took possession.

"Actually, I wanted to show you something if you have time," James said, pulling both women's gazes to him.

"Sure." Erika followed him to the rear of the store where a selection of tiles for the floor, shower and kitchen hung on the wall and populated the shelves.

"I took a look at the bathroom where you want the vanity installed. The bathtub and the tile around it look pretty good but you could stand to upgrade the flooring. Right now, it's a vinyl tile, in okay shape. But I was thinking if you're going through all the trouble of installing a new vanity and toilet, you may as well upgrade the floors."

Erika ran her hands over the black-and-white hexagonal shaped tile she'd had her eye on for a while. She'd had Sam price out the cost of changing the floors when he'd given her an estimate for doing the renovations but she'd only had the budget for necessary repairs—the vanity and toilet weren't just old, they leaked, which ate into her profits. The bathroom floor, as James noted, was okay.

She shook her head. "I got an estimate for changing the floors. I don't have the budget."

"Did your estimate account for free labor and the store's discount on flooring?" He pointed to the sign declaring all flooring ten percent off.

Sam's estimate had definitely included a charge for labor and a ten-percent discount was enticing. She did a rough calculation in her head. It would put her over her budget for the bathroom but only a little.

She cocked her head and looked at James. "Why would you add another reno project to the work we agreed you'd do for free?"

"I have the time and I want to help. That's all there is to it."

She very much doubted that. The price for his time and labor they'd finally agreed upon was already low but she'd been desperate and he'd refused to take any more. It had probably been the first and only time in history where a contractor negotiated the fee down while the customer was negotiating up.

"Okay but only if I pay you the ten percent I'm saving on the tiles. It's fair and it's the only way I'll agree," she added, stopping his protest before it got started.

"It's a deal." He stretched his arm out. She slid her hand in his, sending sparks racing through her body. Her heart thundered in her chest and she found herself involuntarily closing the space between them.

She couldn't take her eyes off his, which she might have felt self-conscious about if his eyes hadn't also been locked on her gaze, the desire she saw in them warming her from head to toe.

"The vanity is on the loading... Oh, sorry. Didn't mean to interrupt anything." Taria's light brown skin flushed and she turned, hurrying back the way she'd come.

Erika took a large step backward, feeling the heat of embarrassment rising in her face. The last thing she needed was rumors about her and James making out in Laureano's hardware spreading through town.

For his part, James didn't look the least bit embarrassed about almost being caught kissing her in public.

He stuck his hands in his pocket and leaned forward, eliminating much of the distance she'd put between them.

A devilish grin, one she found both mildly irritating in its glee and incredibly hot, twisted his lips. "You know that complication you don't have time for right now? I think you might need to make time because whatever this is, it's not going away."

Chapter Fifteen

Taria rang up the tiles and items that were needed to lay them while James maneuvered all the purchases into the back of the van in a way that left enough room for Marcus. Feeling like she was back in high school, Erika had started to explain that nothing had happened between her and James in the tile aisle but Taria had shut down the conversation, saying she wasn't in the habit of sharing other people's business and she didn't have anyone to share it with even if she'd wanted to. That last comment had left her feeling bad for the woman. Taria was probably lonely, having moved to town relatively recently.

Erika made a mental note to invite Taria over for dinner as soon as the renovations were completed, then met James at the van. They pulled into the school parking lot just as the bell rang, signaling the end of the day. The ride home was filled with Marcus regaling them with stories about his day.

She backed the van into the driveway beside the house so the trunk was closest to the door. It would make it easier to move the vanity and tiles from the back into the house.

Marcus got out on the passenger side behind James, explaining in precise detail exactly how he'd made the winning shot in the pickup basketball game he and his buddies played at recess that day.

A flash burst from the trees across from Erika's house, alerting James before his brain actually registered the sound of the gunshot.

He grabbed Marcus's arm and shoved him toward the back of the van, putting the vehicle between them and the shooter.

"Marcus!" Erika yelled.

Without a pause, he drew his gun from the holster at his side. The nerves in his palm pinched as he wrapped his hand around the gun's grip. "Get around to the back of the van and keep your head down," James yelled.

Erika rounded the van on the driver's side and immediately wrapped her body around Marcus in a protective huddle.

A second shot shattered one of the front windows on the house.

James shook his head. "We need to get inside. We're too exposed out here."

Their shooter had gone quiet. It had been nearly half a minute since the second shot, but that wasn't necessarily good news. Although he hadn't seen the shooter, he had a pretty good idea of the approximate area in the trees where the shots had come from. The shooter didn't have a clear line of sight anymore. But that could change quickly. Whoever was shooting at them could be at this very moment moving to get a better angle.

But would he be able to hit his target if it came to that? Just the weight of the gun had set the nerves in his hand to trembling. He had no choice but to try. They were too exposed where they were.

James cut a look at Erika over the top of Marcus's head. "When I tell you to go, run for the front door as fast as you can and stay away from the windows. And Erika as soon as you're safe call Lance."

He hadn't bought for a minute that her hesitancy to call Lance after the break-in had been a way to protect the new B&B's reputation. But someone taking shots at them, that was an escalation that demanded help from the proper authorities.

Erika seemed to agree. She nodded before her eyes fell to his hand, and he knew she'd seen them trembling. "Are you sure—"

"We can't stay here. You know how to use that rifle you were holding the other day. When you get inside, grab it."

She gave another nod.

James peered around the front of the van, looking for any movement in the area the shots had come from. He stepped out from behind the car, firing off several rounds toward the trees and yelling, "Go, go, go!"

Erika and Marcus's footsteps pounded up the porch steps as he got off three more shots, covering them as they made their way into the house.

There was no return fire.

He moved as quickly as he could into the house, slamming the door behind him and turning the dead-bolt into place.

Erika and Marcus sat on the kitchen floor between the island and the stove. She had the rifle in one hand and her cell phone in the other.

"Lance is on his way." She held up the phone, and he heard the sheriff's confirmation come from the other end of the open line.

James crouched down, taking the phone from Erika's hand. "I think our shooter is gone, but be careful coming in."

James ended the call.

"Are you sure the bad guy isn't here anymore?" Marcus's voice cracked and tears streaked his cheeks.

James wasn't sure he'd ever felt such an intense rush of anger, but he wrangled it under control for Marcus's sake.

"I don't know, buddy, but don't worry. As long as I'm here, no one is going to hurt you or your mom."

SOMEONE HAD SHOT at them.

The thought terrified Erika. She didn't doubt for a moment that Roger would have her killed if that's what it took to get guardianship of Marcus. She wouldn't let that happen. She'd never allow Marcus to become like his father and grandfather.

Which meant she'd have to run again.

It would be harder this time. She'd have to figure out what to tell Marcus. He wasn't a baby. He'd demand answers, and he deserved them. And he wouldn't be the only person looking for answers. She'd built a life in Carling Lake she couldn't have imagined ten years ago when she'd fled Los Angeles—her job, Lance and Daisy. Maybe most surprisingly, she'd started imagining a future—running the B&B and, recently, picturing what it would be like to open herself up more, to consider the possibility that she didn't have to be alone.

She shot a glance across the room at James. He and Lance spoke in hushed voices in front of the old fireplace, which she had visions of firing up during the cold winter months. As if he could feel her eyes on him, James's gaze tracked to hers and held for a long moment.

Once Lance and his deputies had arrived, they'd

moved from the kitchen to the library, where they could all be more comfortable.

She sat on the overstuffed green velvet couch, Marcus tucked into her side. He'd been reluctant to take more than three steps away from her, even after Lance's arrival, which was fine with her. Even though she knew they were no longer in immediate danger, her heart was still struggling to catch up.

Still, something didn't feel right about Roger being behind the shooting. Not that she'd put it past Roger to target her. But Marcus? She couldn't see Roger taking the chance that Marcus would get hurt.

Deputy Bridges escorted Daisy into the library.

"I came as soon as I heard. Are you okay?" Daisy sat down beside Erika and threw an arm around her shoulder in a one-armed hug. The action jostled Marcus awake, who'd been dozing on the other side of Erika with his head on her shoulder.

"We're all a bit shaken up but unharmed," Erika answered, leaning into her friend's side.

Daisy chattered on about how the news that someone had taken a shot at Erika was making its way around town, but the only news Erika was interested in at the moment was whatever Deputy Bridges was saying to Lance and James. She couldn't hear them from where she was sitting on the other side of the room but, from the pinched look on all three men's faces, it wasn't good. The three men crossed the library.

"Hey, Marcus, you think I can talk to your mom alone for a minute?" Lance said.

The sleepy haze fell from Marcus's face, replaced by a steely resolve. In answer to Lance's question, he scooted closer to Erika.

She suspected that Marcus's bravado wasn't totally

about protecting her. "It's okay, Marcus. Why don't you show Deputy Bridges that new video game you and Devin can't stop playing?" Hopefully, having Deputy Bridges with him would alleviate some of the fear she knew he was feeling.

"Yeah, come give me some tips so I have a fighting chance when I play against you and Devin from home." Deputy Bridges shot Marcus a reassuring smile.

"Go on. It's okay," Erika said.

Marcus reluctantly rose from the sofa and trudged from the room with Deputy Bridges at his back.

Lance sat on the edge of the armchair across from the couch. James remained standing.

"My deputies combed the area, but unfortunately, we weren't able to find the shooter," Lance began.

Although she'd expected as much, she couldn't help feeling a rush of disappointment. If they could get their hands on the shooter, they might have a chance of nailing down who was behind the various attacks that had been taking place.

"What does that mean? What can we do?" Erika asked.

"Well, the good news is we found shell casings. I'll send them to the state crime lab and forensics will go over them with a fine-tooth comb."

"Okay, what aren't you telling me? I've known you long enough to know when you're keeping something from me." She looked over at James. "What is it?"

James held her gaze. "The three of us were sitting ducks when we pulled up to the house but all the shots were aimed at your side of the car."

Daisy reached for Erika's hand and squeezed. "I don't understand. What does that mean?"

Lance's gaze moved between Erika and Daisy. "We think someone was shooting at you."

The import of Lance's words struck like a fist to the chest. Erika shuddered out a breath. "Someone tried to kill me."

"It's possible," Lance answered.

"The question is who would want to scare you and why?" James said.

"Ellis." Three pairs of eyes locked onto a visibly angry Daisy.

"Daisy—" Erika started.

"Ellis Hanes?" Lance interrupted. "I'd heard he isn't too happy about you opening a B&B. Has he done anything beyond snipe and complain?"

"Not really," Erika said.

"Yes," Daisy said simultaneously.

"He bought off Erika's contractor in a bid to make sure she didn't complete the B&B renovations," James offered.

"And he threatened Erika as she came out of Laureano's hardware store a few days ago. Essentially said she'd better drop the idea of opening a competing B&B or else," Daisy added.

Lance flew out of the armchair. "Why didn't you tell me this before?"

"Because Daisy is exaggerating." Erika shot her friend an angry look. "Ellis did not threaten me. He's not happy I'm opening the B&B, but you can't really believe he'd go this far. I mean my B&B is small potatoes, tiny potatoes, compared to the Carling Lake B&B and his hotel."

"If he didn't see you as a potential threat, he wouldn't have confronted you at all," Daisy pointed out.

It was a sound argument, but still a long way off from proving Ellis had taken those shots.

James's brow furrowed. "Seems like an extreme action to take under the circumstances."

"Ellis mentioned word getting out that your B&B was unsafe," Daisy added pointedly. Her eyes widened. "And that was right after you fell from the bridge. I bet Ellis is responsible for that, too."

Lance held up a hand. "Hang on. I got the lab results back on the rope from the bridge. It was inconclusive so we don't know whether the bridge was deliberately tampered with or if it was just an accident."

Daisy guffawed dramatically. "Come on, Lance. The bridge gives out, someone tries to set fire to the B&B and then Ellis just happens to threaten to spread the rumor that Erika's property is unsafe. That's like three too many coincidences to be coincidences in my book."

"Hanes and I exchanged words earlier this afternoon before the shooting," James interjected. "I came upon him trying to intimidate Erika and while she was holding her own—"

"Of course she was," Daisy huffed.

"—Hanes was not pleased with my butting in," James finished.

Lance's brows knitted. "Not pleased enough that he'd try something like this?"

James shrugged. "You know bullies. They can be volatile when you stand up to them. Especially if they feel threatened. From what I understand, Hanes fancies himself somebody in this town. No telling what he might do when that status is threatened."

The speculation was getting out of hand. Erika couldn't argue with the logic, but Daisy, Lance and

James didn't have all the facts. Maybe it was time they did.

"I'm going to have a talk with Ellis." Lance turned to leave.

"Wait, Lance—" Erika said.

"I know you don't think Ellis would be involved in something like this, but this is my job. You and Ellis had a confrontation recently, and he does have a motive to want to paint your property as unsafe, maybe even potentially hurt you. Considering everything that's going on, it's just sound police work to speak with him."

"That's just it. Ellis isn't the only person who could be behind everything that's been happening. He's not even the one with the most motive," Erika says.

Confusion swept over Lance's and Daisy's faces, but James's expression was neutral, almost as if he expected what she'd say next. But he couldn't, could he?

"What do you mean," Lance asked.

"I'm not... My real name is not Erika Powell. It's Erika Overholt. I was married to Ronald Overholt. Marcus is his son."

"Ronald Overholt, the son of the billionaire conglomerate owner Roger Overholt?" Lance said, stunned.

Erika nodded. "Yes. Roger is not the man everyone thinks he is. Ronald wasn't, either, for that matter. After Ronald's death, Roger threw me out—out of my house and out of the family."

Lance's face scrunched up like he was thinking hard about something. "I know the Overholt conglomerate owns a piece of every major industry in the world it seems like."

Erika nodded again. "Roger stays out of the limelight. He thinks celebrities are low-class, but he's one of the richest men in the country, maybe the world now.

Ronald is Roger's oldest son. Nearly eleven years ago, he was killed in a single car accident. We were in the car together, but I only suffered minor injuries. I had my seat belt on. Ronald was drunk out of his mind and I shouldn't have gotten into the car with him. Shouldn't have let him drive. But I'd learned early in our marriage there were severe consequences to defying Ronald."

Erika's body tensed with residual anger toward Ronald even as her stomach knotted with anxiety, remembering how small and insignificant she'd felt during the years she'd been Erika Overholt.

Quiet stretched across the room.

"Why didn't you ever say anything? Say...something?" Lance asked, shocked.

Erika could see the hurt in her friend's eyes and regret at having put it there flooding through her. "I couldn't take the chance of telling anyone."

"Wait a minute," Daisy interrupted. "How could Roger Overholt throw you out of your house?" Daisy asked, perplexed. "I mean, I know the man is powerful, but it's your house."

Erika pushed to her feet and paced in front of the sofa. A release for some of the nervous energy coursing through her body. "That's just it. I didn't know it, but it wasn't our house. Everything was in Roger's name— the house, the cars, the bank accounts. Everything. I didn't know... I was a very different woman back then. I started dating Ronald not long after my mother died. I was alone and isolated, and I didn't see just how controlling Ronald was. In the first two years of our marriage, he chipped away at my confidence and self-worth until I didn't recognize myself. I didn't have any family, and I knew Ronald wouldn't let me leave, anyway. It would shatter his perfect appearance, and appearances were everything to Ronald. And Roger. Not that I could ever be perfect enough. They both always found fault with the way I dressed, looked, sat, ate—with *me*."

"Emotional abuse is just as destructive as physical abuse but all too frequently ignored or dismissed," James offered.

Erika shifted her gaze to his and was relieved to find understanding there.

"That's what I did, dismissed it. I told myself it wasn't abuse because Ronald never hit me."

"It is abuse, though," Daisy said while rubbing soothing circles along Erika's back.

"I know that now. If I'd been older, had more life experience, I might have questioned how Stepford-wifey Roger's wife, Dianna, was. Or how odd it was that Roger and Dianna's daughter had fled the moment she was old enough."

Lance frowned. "The Overholt family is pretty well-known. I don't remember a daughter."

"That's because Roger disowned her years ago. Before I even knew Ronald. Evangeline. Apparently, she wouldn't allow Roger to control her life. I only know about her because Ronald got drunk enough one night to mention her and told me a bit about her before he passed out. I remember being jealous that she had the spine to stand up to Roger. Sometimes I think Ronald was, too."

"There's something I don't understand, though," James said with a questioning look in his eye. "If Roger threw you out of the family, why all the subterfuge? I get not wanting to keep the Overholt name but it seems like there's more to this story you haven't told us about yet."

"There is. The most important part really." Erika sighed. "I told you perfection was important to the

Overholts, but it wasn't the most important thing. The most important thing was blood, as in Roger Overholt's descendants."

The confused look didn't leave James's face.

"I don't understand," Lance said.

"Roger treated everyone in the family as if they were an extension of him. It was why everyone had to be beyond reproach, unattainably perfect. Roger groomed his sons in his image and, as long as he held the purse strings, they'd do whatever he told them to do. The night of the accident after the doctor delivered the news that Ronald hadn't made it, the doctors told me I was pregnant. I was still trying to process everything when Roger cast me out. I knew I could fight him and probably get something, a nice settlement to keep the Overholt name from being besmirched in the LA tabloids at least, but I also knew the cost of that settlement would be Marcus's life. If Roger knew he had a grandchild, especially a grand*son*, he'd do everything in his power to get and keep Marcus under his thumb. There was no way I was going to let that man anywhere near my son, so I left. Changed my name. Disappeared completely."

"But now you think it's possible Roger Overholt has learned about Marcus and he's behind the shooting today." Lance put her fears into words.

Erika swallowed hard. "Yes. I...don't know who else would come after me like this."

"It's not Roger Overholt," James said, drawing every pair of eyes to him. "Roger Overholt is dead."

Chapter Sixteen

Erika fell back onto the couch, her arms wrapped protectively around her midsection. "How do you…" Erika murmured, suspicion clouding her eyes.

"He's right," Lance interjected, looking up from his phone. "There are a few articles online but I guess, like you said Erika, he wasn't a celebrity so Overholt's death didn't get widespread notice."

James kept his eyes on Erika. Despite Lance's perfectly reasonable assumption that he'd learned about Roger Overholt's demise through the news, James could see that Erika rightly suspected otherwise.

He had what he'd come to Carling Lake for, and he hadn't even had to break any laws. Erika had admitted she was really Erika Overholt. He didn't have documentary proof, but she could hardly deny it after admitting as much in front of Lance and Daisy. He could report back to Ryan, let Erika, Lance and everyone else in town keep on believing that he was just a recently discharged marine figuring out his next steps and fade away.

But he looked into Erika's eyes and knew he couldn't do it.

She deserved to know the truth, even if it meant she'd hate him.

"That's not why I know about Overholt's death." The air in the library stilled. "I know because I'm working for his estate. I work for West Security and Investigations, my family's firm, actually. We were hired by Roger Overholt's executors to find Erika and Marcus."

He kept watching Erika and saw all the blood drain from her face. He felt like he'd been punched in the gut.

"He knew about Marcus. How?" Erika's words were barely a whisper.

"Yes, he knew. How I can't answer but the will directs that all heirs be notified of their bequests at the same time and in the same place, so we were hired to find you. Presumably, you and Marcus have been bequeathed something in the will."

"I don't want it," Erika said quietly. Daisy had rubbed Erika's back again, but Erika shook her off and straightened. "I don't want it." Her voice came stronger now. "I don't want anything from that man. From that family."

"West was only hired to find you and confirm you and your son are Erika and Marcus Overholt. The lawyers will contact you about what's in the will."

Erika sprung from the couch and stalked across the room to stand directly in front of him. "After everything I just told you about Roger and his family, you're going to tell them you know where we are?"

He wanted to tell her he wouldn't, that West would tear up the contract with the estate and return all the money, but that wasn't his call to make. He'd been sent here to do a job.

He reached for her, but she stepped away.

"Don't touch me." Her voice shook with rage. "I can't believe you would do this. I trusted you." She turned and stormed from the room. Daisy shot him a disgusted look before hurrying from the room after Erika.

James started to follow, but Lance stepped in his way.

"Not so fast." Lance's jaw flexed with anger. "She's too angry to hear anything you have to say right now and I have questions."

James felt the muscles in his own jaw tighten with frustration, but he knew Lance was right. Erika was furious, as she had a right to be, and he'd do better to let her cool down some before he tried to explain himself.

"How much did you know about all that stuff Erika just told us?"

"None of it," he practically growled. "West was hired by the estate. Obviously, we knew Overholt was the billionaire owner of the largest private conglomerate in the US but from our point of view, this was a simple assignment to confirm an individual's identity."

Lance's chin rose. "Yet, you've been here for over a week now. How come you haven't already confirmed who Erika is and gotten out of here?"

James sighed. "Because I'm a horrible PI. Technically, I'm not even a PI. I'm just working for the family company while I get my life sorted. I never lied. I just didn't tell the whole truth."

Lance scoffed. "A distinction without a difference if I've ever heard one."

James couldn't argue with the statement, so he didn't.

"Look, if West had sent anyone else up here, they'd have just broken into the B&B and searched until they found some proof that Erika and Marcus Powell were really Erika and Marcus Overholt. I couldn't do that. That's why I'm still here because I—" He stopped short of completing his sentence.

"Because you care about her." It was Lance's turn to sigh.

There was no sense in denying it, not that he wanted to. "Erika and Marcus. I care about both of them."

"So you're sticking around, then? Because I don't think Roger Overholt has risen from the dead to take potshots at Erika."

"Me, either. Erika is angry right now, but I don't know if I buy that the attacks on her and the house are tied to the Overholts."

"So what do you think is going on?" Lance's voice rose a decibel and he slapped the side of his thigh in aggravation.

"I have no idea," James said, feeling his frustration level rising.

"You didn't answer my earlier question. Are you planning to stay now that the cat is out of the bag?"

James nodded. "Yes." Because even though Erika was furious about his deception, he had no intention of leaving her and Marcus until they got to the bottom of whatever was going on and he knew they were safe. He might not even leave then, if he could convince her to trust him again. But that was not a thought he was willing to share with Lance. "I have a question for you. Why aren't you trying to run me out of town on a rail?"

Lance held up his index finger. "I need you. I can't be here with Erika and Marcus all the time. You, however, can."

James barked out a laugh. "Are you kidding me? Erika wants nothing to do with me. The only reason she hasn't kicked me out of this house is because she's so angry she hasn't thought about it. Yet."

"Well then, you'd better do whatever you have to do to convince her that keeping you around is her safest option before she gets around to kicking you to the curb." Lance stepped closer and lowered his voice. "There's someone swirling around Erika and Marcus. I don't know if it's Overholt, Ellis Hanes or someone else altogether, but whoever it is, they've shown themselves to be dangerous. I'm going to need all the help I can get. Are you in?"

He didn't need to think about his answer.

"I'm in."

ERIKA PULLED THE door to Marcus's room closed. She hadn't been sure what to tell him, so she'd kept things simple, reassuring him that Lance would figure out who had shot at them and that he was safe and loved.

But her son was smart and inquisitive. He knew something else was going on. He hadn't pressed when she'd put him off, but she knew her reprieve was only temporary. Technically, she'd been lying to him his entire life. Although he was legally Marcus Powell, that was the name on his birth certificate after all, she'd let him believe a man who didn't exist was his father. She'd let him think his father was a good man who'd been killed in an accident. She'd lied and told Marcus that his father and she were only children, and that both of their parents had already passed on. She couldn't take the chance that he'd one day wonder about grandparents or aunts and uncles and go looking. It had been what she had to do to protect her son, and she didn't regret it.

But now? What was the saying? "Three can keep a secret, if two of them are dead." Now that more than three people knew her true identity, how long could she expect it to stay a secret.

She headed for the kitchen, still thinking, considering whether the best course of action was to pull up stakes and leave Carling Lake. She trusted that Lance and Daisy wouldn't do anything to hurt her or Marcus, but…

Erika pulled up short, surprised to find James sitting calmly at her kitchen table, her bottle of Jack Daniels and a glass in front of him, and a file folder to his right. "What are you still doing here? Where are Lance, Daisy and Deputy Bridges?"

"Daisy went home and Lance and Bridges had to get back to the sheriff's department. Lance said he'd send extra patrols around for the next few days."

"You didn't answer my first question."

"I'm still here because I want to apologize. I am so sorry for not having told you the truth about why I was in town."

His apology took her by surprise and cooled some of the anger bubbling in her chest.

"And I'm hoping you'll hear me out."

Erika stood silent for a moment. She wasn't sure she wanted to hear his excuses. So he was sorry, fine. An apology was worth little at this point. Her secret was out, and she was going to have to make some tough decisions about what to do about it, and quickly.

"Please?" He flashed a smile. And she hated to admit it, but the butterflies still fluttered in her stomach. Traitors. How could she still be attracted to a man who had lied to her, betrayed her and potentially completely upended her life? She didn't have an answer for how—she just knew that she still was.

She sat in the chair on the opposite side of the table from James. He poured two fingers of whiskey into the glass and slid it across the table to her.

She wasn't a drinker. The bottle of Jack had come from Daisy, left over from a rare girls' night in. Did whiskey go bad? Oh, well, she was about to find out because if ever there was a day where she needed a drink to settle her nerves, today was that day.

She took a swig. The liquor burned its way down her throat. "Okay, so I'm listening."

"When I accepted this job, when West Security and Investigations accepted this job, we had no idea why you'd disappeared."

"Isn't it enough that I disappeared? I mean usually when a person goes out of their way not to be found, it's because they don't want to be found."

"Maybe. But it's not that unusual for someone, a family or, as in this case, an executor, to engage our services to find a loved one who has been out of touch for some time. There's nothing inherently suspicious about it, although I'll admit, once I got here and met you, I did wonder why you'd gone through the trouble of so thoroughly erasing your ties to Erika Overholt. That's not easy to do in this day and age."

She gestured for him to pour another shot of Jack. "So why didn't you back off then?"

James sighed. "Because I had a job to do. One I would have never accepted if I'd known why you'd disappeared."

"That's not much of an excuse." She knocked back the second shot and slammed the glass down on the table.

The vein over James's right temple twitched, but he didn't break eye contact with her. "Maybe not, but I'm going to do everything I can to make it right."

"I'm not sure you can. You can't put the genie back in the bottle. Even if you and Lance and Daisy swear not to tell anyone my real name, Marcus knows something is going on. I'm not sure it's fair to keep lying to him."

"Why do you have to keep lying at all? I get your

fear that Roger's obsession with controlling his family would lead him to try to take Marcus from you, but he's dead. He can't hurt you now."

"Can't he? Look at everything that's happened in the last few days. Look at why you're here. He's essentially managed from his grave to send you to track me down. How do I know that whatever his plan is, whatever is in his will, isn't going to be harmful to Marcus?"

"You don't, but like you said, you aren't the same woman you were the last time you confronted the Overholts. You're the strongest woman I've ever known. And now you aren't alone. You have Lance and Daisy. And me."

Erika scoffed. "You? You're not on my side. You work for Roger's estate, which is the same as working for Roger as far as I'm concerned."

"No, I don't. Not anymore."

"What do you mean?"

"I mean, I talked to my brother, and I told him I'd failed. I can't confirm you are Erika Overholt."

"What… I don't understand. I told you my real name. You don't believe me?"

"I believe you but West was hired to find you and get proof—a passport, birth certificate, marriage license—that you are Erika Overholt. I didn't do that. We're going to refund the estate's retainer."

"How can you do that? I mean, won't it hurt your company's reputation?" Was this a trick of some sort? He'd admitted he hadn't gotten the documentary proof he needed to take back to his client. Was this all some ploy to get her to show him some hard evidence that she was in fact Erika Overholt?

James shrugged as if it didn't matter to him at all

whether or not his company's reputation took a hit. "Maybe. Probably, but we'll survive."

"I don't get it. When did you decide all this?"

"I called my brother Ryan, he's the president of West Security and Investigations, while you were still in the back room talking to Marcus. I briefed him on everything that's happened here and we agreed this situation has turned into much more than a simple find-and-identify case." James reached a hand across the table, stopping just short of touching her own. "We are not... I am not going to do anything that could hurt you or Marcus. You have my word on that, Erika."

Her heart urged her to trust him, but she hadn't trusted anyone in over a decade. She wasn't sure she could do it.

"How can I know you aren't lying right now? That you haven't already told Roger's lawyers who I am and where to find me and that they aren't on their way to destroy everything I've built." Or worse, somehow take Marcus from her. Just the thought had her instincts buzzing that she should grab her son and run now.

"I know trusting me is a heavy lift but I think I've come up with a way for us to go on the offensive and maybe figure out what's going on."

"What do you mean *the offensive*?"

"I mean if the Overholts want to know who you are, I suggest you tell them."

"What are you saying?" Erika asked.

"I think you should contact the estate's attorneys and tell them who you are," James said.

The thought sent a sliver of fear singing through Erika. She'd spent the last ten years doing everything she could to make sure the Overholts wouldn't find her and Marcus. She didn't know if she could just walk into their lawyer's office and expose herself and her son to whatever Roger had planned.

"Think about it," James continued. "If you really think the attacks over the last week are tied to Overholt, the best thing we can do is get as much information as we can. And right now that means finding out what's in that will."

"Just call them up and tell them who I am."

"Exactly. The terms of the will require the executor to read the will with all beneficiaries present at the same time and in the same place. I don't know the names of the other beneficiaries, but you were the only beneficiary that the executor couldn't locate. The lawyers are in New York and he's mentioned that the Overholt family is eager to have the will read."

Erika let out a derisive snort. "I bet. Robert, Roger's youngest son, is probably chomping at the bit to get his hand on all those billions."

"Right. So he's not likely to argue if you pushed to have the will reading sooner rather than later."

She dropped her head into her hands. There was some logic to what James was proposing. If she was right and Roger's will was somehow the catalyst for the attacks, knowing what was in the will might make it easier to find whoever was targeting her.

But that would require her to trust James. Could she do that? She wanted to. Sitting across from James at the crossroads of her old life and the life she'd built for herself and Marcus, she knew without a doubt she wanted to believe in James. To trust him.

Somehow, through everything, she was falling for him. Hard.

James grasped her hand, and, as if reading her mind,

said, "You can trust me, Erika. I promise you. You can trust me."

She looked into his eyes and knew he meant every word.

"Okay. I'll make the call."

Chapter Seventeen

James was right about the executors and other beneficiaries being anxious to set up a meeting. Less than seventy-two hours after Erika had made the call to Jenner, Hart & Black, the attorneys handling Roger's estate, she was minutes away from finding out exactly what was in Roger's will and what it had to do with her and Marcus. Marcus had spent the night at Devin's so she and James could leave Carling Lake before dawn and make the three-hour trip to Manhattan. The hour had been too early and her nerves too on edge for much conversation on the drive to the city. For his part, James hadn't seemed to mind the quiet time.

Erika stole a sideways glance at James now as they cleared security in the building where Jenner, Hart & Black had their offices. Lance had increased the frequency of patrol on her street and she hadn't had any problems since the shooting, but James had stuck close anyway, even going with her for the last two days to drop off and pick up Marcus at school. He'd installed the new tile in the bathroom upstairs and stripped the floor of stain in the bedroom floors, staying well past their agreed upon time working on the house. Much to her surprise, Marcus, who'd never before shown a hint of interest in home renovations, had taken to helping

James out after he finished his homework. They had plans to install the vanity and toilet in the bathroom over the weekend.

James insisted that he was only around so much because he didn't want to fall behind on the renovations, but she knew his increased presence, like the sheriff's department cruiser that had been making frequent passes by her farmhouse, were meant as a deterrent to any other would-be attackers. She was no shrinking violet but between the news that the bridge collapsing, the break-in at her house and now someone taking a shot at her, she wasn't too proud to admit she appreciated the company. Or that she was scared.

A young red-haired woman in a black pinstripe power suit met Erika and James as they cleared building security. "Ms. Overholt? I'm Caroline Marx with Jenner, Heart & Black. I'll be showing you to the conference room." The woman nodded at Erika, then shot a glance at James.

"I'm Erika Overholt. This is my friend, James West. He'll be joining me," Erika said, making sure her tone left no room for objection. She didn't know what she was walking into, but she knew Roger Overholt well enough to know that it wouldn't be good. Whatever half-truths he'd told her, she knew James would likely be her only ally in that room.

Caroline simply turned and headed for the elevator bank.

They exited the elevator on the twenty-third floor and passed through the eerily quiet halls until Caroline stopped in front of a set of double doors.

"Here we are." Caroline motioned toward the doors. "Mr. Jenner is already waiting for you."

Four heads turned to watch as Erika and James entered the room.

How many lawyers does it take to read a will?

A short but distinguished-looking man stood from his chair at the head of the long mahogany conference room table. "Alexander Jenner." He thrust his hand at Erika as he approached. "Mrs. Overholt, what a pleasure to finally meet you."

She felt her lips twist into a frown. "It's Powell now." She gave the offered hand a brief shake.

Mr. Jenner blinked twice. "Yes, of course, Ms. Powell," he said, his smile insincere, before turning to introduce himself to James. "I have to tell you, Ms. Powell, your call two days ago came as a welcome surprise." Jenner gestured for Erika and James to take seats at the conference room table. "Especially since our past attempts had been so disappointing." The attorney shot a look at James, who appeared unaffected by the snide comment.

"Well, I'm here now. I presume you've authenticated the photocopy of my passport and birth certificate I sent you after our initial conversation?" Erika and James took seats opposite the cadre of lawyers.

"Yes, of course. We are quite sure you are Erika Overholt." Mr. Jenner settled into the leather executive chair at the head of the conference room table.

When she'd made the call to the law firm two days earlier to say that she was Erika Overholt, Mr. Jenner had been anything but sure she was who she said she was. In fact, she'd have placed him firmly in the skeptical category. Luckily, she'd held on to her old identification, whether to have some link to who she'd been or because some part of her knew she'd need to prove her real identity one day, she couldn't say.

Mr. Jenner glanced at his expensive wristwatch. "We're just waiting on the other beneficiaries. They should be here—"

The phone in the middle of the table buzzed. "Mr. Overholt is on his way in."

The words conjured Roger Overholt's image in Erika's mind, even though she knew it couldn't be him walking through the doors.

Seconds later, Erika heard the conference room doors open behind her.

She took a deep breath, then swiveled the chair and watched her brother-in-law Robert stroll into the room.

Robert didn't seem to register her presence initially, which gave her time to study how he'd changed over the years. Robert's blue eyes were a shade darker than Ronald's had been, but they shared the same lithe, trim frame and wavy dark brown hair. In the ten years since she'd seen him, Robert had grown to look more like his father. She couldn't help but wonder if this was what Ronald would have looked like had he lived. He and Robert had always looked so much alike.

"Mr. Overholt," Mr. Jenner said, rising and extending his hand. "Thank you for making the time to join us on such short notice."

Robert gave Mr. Jenner's hand a cursory shake. "I just want to get this over with. It's appalling how long it's taken this firm to settle my father's estate."

Mr. Jenner cleared his throat. "Yes, well, if you'll just have a seat, we'll get started."

Robert turned toward the table, then stopped. "Erika." He studied her, and Erika got the feeling that he was almost unsure whether she was real or a figment of his imagination. Then his lips flattened into a thin white line. "What is she doing here?"

"If you'll just have a seat, Mr. Overholt—" the attorney gestured again to an empty chair on the side of the table where the other suit-clad lawyers sat "—I'll explain everything."

Robert hesitated for a moment before stalking to his seat.

Mr. Jenner settled himself in his chair once again and opened the folder on the table in front of him. "We're here to read the last will and testament of Roger Overholt." The attorney peered at the group over the top of his glasses. "While it is unusual in this day and age to have an in-person reading of the will such as this, Mr. Overholt had specified several conditions that needed to be met before we, as the executor of his estate, could legally distribute his assets. One of those conditions is a formal will reading. An additional condition was that all beneficiaries be present, in person. As all the mentioned heirs, or their legal representatives, are present, this meeting satisfies those conditions."

The other three lawyers in the room wrote hurriedly on yellow notepads as Mr. Jenner spoke.

"Can we please move this along?" Robert asked irritably. "Some of us have more important things to do than give in to a dead man's whims."

Mr. Jenner shot Robert an irritated look. "In anticipation of this meeting, we have done a valuation of the estate. As of today, Mr. Roger Overholt's estate is estimated to be worth nine hundred eighty million dollars.

Her heart thumped in her chest. Nine hundred and eighty million dollars. It was more money than she could contemplate.

She glanced at Robert and watched a broad smile slide across his face.

"To my only living son, Robert, I bequeath my house

in Los Angeles." Mr. Jenner read the address and some other technical information identifying the house. "The penthouse in New York." The lawyer recited the address for this property as well and mentioned stocks in several companies Erika had never heard of. "Further, although I no longer hold a position on the board, it is my wish that my son Robert be allowed to continue as the CEO of Overholt Industries as long as the Board of Directors determines it is in the company's best interests."

Mr. Jenner's eye skittered nervously over Robert. The atmosphere in the room changed instantly, as if the air now hung heavier, weighted by what the attorney hadn't said.

Robert's eyes narrowed and he leaned forward. "Wait a minute—"

Mr. Jenner raised his hand in a stop motion. "If you'll let me finish reading, I'll answer questions when I'm done."

It didn't take a mathematician to figure out why Robert's mouth had turned down into an uncertain frown. She wasn't certain what the value of the companies Robert had been bequeathed was, but she knew that the bulk of Roger Overholt's fortune stemmed from his ownership of Overholt Industries, which had not been among the names of the companies Mr. Jenner listed.

She felt herself getting lightheaded as a suspicion about what Roger had done with the rest of his estate skittered through her brain.

Everyone in the room seemed to know instinctively that whatever Mr. Jenner was about to say, it would be momentous. The other three lawyers stared down at their legal pads, avoiding looking at any of the others in the room.

Under the table, James reached for her hand, entwining his fingers with hers. She was grateful for the warmth that flowed from him.

Had Roger figured out a way to take Marcus from her? She wouldn't put it past him to reach from the grave to wreak havoc.

"To my grandson, whom I was undeservedly denied a relationship with, but who is and always will be an Overholt, I leave the remainder of my estate, including but not limited to real and personal property, stocks, bonds, securities, mutual funds and all my interests, however found, in Overholt Industries. As he is currently underage, I leave such to him in trust, to be administered by his mother, Erika Overholt, as she should see fit, until his twenty-fifth birthday."

Her stomach lurched as if the floor had just fallen out from beneath her and, in a way, it had. The attorney continued to talk, but all she could hear was a ringing in her ears. Roger had not only known about Marcus, he'd left him with almost everything. It couldn't be true. It didn't make sense.

Robert pushed to his feet, sending his chair rolling backward into the wall of windows behind his side of the table. "What kind of scam is this? You." He pointed, his finger moving along the line of attorneys at the table and stopping at Erika. "You all must be in cahoots with that woman. If you think I'm going to let you steal my father's company, you're crazy!"

Mr. Jenner stood now and looked Robert clearly in the eye. "I resent that accusation, Mr. Overholt. Your father's will is crystal clear, signed and witnessed. I have a copy here for you." He handed copies of the will to Robert and Erika.

The words on the paper were nothing but a blur. She felt nauseous, but pushed the feeling down.

"And, of course, you may challenge the will if you choose. I will tell you, however, your father's will includes a no-contest clause. If your lawsuit is unsuccessful, you'll lose your bequest."

Robert erupted in a litany of curses. The attorneys swarmed, trying in vain to calm him down.

James turned to her. "Are you okay?"

"I honestly don't know. I don't understand why Roger would do this. What am I supposed to do?"

"You don't have to do anything. At least not right now." He squeezed her hand. "You want to get out of here?"

Erika glanced across the room. All four attorneys were still focused on Robert, who was screaming about suing them into oblivion.

"Yes, please."

They both stood, her hand still firmly in James's, and left the room. Moments later, they were outside on the sidewalk in front of the building. The snow had picked up since they'd stepped inside and a biting wind whipped it around as if they'd stepped into a snow globe.

Somehow, she hadn't noticed the building across the street when they'd arrived at the law firm, but now, looking up at the falling snow, she saw that they stood directly across from the Empire State Building.

Was that a sign, an iconic symbol of hope, as the first thing she saw leaving a meeting that had just changed her entire life?

Erika's thoughts and emotions swirled uncontrollably. She let James steer her from the law offices and to the garage where they'd parked.

Roger Overholt had never done a nice or unselfish

thing in his life, so what did his leaving Marcus this money really mean?

And would she be able to handle the fallout when it came?

Chapter Eighteen

Erika hadn't said a word since they'd left the attorney's office and James was starting to worry. Learning that her son was a multimillionaire, and that she was responsible for his fortune, was a lot to process, but it wasn't his primary concern at the moment. "Mo Money Mo Problems" wasn't just a catchy name for a song. The kind of money that had just landed in Erika and Marcus's lap also made them targets for con men, thieves, kidnappers, even worse. When word got out about the inheritance, they'd both need top-of-the-line private security. Maybe for the rest of their lives.

James shot another glance across the car at Erika. She chewed her bottom lip and stared out the front windshield. Even when worried, she was the most beautiful woman he'd ever laid eyes on.

And he was going to do whatever it took to make sure she and Marcus were as insulated as possible from all the craziness that was headed their way.

He'd need to call Lance and update him on the situation. It was unlikely the media would get wind of the boy's miraculous change in fortune this soon but it wouldn't hurt for Devin's deputy father to pick the boys up from school and stay close until he and Erika got back to Carling Lake this evening.

He'd also have to speak to Ryan and get the ball rolling on a top-of-the-line security system for her home. He didn't know if it was still possible, or if Erika would even still want to open her house as a B&B, but at the very least she'd have to institute some sort of background check system for prospective guests. West could help with that as well.

"Where are we?" Erika asked as James pulled in front of a redbrick townhouse in Harlem.

"At my place. I needed to pick up a few things, and I figured we could grab lunch before we head back to Carling Lake. There's an amazing deli on the corner that delivers."

He unlocked the front door of the converted brownstone and led Erika up the two flights of stairs to his third-floor apartment. It was a shotgun-style place with the living room/kitchen space separated from the bedroom by a pass-through bathroom.

He locked the doors, then turned to Erika. "Can I get you something? Water? It's a little early but if you need it, I have wine and the hard stuff as well."

She wasn't listening to him. Her gaze moved around the room, taking in the framed drawings covering the walls. The elevated subway tracks in Far Rockaway. Two old men playing chess on the sidewalk in Harlem. A young girl falling from a bike in Prospect Park. She walked slowly past each one, studying them as if she were gazing at masterpieces hung on the wall of the Metropolitan Museum of Art.

He probably had too many for the limited space, but each of the drawings spoke to him in a different way and he couldn't imagine not being able to look up and see any of them whenever he needed.

Erika stopped in front of a drawing of a marine car-

rying an injured child to safety. "These are amazing.
They look like photos but they aren't, are they?"

"No, they're drawings. Hyperrealist drawings."

She turned to him. "These are yours?" Her eyes
scanned over the other walls. "You drew them all?"

He nodded. "It's a kind of therapy." In more ways
than one.

Erika tilted her head and looked at him as if she
were seeing him for the first time. "They're amazing.
You're an artist."

A blush climbed the back of his neck. Her praise
sent a warm feeling flooding through his body. "I don't
know about that. Look, make yourself at home. The
menu for the deli should be on the kitchen counter. I'm
just going to pack a few more clothes, then I'll call in
our order."

He walked through the bathroom, and into his bedroom, breathing out a knot of anxiety as he did. He
grabbed an overnight bag from his closet. He wanted
to get a few more changes of clothes since it looked like
he was going to be in Carling Lake for a little longer.
He began tossing shirts inside the bag while attempting to work out just what he was feeling.

He hadn't really thought about how it would feel to
have Erika see his art and know he'd drawn it. It had
felt an awful lot like baring his soul.

"I take it from the circle and two stars next to it that
the Reuben sandwich would be your recommendation,
if I asked for one."

James turned and found Erika leaning against the
doorframe from the bathroom to the kitchen. He smiled.
"Definitely, you won't find a better Reuben in the city."

"Why did you get all weird when we were talking
about your drawings?"

"I don't think I got weird." He grabbed a pair of pants and threw them into the bag on top of the dresser.

"Hey," Erika said, coming to stand next to him. "You are so talented. You said you were looking for the next step in your life—couldn't this be it? I think there are a lot of people who'd love to see your art, to own your art."

The owner of the gallery who'd sold his last two etchings said the same thing to him several days earlier. But selling a couple of pieces was different from trying to make a living as an artist. He wasn't sure if he could do it. He wasn't sure if he wanted to do it.

"What were you just thinking about?" Erika asked.

"I actually sold a piece recently. And the gallery has asked if I'd be interested in selling more with them. Maybe even having a small show."

"That's amazing. You should do it. Or if you want, you could open your own gallery and sell directly to people. I'm sure many of the tourists who visit Carling Lake would love to have pictures that reminded them of the lake and mountains. And you might be able to sell some to the hotels and resorts in the area."

Only inches separated them. He vibrated with the need to reach out and touch her. "In Carling Lake?"

Erika's chocolate brown eyes heated. "Anywhere. Wherever you end up setting down roots, I mean." Her voice was little more than a whisper.

"And if I were to set down roots in Carling Lake? What could that mean for us?" He reached out and gently skimmed his fingers down her arm, her skin igniting a fire deep in his belly.

"James," Erika murmured, the desire in her eyes shooting straight to his groin.

He pulled her close, and he was sure she could feel

just how much he wanted her. Dipping his head, he brought his lips within millimeters of her own. "Yes?"

"Yes." She closed the distance between them and met his lips in a demanding kiss.

He deepened the kiss, his body hardening as passion raced between them.

She fit against his body like she belonged there.

He walked her backward the four steps to the bed and eased her down onto it. For a moment, he just stared down at her—breathless, her dark eyes full of desire—and marveled that this amazing woman wanted to be with him. Then he lowered himself to the bed and ran kisses down one side of her neck, then the other. Her moan nearly undid him.

"I want you," Erika said breathlessly, plunging her hands beneath his shirt and running them up his back.

He rose just enough to shed his shirt and allow her to get rid of her top.

Erika wrapped her hands around his neck and pulled his head back down into a kiss that was anything but gentle. She brought her legs up to hug his hips, sending him nearly wild with desire. He pressed into her, running a hand up her leg, to the waistband of her suit.

A moment later, they were both free of all clothing.

For a second, James couldn't speak. He couldn't even breathe.

She was the most beautiful woman he'd ever laid eyes on.

Erika stepped closer. She took him in her hand and stroked his length. He groaned, stepping away just long enough to grab protection. Erika sat on the bed, propping herself on her elbows and watching him sheath himself with passionate hunger in her eyes.

A moment later, he joined her, covering her body

with his own. Erika ran her hands over his back, her eyes locked on his as he positioned himself at her entrance. He ran his thumb over her cheek, then her lips, feeling the softness of her skin as he slid into her. Her back arched, drawing him in deeper.

He held himself there for a moment, in awe that this amazing, wonderful woman wanted to share herself with him this way.

Erika reared up, claiming his mouth in a passionate kiss. Then he began to move and he lost the ability to think about anything other than the woman beneath him. Each moan sent a surge of excitement through him. He was dangerously close to falling over the edge.

"You feel so damn good," he whispered against the soft skin just above her breast.

He slowed his pace and caught her taut nipple in his mouth. Erika gasped in pleasure and he nearly broke again. She stroked her hands over his back and hooked her leg over his hip. Pulling him closer, urging him to sink himself deeper.

James slid his hand between their bodies and cupped her center. Erika moaned, her back arching. He moved his thumb in tiny circles, increasing the speed and pressure until she cried out with pleasure.

He held her until she slumped back against the bed, spent. Then with one swift movement, he surged up and entered her again with one hard stroke. Erika's eyes sprang open, locking onto his. He saw the barely controlled passion surging through him reflected in her gaze.

Erika wrapped her arms around his shoulders and her legs around his waist, pulling him in as closely as she could while he found the rhythm that sent them both to a place he wasn't sure they'd ever come back from.

And he wasn't sure he wanted to.

AN HOUR LATER, Erika sat beside him on his couch, looking sexily rumpled and satiated in one of his collared button-downs. He had to fight to keep his mind from wandering to what she wasn't wearing under his shirt as they dove into their sandwiches with gusto. Apparently, they'd both worked up an appetite from their midday jaunt.

He watched Erika lick dressing from her fingertips and felt desire coil in his chest.

"Why are you looking at me like that?"

His answer was a smile he knew said more than any words could.

She blushed prettily and scooted farther from him on the sofa. "We don't have time for that."

"I can be quick."

Erika laughed, a sound that was quickly becoming his favorite melody. "I don't know if you should brag about that."

He slid closer to her. "I love your lips." He dipped his head and dotted soft kisses along her throat.

She wrapped her arms around his neck and let her head fall to the side, giving him better access. "And I could stare into your eyes all day long. I think they might be one of the most beautiful things God has ever graced this world with."

His lips met hers in a soft languid kiss.

He wanted to do this every day for the rest of his life. He wanted to be with Erika every day for the rest of his life. The only thing that surprised him about the realization was how right it felt.

He could have spent all day making love to her but they needed to talk about next steps regarding her and Marcus's safety.

James rose, chucking their lunch detritus in the garbage before returning to the sofa. "There are a few things we should discuss before we get on the road."

"Like what?" Erika eyed him with suspicion.

He took her hand. "Marcus being a long-lost Overholt is going to draw intense scrutiny the moment the media gets hold of it. And the kind of money he, and through him you, now have access to will make you targets for con men and criminals alike." He could see the wheels in her brain turning, processing what he'd said and what it meant. "You both are going to need full-time security at your home and pretty much anywhere you go for the foreseeable future."

She froze, and he felt her hand turn to ice. "That's why he did it." She shook her head slowly.

He had no idea what she was talking about. "Why who did what?"

"That's why Roger left the money to Marcus."

James rubbed her hands between his own to warm them. "Baby, I'm sorry. I don't understand what you mean?"

"Everything I did—leaving, changing my name, keeping the truth about Ronald from Marcus—I did it all so that Marcus would be a better man than his father, than all the Overholts. And from his grave, Roger Overholt just made it all for nothing. Leaving Marcus that money—" Erika looked into his eyes and the despondency he saw there nearly crushed him. "Roger just made Marcus an Overholt. And there's not a thing I can do about it."

"You could disclaim the inheritance."

"It's not just about the money. How many people at Jenner, Hart & Black know about Marcus? How long do you think it will take before someone leaks that there's a long-lost Overholt heir?"

He would have liked to argue with her, but he knew she was right. There was no way Marcus's lineage could remain secret forever. Pretty soon, Marcus would no longer be an anonymous ten-year-old trying to figure out his way through life. He'd be one of the richest children in the country.

"You saw Robert's reaction." Erika was talking out loud, but the words were more for her than him. Processing the *why* of the situation. "He'll never invite Marcus into the family fold. Roger has just reignited the same type of feud he fostered between Ronald and Robert. Roger may not have snatched Marcus away from me, but this was his last-ditch effort to show me he still has control over our lives."

"Let me talk to my brother. I promise, you and Marcus will have the best security out there."

"I can't... I don't want to live... I don't want Marcus living in a gilded cage. I won't do it."

"West is one of the best security and investigations firms on the East Coast. I'll have him work up a design for a system for your house and a proposal for private security—" He held up a hand when she looked like she'd refuse. "Minimal, discrete protection. I'm just asking you to look at the proposal and think about what I'm saying. This is about your and Marcus's safety, Erika."

He felt guilty the moment he said it. Even though what he said was 100 percent true, it was still manipulative.

From the pinched expression on her face, Erika realized both those things and didn't like it. But after a tense moment, she nodded.

"I'll look at the proposal." She took a step back. "I'm going to take a quick shower and get dressed, if that's okay?"

"Of course."

He waited until the bathroom door closed behind her before dialing Lance's cell number.

The sheriff picked up on the first ring, as if he'd been waiting by the phone to hear how the meeting with the estate executor had gone. James filled him in quickly. When he was done, the silence on the other end of the line stretched so long he had to check to make sure their call hadn't been dropped.

"Well, say something, Sheriff."

"This is…. I don't know what it is. Amazing. Crazy. Weird. Something out of a fairy tale."

"Add potentially dangerous to that list and I'll agree with you."

"I see what you mean," Lance said after a moment.

"I think Deputy Bridges should pick the boys up from school today and maybe keep a close eye on them until Erika and I get back."

James heard a chair squeak on the other end of the line, as if Lance had changed positions. "I'll send Deputy Bridges over to the school now. The last bell won't ring for another hour or so but it won't hurt to keep an eye out."

"Thanks. It doesn't appear that word has gotten out yet, but Robert was irate when he found out Marcus got most of the estate. Who knows what he'll do or say?"

They spoke about the increased security measures that might be needed soon for a few more minutes before James ended the call.

And immediately made another.

James listened to the water running in the bathroom as he waited for Ryan to pick up, and wondered what Erika would do if he slipped into the shower with her.

"James? Are you there? We must have a bad connection?" Ryan's voice shattered the very nice daydream he'd been building.

"Yeah, yeah. I can hear you. I don't have much time before Erika and I need to get back on the road to Carling Lake but a lot of stuff went down this morning."

He ran through a slightly more detailed version of the meeting with the attorneys.

"Sounds like a doozy of a meeting."

"That's one way to put it. I want to know everything there is to know about Robert, his wife, his kids, his best friend and his wife and kids. Anybody who is in any way associated with Robert or Overholt Industries."

"Do you know how many people work at Overholt Industries?" Ryan deadpanned.

"I don't care."

Ryan sighed. "How about we start with the Board of Directors and major executives and work our way from there?"

"Fine," James gritted out.

"Now answer me this, are you just a man obsessed with protecting a woman you have feelings for or in your professional opinion," Ryan stressed the last two words, "is Robert Overholt a real threat to Erika and Marcus?"

James thought about the question. He was plagued by the thought that he'd fall short and Erika and Marcus might be harmed, but the amount of money they were dealing with made people take extreme actions. "Both."

"I guess that's fair."

"Somebody has orchestrated at least two attacks on Erika in the last week. Robert didn't seem like he knew what was in the will but he could just be a damn good actor."

"Okay, but you said the bridge thing and the shots were directed at Erika. Hurting, or even killing Erika, wouldn't mean Robert gets the money, right?"

"No, but maybe Robert doesn't know that. Or maybe he's so upset he doesn't care. But more likely, assuming Robert is behind the attacks on Erika, he's figured that as Marcus's only blood relative, he'd get custody of Marcus, and his trust, should anything happen to Erika."

"Okay, I'll put a guy on it and get back to you ASAP."

"Thanks." The water in the shower shut off. James could hear Erika moving around in the bathroom again. "I also talked to Erika a bit about the potential threats money like that can raise."

"And?"

"She's not happy about it but she's agreed to look at plans for a home security system and private security."

"I can get a team started on that, too. We'll have to send someone out to get accurate measurements. A layout. The works."

"I know the drill. I plan to broach the subject of staying in one of the guest rooms in the B&B until we've got all this sorted out, so Erika and Marcus won't be unprotected."

"Hmm."

"What does that mean?"

"Our job is technically over. I canceled the contract and gave Overholt's executors back their retainer, like we discussed. There's no reason for you to stay in Carling Lake."

"There's a reason," James grumbled. The last thing he was in the mood for was his little brother ribbing him over a woman.

Ryan chuckled. "Oh, yeah. Care to share it with me?"

"No."

He heard Ryan's chuckle turn into full-on laughter before he punched the button on his screen to end the call.

Chapter Nineteen

The multi-head shower in James's bathroom was so luxurious it had Erika entertaining thoughts of what it would be like to step inside every day. It might even make moving to a city like New York worth it.

First, you suggest James move to Carling Lake. Now you're fantasizing about moving in with him. You've lost your mind.

Maybe she had. James's prowess in the bedroom was certainly enough to make any woman go a little crazy. But that was exactly what thinking about a future with him was. Crazy.

He was a war hero and private investigator from New York. She was a mother, part-time reporter and wannabe B&B owner who lived in Carling Lake, New York. Nothing about the two of them together made any sense and she had to remember that.

She shut off the shower and got out. Toweling off, she squared her shoulders and met her reflection in the mirror.

She didn't have any regrets about sleeping with James. She'd wanted him. Truth be told, she'd wanted him from the first moment she'd set eyes on him. Truth really be told, she wouldn't mind having him again. And again. And…

But just because she didn't regret sleeping with James, didn't mean it was a good idea for them to get any more involved with each other. Geography wasn't the only concern. She also had Marcus to think about. And their life was undoubtedly about to take a drastic turn with the addition of the Overholt billions that neither of them could properly comprehend at the moment.

But despite the rational side of her brain cataloging all the reasons she shouldn't, Erika could still feel herself in danger of falling in love with James West.

At least this time she was walking into it with eyes wide open, she thought as she got dressed. With Ronald she'd been so young and the grief of losing her mother still so fresh, she hadn't seen her relationship with Ronald for the abusive situation that it really was until it was too late.

A relationship with James, she knew, was a recipe for disaster, although in a very different way from what she'd had with Roland. He did seem to feel badly about deceiving her, which might make him feel obligated to help her out and hang around until he was sure she and Marcus were safe. But eventually he'd return to New York and his phenomenal shower and she and Marcus would—

She had no idea what she and Marcus would do. A day ago, she had their futures planned out precisely, but now? Would they have to move? She loved Carling Lake and so did Marcus. But it was a small town and she knew that money like the kind Marcus stood to inherit brought with it a host of security concerns she couldn't even begin to contemplate.

Concerns which West Security and Investigations could help her with. Which was why she was going to take a hard look at the proposal from West. She stepped out of the bathroom.

The bedroom was vacant but she could hear James moving around in the living room.

She opened the bedroom door.

James sat at the edge of the couch, typing on a laptop on the coffee table in front of him. He surged to his feet as she stepped into the room.

"Hey. Hi. Hi." He rubbed his hands against the rough denim of his jeans and cleared his throat. His obvious awkwardness helped to set the butterflies in her stomach some. "I made coffee."

He rounded the coffee table and moved into the kitchen.

"Thanks." Erika followed, sliding up next to him and taking the coffee mug he plucked from an upper cabinet.

"Are you having second thoughts about sleeping together?" His voice was rough and she wasn't sure if it was just wishful thinking on her part, but she thought she detected vulnerability.

She smiled up at him, set the cup on the counter and wrapped her arms around his waist. "Well, it would be a little bit too late if I were, but I'm not."

"Good."

She felt his body relax against hers. "But that doesn't mean I don't have a ton of questions swirling through my head. Like what are we doing? Where could this possibly lead? You live here and I live in Carling Lake. And then there's all the stuff with the Overholts. And truly this just seems to be the worst time to start a relationship with anybody. Not that I'm saying we're in a relationship."

James kept his arms wrapped around her but leaned back so he could look down at her. "How about we put a pin in all those questions and revisit them at a later time. Right now we can just enjoy the moment and being here together."

It wasn't the answer she wanted, but the sparks of desire she saw in his eyes sent her questions to the back of her mind.

Her heartbeat picked up several paces and there was a familiar longing low in her body. "Umm…enjoy the moment? I'm not sure I know how to do that." She let a seductive smile slide across her face. "I might need you to show me how."

James's grin bordered on lecherous. He cupped her bottom and hoisted her up. Her legs wrapped around his waist, the feel of his hard length pressed between them, spiking her desire further.

He pulled her into a brief but scorching kiss before starting toward the bedroom. "I think I can do that."

THEIR SECOND GO-ROUND in the bedroom had left Erika feeling boneless. But the tension and anxiety that had melted from her body when she'd been in James's bed increased as they got closer and closer to Carling Lake. The meeting with the Overholt lawyers had raised more questions than it had answered. If Roger knew about Marcus, why hadn't he reached out while he'd been alive? And why would he leave almost all of his fortune to Marcus? There had to be a catch.

James's phone rang, cutting into the silence in the car.

James punched a button on the steering wheel. "Lance, you're on speaker."

"Good to know. How are you hanging in there, Erika?"

"I haven't had a complete meltdown but I'm reserving the right to do so later," she quipped.

"Fair enough. Listen, what's you guys' ETA?" Lance said.

"We're about a half hour out. Why? Is something wrong?" James asked.

"Nothing is wrong. In fact, I finally arrested several of the people involved in that gambling ring. Susan Garraus was among them." Erika stared at Lance in open-mouthed shock. Straitlaced Susan Garraus was the last person in town Erika would have pegged getting involved in illegal gambling. "Wow, I can't say I saw that one coming."

"Yeah, me either," Lance said. "We've got her dead to rights on an illegal gambling charge, but she wants to deal. She's claiming she has information on corruption within the city government, but she'll only talk to you, Erika."

"Me? Are you sure? I'm not exactly Susan's favorite person."

"She wants you. Says she doesn't trust anyone who works for the city not to cover up the information she knows."

She felt her heartbeat speed up again, only this time it was due to the prospect of catching the Carling Lake story of the year. It was a feeling she relished. She shot a look at James. "Would you mind?"

"Why not?" James shrugged. "We're on our way."

A little over a half hour later, Erika and James sat across from Susan in the sheriff's department's interrogation room. Lance had advised Susan that she could have a lawyer present before speaking to them but Susan had waived that right, saying she just wanted to get *this* over with.

Erika was just anxious to find out what *this* was.

"Okay, Susan. Erika is here. What is it you wanted to tell her?" Lance started the conversation off.

Susan shot a disgruntled look at the sheriff. "I wanted to talk to her alone."

"That's not going to happen," James said.

Erika slid a sidelong glance at him. If you didn't look closely, he appeared relaxed, almost as if they were just four friends, who happened to be shooting the breeze in a police interrogation room. But Erika had been around him enough in the last several days to recognize the tension in his shoulders and the tiny vein in the crease where his neck and his jaw met that popped when he was angry or worried.

"What he said," Lance seconded. "My time is valuable, Ms. Garraus, so if you've got something to say, spit it out."

Susan gave Lance another nasty look before turning to Erika. "You were right about the grant."

Erika blinked, confused. She'd pretty much gotten nowhere with that story. "How was I right?"

"We applied for it, Ellis Hanes and I. Only we never planned to use the money to renovate city hall."

"Okay." Erika felt her eyebrows rise a notch. "What did you plan to do with it?"

Susan snorted. "Isn't it kinda obvious? We planned to use it to gamble. Or rather to gamble our way out of the debts we'd run up gambling."

James slid Erika a look. "I guess you won't need my contact with the feds, after all."

"Hang on. What are you all talking about?" Lance pushed away from the wall and came to stand next to the table on Erika's other side.

Susan shot a look at Erika and gave a bitter laugh.

"So you haven't brought your boyfriend up to speed, I see. Smart girl. Men ruin everything, anyway."

"Ms. Garraus?" Lance growled.

"Ellis and I applied for a grant from the federal government to help with the costs of restoring city hall. Only we didn't tell anyone else on the city council because we never planned to use the money for restoration. That damn gambling outfit had sucked both of us in." Susan hunched over in her chair, as if admitting she had a gambling problem had deflated her. "My house is in foreclosure. My creditors are garnishing my wages. Not that it matters. If I worked until I was one hundred I wouldn't make enough to pay back what I owe the bookies." Susan looked up, and what Erika saw in her eyes was almost a plea. "That's why we needed so much money. We were both in so deep only a big win was going to mean anything."

Even though she knew what Susan had done was very wrong, Erika felt sorry for the woman sitting in front of her. "How did you and Ellis come up with this plan?"

Susan's mouth twisted into an ugly scowl. "Ellis. It was his idea. I told him no, several times. But then my debt got so large and he convinced me that as long as we worked together, no one would know." Her expression turned sad now. "And that if we just had enough money to bet big, we could both turn our luck around. Maybe even win enough to actually pay off our debts and give the three hundred thousand to the town and honor the grant."

Erika worked to keep her expression neutral. Of course, the chances that Ellis and Susan would have won big enough to pull off their scheme were slim to none, especially at an unregulated, and more than likely fixed, underground gambling establishment. But gambling was an addiction, and addicts weren't known for clearheaded planning.

"How do we know you're telling the truth about Ellis Hanes?" Lance challenged Susan. "As far as I can tell, there is no evidence, outside of your statement here, that Ellis has anything to do with gambling or this grant you've told us about."

"Lance is right, Susan. Something doesn't add up. Sam Hogan walked off my renovation job because Ellis hired him to update a wing of his hotel. If Ellis is broke, how did he hire Sam?"

Susan scoffed. "Did Sam get the money upfront? Look, believe whatever you want," Susan shot back, "but I'm telling you what I know. Ellis's hotel and B&B haven't been doing well at all these last several years. The buildings do need renovations but between that new resort down Route 283 siphoning off customers and his gambling, Ellis doesn't have two nickels to rub together."

"Maybe," Lance said, "but you've still given us nothing to support that Ellis is involved in any of the things you've told us about."

Susan locked her gaze on Erika. "I know he hired that transient—" Susan made a face "—Brian, to set fire to your B&B while you were in the hospital and then sent him back to bust up the place when the fire plan didn't work out."

"Brian Whitmer?" Erika conjured up a vague picture in her mind of the man. She'd never employed him but she knew he was one of many who picked up work in town during the height of tourist season. If Susan was telling truth, Brian had not only attempted to set fire to the B&B, he'd most likely also broken in and taken those shots at her, Marcus and James.

Damn Ellis Hanes. He could have killed Marcus. It took a moment for Erika to beat back the rage that flared in her chest. By the time she did, Susan was speaking again.

"I made a tape of me and Ellis I discussing the grant. Several, actually. Once we got the money, I didn't trust that Ellis wouldn't somehow try to pin the whole thing on me if it went south. They're at my house in my safe."

Lance's expression still telegraphed his disbelief. "James, Erika, can I talk to you out in the hall for a moment." Lance started for the door without waiting for an answer.

Susan caught Erika's hand as she and James rose to follow Lance. "I want a deal, okay? I'm not going to lie about that. But I asked that you be here because I know you aren't going to just allow them to pin everything on me and brush Ellis's part in this under the rug."

Something Ellis said when he'd confronted Erika in the park the other day jumped into her mind. "Susan, did you tell Ellis that I'd questioned you about the grant?"

Susan nodded. "Yeah, I freaked out. I was convinced you'd figured us out. I called Ellis, told him everything. He told me to keep my mouth shut and you wouldn't have anything to go on."

Erika mentally slotted the puzzle pieces into place. She had thought Ellis's harassment was centered on the potential competition her B&B posed. But she could see how her questions around the missing grant money posed just as big, if not a bigger threat, to Ellis if what Susan said was true. Her inquiries could have pushed

Ellis to go to extremes, like taking a shot at her outside of her house.

James waited just outside the open interrogation room door. "You okay?"

Erika looked him in the eye and answered truthfully, "I don't know."

She turned and led the way to Lance's office.

"What do you think?" Lance asked as he closed the door and took his seat behind his desk.

Erika settled into the chair across from Lance. "I believe her. I always felt she knew more about that grant than she was telling me."

"What she said makes sense," James offered.

Lance sighed. "It does, but I need more than her word to arrest Ellis. Even with the tapes, if Ellis didn't know he was being recorded, they can't be used in court."

"Lance, you have to bring Ellis in. This is about more than the grant. I think Daisy is right. I think Ellis is the person behind the attacks on me."

"Come on, Erika. Just the other day you were sure Daisy was wrong. And you have to admit there's a long way from gambling addict to attempted murderer."

"I know, but that was before we knew how desperate Ellis probably is. You heard Susan. This isn't just about rival B&Bs. Elis is facing potential fraud and embezzlement charges, in addition to the collapse of his businesses. Maybe even arson charges if you can find Brian Whitmer."

"If you believe Susan," Lance pointed out.

"The lady sounded credible to me," James said. "Her statement about Whitmer being hired to set fire to Erika's house fits."

Erika scooted to the edge of her chair. The more she thought about it, the more convinced she became that

Ellis was behind everything. "It makes sense, Lance, and who else could it be? No one else has a motive except Ellis."

"She has a point." James crossed his arms over his chest.

They fell silent.

The wheels in Lance's head were almost visibly turning. "I still don't know if I have enough to bring Ellis in. But—" Lance said, cutting off Erika's next round of arguments "—I can send a deputy to request an audience." Lance's lips twisted. "Nobody is above the law in my town but Ellis is the mayor, so I'll have to pay some deference to the office. And I'll run what we have by a judge and see if I can get a warrant to search his home and businesses."

Some of the tension in her body dissipated. "Thank you, Lance."

Lance shook his head. "Don't thank me yet. You two should go home. Nothing is going to happen tonight."

Erika followed James from the building and to his car. As much as she wanted to be around when Lance brought Ellis in, she was impatient to be with Marcus again. She'd need to tell him about his newfound wealth, but having him in her sights would ease the anxiousness she'd been feeling since finding out about the inheritance.

"You've been awfully quiet since we left the sheriff's station. Something on your mind?"

James gave her a wry look. "Everything is on my mind at the moment."

"You know what I mean. You should be… I don't know…happier. We know who's behind the attacks and I'm sure Lance will have Ellis in custody soon."

"Do we know that, though?"

"I know Lance is probably right about not having enough evidence for the court, but he'll get it. Once Ellis knows we're on to him and that Susan has told us everything, the jig will be up. I'm sure he'll hire an army of lawyers, but there won't be any reason to come after me anymore."

"I'll relax once Ellis Hanes is in police custody. Until then, it's safest if we stay vigilant."

She couldn't argue with his logic. She'd certainly breathe a lot easier with Ellis behind bars.

Deputy Clarke Bridges and his husband, Steve, had a large bungalow about two miles from downtown Carling Lake.

James pulled the SUV to a stop at the curb in front of the house.

Deputy Bridges opened the door. Erika noticed that, even though he was in his street clothes, he wore his gun on his hip.

James must have noticed as well. "Any trouble?"

Clarke shook his head. "All quiet."

"Thanks for taking Marcus to and picking him up from school," Erika said.

"No thanks necessary, you know that. The boys keep each other company, which makes my job easier." Clarke smiled and led them farther into the house. "They are in the basement. I hope you don't mind. I told them they could play video games after they finished their homework."

"Clarke, so much has happened today that I can't bring myself to worry about video games. I'll just have to hope this isn't the game that'll rot his brain."

Clarke chuckled. "Some days are like that." He sobered. "Lance filled me in a bit about what all is going on. Are you hanging around for a while?" he asked, directing the question to James.

James's brow arched up. "For a while."

"Good." Clarke opened the door to the basement and started down the stairs. "Guys, Marcus's mom is here."

The heavy silence that answered sent an ominous chill shuddering through Erika before she reached the last step.

All the lights were on and the video game on the gigantic television screen mounted to the wall was frozen on a fight scene. The door leading outside stood open ominously.

"Boys!" Clarke hurried to the door at the rear of the basement.

James drew his gun and dashed through the open door, disappearing into the home's backyard with Erika at his heels.

Exterior lights at either corner of the house and over the door cast shadows around the home. It took a moment for her eyes to adjust, but when they did, they fell on a prone figure in the snow-dusted grass.

Devin.

Cold hard dread landed with a thud in her chest. She scanned the yard. Footprints led from the back door to the open gate in the fence at the back of the house. She moved toward the gate, but James's hand on arm stopped her.

"We don't know who's out there and you aren't armed. I'll go. You stay here and help the other boy," James commanded before taking off toward the fence, his gun still in his hand.

Every fiber of her being wanted to argue with him. Marcus was missing. He was her son and it was her job to protect him. She'd failed. She had to find him.

But James didn't give her the opportunity to argue. He bolted for the fence, disappearing into the darkness.

A groan sounded from behind her and she turned toward Devin and Clarke. Devin's eyelids fluttered but didn't open. A bump was already growing at his temple. Someone had hit him, and hard from the looks of it.

Nausea roiled in her stomach at the thought of what Marcus might be going through right now. Had he been hit as well? Or worse? She had no idea how long ago he'd been taken. Was he terrified, wondering where she was and why she hadn't come for him yet?

She stood frozen, immovable by the terror coursing through her body as Clarke drew his phone from his back pocket and barked a demand for an ambulance at the dispatcher.

James hurried back into the yard and to her side. His eyes reflected the panic she was feeling. "It's too dark. I couldn't see anyone."

Erika's breath came fast but she couldn't seem to make her feet move, but her body trembled with a primal fear.

Marcus was gone.

Chapter Twenty

Erika listened to the hum of voices in the police station. Marcus had been missing for nearly two hours now, and she'd moved from frantic to numb.

Her son had been kidnapped.

Devin had regained consciousness in the ambulance to the hospital. He'd been able to tell them he and Marcus had heard a noise outside, a sound like a wounded dog, and they'd gone out to investigate. Devin had exited first, with Marcus right behind him. He'd made it a few steps from the door when he heard Marcus groan and fall. He turned to see Marcus lying in the grass, and then something hit him in the back of the head and that's the last thing he remembered.

Lance had put the entire six-man sheriff's department on finding Marcus, and the town of Carling Lake had rallied as well. Search parties were formed and fanned out despite the darkness. Erika knew they'd have to call off the search until morning if they didn't find Marcus soon.

She shuddered at the idea of her son out there, more than likely held against his will. She prayed that whoever had taken him didn't want to hurt him.

James's words from earlier today in his apartment

ran through her head on a loop. *That much money makes you and Marcus targets.*

Was that what this was about? The Overholt millions? She'd give it all away to have her son back in her arms.

James had talked with the attorneys who had assured him they had not released the news that Marcus was heir to the Overholt fortune. And Lance had reached out to Robert and his wife had also denied saying anything to anyone.

That left Ellis.

Lance had sent a deputy to his home, office, and the hotel and B&B. No one knew where he was, and Ellis hadn't answered calls from the sheriff.

Erika had considered whether kidnapping Marcus was some sort of blackmail or revenge scheme. Leverage so that she wouldn't reveal his part in stealing the grant money. What would Ellis do if he found out it was too late? That Susan had rolled on him and it was only a matter of time before Lance had enough evidence to arrest him?

Marcus would be worthless to Ellis then.

She swallowed hard and banished the thoughts that were threatening to overwhelm her.

The entire town was searching for Marcus. Lance had even looked the other way when James called his brother and got West involved in tracking down Ellis via their own sources and methods.

"Here. Drink this."

Erika startled, surprised to find Lance standing over her, holding a steaming paper cup. "It's hot tea. James says you haven't had anything to eat for hours and you need to keep your strength up."

She took the tea, only noticing how cold she was

when she wrapped her hands around the warm cup. She took a sip and cringed at the sickly sweetness from too much sugar. Probably Lance's way of making sure she didn't go into shock.

"Erika, we're doing everything we can." Lance rubbed her shoulder soothingly. "Why don't you go home and try to get some rest."

She shook her head, setting the tea on the table in front of her. "I'm not going anywhere."

"It might be best," James said, coming to stand next to Lance. "If Marcus goes to the house, it would be good to have someone waiting there."

"I called Daisy. She said she'll stay at the house, just in case."

There was no way she was leaving the station. She wanted to know the minute any news about Marcus came in. Not have it filtered through Lance or one of the other deputies who'd only tell her what they wanted her to know.

"Okay, then. Hang in there." Lance gave Erika's shoulder a squeeze before he moved to the other side of the room.

Erika felt her eyes welling with tears. This is why she'd settled in Carling Lake. Because it was a community that looked out for one another. Cared for each other.

She just hoped that if Ellis had Marcus, he'd remember that he was Carling Lake, born and bred, and tap into the community's kind spirit.

James reached out and palmed her cheek. She leaned into his hand, soaking up his warmth and strength. "I saw a cot in Lance's office. You could try and get some sleep."

"I won't be able to sleep until I know Marcus is safe."

She stepped into him and wrapped her arms around his waist, tucked her head into his shoulder and let the tears fall. "I just want my son."

"I know, I know. We're doing everything we can." James cradled the back of her head, his fingers massaging the base of her neck.

His phone rang, and he moved away just enough to pull it from his pocket and glance at the screen. "It's Ryan."

He walked to the other side of the room with Lance. The two of them hunched over a laptop, but from the lack of urgency in their movements, she could tell that this wasn't the call that mattered.

The one that said Marcus had been found.

She started again when her phone buzzed. She was still wearing the suit she'd worn to the meeting with the attorneys and she must have stuck her phone into the pocket at some point.

She had a text from an unknown number. Probably spam.

But the moment she opened the message it became clear this wasn't spam.

If You Ever Want To See Your Son Again, Be In The Parking Lot Behind The Station In Two Minutes. Alone. Tell No One. Your Son's Life Depends On It.

ERIKA LOOKED THROUGH the glass wall of the conference room. There was no one in the small bullpen except the twenty-something civilian receptionist who was speaking into the landline at her desk.

This had to be some kind of cruel joke.

But what if it wasn't? Two minutes didn't give her much time for internal debates.

If it wasn't real, she'd find nothing but an empty parking lot outside.

And if it was from Marcus's kidnapper?

She headed for the door to the conference room.

"Where are you going?" James's question stopped her before she crossed the threshold.

The text had said to tell no one. She couldn't take any chances with Marcus's life.

She turned back to the room, praying her face didn't give away what she was about to do. "I think I will take advantage of that cot in Lance's office."

"Good. You should rest," Lance said, looking away from the computer screen.

James stared at her. For a moment, she thought he was going to call her out, but then the corners of his mouth curved into a smile she couldn't help but find sexy despite the situation.

"I'll come get you if there's any news."

She returned his smile and prayed he'd forgive her for the lie. That is, if there was anything to forgive her for.

She wasn't sure whether she wanted there to be someone waiting for her in the parking lot or not. Unless it was Marcus, neither option was optimal.

Erika walked past Lance's office and headed for the building's rear exit.

The door opened with a soft click, and she stepped out into the night. A dim yellow bulb hung over the door and cast all the light that was to be had in the parking lot.

Her phone buzzed again.

Rear lot.

Erika scanned the parking lot. A dark sedan was parked in the last space at the far edge of the lot, barely visible. Not a single person was in sight.

Almost to the car, a voice called out, "Drop your phone on the ground."

A figure stepped out of the shadows, but Erika had already processed the voice. An icy chill snaked up her spine. "Daisy? What are you doing? You're supposed to be at my house in case Marcus comes home."

"Whether Marcus comes home or not is up to you. Now I said drop your phone."

Erika let the phone slide out of her hand. Erika felt fear warring with fury. The whys weren't clear, but what was clear was that Daisy had something to do with Marcus's kidnapping. "Where's my son?"

Instead of answering, Daisy pushed a button on the key fob in her left hand. The trunk of the black sedan popped up.

"Get in," Daisy said.

"No."

Daisy's right hand came up. Even in the dark, Erika could tell it held a gun. "Get. In."

Erika's stomach roiled, but she didn't move. If she just kept Daisy talking long enough, James or Lance would notice she wasn't taking a nap and come looking for her.

A smile twisted Daisy's lips. "Hoping for the cavalry? I'll never tell them where Marcus is and if I don't go back…"

Daisy left the rest of the statement unsaid, but Erika heard it as clearly as if she'd shouted the words. If she didn't go back to wherever she was holding Marcus, he'd die.

Erika climbed into the trunk, and seconds later she was plunged into darkness.

JAMES WATCHED ERIKA disappear down the corridor leading to Lance's office.

"She's tough. She'll be alright," Lance said from his place in front of the laptop they were using to track the search party efforts.

James knew Erika was a strong woman, but if anything could break her, it would be losing Marcus. What had surprised him was the tumult of feelings he experienced on hearing Marcus was missing. Somewhere along the way, he hadn't just fallen in love with Erika, he'd also come to care a great deal for Marcus. So much so that if Marcus was hurt, he'd hunt his abductor to the ends of the earth, if that's what it took, regardless of how things worked out between him and Erika.

James turned his attention back to Lance and the aerial map on the laptop's screen. Ryan had called in a favor and at first light tomorrow they'd have a chopper in the air to cover the denser areas of the forest and the harder to reach portions of the mountains. And the dusting of snow covering the forest floor didn't help.

He and Lance were identifying those areas and prioritizing the order of the flyovers based on the likelihood that Marcus might be held there. James's phone rang and Ryan's name flashed across the screen.

"Got the background checks back on Robert and his wife. No criminal record or known criminal associates per se. A couple of businessmen who engage in practices that are unethical if not illegal but that's not unexpected." James could hear the flutter of papers being shifted on the other side of the phone. "We pulled Robert's finances—don't ask how. No large or unusual outlays in the last six months. There is something weird, though. It appears that Robert's salary from Overholt Industries goes directly into a trust each month and the trustee gives him an allowance."

James thought about what Erika said about finding out her house and cars were in Roger Overholt's name. "I'm pretty sure you'll find that Robert's house is in his father's name if you look at real estate records. After her husband died, Erika found out Roger, not she and her husband, owned the house they lived in, the cars, everything. It was how Roger exuded control over the family. My guess is the financial arrangement is part of it."

"A forty-year-old man who lets his father keep him on an allowance?" Ryan scoffed. "That's…something." James couldn't argue with that assessment. "Okay, the sister was harder to look into but we are the best so I found some information on her and we'll keep digging."

James felt his forehead furrow as his brain worked to keep up with what Ryan had said. "The sister?"

"Roger Overholt had three kids—Ronald, Robert and a girl, the youngest, Evangeline."

"Right. Erika mentioned a sister. She said the sister has been estranged from the family for years before she even met her ex."

"Estranged is a good way to put it," Ryan said. "There are photos with her and the family in the press until she was about nineteen. The last public mention of her I can find is in a tabloid rag. Apparently, she ran off and married the bass player in a minor league band. Roger disowned her and she, and the band, disappeared from public life."

"But you found her because West Security and Investigations is the best, right?"

"I did. She and her husband moved to California.

They moved a lot until they divorced about six years ago. No children."

"And what has she been doing over the last six years?"

"Not much. She shuffled through a variety of jobs until about a year ago."

"What happened a year ago?"

"No idea. She just sort of fell off the face of the earth. I'm working on it. You'd think with a name like Evangeline Daisy Overholt Hargrove she'd be easy to find but…"

The buzzing sound in James's head blocked out the rest of what Ryan said.

Evangeline Daisy Overholt Hargrove.

Daisy Hargrove.

Daisy was Ronald and Robert's sister.

He'd speculated that Robert might want Erika out of the way so he could claim guardianship of Marcus and control over his inheritance, but he had the wrong Overholt. His theory worked just as well for an aunt as an uncle.

"Do you have a picture of Evangeline Overholt?" James asked.

"Sure. Stand by, I'm emailing it now."

James put his phone on speaker and opened the email from Ryan that had just hit his inbox.

It only took seconds for the picture to load, but he knew in his gut what he was going to see.

Evangeline Overholt aka Daisy Hargrove.

"What is this?" Lance said, leaning in to look at the phone's screen. "Why do you have a photo of Daisy on your phone?"

"Daisy?" Ryan's voice carried over the open line.

"Evangeline Overholt has been living in Carling Lake for the past year under the name Daisy Hargrove."

Lance swore and reached for his phone. "I'll get a deputy over to her house now."

"Ry, we need to know everything there is to know about Evangeline Overholt and Daisy Hargrove. Particularly every piece of property she owns within a hundred-mile radius." James doubted Daisy or Evangeline would be at her house if she had taken Marcus, but it was as good a place to start as anywhere.

He hurried from the conference room toward Lance's office. He'd promised Erika that he'd tell her the moment there was news. And the fact that her new best friend was actually her sister-in-law qualified.

James pushed open the door but stopped short of going in. It wasn't necessary. His gaze swept over the entire office once, twice, three times with the same result.

Erika wasn't there.

Chapter Twenty-One

Bumping around in the trunk of Daisy's car left Erika with a massive headache. Still, that wasn't the reason she was relieved when the car stopped.

Marcus. Daisy must be taking her to wherever she'd hidden Marcus. She'd suffer through a lifetime of headaches to get her son back.

The car door slammed and Erika could hear footsteps crunching along gravel as Daisy approached the back of the car.

Panic rose in her throat. Daisy had a gun and could easily shoot her the moment the trunk opened.

On the drive, Erika had felt around for the release lever that every trunk was supposed to have in case someone got trapped inside. Daisy must have removed it because she'd found nothing. No release lever and nothing she could use as a weapon. She was the only thing in the trunk of Daisy's car.

Erika sent up a quick prayer that James had discovered she was not in Lance's office and somehow figured out where Daisy had taken her.

The trunk popped open.

Daisy waited a foot away, her gun trained on Erika. "Get out."

Erika pushed into a sitting position, then gingerly

stood. She couldn't be sure exactly how long she'd been in Daisy's trunk, but her legs had been immobile long enough that she needed a moment to ensure they'd support her weight.

Daisy jerked her head to the right. "Move."

Erika turned to see what could generously be called a wooden shack several feet away.

Was Marcus inside? The thing looked as if it would collapse under a light breeze. Had Daisy left her son in a hut that could cave in on him at any moment?

Adrenaline pumped through Erika as she hurried toward the structure, but inside she found nothing but an old length of rope and a dirt floor.

She whirled around to face Daisy. "What is this? Where is Marcus?"

Daisy laughed. "You didn't think I'd leave him here, did you? This place is on its last legs! I couldn't treat the little prince like that, now could I?"

Erika's heart thundered in her chest. The little prince. Daisy knew about the inheritance.

"How do you know…"

A slow smile spread over the face of the woman Erika had considered a friend. "How do I know Marcus is an Overholt? Oh, honey, I've known that since the moment I set foot in this godforsaken town. Trust me, it's the only reason I moved here."

Erika's head swam now, not just from the headache, but with confusion. "I don't understand."

"I know, and even though I don't owe you an explanation, I'll explain it to you. You see, about a year ago, I went to see my father. We'd been on the outs for quite a while and, well, it's not easy out here for a divorcee with no real marketable skills." Daisy scowled. "Let's just say he was not open to a reconciliation."

"What does your father have to do with anything? Where is Marcus?" Erika asked, her eyes scanning the shack for anything she could use as a weapon. She'd keep Daisy talking for as long as she could and hopefully get out of her where she'd hidden Marcus, but she couldn't count on James figuring out where she was in time.

"My father has everything to do with everything!" Daisy flung her arms out. Erika flinched when the gun in Daisy's hand swung in her direction, but Daisy didn't seem to notice. "He always has. Always wanted to control everything and everyone around him. And most people let him, but not me." Daisy pressed her gun-free hand against her chest. "I got away from him."

Time slowed down as realization dawned on Erika. "You're Ronald's sister, Evangeline."

Daisy's smile grew wide. "I haven't gone by that name in years. You know, I worried about befriending you. I know we never formally met, but I couldn't be sure how much you knew about me from being married to Ronald. Had you seen a picture of me? Would you recognize me? I should have known when Roger Overholt disowns you, you stay disowned." Daisy's face hardened, but Erika could still see traces of hurt in her eyes.

Daisy was Evangeline. Technically, Erika's sister-in-law and Marcus's aunt. Why hadn't she said anything in the last year?

"You knew about the will, how?" Erika asked, struggling to put all the pieces of the puzzle together.

"My father told me. When I went to him a year and a half ago, it was clear he was in his last weeks of life. It was one of the reasons I asked for forgiveness when I did. I knew he'd require some groveling, and I wanted to minimize that." Daisy spoke as if what she was saying made complete sense. "He treated me like some stranger who had just strolled in off the street, asking to move into his mansion. Worse, actually. He wanted to punish me for having walked away from him, for having refused to let him run my life like he ran my brothers'. As if it's normal for a father to control every aspect of his adult children's lives. That's when he told me about the will. Taunted me about it, actually. He was gleeful about cutting his children out of everything. And don't think for a minute he cared about Marcus. He knew inheriting that kind of money would screw up any chance of Marcus having a normal life and he was proud of himself for doing it."

Roger Overholt had been pure evil until his last moments. Erika wanted to be surprised, but she wasn't. Roger had always been the kind of man who got his jollies from other people's pain.

"So what? Knowing Marcus was the heir, you thought you would come to Carling Lake and ingratiate yourself with us? When did you plan to tell us who you were?"

"When did you plan to tell people who *you* were?" Daisy shot back. "At first, I figured I'd get to know you and Marcus, we'd become friends who were family and then when I revealed who I really was, everyone would be thrilled." Daisy shrugged. "It's not as good as inheriting myself but I could get some money out of you and it would be better than nothing."

"Why'd your plan change?"

"Honestly, I could not take much more of living in this boring town. And the more I thought about it, the less content I was with accepting whatever you and your son decided to dole out to me for the rest of my life. That would be no different from living under my father's thumb."

"So you decided to what? Kill me? Were you behind all the attacks on me and the B&B?"

Daisy's smile sent a chill down Erika's spine. "Ugh, don't you listen? Susan told you, Ellis did all that. Except shooting at you. I still can't believe I missed. With you gone, Marcus would need a guardian and who better than his loving aunt. It could be some kind of heartwarming Hallmark story. The aunt who befriended her nephew, afraid to tell him who she was, until fate stepped in and she was forced to step up."

Daisy had completely lost the thread. There was no way her plan would work. Erika felt panic rising again. She needed to get away from Daisy and find Marcus. "Where's Marcus?"

"Don't worry. I've stashed him somewhere safe and as soon as I've dealt with you, the sheriff will get an anonymous call with his location."

Daisy raised the hand holding the gun.

THE PARKING LOT behind the sheriff's office was abuzz with activity. His stomach had fallen the moment he'd seen Lance's empty office. He'd known something was wrong. Erika wouldn't just take off without telling him. Not unless she felt she had to. Finding her cell phone had only confirmed his worst fears.

Now sheriff's deputies combed the parking lot, but so far they hadn't found anything other than Erika's cell phone.

Lance had already questioned the other deputies on duty and the clerk who worked the front desk. No one had come into the building and no one had noticed Erika leaving.

"James, I've got the video surveillance," Lance called from where he stood several yards away, conferring with one of his deputies.

James hurried over. A black-and-white video played on Lance's phone but it was clear enough for James to see Erika exiting the building and heading toward the rear of the lot.

A figure stepped out of the shadows but their back was to the camera. They'd either been lucky or they'd known where the sheriff's office's security cameras were. What he could tell was that the person was short and slight.

"That could be Daisy," James said.

"The size is right but we can't tell much else from this video."

After several more moments, the person speaking to Erika shifted.

"Whoever it is has a gun." James's voice vibrated, equal parts fear and fury.

They watched in silence as Erika climbed into the trunk of a car. The figure got in on the driver's side without ever turning his or her face to the camera.

"I was hoping we'd catch a break and the recording would confirm or rule out Daisy."

"Maybe we did." James looked at the deputy next to Lance. "Rewind the video to right before the car turns out of the parking lot." The deputy swiped at the screen. "There. Now can you make it bigger? Zoom in on the plate."

"There's no way we're going to get a clear shot of that plate from this video. At least not without help."

"When the car turns out of the lot, the license plate is directly in the line of the camera. Even if only part of it is clear, we can run those digits against Daisy's license plate. It will at least give us some idea if we're on the right track."

"Actually, guys," the deputy chimed in, "I think this is a good picture. I can't make out the last two numbers but the rest is clear. HHJ56."

"Get inside and run that plate against Daisy Hargrove's," Lance ordered.

"I'm going to Daisy's place," James said.

"Let's wait for the plate information. It will only take minutes and could save us time if we're wrong about Daisy," Lance said before turning away and bellowing, "Sampson."

A fresh-faced young deputy jogged over. "I want you to go over to Erika Powell's place. If Daisy Hargrove is there, bring her into the station. Be careful."

"Yes, sir." The young deputy jogged up the stairs leading to the back door of the station. The door swung outward forcefully, narrowly missing hitting Sampson as he reached to open it.

"Sheriff, I got it." The first deputy skirted around Sampson and bounded down the stairs. "I got it. Daisy Hargrove's license plate number is HHJ5629. Those could be the last two numbers of the plate in the picture. And her car is a dark sedan just like the car in the photo."

"Good work," Lance said. "Call Judge Stone and get me a warrant for Daisy Hargrove's residence."

James was already moving toward the area of the parking lot where his SUV was parked.

"Hey!" Lance grabbed his arm before he could get too far. He nodded toward the police cruiser. "I've got the sirens."

James pivoted and picked up his pace. "Let's go."

They arrived at Daisy's house at the same time the

search warrant came through. James was out of the car before Lance shut off the engine. The deputy Lance had sent to Erika's house had already radioed to say that there was nobody home at Erika's.

Daisy's small cottage was in an older neighborhood that looked to be well cared for. The swirling lights on top of Lance's vehicle had attracted the attention of the neighbors on either side.

Lance admonished the lookie-loos to go back into their homes as he dashed up the walkway.

They stood on opposite sides of the front door. Lance knocked and announced himself. There was no response from inside. He nodded toward James. "On my count. One, two, three."

James kicked the door in and followed Lance through the door, his firearm at the ready. If his hunch was right that it was Daisy, not Hanes's paid goon, who'd taken a shot at Erika, that meant she was armed and they had no idea what she might do if she was cornered.

It took no time at all to clear the small house.

Erika and Marcus weren't there.

He hadn't felt this much fear since he'd watched a suicide bomber detonate feet in front of him. Pure paralyzing fear.

"They aren't here." His chest constricted with each word. They had no idea where Marcus or Erika was. Or if they were even still alive.

Lance clasped a hand on his shoulder and gave it a squeeze. "We'll find them. Just keep your head in the game."

James forced himself to take several deep breaths. Lance was right. He couldn't let himself think the worst. Erika was a fighter. She'd proven that by getting away from her controlling in-laws and she'd raised Marcus to be a fighter. They'd both be okay. They had to be. And they'd need him to focus.

He followed Lance back to the front of the house.

"Alright, boys," Lance said, meeting the two deputies that had just joined them. "We're looking for anything that could tell us where Daisy Hargrove is or where she could hold Erika and Marcus."

The four of them reentered the house and fanned out. One deputy headed for the back bedrooms while the second went through the kitchen/dining area. Lance and James moved toward what Daisy was obviously using as the master bedroom.

James began his search with the nightstand next to the bed while Lance threw open the closet doors. The nightstand held the usual clutter of books and discarded receipts on top while the drawer was a hodgepodge of miscellaneous chargers, pens, business cards and other junk that Daisy probably didn't even notice anymore. Nothing out of the ordinary and nothing that gave them any hint as to where she was holding Marcus and Erika.

"Hey, I think I've got something," Lance said, pulling a shoebox from the closet.

Lance set the box on the bed. Inside were dozens of photographs of Erika and Marcus, both alone and together. From the look of it, neither subject had any idea they were being photographed.

"This is…" Lance started.

"Creepy," James finished.

The more they dug, the more obvious it became that Daisy had been following Erika and Marcus for quite some time. James could see how much the boy had grown from the photos near the bottom of the box, which were clearly the earliest ones taken, to the photos closer to the top.

Lance held out one of the photos. "I remember this. This was taken at the Winter Festival last year. Daisy hadn't even moved to town yet."

"She was keeping a low profile or she had someone else taking these photographs for her. Either way, she knew who Erika and Marcus were before she moved to town."

"From the looks of it, she was stalking them."

That's exactly what she'd been doing. The thought was terrifying.

It appeared that Daisy had been planning whatever it was she was doing for a long time. At least a year. And there was no doubt in James's mind it had everything to do with the fortune Marcus had just inherited, although he had no idea how Daisy would have found out about Roger's will.

And it didn't matter. All that mattered right now was finding Erika and Marcus. The photos gave them some insight into Daisy's mind but not what they really needed to know.

Where was she?

"Do any of these photos show a place where Daisy might be able to hold two people without raising suspicions?"

Lance shuffled through the photos in his hand then tossed them on the bed and took another bunch from the box. "No. They're all of Erika or Marcus."

They had to be missing something.

"If they aren't here, Daisy has to have another place where she's keeping them," James said. "You know her better than I do. Does she have a hunting cabin? A boyfriend? Anyplace she would go besides here?"

Lance shook his head. "No other place. No boyfriend. At least, not that I know of."

"There's got to be someplace." James dropped the photos in his hand to the bed and headed for the door. "There's a room at the front of the house that looks like an office. Maybe there's something there."

Lance followed him into the small room, only a little bigger than the closet Lance had pulled the box of photos from. It was only big enough for a small desk and chair and a single two-drawer filing cabinet tucked into the corner.

"I'll take the desk," James said, already rounding it. "You search the filing cabinet. We might need to get into this computer." James tapped the silver laptop on the desktop.

"Unless we can find the password in here somewhere, I'd have to send that to the county forensics guys. I don't have an in-house hacker."

There was no way he was going to waste time sending the computer off. If it came to it, he'd call Ryan, get West's technophile on it. It wouldn't be legal, but he didn't care a whit about legalities as long as Erika and Marcus were out there.

James shuffled through the papers on top of the desk, finding only utility bills for the residence. The first two drawers similarly yielded nothing of interest, but when he tried the third drawer, he found it locked.

He grabbed a letter opener from the pencil caddy and worked the flimsy lock until it gave. The drawer was nearly empty. The only things inside were a letter-size manila envelope and a file folder. He flipped the envelope upside down and a passport and several sheets of paper fell out onto the desktop.

He flipped the passport open quickly and confirmed that, at least according to the United States government, the woman who called herself Daisy Hargrove was in fact Evangeline Overholt Hargrove. He picked up the papers that had been in the envelope with the passport. It was a copy of Roger Overholt's will.

"Lance, I think I've got something," James said.

So Daisy knew about the money. That would support his theory about why she'd have taken Marcus and now Erika.

"What is it?" Lance crossed the room with purpose.

James passed the passport and will across the desk. While Lance studied the documents, James moved on to the folder.

"Okay, so we've got confirmation that Daisy is Evangeline."

James was only half listening. His focus was on the sheets of paper that had been in the folder. Printouts of isolated properties near Carling Lake that were for sale.

"Look at these." James spread the half dozen property listings out on the desk. Lance rounded the desk to view them more easily.

"Properties for sale," Lance said. "You think Daisy bought a place she didn't tell anyone about and is holding Erika and Marcus there?"

"I think it's worth checking out."

"You're right, but we have to prioritize. I need to send two deputies to each property to be safe and I don't have the manpower to search them all simultaneously."

James studied the listings carefully. Most of them were for smallish cabins within forty miles of downtown Carling Lake and off the beaten path. All but one.

"This one." James pointed at a listing of undeveloped lots.

Lance's forehead creased with doubt. "But this is basically just an empty lot. Looks like the original cabin burned down some years ago and there's only an out-house and a storm shelter left on the property."

"Exactly," James said, growing surer this was the place they should start looking for Marcus and Erika the more he looked at the specs versus the other properties. "All the other properties have usable cabins on them, which makes sense if Daisy intended to purchase a weekend getaway. So why was she even considering this other property?"

"Maybe she was thinking about building from scratch," Lance countered.

"We don't have time to argue. We have to begin somewhere and I'm sure this is where we need to start our search."

Lance hesitated for a moment longer. "Okay, you and I can go to the lot property and this one that's not too far away. I'll send my deputies to the other four properties."

James followed Lance from the office, adrenaline coursing through his veins, his heart thundering.

Erika, I'm on my way. Hang in there a little longer.

Chapter Twenty-Two

Erika lunged for Daisy. The sound of a gunshot thundered through the small shack.

One corner of Erika's mind registered a searing hot pain burning her shoulder. But her entire focus was on the woman who had her son.

Erika plowed forward, tackling Daisy around the waist and sending them both into the side of the shack. The walls shook and for a millisecond, Erika wondered if the structure was going to fall in on them. It held, and she and Daisy tumbled to the ground, Daisy losing her grip on the gun. It slid across the dirt floor and into the dark shadows.

Rolling in the dirt, they each fought for a superior position over the other. Daisy clawed at Erika's neck, her hand falling away only after Erika slammed her palm into the other woman's nose.

The blow stunned Daisy and gave Erika a moment to scan for the gun. She didn't see it anywhere. And she had no idea if Daisy had any other weapons hidden away.

Decision made, Erika pushed to her feet and bolted through the door.

She sprang toward the cover of the nearby woods. Thorns pricked her legs through the slacks of her suit but she rushed forward as quickly and silently as she could. She kept an eye out for any other houses or cabins where Daisy might have hidden Marcus but there was nothing but overgrown foliage and darkness.

"Erika!" Daisy's scream cut through the dense woods.

She slid behind a massive tree trunk and held as still as possible. Her breath came rapidly, the sound of each inhale and exhale filling her brain so completely it was hard to make out any other sounds. Was that a footstep?

She had no idea where she was or how far she'd made it from the shack Daisy had taken her to. More importantly, she had no idea where she was headed. Running around in unfamiliar woods was a dangerous situation to be in. Not to mention the snow-covered ground and freezing temperatures. But then again a madwoman with a gun was even more dangerous.

How long had she been standing here? She hadn't heard anything else from Daisy but that didn't mean she wasn't still out there. Waiting.

She could stay here, hiding, but that might also mean she'd die here if Daisy found her.

She couldn't just stand here and wait for Daisy to find her. Peering around the tree, she saw nothing but darkness. Erika moved slowly, hoping the sounds of the nature around her covered whatever noise she might make.

"Erika," Daisy sang. "Come out, come out wherever you are!"

The voice bounced off the trees, making it impossible for Erika to tell which direction it came from. She had to move. She had to stay alive until James or Lance figured everything out and came for her. It was her only chance. And it was Marcus's only chance.

A gunshot tore through the night.

Erika's heart seized. Fear washed over her as she remembered the hot flash of pain from the graze of the bullet. She hit the ground, her arms covering her head.

Daisy had obviously found the gun. That or she had another handy. How much ammunition did she have? A question Erika feared the answer to. Daisy's plan was bonkers but she seemed to have thought it out pretty well. At least from Erika's current vantage point, crouched in the forest.

"I'm getting tired of this game, Erika."

Clinging to the hope that she'd see her son again, she started moving, hunched over, making herself as small as possible.

Brush grabbed at her clothing and left scratches on her face and hands but she kept moving.

"Okay, fine," Daisy's voice came again, but it sounded as if Erika had put some distance between them. "If you're alive, though, Marcus is of no use to me."

Erika froze, terror tearing through every fiber of her body.

"Maybe my best option now is to eliminate whatever witnesses I can and make a run for it. How much do you love your son, Erika?"

She knew it was a ploy to get her to stop running. Daisy had gone through a lot of trouble to have herself declared Marcus's guardian. Hurting him would mean she'd never see the money she'd done all this for. But it was also clear that Daisy was past the point of thinking clearly. The possibility of losing the Overholt fortune forever might just push her to do the unthinkable.

"Okay!" Erika yelled. "Okay, I'm coming out." She

rose, holding her hands in the air and walked in the direction she thought Daisy's voice had come from.

"I should just shoot you right here," Daisy said once Erika faced her.

"No! You don't have to do this."

Daisy motioned with the gun for Erika to keep walking. "Move!"

Erika gave Daisy a wide berth and headed back in the direction she'd run from. At least she thought it was the same direction. She was more concerned about the fact that Daisy was behind her with a gun. There was nothing stopping Daisy from shooting her in the back and leaving her to die.

"You can have the money. It doesn't mean anything to me. If it did, I would have told Roger about Marcus years ago."

"Too bad for you it doesn't work that way."

"It can. I can sign it all over to you." She had no idea if that was true or not but she was willing to say anything at this point.

"You expect me to believe you'd just hand me hundreds of millions of dollars and not tell your boyfriends about all this. By the way, I would like to know how you got the sheriff and the hot new guy wrapped around your finger."

Erika ignored the last statement. "I'll say I took off to look for Marcus. Tell me where he is and I swear, I'll never say a word."

"I wish I could believe you. I was kind of starting to like you," Daisy said as they stepped out of the woods and into the clearing in front of the shack. Apparently, she hadn't gotten very far at all. "Back inside." Daisy poked the gun in Erika's back.

Once inside the shack, Erika turned to face Daisy. "Daisy, don't do this."

"Blah, blah, blah. You're a writer. This is repetitive."

Daisy's arm rose but the sound of a car's engine in the distance had them both jerking their attention to the door.

Taking advantage of the distraction, Erika charged, grabbing Daisy's hand that held the gun and shoving her shoulder into her stomach at the same time.

They hit the ground hard. Sharp pain radiated through Erika's hip and down her leg but she didn't let go of the gun.

She slammed Daisy's wrist against the ground— once, twice. The third time Daisy's hand opened and the gun fell free.

Erika lunged for it, not wanting to lose sight of it this time. But before she could reach out and grab it, Daisy yanked her back by her hair. "Where do you think you're going?"

Erika fell on top of the other woman. If she couldn't reach the gun, she'd have to make sure that Daisy didn't get it, either.

Shifting her weight, Erika hooked her legs one over each side of Daisy's hips, straddling the other woman. She plowed her fist into Daisy's face, snapping her head to the side.

Daisy howled and thrust up with her palm. Blood spurted from Erika's nose and the pain had stars bursting in front of her eyes.

Daisy seized on Erika's moment of disorientation to flip their positions. Daisy wrapped her arms around Erika's throat. "You had to do this the hard way, didn't you?"

Erika grabbed at Daisy's hands, fighting to get air

into her lungs. Daisy was petite, but greed, rage and adrenaline had given her a boost in strength. Prying her hands loose wasn't going to work. Erika pulled back her fist and plowed it into Daisy's gut.

Daisy doubled over, losing her grip on Erika's neck.

Erika rolled to her side, coming face-to-face with the gun Daisy had dropped. Her lungs greedily sucked in air.

"Enough." Erika turned to find Daisy standing over her, the hammer that had been hanging on the wall clutched in her hand. "This ends now."

Without thinking, Erika reached back for the gun, bringing it up in an arc.

Daisy blinked, her eyes widening in surprise.

Then Erika pulled the trigger, and another deafening roar rocked the small shack.

THE SOUND OF a gunshot tore through the night as Lance stopped the sheriff's cruiser behind a dark sedan.

"That was a gunshot." James bolted from the car, ignoring Lance's shout to let him call for backup. The cruiser's headlights cast light onto the small wooden shack on the property. James pulled his gun from his holster as he ran toward the door to the wood shanty.

He burst through the door, assessing the scene in the space of a breath. Daisy writhed on the ground, bleeding from a wound to her right upper thigh.

Erika stood several feet away, a gun pointed down at her former friend. "Where. Is. Marcus?"

Daisy's only answer was a mewling sound.

If Erika had registered his presence, she didn't show it. Since the last thing he wanted was to startle her, he kept his voice low when he spoke. "Erika, baby, you can put the gun down now."

She blinked at him through glassy eyes.

James felt a stab of anger at the sight of her bloody nose and the start of swelling around her left eye. He pointed his gun at the ground. In his peripheral vision, he saw Lance come through the door.

Erika turned her attention back to Daisy. "She's going to tell me where my son is." She held the gun out in front of her.

"You don't want to do this, Erika," Lance said.

Erika kept her eyes locked on Daisy. "She's going to tell me where my son is!" she yelled.

"I think he's here," James said.

Erika's head snapped in his direction. "Here?"

"On this property. Lance and I found the listing for this property at Daisy's house. It mentions a root cellar. Let Lance take care of Daisy and we can go look for Marcus."

Erika only hesitated for a moment before lowering the gun.

Lance moved in quickly, rolling Daisy onto her stomach and slapping his handcuffs around her wrists. He stepped back and used his radio to call for an ambulance.

"Where is this root cellar?" Erika asked, stepping into James's arms.

He held her tightly and relished the feeling of having her safely in his arms for a moment before answering. "I don't know exactly, but the property didn't look that big. I'm sure we can find it."

"Here," Lance said, moving over to where they stood. He unhooked the flashlight from his duty belt. "Take my Maglite. I'm not going to tell you we should wait for backup to arrive but I will say be careful."

James gave Lance a brisk nod of thanks and stepped

back into the darkness. If he thought he had a chance of doing anything other than angering Erika, he'd have suggested she wait with Lance while he searched the property. They didn't know if Daisy had been working alone or what they would find if they found the root cellar.

If they were too late to save Marcus.... He wanted to protect Erika from that possibility as long as he could.

He walked in a grid pattern, Erika at his side, sweeping the flashlight over the ground in front of them. The foundation of what had likely been a cabin in the past was still on the property.

"There." Erika pointed, hurrying toward a spot about thirty paces from where they currently stood.

He could see it now, too. A wood door in the ground, a metal hook for a handle. Erika reached for the handle and pulled to no avail. She grabbed the handle with both hands and tried a second time.

"Hang on," James said, holstering his gun. He thrust the flashlight at Erika. "Hold this and stand back. We don't know who or what is down there."

He waited until Erika had moved away, then pulled on the handle.

The door was heavy but gave with little resistance, which he took as a sign that it had been opened recently.

James pulled his gun and took the flashlight from Erika. "Stay behind me."

They started down the stairs, each one creaking as they did. If there was someone down here, they knew they had company.

James panned the flashlight over the cellar, stopping when it landed on a cot in the corner. A small body lay prone on top, perfectly still. Marcus. His heart felt as if it was being squeezed in a vise. Beside him, Erika let out a wrenching sob.

Marcus's arms were behind his back, his ankles tied together and dirt-stained tear tracks ran from beneath the blindfold he wore, but he looked to be physically unharmed.

"Hello?" Marcus said, his voice small and hoarse from crying.

"Marcus!" Erika ran across the cellar.

"Mom!"

The sound of the boy's anguished cry for his mother tore James's heart in two. Marcus looked to be unharmed but the emotional scars from the situation could take time to show. And even more time to heal. For Marcus and for Erika.

There was bound to be a long road ahead for both of them. In that moment, James knew that he wanted to be there and travel that road with them. For the rest of his life.

Erika threw her arms around her son, holding him as they both wept with relief. James freed Marcus's hands and legs from the ropes that had been used to bind them.

Erika eased the blindfold from her son's eyes.

The flashlight gave off the only light in the space, and Marcus blinked against the sudden change.

Marcus threw his arms around his mother, and Erika drew him in, dotting his face with kisses.

James caught her eye over Marcus's shoulder. She smiled and reached out to him.

He took her hand and let her draw him into the hug. He wrapped his arms around the woman and child he'd lay down his life for and thanked the heavens they were safe.

Chapter Twenty-Three

"Okay, let's clean up these breakfast dishes and get to work on that science project," Erika said, carrying her plate and empty coffee mug to the kitchen sink.

"But, Mom, it's Saturday," Marcus whined.

"Exactly, which means you only have two days until it's Monday and the project is due. So let's get it done."

Marcus took his dirty plate to the sink, grumbling under his breath about the unfairness, before heading to his room to get to work.

She ignored him and began rinsing their dishes before stacking them in the dishwasher. The bullet that grazed her arm would leave a scar but nothing more damaging.

Marcus however had suffered through nightmares for the first several nights after the kidnapping. She'd made him an appointment with a local therapist and that seemed to have helped. He'd taken the news about his father and long-lost relatives surprisingly well. He'd taken the news about suddenly becoming a billionaire even better, starting a draft Christmas list, although it was only February. They'd already had one long talk about their newfound wealth and the importance of principles, values and character, and she could see several more similar talks in her future. But Marcus was a good kid. She had faith the money wouldn't corrupt him.

Keeping Marcus's existence out of the public eye had been impossible after Daisy's arrest. James's brothers Ryan and Sean had rolled into Carling Lake the day after they'd found Marcus with several other men and enough equipment that you'd have been forgiven for thinking they were about to launch a shuttle into space. Installing the security system took three days, but she had to admit she'd never felt safer. Especially since they'd also left bodyguard Tess Stenning behind.

Although she had vowed to be far more careful about who she befriended in the wake of Daisy's betrayal, she'd found Tess to be a consummate professional with a quick wit that was disarming.

Tess was the first paying guest at the B&B, but she hadn't been the only paying guest. Tess had shown up in Carling Lake, along with Brandon West, James's lawyer brother. Brandon had been a godsend, explaining what to expect while Roger's will was working its way through the system and putting her in touch with a financial planner and accountant with experience in handling the amount of money Marcus was about to come into. Guess you couldn't just walk into Bank of America and open a billion-dollar checking account.

She'd also had Brandon reach out to Robert through his lawyers. She would never forget what Roger and Ronald had put her through but maybe this could be an opportunity for the family that left to start anew. Without Roger's menacing presence lurking over the Overholts, maybe they could build some semblance of a functional relationship. So far she'd heard nothing from him, though. Not about fighting the will or getting to know Marcus.

For the hundredth time, she glanced out the window over at the now-empty structure next door. Technically, James still had a few days left on his lease, but the cabin had been vacant for the last two weeks and three days, ever since he'd headed back to New York.

They'd spoken every night since he'd left, but conversations had become more and more strained. With each passing day, the question that neither of them seemed to want to tackle grew bigger and bigger. Where was their relationship headed?

In those moments in the back of Daisy's car, the answer to that question had crystallized for Erika. She wanted to be with James.

But pride and fear had kept her from telling him as much before he'd left for New York, even though part of her suspected he felt the same way. Thankfully, she'd only been grazed by the bullet to her arm and hadn't required a stay in the hospital. James had stuck around long enough to make certain she was okay and to finish the renovations on her house but then he had to go back to New York, giving her no sign about when, or if, he planned to return. The last two weeks hadn't been a complete downer, however. Brian Whitmer had been arrested by authorities in Ohio during a traffic stop. It hadn't taken much convincing to get him to confess. Ellis had hired him to set a small fire at the B&B to bolster Ellis's claims that it was unsafe for visitors. When James thwarted the arson attempt, Brian had returned, intending to cause enough damage to keep the B&B from opening on time.

Ellis had come to him again, desperate and nearly crazed. He'd decided that if Erika opened her B&B, then that would be the final straw for his family's hospitality company. Never mind that the debt he'd amassed stealing money from the company to support his gambling habit. But desperate people weren't always the most rational. Brian had cut a deal to testify against Ellis and a few days after his arrest, Canadian Border Services stopped Ellis trying to cross into Ontario using a fake ID.

Of course, Ellis denied any involvement and claimed the fraudulent grant was all Susan's idea, but Lance seemed confident that there was enough to put Ellis away for several years. Ellis's sister had stepped up to manage the B&B and hotel but no one knew for sure what was going to happen to the family's businesses.

Unlike Ellis, Daisy appeared to be eager to take a plea. She'd been arrested and charged with two counts of kidnapping, the assault on Devin and a host of other charges. Robert had put out a statement disavowing Daisy's actions and stressing that she hadn't been a part of the Overholt family for many years. With multiple attempted-murder and kidnapping charges, among the many other charges she was facing, throwing herself on the mercy of the court was the only way she was ever going to see the light of day again. She was looking at decades in prison and Erika hoped she ended up serving every minute. As far as she was concerned, it was the only way to ensure Marcus's safety.

Her phone rang as she started the dishwasher. The main number for the *Carling Lake Weekly* scrolled across the screen.

"Erika, it's Aaron." Her boss's voice boomed through the speaker. "I know it's the weekend, but I just had a story come across my desk that I want you to get a jump on."

She'd already given Aaron her notice but had agreed to stay on until he could hire someone to fill her position.

"What is it?"

"I think it would be better if I explained it to you in person. Can you come into the office now?"

"I have to find someone to stay with Marcus."

"Bring him. He can sit at Margaret's desk and play on the computer."

"We'll be there in fifteen minutes."

She disconnected the call and hurried an excited Marcus into the car.

It wasn't often that Aaron got a hot tip on a story. Actually, in the eight years she'd been working for the *Weekly* this was the first time she could remember it ever happening.

The *Weekly*'s lobby was pitch-black as she pulled open the doors. She grabbed hold of Marcus's hand as they stepped into the dark space.

"Hello? Aaron? Are you here?"

The overhead lights rose slowly. The framed *Weekly* covers that had graced the lobby walls since she'd started working for the paper were gone, replaced with drawings Erika immediately recognized as James's work. Multiple pieces hung on the wall. Some of them she recognized from his apartment, but others were unfamiliar.

A black-and-white drawing in pen depicting the *Weekly* building. A rendering in color of Carling Lake and the surrounding mountains.

An easel stood in the middle of the space. On it was a canvas-sized drawing of her and Marcus laughing, their arms wrapped around each other.

"Cool," Marcus said in an almost reverent whisper.

"While I was in New York…" A familiar deep voice came from above their heads.

Erika pulled her gaze away from the drawing and

watched as James descended the stairs leading from the upper offices, wearing a dark suit and white dress shirt.

"...desperate to be back here with you and Marcus, I'd close my eyes, and that's how I envisioned you two."

"You were desperate to get back to us?"

James came to a stop, feet from her. "Honey, you have no idea. I wasn't back in New York for ten minutes before I realized my home was with you and Marcus."

"But when we spoke on the phone... I wasn't sure..."

James took her hands in his. "I wanted to give my brother two weeks' notice, and I needed to sublet my apartment. And I wanted to finish this. A grand gesture of sorts. I've decided to take your advice. Aaron has agreed to rent the *Weekly*'s lobby to me to use as a gallery here in Carling Lake. I'll also have a few pieces with a gallery in New York and the owner is going to help me get the word out about this place."

Erika's heart thundered with excitement. "So you're moving here, to Carling Lake, permanently?"

"If you'll have me?" James gave a tentative smile, his gaze moving from her to Marcus and back.

Erika looked at Marcus. "What do you say?"

"Yes! Yes! Yes!" Marcus beamed.

Erika wrapped her arms around James's neck, pulled him close, and smiled. "I guess it's unanimous, then."

"I love you, Erika Powell."

"And I love you, James West."

* * * * *

COLTON'S SECRET SABOTAGE

DEBORAH FLETCHER MELLO

To my Pretty Princess and Crown Prince,
You two are joy and sunshine on the darkest days!
Know that you are much loved, now and always.

Chapter One

"I love him. I've never loved anyone as much as I love Mark. He makes…well…he makes the sun rise for me in the morning. We're going to be so happy together!"

The petite redhead with the pixie haircut smiled sweetly into the camera. She batted the extensive length of her false eyelashes, the accessories looking like large bugs over her eyes. Her name was Darla Campbell. *Darla Campbell of the West Virginia Campbells*, as she often proclaimed. This was her last confessional interview before the final champagne ceremony where former pro-football player Mark Hewett would select one of two finalists to be his happily-ever-after.

Darla was a contestant on the television show *Lasting Love*. And Darla loved to play to the camera. Her on-air antics had brought the drama to the reality TV show, skyrocketing it to first place in its time slot. Darla earnestly believed she was a shoo-in for the top spot, the deal sealed with a bathroom blow job when Mark had been on a dinner date with the other finalist. Heather, a mousy, timid administrative secretary from the Bronx, had not been happy and the confrontation between the two women had been fodder for a really bad B movie.

"I will be a wonderful wife for Mark. There's nothing I wouldn't do for him," she concluded, even managing to squeeze out a tear or two. The woman smiled as she swiped her fingers against her cheek.

Naomi Colton wanted to gag. Instead, she gave the redhead a bright smile. "One last question, Darla. Have you told Mark about your boyfriend back home?" Naomi flipped through the notes on the clipboard she carried. "I'm told his name is Kramer. Kramer Wingate. Is that correct? Kramer says you two are an item and that you're three months pregnant with his baby."

The redhead's earnest expression dropped, hitting the floor like a ton of bricks. Her tone was no longer sweet and syrupy. Her voice rose an octave and she reminded Naomi of a kid who'd gotten caught with her hands in a cookie jar. She was stunned and not able to think fast on her feet as she stammered. "Kramer? He... Well... No... Kramer and I haven't been together for weeks. I don't know why you would even bring this up now!" she said defiantly.

For the briefest second Naomi felt bad for manipulating the storyline. But it was those exploitations that put the reality in unscripted television. It was what she was paid handsomely to do and do well. Besides, something told her that no matter where Darla landed when it was all over, the young woman would be standing tall on her stilettos, still batting her eyelashes for attention some man would gladly lavish on her.

Naomi smiled sweetly. "He's the one who called the

show to tell us you two were together. At this point, since you never mentioned him on your intake interview, we'll just have to believe he's an old flame looking for fifteen minutes of fame."

"That's it! He's just sour because I dumped him for bigger and better."

Naomi forced another grin to her face, and she nodded. She didn't bother to mention that they planned to bring Kramer on as a surprise guest right before Mark made his final choice. Besides, Heather had become a fan favorite. Heather was the underdog, and the audience was rooting for her. Throwing a wrench in the midst of this love triangle would make for good television. And if it looked like Mark might still be leaning toward Darla, they could bring up the pregnancy question that she had conveniently dodged. Naomi suddenly wondered if they could ask Darla to take a pregnancy test. She made a mental note to call the legal department and ask. Naomi wanted to do something to up ratings even further, and bringing the drama in the final hours was sure to do just that. If the reality dating show was renewed, at least Naomi had made certain the next junior producer who had her job would have an easier go of it.

With a degree in communications from the University of Colorado Boulder, Naomi had initially considered a career in public relations. But sitting behind a desk writing press releases had not been her thing. For a brief minute she'd considered being on-air talent but that had been a total disaster. From that failure Naomi discovered she liked being behind the camera far more than being in front of it. She'd started on the production team for a children's comedy show, cutting her teeth as a production coordinator. From there she'd steadily moved up the ranks, securing this gig with *Lasting Love* four seasons ago. The show filmed in a private home in Beverly Hills and afforded her the ability to sleep in her own bed at night. Now, in less than forty-two hours, she'd be adding executive producer to her résumé, sitting at the helm of her own reality show. From development to completion this season was hers and hers alone, and there'd be no relationship drama that she or anyone else would have to manipulate.

She gave Darla another smile, dismissing her with a nod of her head. As the young woman sashayed away in a bikini that was more string than fabric, Naomi blew a loud sigh, thinking her current day job babysitting the talent couldn't be over soon enough. Tomorrow she'd be in charge on a new show and the talent would be someone else's problem.

PHILIP REES WAS sound asleep when his cell phone began to buzz for his attention. It was the first day of a much-needed break and despite his curiosity he had no intentions of answering whoever was calling. He rolled to the other side of the king-size bed and pulled a pillow over his head. Just as he was about to doze back off, the house phone rang, sounding like an alarm gone awry. No one ever called him on the house phone. No one but a few close professional friends and his superiors at the Boulder Police Department. He heaved a

deep sigh, reaching toward the nightstand for the telephone receiver.

"Hello?" His tone was groggy.

Police Chief Theodore Lawson greeted him warmly.
"Good morning, Detective Rees. I didn't wake you,
did I?" Chief Lawson helmed the Blue Larkspur Police Department and Philip had worked with him on a
few cases previously.

Philip sat upright in his bed. He swiped the sleep
from his eyes and took a deep breath. "No, sir, Chief!
Good morning! What can I do for you?"

"I know you're on holiday, son, but we need you. The
state's cybersecurity office has reached out for our assistance. Their team needs someone to go undercover
on a case and you're the best man for the job."

"There's no one else available, Chief?"

"I specifically recommended you, Detective. And
I've already cleared it with your superiors. They've
agreed that I will be your point of contact. This one's a
little close to home and not only do I need your discre-
tion, but I trust you'll get the job done. You'll be doing
me a big favor."

Philip sighed, just the slightest gust of air blowing
past his lips. This would probably go down as the short-
est vacation in history. Because there was no turning
down a police chief, even if the man wasn't his own
commander, most especially if it was personal and he
was asking nicely. Philip had the utmost respect for
Lawson. Eighty-one years young, Chief Lawson was
a staple in the law enforcement community. He'd been
doing his job since forever. He did it well, and the offi-

cers who followed him held him in the highest regard. Philip was no exception.

"I can be in your office in an hour, sir."

"Thank you, Detective. I'll fill you in on the details when you get here," the chief said as he disconnected the call.

Philip lay back against the pillows and closed his eyes. He was tired and his body hurt. It had barely been twenty-four hours since he'd come off his last case. He'd successfully halted a trafficking ring that had been terrorizing the local high school. No shots had been fired and he'd gotten a dozen teens out unscathed. Sleep had been the only thing taken from him and he'd been looking forward to simply closing his eyes and shutting the world away for a few good hours.

He sat upright and threw his legs off the side of the mattress. Sleep would have to wait. If he were going to keep his promise and make it to the station within the hour, he needed a hot shower, a steaming cup of coffee and a prayer.

Minutes later, he stood beneath a flow of hot water feeling each sinewy muscle begin to rejuvenate. He knew that once he finished that hot cup of coffee, he'd feel like a new man. He had been doing this for most of his career with the Boulder Police Department. He'd joined the force right out of college. His first assignment had been traffic control, and he didn't miss those days! The promotions had come swiftly as he proved himself with each case. He kept his head down, played by the rules and got the job accomplished. Believing in the integrity of the law, he held himself and others to a high standard. In the process, he had made quite an impression on his superiors and the other officers, who looked up to him. But it was when he found himself working undercover, as a detective, that he knew he had found his calling.

Most of his assignments had been white-collar crimes. He'd don a silk suit, paisley necktie and show up to work, his fellow officers teasing him about how he looked like a *GQ* model. There had been the one time he'd gone under for the narcotics division, assuming the identity of a biker on the run from the police. That had almost gotten him killed. Each time, though, he'd taken down the bad guys, prevented civilians from being injured and righted a wrong. He loved what he did and now the chief needed him to mask up like a caped crusader and do it again.

As he lathered himself up for the third—or maybe it was the fourth—time, he made a mental checklist of the things he would have to cancel or reschedule. His dentist was not going to be happy with him. His mother was really going to be pissed!

NAOMI WAS BORED to death and not even her collection of Maroon 5's greatest hits was helping. The drive from her Los Angeles home to Blue Larkspur, Colorado, had already taken nine hours, and depending on traffic, Naomi had at least six more hours to go. She had recently flown home for her brother Caleb's wedding and back again for work, and she was starting to think she should have flown this time.

The decision to drive had seemed like a good idea

when she'd made it, thinking that it would give her time to clear her head before diving right into the production of her new series, *In the Saddle*. Clearly, she thought as she sat in heavy traffic, she'd been wrong.

It was also meant to give her time to take a breath before returning to family who would surely have something to say about her career choice. Naomi was one of twelve children born to Ben and Isadora Colton. There were the two eldest, twins Caleb and Morgan, and then fraternal triplets Oliver, Ezra and Dominic. Next was her sister Rachel and then brother Gideon, followed by a second set of twins, Jasper and Aubrey. The youngest brother in the family was Gavin and lastly came Naomi and her fraternal twin Alexa. Naomi was the baby by three minutes and twenty-nine seconds.

Their father had been Benjamin Colton, judge for Lark's County. He had been the love of Isa Colton's life. They had fallen in love, married young, and had a dozen children during their union. He had been a staple in the community, thought to be fair-minded and generous of spirit. Her mother had been devoted to Ben Colton, and their social and philanthropic ventures had made it possible for them to move in the elite circles of Colorado society. From all Naomi remembered, life had been all cotton candy and sugarplums back then.

Sadly, life turned on a dime for all of the Colton offspring when their father was indicted on a lengthy list of corruption charges. He'd been accused of taking bribes and kickbacks from private prison owners and juvenile detention centers to sentence more kids and adults to their facilities, whether they were guilty or not. He had been removed from the bench and was about to stand trial for his misdeeds when he died in a car accident, not paying attention on an icy road.

Suddenly cotton candy was day-old bread and butter, and life had become dismal at best. Naomi remembered her home being full of life and laughter and then just like that it was all gone. She'd been six years old then and would learn what had happened as she grew older but at the time, she remembered feeling like a cloud of darkness had fallen over them and they couldn't find their way free. They were ostracized by the community and pitied by their former friends. Isa was forced to re-build her life and her children's, and nothing had ever again been easy. But they had each other, and each other had been more than enough. Naomi couldn't fathom any other family being as close as theirs. Her brothers and sisters were her best friends, even when they were at odds with each other.

Most of her siblings believed Naomi's foray into tele-vision was either a fluke or a phase that she should have gotten over years ago. Not even her own twin, a deco-rated United States marshal, saw it going anywhere. But Naomi was determined to prove them wrong. What none of them knew was that she wasn't approaching this haphazardly. She'd done her research. She could tell you everything you needed to know about the de-mographics of her target audience, what shows were trending successfully and what people wanted to see. She sensed most were tired of relationship drama and woes that mimicked their own failed love lives. They rooted for the underdog, and they loved seeing your average Joe or Joanne accomplish the unfathomable.

She'd been working for months behind the scenes to raise the money and support she needed to make this happen. Convincing a production company to partner with her had taken a round of meetings and a lot of begging. She had immense faith that she had a winning formula with her new series, and she was determined that it would be the first in a long line of number one television shows on her IMDb profile. Her short-term goal after this program's success was to produce a successful, non-reality production with national distribution. Something along the lines of *60 Minutes* or *Dateline*. And in the long term, she hoped to one day helm her own television station. She had vision and she wasn't unwilling to work hard for her big dreams. Thinking about it, Naomi started shimmying her shoulders to a Taylor Swift tune.

She considered it a major coup that her siblings Jasper and Aubrey had agreed to let them film on their property. The duo owned and operated Gemini Ranch, a sprawling one-hundred-acre expanse of land in Blue Larkspur. Gemini Ranch boasted stunning open pastures and beautiful wood cabins that surrounded the main lodge. There were barns, outbuildings and staff cabins. From its very popular cattle drive to skiing and snowmobiling in the winter, the ranch hosted activities all year round.

It wasn't lost on Naomi that she'd probably been given the gig because of her familial ties, the production company willing to give her a chance since her connections meant a reasonable discount in their half of the production budget.

Weary of the stop-and-go, the multitude of cars trying to weave their way around an accident, Naomi eased toward the far-right lane and the next exit that would take her to a line of eateries and filling stations. When she was finally able to turn off, McDonald's was her first stop. Minutes later, with a bathroom break behind her, and a double fish filet sandwich with fries and a soda settling in her stomach, she took a seat on a rock wall outside the building and stretched her legs. She pulled her cell phone from her pocket and depressed the first speed dial number. Isa Colton answered on the second ring.

"Hi, Mom!"

There was the barest hint of urgency in the matriarch's tone. "Naomi! Where are you? Is everything okay?"

"Everything's fine, Mom. And I'm about five, maybe six hours away."

"So that's probably six, maybe seven hours away," her mother said facetiously, knowing Naomi sometimes exaggerated how quickly she'd make it, or underestimated time and distance. "You've been driving all day. You should probably stop and get a hotel room for the night."

"I'm fine. I stopped to rest and get something to eat."

"I hope you ate something healthy, Naomi."

"I had fish."

There was a moment of hesitation and her mother

chuckled. "A fast-food sandwich from the Golden Arches is not fish."

Naomi laughed. "Nothing ever gets past you!"

"I'm the mother of twelve. There's little you could do that I haven't seen before or done myself. So, tell me more about this show you're producing?"

"I'm excited, Mom! If I get it right, it could be the turning point in my career." Exuberance bubbled up in her tone.

"Naomi, have you thought about what you'll do if it doesn't work out? Everyone should have a plan B. Maybe consider coming home and working…"

Naomi interrupted her mother. "Please, don't start. Just let me have this moment before you all start giving me advice I didn't ask for."

"And don't you be rude, Naomi Colton. That advice may be exactly what you need. It never hurts to have options."

Naomi rolled her eyes skyward. What she needed was a nap, but she didn't dare say that to her mother. Instead, she changed the subject. "Maybe I will get a hotel room and hang out for a day. Production doesn't start until next week and I could use a day or two to clear my head."

"Well, if you're tired you should definitely not be driving. And if you need me to, I can send one of your brothers to come get you."

"Mom, I love you but I'm going to change the topic back to my new show. Because that makes me happy and you worrying about me isn't any fun."

"One day I hope you have a daughter just like you, so you'll know exactly what I go through with you."

"Is that some sort of curse?" Naomi said with a chuckle.

Her mother laughed with her. "I am just saying! So, tell me, what is it about?"

"It's kind of a cattle drive with inexperienced city folk, summer-camp-style. We're bringing contestants who are not familiar with ranch life together and putting them through a series of obstacles. Essentially, we'll eliminate one person each week and crown a winner at the end."

"That's what you wanted to do when you were a little girl!" Isa gushed.

"I did! I can't believe you remembered that!"

"There's very little a mother forgets. You had that rocking horse your daddy got for you and your sister. Alexa couldn't have cared less about hers, but you were always riding yours. You'd turn a jump rope into a lasso, jump on that thing and start screaming about being in the saddle. It used to tickle your father every time you did it."

The two women laughed heartily at the memory.

"So, what are you calling this show?" her mother questioned.

Naomi grinned into the receiver of her cell phone. *"In the Saddle!"*

"IN THE WHAT?" Philip questioned, his entire face dropping into a deep frown.

"In the Saddle. You'll be part of the production

team," said the chief. "In fact, you'll be reporting directly to the production manager, I think. I'm not sure where they plan to put you, but just in case, be able to swing a hammer while you keep an eye on your mark and gather any intel on what he might be up to."

Philip flipped through the manila folder the police chief had passed to him. The "mark" was a man named Brad Clifton. Brad was a technical wizard who owned a large security company. Now, apparently, he was also a contestant on some new reality television show. Brad was suspected of selling company secrets to the Russian mob and Philip was to keep an eye on him. At first glance, the assignment looked easy. But Philip had learned early on in his career that nothing was ever easy, no matter how it looked.

"Where did they get their intel? Can we trust it?"

"His business partner reached out to the police department's cyber squad and provided them with information that Brad is selling their company's tech secrets. They believe he'll be using his role as a contestant on that show to reach his buyers undetected."

"So, our mark is on a reality show to learn how to ride a horse?"

"It's a bit more than that," the police chief responded. "The contestants are going to be put through their paces in a series of Wild West adventures to test their survival skills."

Philip shook his head slowly. "You mentioned this being personal. Do you know Brad Clifton?"

"I don't. Are you familiar with the Colton family?"

"I met District Attorney Rachel Colton a few years

ago, when I had to testify on a case she was heading. And I know she has family that owns the law firm, Colton and Colton."

"Yes, her brother and sister are both attorneys, too. Morgan and Caleb also run The Truth Foundation, working to exonerate the wrongfully imprisoned," Chief Lawson said with a nod. "Well, their mother, Isa Colton, is a dear friend of mine. Her daughter Naomi Colton is producing this television show and they're filming at Gemini Ranch, which is owned by two of her other children."

"Keeping things in the family, I see."

The older man shrugged. "Something like that. Anyway, I need someone I trust to keep an eye on things. We don't know what this Clifton guy is planning and if he does do something that might put Naomi at risk, I want you there to keep her safe," the chief said.

"Naomi Colton." Philip nodded again, then sighed heavily. "So, how long is this assignment?"

"From what I know, and don't quote me, production is supposed to last about four, maybe five weeks. But you'll get all the details tomorrow. You report to Marvin Taylor at eight o'clock. Marvin is the production team manager. He'll give you your assignment and walk you through everything you need to know."

"Am I working under an alias?"

"No, not necessary. The cyber team has linked you to a whole other profile. If anyone's looking for you, they'll find a regular, hardworking guy with a nonde-script history. Nothing that will throw up any red flags."

"Does the man I'm reporting to know I'm undercover?"

"Marvin? No. He doesn't know anything. No one will know. The guy you're replacing won an all-expenses-paid trip to the Bahamas. He's being paid nicely to take an extended vacation. It was an opportunity we made sure he couldn't turn down."

"I want to go to the Bahamas!" Philip feigned a pout, laughter pulling at the muscles in his face.

Chief Lawson chuckled warmly. "You won't regret this. How often does anyone get the chance to say they worked on a television set?"

Philip laughed. "I'd still rather be in the Bahamas."

Chapter Two

Naomi hadn't realized how much she missed her family until she was standing in the middle of a paddock hugging her big sister. She and Aubrey were spinning each other around in a circle like they were kids again playing London Bridge. Jasper stood off to the side, his arms crossed over his chest as he eyed the two women like they'd lost their collective minds. Like they hadn't just seen each other at their brother's wedding. He evidently was not amused, although he too had expressed how glad he was to see his sister back home with them.

Jasper shook his head. "I need to check on the renovations down at the main lodge. I'm going to let you two do that girl thing you Colton women do. Come talk to me when you're done."

"I will," Naomi said, still hugging tightly to her sister. She blew her brother a kiss.

The two women looped their arms together and began to walk. It was hot, the outside temperatures steadily rising. A herd of cattle grazed beneath a few shade trees in the distance, near a stream of water, and Naomi would have bet if they stood still long enough, they'd see steam rising off the blades of grass that hadn't turned color under the summer sun.

"So, what's been going on with you?" Naomi asked. "How are you and Luke doing?"

"My Luca and I are doing exceptionally well. Being in love is amazing!" Aubrey answered.

"That's because you're still in that honeymoon phase of your relationship. Give it another few months, and then let me know."

"Why are you being so cynical?"

"I'm not cynical. Just pragmatic. I've had more than my fair share of failed relationships. I know not to trust all the glitz and glamour. Your relationship is like a shiny new toy right now, but give it time. It'll get dull on you."

Aubrey laughed. "Says the woman who hasn't had a new man since forever."

"Exactly!"

Both chuckled warmly as they continued to stroll slowly.

"I really appreciate you and Jasper letting us film here on your property," Naomi said. "I can't begin to tell you how much this means to me."

"We need to thank you. Usually, the ranch is booming with business this time of the year, but that storm last month did a ton of damage. Since it only made sense to close down until we could get the repair work done, we've had to juggle the budget to keep the ranch hands paid. Renting the space for your project gives us more than enough income to keep everyone working and relieve some of the renovation expenses. The timing could not have been more perfect."

"It made sense for me, too. This was the ideal location and since I suddenly have a little juice with the production company, I asked nicely. Then I begged!" Naomi cut an eye toward her sister and the duo burst out laughing.

They sauntered slowly toward the barn. "Where are you staying while you're here?" Aubrey asked. "Because you can always stay with me at my place if you want."

"And be a third wheel with you and your Italian boo? That would be a no! I plan to hang out with Mom for a night or two, then I'll move into that spare room in the office. I like to stay on set when I'm working on a project with a tight timeline and this one is super tight."

"Is that why your set decorator person put a cot in there?"

"That would be correct!"

Aubrey rolled her eyes skyward. "Well, my Italian boo is on deadline. He's locked in his office, so you will probably not see him much while you're here. At least come over tonight and get drunk on that cheap wine you like so much. I'll call Rachel and make her come, too. We can catch up."

"I can't do it tonight but let's plan on doing it soon. We haven't had a sisters' night since Caleb and Nadine's wedding. By the way, are they still married?"

"Happily married. You really should give it some consideration."

"Since that requires a man I actually like, I don't see it happening anytime soon."

Aubrey chuckled. "You usually like most of the men you meet. How many one-night stands do you have under your belt so far?"

"I don't like what you're trying to imply. I don't like it at all. Just because I exercise the options of my sexual freedom on a regular basis gives you no reason to judge me."

"You're a ho. And I'm telling Mom you're a ho."

"I am not! Tattletale!"

They dissolved in giggles. Naomi hugged her sister one last time. "I need to go see which of my crew has checked in and get some actual work done. I'll text you later and let you know when I should show up at your house. And don't forget I like chocolate cake with my wine."

"I think Rachel's allergic to chocolate."

"She is not!"

"She might be!"

"Good, then more for me!" Naomi concluded, a wide grin on her face. She turned and began to jog slowly back to the other side of the ranch, her sister laughing as she stared after her.

PHILIP'S NEW BOSS talked fast and said very little. He was a rotund man who was as wide as he was tall, with fire-engine red hair and a really bad comb-over. He was also annoyed to be saddled with a newbie on the first day of production and had no problems letting Philip know that he was not happy about him being there. He tossed him a hammer and a set of plans, and pointed him toward a stack of wood planks. Then he proceeded to ignore him for the rest of the morning.

After a good thirty minutes, Philip figured out that he was building a platform and podium with a decorative post and rail fence along each side. The instructions were clear enough and he was able to start building with some confidence that he could do it without any assistance. He thought he was doing reasonably well until Marvin came to critique his work. Marvin wasn't unhappy but he wasn't overly thrilled, either. But his tone had changed substantially, and it was looking like the two would have no problems working together.

"How long have you worked construction?" the man asked him.

Philip shrugged his broad shoulders. "My father taught me when I was a boy. I've done odd jobs off and on for most of my life."

"He taught you well. But you've got natural instinct that can't be taught," Marvin said casually.

"Thank you." Philip continued hammering at the project. But he had questions. "So, how does this work?" he asked. "We put things together and then what?"

"Most times we build it and break it down at the end of shooting. We don't have a lot to put up on this job. Just some backdrops, the piece you're working on and a few random projects. It'll go fast. Then we'll hang around in case the boss lady needs us for any odd jobs."

"The boss lady?"

"Naomi Colton. She's the producer on this series."

"I look forward to meeting her."

Marvin cut an eye in his direction. "You worry about that wood and stay out of the lady's way. She's not looking to be your friend." His tone was protective and chastising.

Amused, Philip laughed. He held his hands up as if he were surrendering. "I promise! I won't be a problem."

"You better not be!" the older man quipped. He gestured for Philip to get back to work.

The moment was interrupted when a young woman rushed in screaming Marvin's name. Her exuberance beat her through the door as she squealed loudly. Hurrying to the man's side, she threw her arms around his neck and hugged him tightly.

Philip stood upright and stared. She was well over five feet tall with a slender build and a mesmerizing smile. She wore denim jeans that fit her snugly and a vintage Jefferson Airplane T-shirt. Her hair was a medium brown and hung straight down her back, a gray headband holding the strands in place. The style showcased her facial features: chiseled cheekbones, a pert nose and ocean blue eyes that shone as bright as late-night stars.

"Naomi! It's good to see you!" Marvin chimed warmly.

"I'm so glad you were available. I didn't want to do this without you."

"I'm happy I was available, too. I can't tell you how proud I am of you. You said you'd do it and now look where you are? Producer!"

"I couldn't have done it without support from friends like you, Marvin."

NAOMI SUDDENLY PAUSED, her attention turning to the man staring at her so intently. He was very easy on the eyes, and she imagined he garnered much female attention wherever he found himself. He was tall, standing easily over six feet and an inch or two. He wore Levi jeans like a second skin, and he was bare-chested, glistening under the barest hint of perspiration. He was lean and well-muscled with a rich umber complexion. His hair was black and cut short, the strands tightly coiled. He sported a hint of a goatee and a mustache. He had the sultriest light brown eyes and Naomi suddenly imagined herself getting lost in them. His smile was inviting, and he had her thinking all kinds of things that she had no business thinking.

She grinned. "And who do we have here?"

Marvin rolled his eyes, not at all amused. "This is Phil. He'll be working with me."

"What happened to Frank?"

"Frank won himself a vacation. I'm sure he's lying on a beach right now with a drink in his hand."

Naomi extended her hand. "It's a pleasure to meet you, Phil. I'm Naomi Colton."

Philip smiled warmly, a picture-perfect bend to his mouth. "Philip Rees," he said as his palm slid sweetly against hers. He tossed Marvin a look. "My mother named me Philip. *Not* Phil. And the pleasure is all mine." His gaze shifted back to Naomi and the two locked eyes.

Naomi chuckled. "Philip it is, then. Welcome to the team, Philip!"

"I appreciate the opportunity."

Marvin looked from one to the other. He shook his head and took a step between them. "Well, *Philip*," he said, putting emphasis on the man's name. "*Philip* needs to get back to work."

Philip laughed. "Yes, sir!" He winked an eye at Naomi, who shot back a grin. "You have good day, Naomi!"

"You, too, Philip. And I'm sure I'll see you around."

MEN LIKE PHILIP Rees were a distraction, Naomi thought. They were too pretty for their own good. Women flocked to them like bees to honey and most could easily manipulate a situation with their good looks and charming personalities. He had winked his eye at her, and it had felt almost salacious. She was also thinking that she needed to put out a dress code of sorts. Him bare-chested had her tongue-tied. She couldn't walk into a room with him half-naked and suddenly be distracted by thoughts of pressing her hands against the warmth of his skin to tease him with her fingertips. Because she'd imagined herself teasing him until he called her name over and over again as he begged for more. Naomi shook away the reverie and took a deep breath. Clearly, Philip Rees would be a huge distraction. A familiar voice suddenly interrupted her musings.

"What's got you smiling like the Cheshire cat?" Jasper asked. His expression was smug, his eyes narrowed as he stared at her.

"I wasn't!"

"Yes, you were."

"I was not! Why are you spying on me?"

Jasper laughed. "Spying? That's a bit of a stretch, Naomi."

She changed the subject. "How can I help you, Mr. Colton?" she said haughtily.

"Well, Ms. Colton," he said jokingly, "my staff and I are delighted to welcome you and your film crew here to Gemini Ranch. We want to make your visit here as pleasant and carefree as possible, so if there is anything we can assist you with, please do not hesitate to ask."

Naomi laughed. "Do you practice that in the mirror?"

"About twenty or thirty times before every new group arrives for a visit." He laughed with her.

Naomi reached to give her brother a hug, the two holding tightly to each other. "And business is good?" she questioned when she finally let him go and took a step back.

Jasper nodded. "Business is good. The bills are paid, the staff is happy, and our sister has stopped micromanaging me. I have no complaints."

"I thought it was you who micromanaged her?"

"Did Aubrey tell you that?"

Naomi laughed. "Are you denying it?"

"I have no knowledge of what you're implying. But tell Aubrey I will get her back for that."

"Not me. No one gets between me and my twin and I don't get between you and yours."

"Chicken!"

"Cluck-cluck!" Naomi said, doing a poor imitation.

"I can't with you." Jasper grinned. He changed the subject. "How are things with you? This television series is a big deal. The crew you have working for you is a good group."

"You've been talking to them?"

"Here and there as they've been getting settled. They're excited about doing this project with you."

"I'm excited."

"Have you thought about what you'll do after? If this doesn't go the way you hope?"

"Did Mom tell you to ask me that?"

"No, she didn't. This is all me and I just wondered if you have a backup plan."

"I've been taking pole dancing classes so I can work the pole for tips. I hear it's big business if you can get your leg up over your head and spin up the pole and back down again," she answered flippantly.

Jasper shook his head. "So, you don't have a plan."

"I would appreciate it if you all would let me fail, then offer to help pick me up. Right now all you're doing is getting in my way and trying to make me trip over my own two feet."

"That's not what we're trying to do. We just want you to have options. You can always come back home. There's always a job here for you."

Naomi stole a glance at her wristwatch. "I love you, big brother! But you and your demon twin are not going to make me muck stalls for a living."

Jasper shrugged. "Because pole dancing is so much more glamorous."

Naomi reached to kiss her brother's cheek. "That and I do a mean striptease. I've almost perfected my twerk, too!"

"You need an ass to twerk with, Naomi. You were cursed with a Colton ass. Flat and lackluster."

"Why are you looking at my ass? That's so gross!"

Jasper hooted. "Exactly, flat and gross!"

Laughing with him, Naomi flipped him her middle finger before turning and heading toward the makeshift space that would serve as her office, workroom and temporary home. It was one of the few cabins on the property that hadn't suffered any damage or needed to be restored. The wood structure was sturdy and welcoming, her sister's decorative touches making it feel homey. Behind her, her brother's guffaw rang sweetly in the air as it faded into the distance.

Chapter Three

Naomi stood staring at the oversize corkboard that rested against the wall. Twelve photographs had been lined neatly in two rows. The call sheets were pinned in one corner, detailing the daily filming schedule. Naomi's friend Janice Christian had been hired as the assistant director on the show; Janice's husband, Jude Christian, was the director. Janice had nicely created the call sheets based on the director's shot list. Filming locations, cast call times and the shooting schedule were laid out in black-and-white for the cast and crew to know where to be on set and when to be there. Jim Bauer, the assistant producer, stood at Naomi's elbow, evidently forgetting that she was in charge and not him.

"The limousines will pick up the cast and deliver them here. There will be a cameraman and an intern in each to get the shots of them being surprised at being selected and their reactions as they travel here to the ranch. Three of them," he said pointing to the pictures pinned on the board, "Brad Clifton, Carl Barker and Constantine Meza have already been notified. Because they had to travel farther than the others, I decided to extend the offers in advance. We'll pick them up from the hotel, maybe shoot a meet and greet with the three as they size each other up."

Naomi gave him a quick glance. "Why does the cast look like a fraternity photo for Sigma Alpha Epsilon? I specifically said we wanted a diverse cast. Male and female. White, black and other." She waved her hand toward the corkboard. "This won't work."

"I thought it would make for a more action-oriented show. I think viewers will respond more favorably to twelve all-American studs vying for the win each week."

Naomi shook her head. Months ago, they'd narrowed the selections down to thirty potential candidates. Of the thirty, the final twelve were supposed to be surprised just twenty-four hours from the start of filming, being made to drop everything in their lives to compete for the one-hundred-thousand-dollar prize. Taking a step forward, she snatched six photos from the board and dropped them to the floor. "Where are the photos of the other candidates?"

Jim's eyes narrowed substantially. "I really think…"

Naomi snapped. "You're not getting paid to think, Jimbo. You're getting paid to execute my vision for this production. And I envision a little more than what I'm seeing here. I'm not interested in six episodes of frat house escapades."

Jim tossed a look over his shoulder while the others in the room pretended not to hear the conversation between them. Much like her, he too was hoping to make a name for himself in the industry. He would not have been her first choice for an assistant producer, but the production company and the men with the money had thought him an excellent choice. Most especially because his father headed one of the most prestigious studios in the film industry. Picking her battles wisely, Naomi had smiled and nodded, thinking she'd be able to keep the man on a short leash and rein him in when necessary. It suddenly felt necessary.

Naomi gestured for the film student who would be working as her personal assistant. "I'm sorry, what's your name again?"

"Felicia. Felicia Darby."

"Felicia, would you find me the folder with the prospective applicants, please?"

"Yes, ma'am!"

Naomi cringed and shook her head emphatically. "I am not that old! Please, call me Naomi."

"Yes, ma'am!"

Jim laughed, his upper lip curling awkwardly. Naomi's brow furrowed with annoyance as she gave him another look. Admittedly, she deserved it for snapping at him, but she was in no mood for his snark. Felicia was holding out the folder to her before she could tell him what she thought. She bit back her words and moved to a wooden chair that sat behind a small desk. Flipping through the photos, she could only begin to imagine what Jim had to be thinking to make the selections he'd made. Then again, all of the candidates he'd selected looked much like him—blond-haired and blue-eyed, from wealthy, pedigreed families. Each one was prettier than the other. Women would have loved them, men would have envied them, and theirs would have been a whole different show from the one she planned. Bless his heart, she thought, her head shaking slowly from side to side. He'd tried it!

Minutes later she moved back to the board. She snatched one more away and pinned seven new photos. She took a step back and folded her arms over her chest. "What do you think?" she asked, directing the question at Jim. "We'll keep the three who've already been notified, but I think this is a better lineup."

He stared, his gaze moving slowly from one image to another. He pointed his index finger. "The beauty queen might be problematic. She's high-maintenance to the nth degree."

"Exactly. High-maintenance having to rough it will make for great entertainment."

"I'll bet you a dime to a dollar that one of my five will take the top prize."

"My money's on the lawyer," Felicia interjected as she pointed to the photo of a handsome redhead who looked like a lumberjack on steroids. "He's cute," she giggled.

Naomi grinned. "I'm betting the nuclear physicist will give them all a run for their money!"

Jim shrugged. "It'll be a good mix," he finally acquiesced. "We'll arrange for transportation. They'll all arrive here the day after tomorrow."

"Let's make us a television show," Naomi exclaimed excitedly.

PHILIP HAD QUESTIONS and he wasn't sure where to get the answers about Clifton. For the moment he could wait until he knew all the players and the places. Those on the crew were friendly enough and he'd gotten a few tips and pointers from the lot of them. Marvin had finally warmed up to him and he could actually see the two of them eventually becoming good friends. The older man was exceptionally protective of Naomi Colton, and he found that intriguing. He was also a storyteller and he gossiped endlessly about everyone. Most concerning at the moment was the gossip about Naomi's assistant producer. Apparently, Jim Bauer had a history of not always playing fair. That unsettled Marvin, and for reasons Philip couldn't begin to explain, it now worried him, too.

He gasped for air as he ran another lap along the border between the open fields and a line of tall trees. It was hot, with a hint of humidity, which made it feel even hotter, slightly sticky and deeply uncomfortable. But he pushed himself, needing to exercise his muscles and challenge just how far he could push his body if he needed.

In the distance he recognized Naomi as she stood in conversation with members of her staff. He stopped to stare, using the moment to catch his breath. He leaned with his palms pressed to his thighs, sucking in oxygen, before standing upright and laying his hands on his hips. Even from afar you couldn't miss how attractive Naomi was. She had an easy beauty, a girl-next-door type of energy. He'd bet she'd been a cheerleader in high school, running with the popular crowd, and not giving boys like him an ounce of attention. He himself had been nerdy with oversized glasses on a large head and big feet that had kept him off balance. Often, he'd been the punchline for a bad joke and the object of his school's bullies. It wasn't until his senior year that he'd grown into his size, his body catching up with his feet and his head. And even then the girls hadn't given him a lot of attention.

He imagined that back then, Naomi would've dated jocks, and now, artistic types who drank organic juices and seaweed. The thought made him chuckle as he continued to eye her from the distance.

She talked with her whole body, arms and hands waving with her words. Her face was animated, the length of her hair swaying as she laughed. And she was loud. Boisterously loud! Philip had never found that attractive in a woman before, but there was something about Naomi's exuberance that drew him in and made him want to join in her enthusiasm. There was something he liked about her, but he couldn't quite put his finger on what that was. The women in his past had all been pretty packages with mediocre content. Women his mother hadn't thought worthy of their family name and his mother's opinion was important to him. Admittedly, his attraction to his former lovers had been purely physical, but he had hoped that their inside characters would have matched their outsides. Most times he'd been wrong, currently batting a solid zero in his love life.

He took one last deep breath and stretched his arms high above his head. Shaking away all thoughts of the beautiful woman, he cleared his mind, then took off running, wanting to put the last lap of his exercise routine to rest.

"HE'S STARING AT ME," Naomi mumbled under her breath. "I really think he's staring at me. Why is he always staring at me?"

"Who?" Felicia questioned as she quickly glanced from one side to the other.

Naomi gestured with her head to the man standing in the doorway behind them. "Jim," she whispered. "He's always staring. He's like a stalker."

Felicia giggled. "You're funny! He is a little strange, though," she said, her voice dropping an octave.

Naomi rolled her eyes skyward. "Strange is putting it nicely. Keep an eye on that one."

The two women laughed heartily. Movement out of the corner of her eye drew her attention. Naomi turned to see Philip with his hands resting against his waist as he lifted one foot against his buttocks and then the other, seeming to stretch the muscles in his legs. She stared after him, admiring the near perfect curve of his backside and the long legs that were solid like tree trunks.

Although she would never admit it, she was curious to know more about the man. But mixing business and pleasure on the set was a definite no-no, and not a line she had ever crossed. But something about Philip-not-Phil had gotten under her skin, latching on like a rampant Carolina kudzu. She couldn't begin to explain it and was feeling slightly foolish about how she was feeling. She didn't anticipate any free time where they could sit and have a casual conversation, but she could hope, and hope always proved to be a nice distraction when things began to stress her. She shook the thought from her head.

"So, I interrupted you," Naomi said. "Was there something you needed from me?"

Felicia nodded. "The production company called, and they want you to give them a call back. There is some concern about one of the contestants."

"Did they say which one?" Naomi asked.

"No," Felicia said. "Just something about one of them failing his background check."

"Damn, damn, damn!" Naomi exclaimed. She shook her head. "Heaven help me. Like I really need this right now." She sighed, turning back toward the office to place that call. She muttered loudly. "Just let it be one of the frat boys that Jim picked."

THE NEXT MORNING, activity around the ranch had increased tenfold. People were scurrying from one side of the property to the other. Limousines and luxury buses had begun to roll in shortly after breakfast and Naomi followed behind Jude, the director, and the camera crew, her arms folded across her chest as they welcomed the contestants. As each stepped out of their vehicles one after the other, the cameraman was there to get a reaction shot, zooming in on smiling or annoyed faces and capturing their first words.

Philip stood off to the side, eyeing the activity with nominal interest. There was only one contestant that he was waiting to see, and when Brad Clifton stepped out of the car that carried him, Philip pulled himself upright and stared.

Brad Clifton wore an air of arrogance like an oversize trench coat. He was not the nerdy tech guy Philip had expected. He looked like your average Joe who'd had a makeover. He wore glasses with large, bright white frames and his thick black hair had been slicked back with pomade to tame his curl. Someone had styled him in a dark suit that flattered his slim frame, but he kept pulling at the collar of his white shirt as if he wasn't comfortable. His smile pulled from ear to ear and when Naomi stepped forward to say hello and introduce herself, he pumped her arm as she shook his hand.

From where he watched, Philip sensed that Brad was not going to be one of her favorite competitors. He chuckled softly to himself, then headed in the direction of the main lodge, where the twelve competitors would all gather to start their first challenge of the show. Hopefully, Philip thought to himself, no one would notice him standing quietly in the background as he got a closer look at the man whose criminal ventures had brought him there.

"WE HAVE A PROBLEM."

Naomi shook her head before turning her attention toward Jim. Her second-in-command looked frustrated, his cheeks beet red. His clothes were rumpled, and he looked like he'd been dragged through a puddle of mud.

"What's wrong now?" she asked.

Jim pointed toward the corkboard. "Contestant number six is headed to the emergency room."

Naomi's eyes widened. "What the hell happened?"

"He was getting to know his horse, spooked the animal, and it threw him off, then kicked him."

"Kicked him?"

"Nailed him good. It looks like he threw out his back and he might have a concussion. I highly doubt that he'll be able to come back."

Naomi stared down at the board, her hands resting on her hips. Number six was the attorney who looked like a lumberjack. She would have known his fire-engine red hair anywhere. His name was Carl Barker, and he had been considered a potential front-runner. The cameras loved him, he had personality and his cutthroat approach to life would have made him a fan favorite or a perfect villain. She shook her head a second time. "Please, tell me he signed all his waivers before he went trekking down to the barns. We do not need a lawsuit!"

Felicia waved his folder in the air. "All signed, sealed, and sent to Legal."

Naomi heaved a sigh of relief, suddenly feeling bad that she had to consider being sued even before expressing her concern for the man's well-being. It was an aspect of her position that she truly detested. Carl was headed to the hospital, battered by a four-legged animal. He was a big guy but clearly, his size hadn't helped him. Production had barely started, and she was ready to pull her hair out.

"What do you want to do?" Jim questioned. "We can always go forward with the remaining eleven contestants. We got the horse kick on film, so we can just write it in and eliminate him at the start of the show."

"Ten," Felicia interjected. "The nuclear physicist had a felony drug conviction on his record. He left this morning."

Jim shook his head. "He's being replaced with the

grandmother from Topeka. She was going to be the last to arrive later this evening."

"We need twelve contestants," Naomi stated, not needing to remind him that they were contractually obligated to provide a lengthy list of must-haves with a dozen contestants competing at the top of that list. "Who else lives close enough that we can get them here tonight?"

"The closest potential candidate has already declined. He booked *Jeopardy!* Anyone else can't get here until the day after tomorrow."

"That's too late!" Naomi groaned. She dropped her face into the palms of her hands and covered her eyes. She needed a warm body to replace lumberjack Carl. Her mind raced as she considered her options, feeling like she really didn't have any. She suddenly snapped to attention, staring one more time at the pictures pinned to the corkboard.

She grabbed her walkie-talkie from the desk and headed toward the door. "I'll be back," she said. "Get me an update on Carl, send him some flowers with our regrets, and let's get everyone ready for tonight's challenge."

"Where are you going?" Jim called after her.

Naomi grinned. "To get us a replacement. And he's going to be perfect for the show!"

Chapter Four

Naomi made a mental note to ask Aubrey or Jasper for a dedicated golf cart or truck to get her around the massive property. Why she was racing on foot from point A to point B trying to find the new handyman was mind-boggling. She'd twisted her ankle stepping into a gopher hole and her back was starting to hurt, but she used the time it was taking to gather her thoughts and figure out what she needed to say to convince the handsome man to help her out. Because Philip-not-Phil was going to be her twelfth contestant, no matter what it took!

There was no way he could ignore her pleas, she thought. He seemed like he would be a nice guy and nice guys were always willing to help when called on. At least the few she'd known had been. He would help, she mused, trying to convince herself so she could convince him.

Minutes later she found him hammering nails into a length of plywood. He and Marvin were laughing together like old friends. She almost hated to break up their budding bromance. Almost. This was far more important, and they'd get over it, she mused. Stepping into the space, she looked from one to the other as both men came to an abrupt halt. They both looked at her and then at each other, confusion washing over their faces.

Marvin took a step forward. "Are you okay, Naomi? Do you need something?"

Naomi nodded her head. Her gaze locked with Philip's when she turned toward him. He had beautiful eyes and she suddenly imagined herself swimming in the depths of them. Naomi gasped, her heartbeat suddenly racing like a drumline gone awry. Her brain felt fried, and her words caught deep in her chest. She opened her mouth to speak, and something like a mousy squeal slipped past her lips. Just like that Naomi completely forgot the speech she'd just spent the last twenty minutes practicing. She sucked in a deep breath, gasping like a fish eager to be submerged in water, and then she grabbed his hand, pulling him along behind her as she headed back out the door.

PHILIP WASN'T SURE what to make of the moment. Naomi was literally dragging him along with her. Her face was red and a line of perspiration dripped over the round of her cheeks. She actually looked like she might implode, and he was starting to think that he might need to worry.

Her fingers were tangled between his and he squeezed her hand. "Hold up," he said as he came to an abrupt stop. The gesture threw her off balance and she fell back against him. It surprised her, and him, throwing him off guard as they both lost their footing and fell, rolling together down a grassy knoll.

Naomi swore, a litany of profanity spilling past her

thin lips. As she sat upright, she began to laugh, tossing her head back as tears rained down her cheeks.

"Are you okay?" Philip questioned as he pulled himself upright, brushing his palms against his denim jeans.

Naomi was laughing too hard to answer. And before he knew it, he was laughing with her. She sucked air deep into her lungs. Her laugh transitioned into a loud chuckle and then a slight giggle, before her face turned serious again. She sighed. "I am so sorry!"

Philip shook his head. "As long as you're okay. I don't think I broke anything, so I'm good."

Naomi shook her head. "I'm glad you're not hurt but...well..." Her eyes suddenly widened.

Something large moved behind him and when he turned to see what it was, Philip found himself eye to eye with a cow. A very large, very disgruntled cow with more bovine friends standing behind it. The animal snorted, spewing spittle in his face. Philip scooted in the opposite direction, moving to put some distance between him and the bovine. It was then that he realized he and Naomi were sitting in a field of cow patties. He wrinkled his nose, the smell of manure rising into his nostrils. He cursed, his words loud and abrasive.

"We are definitely sitting in that!" Naomi said, giggling nervously again.

Philip shook his head. Standing, he reached out a hand to help her to her feet. "So, do you want to explain *why* we're sitting here? What's this all about?"

Naomi brushed grass and dirt from her backside, then swiped both hands against her pant leg. "I need you to be a contestant on my show."

He tilted his head ever so slightly. "Excuse me?"

"You heard me. One of my contestants fell off a horse and has to pull out of the show. I want you to take his place."

"Your horse show? You want me to be on your horse show?"

"It's not a horse show. The premise of the show is city folk meet the Wild West. You'd be put through a series of rough cowboy escapades. Those less successful will fall off the saddle at the end of each cycle. We're only filming for four weeks, and I need to create eight dynamic episodes in postproduction. The final two contestants will compete in a ride-off, with the winner receiving a hundred thousand dollars. I'll be right here to help guide you along. Doesn't the prospect of winning all that money tempt you even a little?"

"Not at all. Sorry." Philip shrugged his shoulders, pushing them skyward. Being front and center as part of the cast was not what Philip had signed on for. He didn't have any interest in challenging his own skills. As a kid, he hadn't wanted to play the cowboy, only the Indian. In actuality he couldn't have cared less about being on a horse or living in a tent. Besides, joining the cast would mean a whole other level of eyes researching his background and despite Chief Lawson's assurances, he didn't want to risk them uncovering something they didn't need to know. He shook his head.

Naomi persisted. "Are you scared? Because the challenges really aren't that hard. And we have all kinds of safety protocols in place. Besides, some of it will test your intellectual abilities to see if you need brawn or brains to survive. And we know you have a brain, so why not do it?"

Philip laughed heartily and shook his head emphatically. "No," he said firmly. "That's not going to happen. I really like what I'm doing. I don't need to do anything else."

"Don't say that. If I can't convince you to help me, it's all over." She tossed up her hands in frustration.

"You're being a little dramatic, aren't you?"

"Not at all. This is important to me."

Philip stared at her, noting the way her brow furrowed and her nose twitched. He sensed she wasn't a woman who cried easily but her lashes now glistened with tears. He suddenly found himself wondering what would happen if he leaned forward and captured her mouth with his, kissing her until her face was flushed and her body trembled in sync with his. That was another reason he couldn't consider her request. Being a contestant would put him in closer proximity to her and in that moment, he wasn't sure he could handle it.

He shook the clouds from his head and took a deep breath to clear his thoughts. "Why me? There are at least a dozen guys on the production crew that you could recruit. So, why do you want me?"

NAOMI MET HIS stare with one of her own, eyeing him intensely. She didn't bother to tell him the obvious. He was handsome, intelligent and charming, and if he were willing to play, she predicted the viewers would fall in love with him. Instead, she said, "Because from what I can tell, you're kind, and I believe that you will help me out simply because I need assistance. And you won't expect anything in return. There's not a whole lot of that left in this world and I want my audience to see it. You're one of the good guys and we need to see more men like you on network television."

"More men like me?"

Naomi nodded.

"So, you need a Black guy and I just happen to fit the bill?"

Naomi shrugged. "You being Black is only an issue if you make it one. But yes, you being Black is definitely a benefit. I'm not going to lie to you. I need more diversity in the cast and another white guy won't give me that."

Shifting his feet, Philip turned to stare at the herd of cows that seemed to be watching them from a distance. They too looked like they were waiting for him to answer. This wasn't how he had planned to keep an eye on Brad Clifton. But, he mused, it might make watching the man even easier. He also couldn't risk blowing his cover, and turning her down might get him removed from the set. He couldn't afford to be fired from the job and unable to do what he was really here to do.

He turned back toward her. She was chewing nervously on her bottom lip, and he suddenly wondered a second time what she might taste like if he pressed his mouth to hers. A layer of heat wafted like morning mist between the two of them and he felt his muscles starting to tighten through his southern quadrant. He took a deep breath of rank air to stall the sensation. Gesturing with his head, he pointed her back up the incline they had rolled down. "Let's keep walking while you tell me more about what I'm getting myself into," he said softly. "Then I need to go get a shower. You might want to get one, too." He skewed his face then gave her the faintest smile.

Naomi's grin was canyon-wide. She jumped excitedly, then threw herself against him in a deep bear hug. Kissing his cheek, she practically screamed into his ear. "Thank you! Thank you so much!"

"Please don't knock me down again," Philip said. "I don't think Clarabelle over there would appreciate it."

Naomi turned and headed back up the hill. "Except you were the one who knocked me down," she said with a deep giggle.

Philip laughed. "You're kidding, right?"

"It's my lie and I'm sticking with it!" Naomi quipped as she tossed him a look over her shoulder.

Smiling, Philip nodded, feeling a little less bothered by his own tall tale.

IT WAS NOT the morning he'd anticipated, and it certainly was not going to be the next four weeks he'd initially prepared for. Philip stood beneath a flow of warm water still conflicted about what he'd just agreed to. He felt slightly bewitched by Naomi Colton's persistence, her vivacity. She'd shouted at the top of her lungs, jumping up and down excitedly. It had almost made him want to jump up and down with her. Almost.

Naomi Colton was unlike the women who usually crossed his path. The last woman he'd dated had never read for the pleasure of seeing words on a page and feeling a story unfold in her heart. Joy for her was a perfect selfie and the addition of followers who complimented her latest hairstyle. It was rare that she'd had a thought of her own; she'd always been looking to him for his approval. Her name had been Tiffany something. She had been arm-candy galore, and now, he could barely remember her full moniker. Something about that didn't sit well in his spirit.

Tilting his face and head beneath the warm spray, Philip pressed both palms against the tiled wall and leaned his body forward so that the water ran over his back and shoulders. The shower was soothing, easing the tension out of each muscle. He had lathered himself once, twice and a third time, and finally the stench of animal no longer clung to his nostrils.

An hour after their encounter, after a mountain of paperwork and a multitude of promotional shots, he was now getting ready to make his entrance onto Gemini Ranch. One of the production assistants had spent a good thirty minutes prepping him for how to step out of the limousine and act surprised. Or indifferent. Depending on his mood and the character he hoped to represent to a national audience. It had been a lot to take in, most especially since he couldn't get thoughts of Naomi out of his head or forget the target of his first mission. Whether he liked it or not, Brad Clifton was still his one and only priority, whether he was learning how to rope a bull or hammering nails into boxes for one of the sets. Everything else was secondary and he didn't get the impression Naomi Colton would accept being second to anyone or anything.

HE SAID YES! Naomi was still happy-dancing like she'd won the biggest prize at the state fair. Philip agreeing to join the cast of her show was pure icing on some very sweet cake and it had made her entire day. She was also planning to ensure it made her entire project. Most especially because Jim had balked at her choice. He'd thought another woman would have been a better selection and made sure to tell her and any of the other crew who bothered to listen. He had wrecked her last good nerve shaking his head and grunting at her, so she had hugged him. Covered in cow and smelling like the outdoors, she'd wrapped him in a bear hug, holding on tightly. He'd been surprised. Then he'd been annoyed. So much so that he'd stomped out of the office, heading for a shower.

She shook her head, then she and Felicia had laughed heartily. She would apologize later, she thought, and not because she regretted doing what she'd done. She'd say sorry so if it came back to bite her in the ass later, so at least her apology would be on record. Although she'd profess loudly and often that the show was her baby, she still had to answer to the men holding the purse strings. She wasn't one to bite the hand feeding her. But worrying about Jim wasn't high on her priority list. For the moment, she needed to focus on her next steps.

Philip would be the last contestant to *arrive* on set. They would film his arrival in the next few hours, then rush him to wardrobe to change. The first challenge scheduled for later that evening would set the tone for the rest of the competition, and she was eager for them to get started. She headed toward the main house, taking a slow stroll as she reflected on the lengthy list of tasks on her to-do list.

And then she thought about Philip. Tall, dark and delicious Philip! He was a good-looking man and he rolled with her quirky sense of humor. They had laughed together, and it had felt as natural as breathing. He had taken their little accident with the grace and patience of Job. She hadn't known what to expect, and his concern for her well-being and his calm demeanor had been refreshing. She didn't imagine many men would have been as conciliatory. That alone had her wanting to know more about Philip Rees…

Chapter Five

Filming had officially started. Naomi stood off to the side as Philip stepped out of the oversize SUV that had been sent to pick him up. He had changed into a pair of khaki slacks, a white dress shirt and a paisley-print necktie. He cleaned up nicely, she thought as she chewed anxiously on her bottom lip. He smiled warmly as the show's host stepped up to shake his hand in greeting. When the director shouted, "Cut," Naomi had to contain her enthusiasm. She let Jim step in to point Philip toward the cabin where he'd be given his supplies for the next four weeks, or for however long he lasted. She fought the urge to follow. Instead, she headed toward their host, famed country singer Montgomery Burch.

Monty, as he was known to his family and friends, was renowned in the Nashville music scene. He'd been a legendary staple at the Grand Ole Opry. The winner of multiple Grammys, he was high-profile enough to give the show credibility. Signing him had taken some serious negotiating, and it was only when she'd convinced him that the show would pull him out of obscurity that he'd agreed to come on board. He sauntered in her direction, smiling as he met her halfway.

"Monty, welcome!" Naomi exclaimed. "Did they get you settled in okay?"

The man leaned to kiss her cheek. "They did. This ranch is something! I'm excited to be here."

"We're excited to have you. We're going to go ahead and film your introduction. Then you'll be able to rest a bit while we get set up for the first challenge."

"Sounds like a plan," he exclaimed.

Minutes later, Naomi, Monty, the camera crew, the director and production assistants all stood at the entrance to Gemini Ranch. They'd been able to set up swiftly and their timing was on point, the sun just beginning to set off in the distance.

Naomi gave everyone a nod and a smile. "Quiet on the set!" she cried.

Another film student—and there were a few on set to help keep the costs down—was serving as the clapper loader. He held the clapper board high, calling out the scene and take numbers to assist in synchronizing the picture and sound in postproduction. When he slammed the hinged clapper stick, the director called out. "Rolling film. Action!"

Monty strode slowly into the camera frame, his expression serious. He led a beautiful black stallion behind him, the massive horse ambling in time with his stride. When he reached his mark, the cameraman zoomed in on his face, and Monty recited his monologue. No one would ever know he needed a teleprompter to help him.

"Welcome to Gemini Ranch. Twelve strangers have

been invited here to prove they can out-wrangle the competition. The contestants will lock horns in a number of grueling challenges, as I, and a panel of experts, judge their skills, knowledge, grit and passion. We've brought together a diverse group of men and women from all across the nation to vie for the prize of a lifetime. Proving they have what it takes will separate the cowboys from all the others and make for some explosive drama. One by one, we'll see who falls, and who can stay in…the saddle!" Monty smiled and winked, then he threw himself atop the horse, turned it around and rode off into the distance.

"Cut!" The director stood. He and Naomi stood in quick conversation.

Monty galloped back. "Told you I could get it in one take," he gushed, the comment directed at Naomi.

She smiled. "Yes, you did, and you did a great job. But I need you to deliver that last line one more time."

The man looked confused. "One more time?"

"Yes," Naomi said. "Just the last line. This time, I need you to pause before you say *in the saddle*, since that's the title of the show."

Monty stared, his expression blank. He finally nodded. "Okay," he said. "But let's shoot the whole thing over so it flows. I can't have you editing my segments together making me look like I didn't know what I was doing."

Naomi gave him her sweetest smile. She'd anticipated him being a prima donna but had hoped it wouldn't start so early. They were already setting him up to do the shot a second time, so she didn't bother to respond. She folded her arms over her chest as the clapper board sounded and the director yelled, "Action."

Monty delivered his second performance. "One by one, we'll see who falls, and who can stay…in the saddle!" He flashed that bright smile but didn't bother with the wink. She watched as he and the horse took off, heading toward the stables instead of turning back around.

She and Jude gave each other a look.

"We got the shot," Jude said. "But you're going to need to rein him in. It's too darn early for tantrums and he has a lot of camera time."

Naomi sighed, her head beginning to throb with what she was sure was the first of many headaches to come.

PHILIP WAS STILL questioning what he'd gotten himself into. Each of the contestants had been corralled into the barn for a quick meet and greet. From what he understood, each morning they'd be trained to complete a task on the ranch. A team of mentors would guide and put them through their paces. Later they would compete to see how they were able to execute what they had learned. Those same mentors would offer their input on who should stay and who should go. Although he was physically fit, he was no cowboy and not a huge fan of livestock. The prospect of the challenges to come was somewhat daunting. He wasn't, however, going to let it show.

There were lights and cameras posted in every corner of the barn. The crew was moving about like an army of ants putting things into place. The other contestants seemed to be taking it in as Philip was, somewhat awed by the frenzy to get the perfect shot. It showed in their expressions, but he maintained a poker face. He would have liked to have seen her and have her see him since he'd cleaned up from their morning debacle. This was his second wardrobe change, the production assistant explaining that they would edit the film to make it seem like a different day. The magic of television, he thought, shaking his head.

He wore black. Black leather cowboy boots with a steel heel. Black denim jeans, a matching black button-up shirt, and a classic, black felt Stetson. An audio pack and microphone were strapped beneath his shirt to capture any conversations he had.

Philip looked the part, but he wasn't feeling the role he was supposed to be playing. He likened himself to Bass Reeves, the first Black, deputy US marshal west of the Mississippi River. Reeves had been born enslaved, gaining his freedom sometime during the Civil War. He too had been a law enforcement officer, believing in the tenets of civil obedience. Philip doubted, however, that Reeves had ever been subject to the whims of a woman while working undercover.

He was suddenly pulled from his thoughts when someone tapped him on the shoulder. He turned to see a stunning woman with jet-black hair that fell down her back. A wide grin spread across her face.

She extended her hand in greeting. "Hi, Grace Daniels, and you are?"

Philip smiled back. "Philip. Philip Rees. And it's a pleasure to meet you, Grace Daniels."

"So, what is it that you do?" she questioned, still holding tightly to his fingers.

"I'm a handyman," he answered.

The woman's large smile dimpled her cheeks. "A handyman? Huh! I just bet you are!"

They both laughed as the woman gave him a quick nod and moved on to introduce herself to the others. Philip wasn't interested in working the room. He was polite, but not overly enthusiastic. He let the other contestants come to him.

By the end of the hour, he'd met and shook hands with Stefan, the college student; Harold, the mechanic; Josiah, the entrepreneur; Fred, the tractor trailer driver; Hannah, the grandmother of seven; Constantine, the plastic surgeon; Juan-Carlo, the DJ; Melissa, the Mary Kay representative; Malia, the airline pilot; and of course, the tech nerd. Brad Clifton. His new friend Grace was quite the social butterfly, pulling the others over to introduce them. Grace was a former Miss America representing the great state of Texas. Now she owned and operated a nonprofit that provided small houses for the homeless.

They were quite a mixed bag of chips, a diverse group of ethnicities and ages. What they each had in common was a desire to prove that they were more than what people assumed them to be. Their lives had become stagnant, making them feel like it was necessary to prove they were worthy of so much more. And then there were the few who only saw the dollar signs, wanting the cash prize at the end to get out of debt and pull themselves from their current social and economic status. Philip didn't fall on either end of that spectrum and he suddenly felt out of place, a red circle being pushed into a black square. And what would he say when asked about his motives, he thought. Because he knew questions would come from the other contestants, and he was almost certain he would have to make up his answers on the fly.

It didn't take long for the meet and greet to become a dick-swinging competition, the testosterone in the room rising to a combustible level. Everyone was assessing their competition, determined to one-up whomever they could. Philip, however, sensed that despite the bravado of a whole lot of his male counterparts, it was some of the women who actually came off looking ballsier.

An associate producer eased to Philip's side. She was a young woman, looking like she'd just graduated from high school. Her name was Helen, and she had the exuberance of a hamster spinning on an exercise wheel.

"Phil, hey! You doing okay?" Helen said, greeting him cheerily. She didn't bother to wait for his response. "We really need you to move around the room. You've been standing in this one spot since you arrived. The camera loves you and we want to make sure we get plenty of great shots of you with the other contestants. Maybe you could go join the men on the other side of the room?"

Philip gave the woman a side-eye. "No," he said firmly. "And my name is Philip, not Phil. Thank you."

Helen looked stunned, not sure how to respond. She opted to say nothing, just giving him a nod as she scurried back over to the crew. It was then that Philip noticed Naomi had entered the space, standing with her arms folded over her chest as someone whispered into her ear. Philip watched as she glanced up to stare in his direction, the slightest smile pulling across her face. Before he could react, Grace was once again standing at his side. She stood with her palms clasped together in front of her as she leaned into his side, so close that he could smell the lavender rinse she used in her hair. He shot Naomi a quick look as she watched them, her eyes darting from where they stood to the monitor capturing the moment. Philip took a deep breath and held it in his lungs to stall the rise of anxiety that suddenly pulled at him.

Grace's tone was flirtatious. "So, are you just shy, or antisocial? The others are trying to get a read on you."

Philip gave her a smile. "I'm just taking it all in."

"Well, I have a proposition for you." She leaned even closer. "I've watched enough reality television to know that the right alliance can make or break a competition. I think a handyman will come in handy. And people tend to underestimate what I can do. And we're pretty together," she said matter-of-factly. "So, what do you say about the two of us teaming up to win this thing!"

"We may need more than just the two of us," Philip responded, his gaze sweeping around the room.

"I agree. Anyone else you like?"

Philip paused, his eyes shifting to where Brad Clifton was talking to the DJ and the airline pilot. "What about the tech guy?" he questioned.

Grace winced. "There's something creepy about that one."

"What's that saying? Keep your friends close and your enemies closer?"

The woman shrugged her narrow shoulders. "Maybe, but I like Constantine and Malia. Melissa, too."

He nodded. "Then let's form that alliance," he said.

Grace looped her arm through his, perfectly manicured pink nails trailing the length of his arm. She pulled him along beside her. Philip felt just uncomfortable enough to suddenly worry what Naomi might think. He stole a quick glance in her direction. She was watching him intently, but he couldn't read her expression. Then he wondered why it even bothered him.

So, Philip was making friends, Naomi thought as she watched him and the beauty queen walk off together. She shifted her attention to the camera monitor, noting how much the lens loved him, and her. In a different show, with a different cast, Naomi would have played on that, making them a couple even if they weren't. Now, though, she was feeling something like jealousy in the pit of her stomach, and the wealth of emotion surprised her.

She had the camera tech roll the film back so that she could hear the audio. She eased a set of earphones onto her ears. When she took them off, she blew a sigh of relief. Clearly, Grace was the aggressor. Philip was playing the game. At least, that was what she wanted to believe although his bright smile and the shimmer in his dark eyes might be telling a different story.

She turned to Helen. "Shut this down and start

prepping them for the first challenge. We need to stay on schedule."

Helen nodded. "Yes, sir, boss lady!"

With one last look toward Philip and the beautiful woman still hanging onto him like fungus, Naomi turned on her heels and headed out the building.

Chapter Six

When Philip and Naomi saw each other the next day, Philip was standing atop a piece of yellow tape in line with all the others. Brad stood on his left side. Grace stood on his right. Filming was a series of takes and re-takes as Monty, their host, tried to remember his lines. He sipped once or twice from a silver flask and celebrated when he nailed his monologue. Philip was finding the entire process tedious.

Naomi smiled, her eyes skipping past him after the director yelled, "Cut," and they all stopped standing at attention. She took a moment to thank them all for their efforts.

"I hope everyone's having a great time?" she exclaimed.

A chorus of yeses and yeahs answered her.

She smiled. "We had a great first event. Congratulations to Grace and Melissa. You two ladies have gained an advantage in the next competition tomorrow."

A round of applause rang through the air.

"We're very excited to have you all on this journey with us. And just imagine, our first winner ever is standing right here in this room, ready to make history as the first winner of *In the Saddle*, and it may very well be you!" She clapped her hands together excitedly and her eyes paused on each face, hesitating slightly as she and Philip locked gazes.

She continued. "We know today's been a long day and tomorrow is going to be equally grueling. We're going to release you all now so you can get some rest. Sleep well and we'll start filming again at nine o'clock after everyone has had breakfast. Good night!"

One by one the cast sauntered past Naomi and her crew, bidding them all a good night. She made a point to speak to each person individually, so Philip purposely hung back until he was last in line. His smile was smug as he wished Helen and the others well. He turned his attention to Naomi. "So, Ms. Colton, do you have any plans for the evening?" He gave Naomi the sweetest smile.

"Just work, Mr. Rees. Putting together this series will occupy my time twenty-four seven until we get that last shot of the winner."

"I'm duly impressed. You've got quite an operation here. Although I wasn't aware I'd have to sleep on the ground in a sleeping bag."

"I didn't tell you about that?"

"No, you didn't," he said. "In fact, I'm starting to think that there's a lot you forgot to tell me about participating in this show."

Naomi grinned. "Not really. Most of it will surprise you like it'll surprise everyone else. You'll do just fine."

She grabbed her bag and moved toward the door. "Come on. I'll walk you to your tent."

"Define *just fine*."

"You seem to be making friends and forming alliances. I don't anticipate you'll have any problems. Grace is already showcasing how adept she is at orchestrating things. I have no doubts that if you need help, she'll be more than willing to assist you."

There was a moment of pause as Philip reflected on her words. He chuckled softly. "Why do you sound jealous?"

"Jealous? Please!"

Philip shrugged his shoulders. "I'm just saying what it sounds like. For the record, though, Grace is not my type."

He said that with a hint of amusement in his tone, not wanting to admit that Grace was exactly the type of woman he had previously dated. All fluff and sugar in a pretty package.

"You have a type?"

"Don't we all?"

"And exactly what is your type, Mr. Rees?"

Philip pushed his hands into the pockets of his jeans. They had just stepped into the area where twelve tents had been pitched beneath the trees. Most of the cast had retired for the night, but Brad, Harold and Fred sat in a circle around a firepit, still talking.

"Are you going to be safe walking out here alone?" Philip asked as they came to a stop in front of the tent he'd been made to pitch for himself earlier.

"Don't change the subject. You didn't answer my question."

"What question was that?"

Naomi tossed him a look, frustration and curiosity holding hands. "What's your type?"

Philip laughed heartily. "You!" he answered finally, and then he gave her a nod, stepped through the flaps of his tent and closed it behind him.

He could still hear her giggling as she moved off into the distance and he couldn't help but laugh with her.

Philip stood in the center of the tent feeling slightly squirrely. He had surprised himself with his answer. But the honesty behind that single word suddenly had him rethinking his priorities. He wasn't there to flirt with Naomi Colton and his attraction to her was starting to be a distraction he couldn't afford. But the beautiful woman had his full attention. She was exactly his type: funny, spirited, driven. Saying it aloud had been the most honest thing he'd said to her since he'd gotten there. But he had to remember why he was there. He wasn't a contestant. He was there to catch a bad guy and make sure no one got hurt in the process.

HE'D BEEN JOKING, Naomi thought. Teasing her. He didn't know her well enough to know if she was his type or not. Then again, she didn't know him well enough to discern whether or not he was joking. Either way, she had to admit that their encounter had been a pleasant way to end her day. What she couldn't deny was the physical attraction between them. Because the nearness of Philip Rees left her needy and wanting and it had been a while since she'd last *wanted* any man. She paused, trying to remember who and when. When nothing, or rather no one, came to her, she shook her head.

It had been too long and not for lack of interest or trying. Naomi was just particular about the men she spent time with, and living in Los Angeles, she found too often that they were too pretty, too self-absorbed and too obsessed with breaking into the business. Men interested in a long-term relationship were far and few between. She'd also gotten set in her ways. She liked her space and her time, and she was a tad selfish, not wanting to share either if she didn't have to.

Philip should be flattered that she was even thinking about him. Not that he would ever know. But she was. Thoughts of the man were spinning hard through her head and she knew he would occupy every minute of her dreams when she finally fell off to sleep.

When Philip was certain Naomi was no longer in the vicinity he stepped back out of his tent and moved toward the firepit, taking a seat with the other men. They all greeted him warmly.

Brad tossed him a look and then nodded his head. "We'd offer you a beer, but all they've given us is some generic soda pop."

Philip laughed. "Not a problem. I just came to shoot the breeze with you guys for a few minutes before I call it a night."

"So, what do you think?" Brad questioned. "Is this starting out the way you thought it would?"

Philip shrugged. "No! I didn't expect to get beaten

by two women in the first challenge." He thought back to their first contest, a series of endurance tests that ended with them having to solve a puzzle of sorts. The women had done okay in the endurance portion where they had to navigate their way through a massive hay maze, but had murdered them with the puzzle, configuring the schematics of a wood barn with pieces the size of small toddlers. They had laced their last piece together minutes before the lot of them had even come close to figuring it out.

The men laughed, echoing his sentiments.

"They're some tough old birds!" Fred the truck driver said.

"I doubt they'd appreciate being called old, or birds," Philip said.

"Yeah, dude," Brad intoned. "They catch that on camera and suddenly you're a bad guy, the headlines proclaiming you're misogynistic, racist, intolerant or whatever else is popular to call out at the moment."

"You got to be politically correct. Especially on camera," Harold the mechanic interjected.

They all responded with head nods.

"So, what do you do again?" Fred questioned, the comment directed at Philip.

Philip shifted in his seat. "Construction. I was actually working with the crew here on set when they lost one of their contestants. I was recruited last minute to fill in."

"Sounds like someone might have a thing for you," Brad interjected.

Philip laughed. "Nah, dude! I was the only one who passed the background check."

There was a round of chuckles.

"Did I hear you say you're in computer technology?" Philip said to Brad. "You're a programmer, or coder, or whatever it is they call it?"

Something like annoyance flushed Brad's face. "I own a security firm. We develop security technology. It's a little bit more than just coding."

"All that technology stuff is above my pay grade," Philip said. "Give me a stack of wood and a hammer and I'm a happy man!"

"I like you," Fred chimed. "I can appreciate a man who looks for the simple things in life, because I believe technology will be our downfall."

Brad shook his head. "On that note I'm going to leave you country bumpkins and head to bed."

Philip laughed. "Country bumpkins? Really?" He struggled to not let his annoyance with the man show. It had taken no time at all for him to know he didn't like Brad, and he assumed Brad probably didn't like him, either.

"If you can't see that technology is the wave of the future, I can't help you," Brad shrugged. "You need to get on board or you're going to get left behind."

"We'll agree to disagree," Philip responded with a shake of his head. He hadn't come to argue morality, ethics, or politics with a man who clearly thought little of others and only himself. Philip had been raised to always consider his fellow man in his actions, and he did that even when he was undercover pretending to be someone else "Because I think the simple ways of our ancestors will continue to endure when technology fails us. And I think this experience will prove that to all of us."

"And you hug trees, too, right?" Brad yawned and stood, stretching his arms upward.

Fred laughed. "You're the one who might be hugging a tree or two in the next week. Your technology isn't going to help you win this competition."

Philip reached out his hand to slap palms with the man. Their chortles rang warmly through the late-night air.

SHORTLY AFTER MIDNIGHT, Philip was still awake, tossing and turning inside the sleeping bag that would be his bed for the next few weeks. The production company had provided cots so they would at least be off the ground but his was too narrow and too short for his frame. There was no level of comfort as he reasoned the ground might be a better choice if he hoped to get a good night's rest.

He also couldn't get thoughts of Naomi out of his head. She'd become an itch he couldn't reach, lying beneath the first layers of his skin as it dug deep toward the center of his core. She brought a sense of joy to each of their encounters that was both unexpected and pleasant. She had this incredible laugh that brightened her face and seemed to lift her whole body. It left him feeling like he was walking on air. He enjoyed those moments. He found himself wishing for more of them. And then he had to remember. He wasn't there for Naomi Colton. He was there for Brad the tech guy, who found no value in hugging trees.

Philip had rolled from one side to the other for the umpteenth time when he suddenly smelled smoke. He sat upright, the gesture so abrupt he caught a cramp in his left calf. Ignoring the pain, he pushed himself out of the bed, stumbling over his own feet. The sound of nylon sizzling sounded through the air, and he realized his tent was on fire, flames having already eaten the entire back side of the tent. He grabbed his duffel bag and rushed through the front flap, yelling at the top of his lungs.

BY THE NEXT MORNING, Naomi had received fifteen telephone calls about the fire in the cast housing area. Eight of them had come from Jim. Jim in a panic. Jim confused. Jim becoming resigned to the situation. Jim panicked some more. By the time she reached the space where each of the contestants had pitched their tents and were sleeping, the fire had been put out. In total, three tents had gone up in the flames. A crowd of cast and crew was gathered about in small groups, assessing the situation. Philip stood off to the side, his arms folded across his torso. He was bare-chested and shoeless, wearing nothing but his boxers. His expression was stoic. Grace moved to his side, drawing her hand against his broad back. He flinched from her touch and if Naomi hadn't been watching him so closely, she would have missed it.

Jasper and Aubrey stood with two of the other contestants and her production assistants were passing out cups of coffee to anyone who wanted one. Melissa was sobbing, her few possessions she'd brought with her having gone up in flames.

Jim hurried to her side, visibly flustered. "We need to call the fire department, but your brother said it's not necessary," he shouted as he threw up his hands.

"The fire is out," Naomi answered. "What else do you want them to do?"

"This could shut production down! Careless, just careless," the man muttered.

Naomi took a deep breath, blowing it out slowly before she spoke. "No one's shutting production down. Did anyone get hurt?" she questioned.

Jim shook his head. "No. That guy Philip got everyone out safely. But we lost three tents. His, Melissa's and Fred's. Melissa is just devastated! She could have died!"

Naomi blinked rapidly as she took in the comment. She took another deep breath. "Thankfully, no one was hurt. We can replace the few possessions they each lost. Have Felicia take them shopping as soon as the stores open for any personal items they need and tell her to pick up three tents while she's out. We'll delay filming until after lunch to give everyone an opportunity to collect themselves."

"We can't afford to delay production."

"We'll make it up on the back end. If we cut back on the bios, we should be good. We just need to keep going and I'll figure out where we can cut back and fix it. We'll still come in under budget if we're smart about what we do."

"I'm not so sure about that," Jim quipped.

"Well, I am," Naomi snapped back. She glared in

Jim's direction as she stepped away from him. She moved to where Melissa was still weeping openly. "Are you okay?" she asked.

"I think I should go home. This is all too much! My tent burned down!"

"I'm so sorry that you've had to go through that, but I hope you'll get some rest and think about staying. We are going to replace your personal items and will have a new tent up for you before the end of the day. Until then, I'll arrange for you to stay in one of the cabins for the rest of the night. What I don't want is for you to allow this one moment to spoil this entire experience for you."

"I don't know…"

"Just give it some thought, and we can talk again tomorrow." Naomi tapped her gently against her forearm and smiled sweetly.

The other woman smiled back and nodded. "Okay. I'll give it some thought," she said.

"That's all I can ask." Naomi moved to where Jasper and Aubrey stood, the twins seeming to have a telepathic conversation that only they understood.

"Hey, do we have any idea how this happened?"

"Your guy Jim seems to think someone didn't put out the firepit properly." He pointed to where Naomi had seen the male contestants sitting earlier.

"What do you think?" she asked.

"I think it's possible, but we'll really never know for sure. Your people were able to get the flames out as fast as they could but those nylon tents went up fast. The supplies can be replaced. We're just grateful no one was injured."

"Do you think you can put my tentless contestants up in one of the cabins for the rest of the night?"

Aubrey nodded. "It shouldn't be a problem. Is one night enough?"

"More than enough. I need them back in the game later this afternoon. It'll be back to tent city for all of them."

Jasper took a step closer, his voice dropping an octave. "Are you okay? You look flustered."

"Jim just likes to push my buttons. He made a stupid comment about shutting down production. He just irks me." Naomi threw Jim a look over her shoulder. He was tapping Melissa against the shoulder. She couldn't explain it, but she was certain he was stirring up the woman's fears and making no effort to calm her concerns. Jim had a way of parlaying negativity for his own benefit, and she suddenly felt like she might need to worry about the knife he surely had pointed at her back. She took another big breath and shook the thoughts from her head.

"I'll go prep the bunkhouse," Aubrey said.

"Thank you."

"I need to go check on the horses," her brother said. He leaned to kiss Naomi's cheek. "Get some rest. You get snappy when you're tired. And I'm sure Jim didn't mean anything by what he said."

"Oh, he meant it," Naomi muttered before wishing the duo a good night. "Just hang tight for a minute and I'll have the contestants follow you down to the bunkhouse," she said.

Aubrey nodded, folding her arms over her chest.

She gestured for one of the production assistants, a

college student whose name escaped her. She gave him a smile. "Would you find Fred, please, and then walk him and Melissa to the cabin. My sister will show you where they're staying."

The young man nodded. "I know where he is. I'll get him."

"Thank you. I'll grab Philip and meet you all there." Naomi didn't miss the raised eyebrow her sister directed toward her. She suddenly regretted telling Aubrey about their encounter in the cow pasture. "What?" she mumbled tossing a look over her shoulder.

Aubrey shook her head, her own voice dropping to a loud whisper. "Nothing. Now, which one is Philip?"

Naomi felt herself blush, grateful that no one else could see it in the dim light. She gestured with her head. "Tall, dark and handsome over there."

Philip was still standing like stone. He seemed to be silently studying each of them, forming his own opinions about all that was going on. She was curious to know what he was thinking.

"He is cute," Aubrey said. "Is he single?"

"I don't know, and it doesn't matter. Nothing can happen between us. Nothing!" Naomi raised her voice ever so slightly, then shot a look in his direction. "Nothing at all," she repeated one last time. "And I don't need you hammering me about him."

"Okay…why are you being so defensive?" Aubrey asked.

"I'm not," she insisted.

"Yes, you are. It sounds like someone might be interested in tall, dark and delicious."

"I appreciate your cheap jokes but I'm not in the mood right now."

Aubrey laughed. "Just tossing in my two cents. And you can keep the change!" She turned, giving Naomi one last wave before heading down to prep the beds for her newly acquired guests.

"Thanks, sis!" Naomi called after her.

"Love you, too!"

Naomi sauntered to Philip's side, crossing her arms over her chest.

"How are you doing?"

Philip shrugged, turning to give her his full attention. "I'm fine. I'm just glad no one was injured."

"So am I." She inhaled, drawing air deep into her lungs. "Jim thinks it was the firepit that started it. That the guys didn't shut it down properly."

Philip shook his head. "That's not possible. I saw Fred put out the flames in the firepit. He made sure to water it down and then he shoveled it. That was at least an hour or two before the fire started. And the blaze started in the back of the tents, not the front. There's no breeze, so it's not possible any embers lasted that long and blew against the tent, starting the flames."

"So, what are you saying?"

Philip's gaze locked with hers. He took a step into her space, standing so close that she could smell the faintest scent of cologne on his skin. His shoulder brushed ever so gently against hers as he leaned closer to whisper in her ear. "I think someone started that fire on purpose."

PHILIP REES WAS a conspiracy theorist and an agitator, and now he had her side-eyeing everyone on set. His words were playing over and over again in her head. And maybe he wasn't all those things, but he had voiced out loud what she'd been trying not to think and definitely wouldn't have said out loud. She was just grateful that he'd only said it to her and had promised not to repeat it to anyone.

Naomi was pacing the floor. She wasn't happy and she wanted someone to blame for her frustration. To cover her backside, she'd drafted an email to the production company. Hearing it from her first allowed her to downplay what she knew Jim would blow out of proportion. She knew he was beside himself with anticipation, hoping to tattle to the powers in charge.

Now she just had to figure out if Philip's theory was right. If someone had started the fire deliberately, who had done it and why. Like she needed one more problem to add to her list. She threw her body down onto the cot and lay back against the paper-thin pillow. She was tired but doubted she'd be able to sleep. She had too much on her mind, and for whatever reasons, Philip Rees kept creeping front and center in her head.

PHILIP WAS ONE of the first to rise the next morning. With Fred the truck driver, and his new partner Grace, he walked down to the commissary area for the morning cup of coffee. Grace was overly enthusiastic about what would come. Philip didn't have the same sense of excitement, but he could appreciate her excitement as she rambled on about what they might have to do and the alliance she thought would give them a leg up on their competition.

"And what about that fire last night!" Grace exclaimed. "I'm so glad everyone was safe!"

Fred shook his head. "I was sure I put that pit out. That's something I don't play with. Fire ain't forgiving."

Philip nodded. For just a split second he had drifted off into thought, seeming not to hear anything either of them was saying. Neither of his companions appeared to notice that someone had snatched his attention and he was focused intently on the man slowly sauntering in their direction.

Brad Clifton had stepped out of the trees that bordered the property, coming from the opposite direction where the tents were. He was up early, and Philip wondered where he had gone and whom he had been with. He walked with a wave of confidence, practically skipping in their direction. As he drew closer, he pushed something deep into the pockets of his khaki pants. He adjusted his shirt, tucking the hem into the waistband. As he moved closer there was no missing his smug expression, like he'd just accomplished something to be proud of.

Brad cut a narrowed eye at Philip as he moved toward the coffeepot. "How'd you two sleep last night? I'm betting where you slept was far more comfortable than where the rest of us slept."

"You jealous?" Philip asked, a hint of sarcasm in his tone.

"Not at all. I'm hoping all that pampered treatment

you received will make you soft. It'll help me to eliminate you early in this game."

Philip chuckled, his head waving slowly from side to side. "Wishful thinking will get you nowhere," he responded.

"So, where are you coming from?" Grace questioned Brad as she moved to Philip's side. She gestured toward the woods and Philip smiled. He could have hugged her for that observation, taking the onus off him to ask the question he too wanted an answer to. She didn't have a clue what she'd done for him. He focused his stare on Brad's face for his reaction.

Brad's eyes widened, and he suddenly looked nervous. He shrugged his shoulders. "I just went for a morning walk." He changed the subject. "So, what do you think they're going to have us do today?"

"Whatever it is, I have an advantage." Grace grinned.

"Like an advantage is going to help you," Brad scoffed. "Don't you know some of the guys are gunning for you women? Not me, of course, but I've heard some of the men say that eliminating you early shouldn't be too hard to do."

"You wouldn't do anything like that, right?" Philip said.

Brad winked an eye. "Of course not. Healthy competition is good for the soul."

Grace rolled her eyes. "You need to have a soul first," she countered. She turned her attention to Philip. "Can I get you a cup of coffee?"

"I'm good," he answered.

The woman smiled. "I'm going to grab a seat and

maybe one of those muffins. Just let me know if you need anything," she said, putting an emphasis on that last comment. *Anything!*

Brad took a step closer. "You hit that, didn't you?"

"Excuse me?"

"Her!" He tilted his head in Grace's direction. "If you didn't, you can! She is hot for you!" He smacked his lips as he leered at the woman.

Philip sighed, a heavy breath of warm air blowing past his full lips. "I have no idea what you're talking about, and something tells me I'm not interested." He lifted his eyebrows and grinned at the other man.

Brad laughed. "I get it. You're trying to be discreet." He tapped Philip on the shoulder. "We should partner up. You and I can take this thing all the way to the final two. Give it some thought," he said as he turned, moving toward the table of breakfast foods.

Philip's wide smile dropped as soon as Brad turned his back to him. Brad was an obnoxious ass, he thought to himself. But partnering up with him might give him an edge to figuring out what the man had up his sleeve.

Where had he gone hiking? Had he been alone in those woods, or did he meet up with someone? And why join a reality television show if he was spilling corporate secrets, knowing that eyes and cameras would be on him 24/7? Still having more questions than answers, Philip followed after them.

Chapter Seven

Minutes after Philip had downed two carrot cake muffins, a plate of bacon and a cup of hot coffee, Naomi stood at the front of the room, gesturing for his attention. She also called for Fred, Hannah, Josiah and Harold.

"Good morning," he said as he strolled slowly to her side.

"Good morning! Did you sleep well last night?" she asked.

"It was a good night. I'm going to miss being in a real bed when I go back to my tent."

Naomi giggled. "Sorry about that. You'll get over it, though."

He laughed.

She greeted Fred and Hannah, who had joined them. Josiah gestured for her to give him a quick minute while he finished the last of his eggs, then he and Harold followed.

"I need Fred, Josiah and Harold to meet Jim at the main house. We need to film your contestant bios this morning. It shouldn't take too long and then you'll be able to relax for a moment before the event this afternoon.

"Hannah, I understand that you've never been on a horse before, and you, Philip, have, but you don't have much horse-riding experience. Is that correct?"

Both nodded.

"I'm not partial to big animals," Hannah said. "I understand this is a ranch and horses go with ranches, but I'd prefer to stay clear of the horses and the cattle if possible."

"Well, I'm hoping we can ease some of your fears. Unfortunately, we have a few challenges that will require you to ride if you want to compete."

The grandmother started to tap her toe in the dirt. She didn't look happy as she contemplated her choices. "I'm going to need to think about it," she said, turning away and moving back to a table to sit down.

"Okay, then," Naomi muttered under her breath. "You do that." She jotted notes onto her notepad before turning her attention to him. "Are you willing to get comfortable with the horses, Mr. Rees?" she asked.

He took a step toward her, his voice dropping an octave. "I'm always willing to try, but I can't make any promises I'll be good at it."

His sultry tone was like warm butter against her ears. Her feminine spirit began to pulse for attention, and she was suddenly flustered by the nearness of him. Her eyes skated around the room to see who might be watching the two of them.

Taking a deep breath, she turned back to him and smiled. "Something tells me you're probably pretty good at everything you try," she said, her own words a loud whisper.

"Do you ride, Naomi?" he asked, sounding like he was asking something completely different from what he'd actually said.

"Ride?" she asked, thrown off by the hint of innuendo in his tone.

Philip smiled. "Horses. Do you ride horses?"

"Uh, yes. I'm sorry. Yes, I do ride horses."

He stood staring at her, seeming to study the line of her profile and noting the placement of each pore against her porcelain complexion. Naomi stared back, the intensity of his eyes like a beacon pulling her in. Whether either was willing to admit it or not, something was brewing between them. Something neither wanted to define or was in a position to enjoy.

Naomi took a step back, throwing a questioning look in his direction. "Yes?"

Philip chuckled. "You called me over, remember? Something about horses?"

She shook her head, still feeling out of sorts. "I'm so sorry. You need to head over to the stables. They'll pair you up with a mount and get you comfortable being in a saddle. They have the best team of experts on staff."

"Should I ask for anyone in particular?" Philip asked.

"No. They're expecting you. Once you're done, find Jim. He should be ready to film your bio by then."

Naomi turned, moving toward the exit. She turned back around when Philip called her name.

"Maybe you and I can ride together sometime," he said. "I'm sure you can give me some pointers." His smile was infectious, lifting the lines of his face with promises and probably a lie or two, she thought. In the past she hadn't dated the most honest men. A few had taken the art of lying to a mastery level. One in particular, a film producer, had wined and dined her for weeks until she discovered he had two wives and a mistress. Nothing out of his mouth had been the truth. After he'd been exposed, she'd packed her trust issues away with all her other baggage, swearing off men for good.

There was a moment of pause as they locked gazes one last time. Time seemed to stand still, waiting for one or the other to give. Naomi pressed her palm to her abdomen and sighed. She spun around on her heels, tossing him a smug look over her shoulder. "I really don't think that's a good idea. I might hurt you."

As she walked away, she heard the sound of Philip's mischievous chuckle billowing through the morning air.

THE ANIMAL STARING back at Philip was a purebred Appaloosa named Bubbles. The name came from the distinctive snowflake spotting that covered his chocolate brown coat. The horse was evaluating Philip equally as hard as Philip was gauging him, as the two looked each other in the eye. The gelding whinnied and nuzzled Philip's face.

"Looks like you've made a new friend!" Gemini ranch hand Kayla St. James declared. She laughed warmly as she ran her hand down the horse's neck. Her dark brown hair fell in a neat ponytail down her back and her green eyes shimmered in the light.

"I might need a friend," Philip answered as he stroked the animal's muzzle. "Hopefully he'll still like me when I'm on his back."

"He's a good boy" she cooed. "He'll be fine. And so will you." She winked her eye at him. "Now that you're familiar with the saddle, let's see you get it on him. The first thing we want to ensure at all times is that the horse is protected. Saddles can weigh up to fifty or sixty pounds, so you want to start with a solid, thick-cushioned pad between the animal and the saddle." She pointed to the padding hanging on the post. "Place that on his back," she said. "And if you want to add a decorative layer of protection you can then put a blanket atop that."

Philip nodded, laying the cushioned pad on the horse's back. "First, I'll need you to throw that blanket on his back and center it." Kayla handed him a Western-print blanket in blue and white, which he lined up with the pad.

"Good job," she commented. "Now I want you to lay the saddle on the blanket. Don't just drop it on his back. Lay it gently and then walk from one side to the other to ensure it's even on both sides and the blanket and cushion are smooth."

Philip took a deep breath and followed her instructions. The saddle was heavy and it took a moment to make sure it was in place. When Kayla nodded her head at him, he relaxed, feeling more confident about what he needed to do and how he should do it.

Kayla then showed him how to bring the saddle's front and back girth down and check that it fit properly. She led him back to the horse's other side. They started with the front first, and then the bucking cinch in the rear. "Reach underneath the horse for the strap and pull it up through the securing ring. You want to tighten the cinch enough to keep the saddle in place, and loose enough to keep the cinch from straining his breathing. And this is very important. The guy who had to leave early claimed to know what he was doing, and I discovered his saddle hadn't been tightened properly. That fall could have killed him!"

"I surely don't want that to happen."

"You got this!"

Complying with the instructions, Philip bristled slightly when Bubbles neighed his displeasure. The horse shimmied from side to side. Philip's eyes widened and he tossed Kayla a look.

The young woman laughed. "Your hands must be cold," she joked. She gave him a nod.

Laughing with her, Philip tried again, the outcome more successful the second time around.

"Good job," Kayla said. "Are you ready to mount him?"

"I can do that, I think. I've been atop a horse before. I'm just not good at riding. But my father used to say that what you do most, is what you do best."

"Your father was a smart man."

"He had moments!"

She smiled as she watched him secure his foot in the stirrup and swing his leg up and over the top of Bubbles. He was visibly nervous and the horse seemed to sense his discomfort.

"You need to relax," Kayla said softly. "He is now an extension of you and your emotions. He can feel you being nervous and that will make him nervous. He needs you to trust him so he can trust you."

"I'm trying, but it's high up here and I'm not a fan of heights."

Kayla laughed. "You men are such babies!"

"Just a few of us." Philip chuckled. He took a deep breath and stroked the horse's neck with his large palm. "Good boy," he murmured.

Kayla grabbed the reins and guided Philip and his horse out into the corral. Four young men sat on the fence, all glued to their cell phones. Kayla shook her head, annoyance furrowing her brow.

"Everything okay?" Philip questioned, noting the change in her demeanor.

She rolled her eyes skyward, gesturing toward the teen brigade with her head. She shouted, her stern tone grabbing their attention. "Gentlemen! What are we doing?"

A tall, lanky young man with aqua blue eyes who hadn't yet grown comfortable with his height jumped from the fence. One of his cohorts followed, a short and stocky kid who was biting nervously on his fingernails.

"Sorry, Miss Kayla!"

"Y'all didn't have school today?"

"We got out early," the tallest answered, "and Mr. Colton said we could come get in some hours for extra credit."

"Well, Dillon, I'm sure Mr. Colton meant for you to earn that extra credit doing some work, not playing on your cell phones."

"You were busy," Dillon responded. "We didn't want to bother you."

"I was not that busy," Kayla said with a shake of her head. "Those stalls need to be mucked. Let's get to work, please."

Philip was still sitting atop the horse, the students pausing to stare up at him.

"Are you on that television show they're filming?" one kid questioned.

"I am," Philip answered.

"Hard to win if you can't ride a horse," the other kid muttered under his breath before sticking a finger back between his teeth.

"Don't be rude, Ethan," Kayla admonished. "Mr. Rees can ride. Now, get to work, please."

"That other guy could ride, too, and look what happened to him!" Ethan murmured.

Philips slid down as the teens all pocketed their cell phones and headed inside the stables. "Friends of yours?" he asked.

Kayla chuckled. "Students from the high school. We mentor them through their school's 4-H program. They're great kids, but if you aren't firm with them, they'll run all over you. And those darn cell phones drive me to distraction! They can't go five minutes without checking their messages, or their tweet feed or whatever it is they say they can't live without."

"Some of us adults are just as bad. We have a few contestants going through serious withdrawals not being able to access their cell phones."

"You're not one of them, are you?" Kayla questioned.

Philip shook his head. "No, ma'am!"

Kayla grinned. "Don't ma'am me. I'm not that old."

Philip held up his hands as if he were surrendering. He smiled back. "I know, but you're tough as nails and I don't want to get on your bad side."

"Then you need to get back on that horse so we can work on your technique."

"Yes, ma'am!"

An hour later, she applauded Philip's efforts. He had taken the horse through its paces, or rather the horse had worked him, but either way, Philip felt more confident about his ability to control the large animal and extremely comfortable sitting in the saddle and maneuvering the two of them from place to place. As he jumped down off Bubbles, Kayla moved to his side.

"Nice job, Philip. You should be very proud of yourself," she said.

"Thank you. I couldn't have done it without you. Naomi said you were the best." A flutter of energy flickered through his midsection as he revisited his early encounter with the stunning woman. He hoped to see her again soon. Kayla speaking pulled him back to their conversation.

"That's true," she responded, her expression smug. "I am good at what I do! Thank goodness you're a good student or you might have ruined my perfect record. Then I would have had to bury you on this ranch and report you missing."

"Now I'm really scared," Philip joked.

Just then, Philip noticed a man he'd seen earlier on

the ranch standing there and watching them, his expression tinged a dark shade of unhappy.

"Hey, Jasper!" Kayla nodded at him, a bright smile pulling across her face.

The man named Jasper ignored her greeting and demanded curtly, "What's going on here?" His gaze shifting from Philip to Kayla and back. He stiffened his shoulders, seeming to pull himself taller. "What's he doing here?"

Kayla's eyes narrowed ever so slightly. "I was just helping Philip get comfortable with the horses."

"Philip?" Jasper's brow lifted, his eyes skating from the top of the other man's head down to his toes. "You're with the production company, aren't you?"

"I'm one of the contestants," Philip answered. "And you are?"

"Jasper Colton. I co-own Gemini Ranch."

Philip nodded. "Well, Kayla's been wonderful. She's an excellent instructor."

Jasper didn't bother to answer. Instead, he turned toward the woman abruptly. "You have other things to do. If the contestants need help, I'll help them."

Philip turned his own gaze back toward Kayla. She visibly bristled, a wave of emotion washing over her expression. "Did I miss something?" she asked.

"No," Jasper snapped. "I just don't want you distracted from your responsibilities."

The young woman took a deep breath as both hands clutched the sides of her waist. She blew the air out slowly as she chose her words carefully. "Jasper Colton, you know darn well I would never allow anything to interfere with my responsibilities here on the ranch."

"That's not…" he started.

She held up her index finger, stalling his comment. "And I take offense at you implying that I would."

Jasper's mood seemed to change, his attitude doing a one-eighty. "Kayla, I didn't mean…"

She shook her finger a second time. "I'm not done. Now, your sister requested I be here to help Philip and any of the other contestants who wanted help. That was also one of my responsibilities for today."

Jasper tossed his hands up. "Naomi doesn't give orders around here!"

"Naomi didn't make the request. Aubrey did."

Eyes wide, Jasper stammered. "Aubrey? Why…what does… Aubrey?"

Kayla shook her head. Attitude painted her expression like bad makeup. "I suggest you ask your twin. I was only following directions," she snapped back.

She gave Jasper her back as she turned to face Philip. She smiled sweetly. "Just remember to relax and you'll be fine. You're actually a natural and the horse likes you. And if you need any additional help, I'm here. I can answer any questions or give you pointers if you need them."

Philip nodded, acutely aware that Jasper Colton was shooting daggers in his direction. "Thank you. I appreciate that!"

A familiar voice suddenly called out from the barn door. "Hello!"

Philip smiled as Naomi moved to where they were

all standing. Jasper was still trying to decide what to do or say and Kayla had moved on, heading in the opposite direction.

"How'd he do?" Naomi questioned.

Kayla tossed a look over her shoulder. "Really well. He'll be able to hold his own with no problems."

"Thank you. Hannah is the only other contestant who's not comfortable being on a horse. She was supposed to come see you, too, but I think she got cold feet. She's scared of horses. She had hoped to use this experience to overcome that fear."

"If it'll help, I'll try to find her and ease her mind."

Naomi clutched her chest. "Do you mind? I would really appreciate it."

"It's not a problem." Kayla tossed another look over her shoulder. Jasper was still staring at her, and she suddenly seemed on edge again. She shook her head.

Naomi frowned. "Is everything okay?"

"Your brother's just an ass," Kayla said bluntly. She waved a dismissive hand. "It's nothing. I'm just being sensitive."

"No. He can sometimes be an ass."

"I shouldn't have said that. I apologize."

"No apology necessary," Naomi said. "But if you need to talk to someone, just find me."

The two women hugged and Kayla made her exit. Naomi moved to where the two men were standing. She gave Philip a quick smile before focusing on her brother.

"What did you do to Kayla?"

"I didn't do anything. Why? What did she say?"

"She said you were an ass."

Jasper flinched. "I need to go apologize," he said. He tossed Philip one last glare and then he hurried after the other woman.

"What was that all about?" Naomi asked, meeting Philip's gaze.

"I think your brother likes her."

"Jasper likes Kayla?"

Philip shrugged. "I think he's got it bad for her."

Naomi laughed. "Kayla's always been like one of the guys. Besides, she's intelligent and way out of his league."

"Ouch! You don't mince words, do you?"

"I'm direct and to the point."

"And what's your type?" Philip asked, changing the subject. "I did tell you mine."

"No, you didn't! And you need to stop flirting with me. It's unprofessional."

Philip laughed. "Who's flirting with who?"

"I have *not* flirted with you."

"Yes, you did, and you tried to take me for a roll in the hay on our first date."

"Ha ha. You have jokes. That was so not funny. I can't *date* you, you know that."

Naomi eyed him from head to toe and back as Philip took a step forward, closing the distance between them. Something decadent danced between them, slowly building to something neither expected. It teased their sensibilities and left them wondering a lengthy list of what-ifs. A wisp of hair had fallen in her face, and he eased it out of her eye with the pad of his index finger. He dragged it slowly behind her ear, gently caressing the side of her face. She felt herself shiver beneath his fingertips.

Naomi gasped, his touch throwing her off and leaving her discombobulated. She shook her head. She took a big step backward, needing to put some distance between them. "You need to head back to the main building. We have to film your bio and get some candid shots of you."

Philip nodded. "Are you going to walk me there?"

"You're a big boy. I'm sure you can find your way without me."

He smiled. "I can. But I'd much rather sneak in a few extra minutes with you. Learn something new about you that you haven't told me yet."

Naomi slowly backed her way toward the barn door. "I'd invite you to tag along but you're going to need those few extra minutes finding someone who can help you put your horse up," she said smugly.

PHILIP WATCHED AS she made her exit, leaving him standing alone. It was then that he noticed the boys from earlier, eyeing him intently. He shook his head.

"Dude, I think she shot you down," Dillon said.

His friends nodded in agreement.

"Women can be vicious," Philip said as he began to undo the saddle.

"That's why I stick to video games," Ethan added.

Philip laughed. "You might be on to something there."

There was a moment of pause as he stripped the equipment off the large animal, the boys giving him points. "Hey," he said, after Bubbles was back in his stall and chomping on hay. "Can I ask you guys something?"

Dillon shrugged. "Sure! What's up?"

"Tell me about the other guy who could ride. What happened to him?"

THINGS WERE BACK on track and Naomi could not have been happier. The morning had gone well and the afternoon even better. She stood with Jude, the show's director, as they both watched the captured shots of the players on the monitors.

The second competition had started with Grace and Melissa accepting their advantage and being named team leaders. Then each selected five players. Naomi wasn't surprised when Grace's first pick was Philip. Melissa chose Brad. Grace added Harold the mechanic, Malia the pilot, Constantine the plastic surgeon, and Fred the truck driver. The others joined Melissa's team and then the games were on.

Moving the contestants down to an empty pasture that had been configured for their next task, Jim was like a kid on the playground. He had them laughing and wound up with excitement. He sometimes came in handy, Naomi thought. But like she knew he would, he couldn't wait to call the production company to tell them what had happened with the fire and to criticize how she had handled the situation. Luckily her message had been the first thing they'd read that morning. Him adding to that had not fallen in his favor. Now he was trying to redeem himself.

Identical metal enclosures had been set up in the middle of the pasture. Ranch hands would be helping to steer cattle toward them. Most of the players were comfortable atop a horse and would be partnered with someone from the ranch with more experience to guide them. As a team, the contestants had to repair and re-hang a new gate on the enclosure and ensure none of the cattle could escape. What they didn't know was that one side had not been secured and needed to be shored up before the cattle arrived. But they had been told to ensure their enclosure was secure. Once that was completed, they had to unload twenty-five bales of hay and load food bins with bags of feed. The work would be physical and strenuous and would test them in ways few imagined.

Philip took a leadership position right from the start. He and the beauty queen seemed to be working nicely together, Naomi thought as she watched them huddle with the rest of the team and then begin to delegate tasks. Grace kept looking to him with doe eyes that played well on the screen. Naomi could already imagine social media going wild as they pondered the connection between the two. At one point, Philip reached out and wrapped an arm around Grace's shoulders. The gesture was friendly and supportive, but for some reason it hit Naomi the wrong way. Something that felt like jealousy punched her in the gut and the intensity of it surprised her. She struggled to not let it show on her face, fighting to keep her expression devoid of any emotion.

From the onset of the contest, it was clear that the team that had nicknamed themselves Beauties and the

Beasts were in a league of their own. Steps ahead of the group dubbed The Winning Pack, they took the win easily, their time from start to finish some twenty-six minutes faster. The players breathed a sigh of relief when they discovered there would be no elimination. Not this round. With their celebratory hugs and cheers in the proverbial film can, Naomi didn't bother to comment on the hug that Grace had given Philip. Jim, however, felt it necessary to add his commentary.

"Looks like we might have a romance brewing," he said.

"Excuse me?" Naomi responded, pretending not to know who or what he was talking about.

"Your guy Philip and the beauty queen," he said, gesturing toward the duo with his head. "They're getting very friendly with one another. We might want to play on that story line."

"We're not filming a dating show, Jim. Let's just stay focused on the contests and the Wild West aspect of their interactions here at the ranch."

"And let's be bored to death," Jim concluded. "You know better than anyone that we need to spice it up for the ratings. If those two give us the spice, then we need to capitalize on it."

Naomi bit back her response, needing to choose her words carefully. But before she could answer, a blood-curdling scream rang through the late-afternoon air. She and Jim turned at the same time, searching out what was going on.

The herd had broken through an opening in the enclosure. Hannah had been standing alone on the other side of the fencing. As the cattle bolted free and the gate swung open, slamming into her, she was trapped, the massive animals stampeding past her.

Naomi felt her heart stop, blood rushing to her head as her mind began to race. Then she took off running. "Get the paramedics up here," she shouted. "Now!"

SOMETHING DIDN'T FEEL right after today's events, Philip thought. He sat inside his new tent. The others had begun to gather outside, the beginnings of a fire starting to crackle beneath the night air. He would join them, but he needed a few minutes to gather his thoughts.

Hannah had been eliminated from the competition. She had been ready to leave even before the accident. It hadn't been the experience of a lifetime that she'd been hoping for. Thankfully, she had only suffered a few minor bumps and bruises after being brushed by the stampeding cattle, but the moment had scared her. She was done even before their illustrious host had proclaimed her no longer in the saddle. Hannah hadn't given a rat's ass about that saddle, and as she'd departed, she had no problems letting them all know.

He'd been certain the gate to the enclosure was secured before they started unloading the heavy hay bales from the truck. He and Fred had both checked each panel carefully, discovering the one loose side that had been left to throw a wrench in the competition. He would have bet his own life on that. The other team had missed theirs, eating up valuable time regathering their cattle before they could move on to the hay and feed.

Philip couldn't be certain, but there was no way that

panel had come loose without some human intervention. Someone had purposely loosened that gate. And now he was left wondering who had done it and why.

Chapter Eight

Brad was telling the story about one of his many exploits where he'd bested someone who lacked his intellectual acumen and abilities. Someone who didn't have his financial resources, or his wit and charm. He apparently fancied himself quite the people person. He was animated, his arms waving about as he jumped to his feet to make a point. Someone laughed, which seemed to further fuel his mood.

For the briefest moment Philip considered challenging him, aware that an argument would ensue, and then he changed his mind. Knowing what to expect, he was already weary of the conversation. He took an empty seat in the circle, extending his legs out in front of him. It was warmer than normal and the heat from the flames only added to the discomfort, but Grace and company were toasting marshmallows and making s'mores. Someone handed him an ice-cold bottle of beer, and though he wasn't a big drinker, the brew hit the spot after their long day.

"We were talking about Hannah before you got here," Brad said. "I was saying that this is how the game works. You eliminate the weak right off the bat to level the playing field. Then the smarter players will cut the stronger players down at the knees. That's when the real cream of the crop rises to the top."

"He said he expected you to go down in the third or fourth round," Fred said, giving Philip a side-eye. "Me, too."

Brad nodded. "Everyone knows you two are strong. They can't beat you with brute strength, so it only makes sense to shut you down sooner than later. You two would definitely be considered a threat."

"And where do you stand in the mix?" Philip asked.

Brad chuckled. "I plan to be the guy standing alone at the end, wearing the crown and winning the hundred thousand dollars."

Grace rolled her eyes skyward. "It's a saddle and you're supposed to be sitting in it. Or didn't you read the memo?"

The circle laughed. Even Brad chuckled, oblivious to the woman's disdain for him. She gave Philip a look and he winked an eye at her, giving her the slightest salute with his can of beer.

"What do you think they have planned for us tomorrow?" Harold asked.

"Something easy, I hope. I hurt!" Josiah the entrepreneur interjected.

"I do, too," Constantine the plastic surgeon added. "Which is why I'm going to say good-night. This has been fun, but I need some rest."

"That's a good idea," Philip said. He stretched his arms up and over his head.

"Really?" Brad said. "How soft are you?"

"I'm soft, soft," Philip quipped. "Should make it easy for you to take me out and send me home."

Brad laughed. "You should be so lucky."

"So should you." Philip chuckled as he took another swig of his beverage. "So should you."

Grace stood. "I'm going to say good-night, too. Y'all try not to burn anything down this time, please!"

"Don't you worry about that, pretty lady," Fred said. "I'll double-check it tonight, for sure."

As she eased past Philip she leaned to whisper in his ear. "If you need *anything*, anything at all, you know where to find me." She let her cheek brush gently against his as she pulled herself upright and headed toward her tent. She tossed him one last look over her shoulder.

Philip lifted the bottle of beer to his lips and downed the last of it. He didn't miss the other men staring at him, amusement dancing across their faces. He shook his head and chuckled softly.

"Dude, that woman wants you! She wants you bad!" Stefan the college student exclaimed. He gave Brad a fist bump, the two grinning like Cheshire cats.

Philip shook his head, not bothering to comment.

Fred interjected, "When you boys grow up, you'll learn that waiting for the right woman means more than settling for just any woman."

Philip smiled. "How long have you and your wife been together, Fred?"

"Twenty-seven years!" the man said proudly.

"Are you saying that you would turn that down if

presented with the opportunity?" Brad asked. He folded his arms over his chest, his hands tucked beneath his armpits.

"I would," Fred answered. "I don't need that. I have the best woman in the whole wide world."

Brad pointed a finger at Philip. "Well, *he* doesn't have a woman, so why shouldn't he see where it goes?"

Philip smiled. He suddenly thought about Naomi and the emotion that was brewing between them. There was something special there. Something he hadn't known he needed. In that moment he knew that when he was able, he planned to explore it to its fullest. Brad's curiosity had his head spinning, throwing him squarely into his own feelings. He took a breath, blowing it out slowly before he spoke. "Actually, I'm in a new relationship and since I'd like to see where it can go, I'll have to take a hard pass."

"How new is new?" Brad questioned.

He shrugged. "We only met recently, so it's very new. But I don't plan to start it off sleeping with some other woman. What kind of man would that make me?"

"A smart one!" Brad quipped. He laughed and the twentysomethings in the group laughed with him.

"I don't like you," Malia the pilot said, staring at Brad intently.

Brad shrugged. "Just like a woman! You want to be one of the guys and then get your bras twisted in a knot when you don't like our jokes."

Philip bristled, not liking that Brad had lumped all men into his warped thinking. Philip the detective would have spoken up. Philip the handyman turned contestant bit back a response.

Malia rolled her eyes skyward. "On that note, I'm going to say good-night," she said rising from her seat. She tossed a look at Philip and Fred. "Thank goodness there are still good men like you two out here."

Fred laughed and Philip winked an eye at the pilot. Brad snarled.

"I think I'm going to head to bed, too," Philip said. "I'm sure tomorrow's going to be a long day."

"I'm sure you're right. I think I'm going to head there myself," Fred responded. "Rest well, bro!"

Philip tossed Brad one last look. The man had reached for another beer, tossing it back in one large gulp. Something about him was suddenly off, Philip thought. Brad seemed nervous for no good reason. As Philip reached his tent, glancing around one last time, Brad rose from his seat, then headed in the direction of the latrines. Philip watched as he disappeared in the darkness, the faintest sliver of moonlight casting shadows across the sky. He stood as still as stone and moments later he didn't miss the glow from a small flashlight headed across the fields toward the tree line.

NAOMI STARTED EACH morning watching the raw, unedited footage shot the previous day. The dailies were lengthy and sometimes boring, but they allowed her to assess the performances, aesthetics and cinematography. It gave her direction for what they would need to capture for continuity, to ensure they had a great show when the film was finally edited. With the tight budget and short schedule, they needed to be as precise as they could be.

There were cameras placed all around the ranch wherever the contestants might congregate. Although they knew the cameras existed, it took no time at all for most of them to forget and stop *performing*. To be as authentic as they could possibly be. Naomi had watched the footage from the previous evening multiple times, rewinding it over and over again. The first time had left her in her feelings as she watched the beauty queen practically throw herself at Philip, whispering something dirty in his ear. Okay, Naomi thought, maybe it wasn't dirty. Maybe it was an invitation of an adult variety. Whatever it was, her leaning into him, pressing her face against his, didn't sit well with Naomi. It didn't sit well with her at all.

Philip's response to Grace had left her curious. He hadn't shown an ounce of emotion, seeming to ignore the transgression. It also left her at ease, knowing he hadn't taken the bait. The men had found their interaction entertaining but it did nothing but annoy Naomi. She rewound the tape yet again, watching for that moment when Philip had dismissed the beauty, his disinterest written on his face. If they had been filming a dating show, that look would have been pure television gold. At the moment, though, that whole scene was a source of irritation and not how she had hoped to start her new day.

They would be filming most of the morning and all afternoon. It meant Naomi would have to spend far too much time trying to keep a tight rein on Monty, who seemed to be devolving each time he was on camera. Their illustrious host bored easily, drank frequently, and rumors about him being a total diva were proving to be true. His tantrums had become fodder for one joke too many, but he was the least of her problems.

The day's challenge was a Wild West relay race. It involved a lot of moving parts that couldn't be controlled by the producers. Outcomes would solely be determined by brawn and brains, and there would be a double elimination, with two persons from the losing team heading home when it was over.

They had planned five activities for the relay race. The contestants would have to prove themselves on basic skills necessary to work on a ranch. Each team would pick one person per task to complete for their team. They would be judged on their speed on horseback, strength to haul hay, the smarts to fix a flat tire, determination to catch a calf, and the ability to then lift that calf up and run with it. It would be a timed event and who they designated to do what task could make or break a team.

"We have a problem!" Felicia came to Naomi, pulling her from her thoughts. "Actually, we have two problems."

Naomi shook her head. That was the last thing she wanted to hear. "What now?" she asked.

Felicia wrung her hands together, nervousness blanketing her expression. "Your brother needs you to come to the barn. He says there is something wrong with the calves."

Naomi gasped. "What could possibly be wrong?"

"He said the vet is on his way but it's not likely you'll be able to use them today."

"I need them!" Naomi snapped.

The young woman shrugged, obviously not sure how to respond.

Naomi pressed her face into the palms of her hands and took a deep breath. She looked back up, meeting her assistant's stare. "I'm sorry. I didn't mean to snap at you."

Felicia nodded. "It's okay, I understand. Jim says you've been under a lot of stress."

"Jim said that?"

She nodded again. "I think he's worried about you."

"I just bet he is," Naomi mumbled under her breath. She bit back what she wanted to say, containing the rise of emotion that threatened to have her ranting like a mad woman. Because she knew Jim was not concerned about her well-being. "Where is my brother?" she asked instead.

"Down at the barn."

"At the barn. You did say that, didn't you?" She paused. "And what's the second problem?"

"Constantine has pulled out of the competition. He's afraid of injuring his hands and doesn't want to risk it. So you now have ten contestants left. Not eleven."

"Well, at least we can make that problem work in our favor." Naomi hurried out the door and raced toward the barn.

A crowd had gathered in the barn, Gemini ranch hands and the film crew and cast all looking somber. A few were teary and her brother looked like he might cry. Or explode. Or both. He stood with his hands on his hips and his shoulders slumped forward as if the weight of the world had landed on his shoulders.

The man who Naomi assumed was the vet squatted above one of the animals, his left hand stroking the little creature gently. He held a syringe in his right hand and slowly injected something into the baby animal's neck.

She eased to Jasper's side. "What happened?" she asked, her voice dropping an octave.

"The vet thinks they got into something toxic."

"Toxic?"

"Something poisoned them. They're dying. We have to put them down to keep them from suffering."

Naomi's eyes widened. She suddenly thought of Aubrey and how much her sister loved their animals. Remembering how she and Luca had saved a calf as they'd gotten to know one another. Naomi couldn't begin to fathom how such a thing could have happened. She shook her head. "How many?"

Jasper pointed to a far corner. Six young cows lay postmortem. Tears suddenly misted her eyes, pressing hot against her lashes. It took everything in her not to burst out sobbing. The hurt seemed unfathomable, and all she wished was that she could have prevented their suffering. She wrapped her arms around her brother's waist and hugged him, pressing her face to his chest. Jasper hugged her back.

"How could this have happened?" she questioned, her voice a loud whisper.

"The vet seems to think it might have been toadstools in the fields where they graze. He'll do an autopsy to make sure."

"Don't they instinctively know not to eat certain grasses or mushrooms?"

The vet had moved to where the two stood and answered the question for her. "In general, we don't think livestock will actively seek out and eat toxic mushrooms, but we don't really know much about the palatability of each species. Obviously, we eat mushrooms that are not toxic, and we know they can be delicious. They could very well just have been in the dense grass where the animals were grazing and been consumed as they were feeding. It could have been in their feeding hay or baleage on a field. We may never know for sure."

Naomi's eyes narrowed. "What's baleage?" she asked.

"It's grass that's been baled and wrapped soon after cutting. It minimizes the risk of loss, should it rain," Jasper answered.

The vet nodded. "It's very possible some fungus pieces were growing up through the vegetation and were consumed as the animals ate the hay. How close to the edge of the pasture do you allow them to go? If they went exploring near your tree line at the edge of the pasture, or under some trees, they could have found them there, especially if they were curious or hungry. Unfortunately, there are a lot of potential scenarios, and we may never know."

Jasper nodded. "I appreciate you coming out, Dr. Phelps."

The two men shook hands. "Keep your eyes on the

rest of the herd," the veterinarian concluded. "What's unusual is that so many of them would get sick at the same time. Usually one, maybe two, but not more. Just call if you need me to check on any of them."

Naomi wrapped her arms around her torso, hugging herself tightly. She watched as Jasper walked Dr. Phelps out of the barn. He and a team of ranch hands returned minutes later, moving swiftly to gather up the dead cattle for burial. She suddenly felt lost, not sure what she should do next as she struggled to focus. This was not supposed to happen, and she felt responsible, like she'd purposely dropped bad luck down upon her family and the ranch. She heaved a deep sigh as she moved back to her brother.

Jasper spoke before she could say anything. "I only have one calf left and he's too small for your competition. I can probably borrow a few, but I can't make that happen until tomorrow and it might cost you."

"Don't worry about that right now," Naomi responded. "We'll figure it out. Is there anything I can do to help you?"

Jasper shook his head. He was staring across the way, his eyes locked on Kayla, who'd just arrived with Aubrey to assess the damage. The two women stood in conversation, visibly distressed.

"I need to go update them," Jasper said, gesturing in their direction with his head.

"Tell Aubrey I'll call her later," Naomi said as her brother moved away.

With one last glance, Naomi turned in the other direction and walked out the barn, heading back toward the office. Outside, she found Philip waiting for her. She was surprised. Under different circumstances she would have been pleased. In the moment, though, she couldn't have cared less.

"Are you okay?" he asked.

"No," she said firmly. "I'm not okay. Not at all."

"Do you want to talk about it?"

"None of this makes any sense."

Philip nodded. "I agree. I think someone's trying to sabotage you."

"Excuse me?" Her head snapped as she turned to stare at him.

"Sabotage. Someone is making these accidents happen on purpose."

Her eyes widened. "What makes you say that?"

"First, you lose a contestant who falls off a horse because his saddle girth wasn't tightened properly. From what I heard he was an experienced horseman, so that doesn't sound like a mistake he'd make. Then the tents catch on fire, but the fire starts in the back, away from the firepit. How'd that happen? Another contestant gets mowed down by cattle because a fence that had been hinged and closed was suddenly not hinged. Now the calves you needed just drop dead for no apparent reason. It's just too convenient and too many accidents to be random." Philip shrugged his broad shoulders.

She continued to walk, with him beside her. Thoughts were spinning in her head faster than she could catch them. Questions firing one after the other, searching out answers she didn't have.

Who would want to do this? Was it possible someone on her production crew had it out for her? Could it be Jim, and was he that evil? What about her family? Was it a vendetta against the Colton name for her father's sins? Or a disgruntled employee who'd butted heads with her brother Jasper? The list was potentially longer than Naomi could begin to fathom.

"You haven't mentioned this theory to anyone else, have you?" she asked.

Philip shook his head. "No. No one, but I think you need to contact the authorities and ask them to investigate."

"Thanks for your opinion, but I don't need anyone panicking. I'd appreciate it if you kept this to yourself."

"What do you plan to do?" he asked.

"I don't know yet."

"If I can help…" he started.

Naomi shook her head. "Just keep this to yourself, please. That's all the help I need for now." She didn't bother to add that she worried about putting him or the others at risk. Not knowing who was gunning for her, she didn't know how far they were willing to go. She was scared but she didn't want him to know that, determined to keep up a brave face. She gave him a faint smile.

Philip suddenly reached for her hand, entwining his fingers between hers. His palm kissed her palm gently as they came to a stop. "I can help if you let me, Naomi. I…" he hesitated, suddenly seeming to consider what he should, and could, say. He stammered. "I…well…it's…"

Naomi snatched her hand from his, the gesture abrupt. His touch had burned, heat rippling with unexpected pleasure deep in her core. It surprised her, the intensity so unexpected that she wasn't sure how to handle it. Or him. "Sorry," she muttered. "I'm just…well…"

PHILIP NODDED HIS UNDERSTANDING. He too hadn't expected the sensations that had come over him as his whole body flooded with emotion. He was feeling protective of this woman, needing to ensure her safety when he wasn't really sure who he needed to keep her safe from.

He had played everything over in his head more times than he cared to count. He knew Brad was up to something and he still didn't know what that was. But Brad was trying to trade secrets, he reasoned. Brad had no reason he knew of to bring down a reality television show. He had nothing to gain and no connection to the Colton family that Philip was aware of. These accidents felt personal, intended to hurt Naomi or her siblings directly. The list of things he didn't know was twice that of what he did know. But what he was certain of was his determination to protect Naomi.

He didn't have the words to say that to her and so he said nothing. They returned to walking side by side until they reached the door of the small cabin.

"I'll meet everyone down by the tents in thirty minutes," she said. "If you can help pull them all together, I'd appreciate it."

"I'll go round up as many of them up as I can," Philip said softly. "I'll see you then."

Naomi watched as he turned, moving to walk away. She suddenly called his name and took a step toward him.

"Yes?" Philip's gaze skated slowly over her face, noting the tension that pulled the muscles tight. There was a twitch along her right eye and he suddenly wanted to pull her into arms and hold her until she could relax and be well.

"Thank you," she said, giving him the slightest smile.

Philip's heart skipped a beat and then a second. He returned the gesture, then turned, hurrying off in the opposite direction.

Chapter Nine

"We're going to shut down production until tomorrow morning at eight," Naomi said, issuing instructions to her crew later that afternoon. Since her earlier encounter with Philip, she'd had much to think about. His concern for her had been refreshing, but it had put her in a mood, leaving her feeling out-of-sorts. He'd been kind and considerate and then he'd touched her, the gesture meant to be comforting. Instead, it had left her raging with desire. Desire she had no business feeling and she couldn't follow through with. She shook the thought and continued, "Let's get everything ready for the next competition so we can go without any interruptions. Plan on tomorrow being a full day of filming."

"What about the calves?" Jim questioned. "Can we proceed without them?"

Naomi nodded. "I have another idea. I just need Jasper to confirm we can do it. He should be texting me in a few minutes. If not, we'll wait for him to find us new calves and save it for another day. Then we'll just add it to another contest."

"I think we should shut down production until…" Jim started.

"And shutting down production longer than a day is not an option. We're going to finish this show on time and under budget and I'd appreciate you trying to help rather than interfere with me doing that."

Jim bristled. "I was trying to help you. Maybe if you took advice from those of us who might know some things, you wouldn't have these problems."

Naomi gave the man her sweetest smile. "I do appreciate your help, Jim. I really do, but there are times your advice feels anything but helpful. And I say that with the utmost respect."

He stood staring at her, pondering her comment. "Whatever," Jim muttered. He crossed his arms, his thin lips pushed out in a pout.

"Jim, I really need you to cut me some slack. I understand you're frustrated. We all are. But if you would just trust me, I promise we can make this work."

He shrugged. "I'll go put the rest of the crew on notice," he finally said.

"And I'll go talk to the contestants." Naomi nodded her head.

He was still muttering under his breath when he made his exit. Naomi rolled her eyes skyward, trying not to let her frustration with the man show.

Jude and his wife moved to where she stood. "How can we help?" Janice asked. "You know we've got your back. Whatever you need, just ask."

"I do need a favor," Naomi said. "I need to figure out how we can tighten the budget. Can you two revisit the

shooting schedule and see if we have any wiggle room
to make up for the time we lost today?"

Jude nodded. "I think we can actually cut some time
from the schedule toward the end. Once you get down
to your last four contestants, we do all-day shoots, and
weed them out faster, maybe two persons per day instead of the one originally planned. If we can make it
work, we might be able to shave two, maybe three days
off that last week."

Naomi nodded. "If you two can get with Felicia and
give me a revised proposal with the new numbers and
an updated call schedule, I would really appreciate it."

"We got you," Janice said.

"I'll be back to help as soon as I finish with the contestants," Naomi said as she headed toward the door.
She felt a hint of excitement rise with her tone. "Let's
get to work," she said eagerly. "We can still make this
work!"

And Naomi earnestly believed that. She believed if
she put her head down and pushed forward everything
would fall into place as she had initially planned. Despite her concerns for her team and the contestants, she
believed that as long as she paid attention to every detail, she could keep them all from harm. She had let her
guard down, trusting others to do their jobs and have
her back. Now she feared that trust may have been mis-
placed. But she was determined to focus on the positive.
Naomi refused to be bested by some coward playing
with her livelihood. Walking to the contestant tents,
Naomi used the time to reflect on Philip's suggestion.
He had verbalized what she'd been thinking and hadn't

wanted to say out loud. What she hadn't wanted to believe about anyone in the cast or the crew. But how had he put it all together, and why was he even thinking about it? Something about Philip's concern and desire to help just didn't feel right. Or maybe it felt too right and necessary, a man stepping up to be her superhero. Again, Naomi was looking for things to worry about that weren't there. After all, Philip had experience that might give him insights that others didn't have. Or not. Who was he, really? Now Naomi had questions whose answers she didn't know where to even begin to look for.

They were all seated around in a circle when she arrived. Grace and Malia both still appeared distraught, sitting side by side comforting each other. Philip leaned against a tall pine tree, his arms crossed over his chest. His eyes skated back and forth as if he were trying to read the situation. He smiled at her as she stepped into the midst of their group. She didn't smile back, her expression stoic. In that moment, as everyone quieted down, waiting for her to speak, she couldn't get something the man had said out of her head. Her eyes moved from the firepit to the tents to that pine tree and back. Jim had proclaimed negligence responsible, saying one of them hadn't put out the flames properly. So why hadn't that tree or the pine straw that littered the ground ignited first? Both were closer to the pit than the tents. Philip had insisted the inferno had started in the rear of the tents, making it highly unlikely for a burning ember from the pit to jump that far. But how was he so certain? Even if she could concede that one fact, the rest of it still didn't make any sense to her.

She stared at him briefly and he gave her the slightest nod of understanding. Then her gaze shifted over the faces of the remaining contestants, her mind racing. Wondering if any one of them could be trying to take down her show.

"So, WHAT ARE we supposed to do for the rest of the day?" Stefan questioned.

"What you do every day," Melissa answered. "Absolutely nothing."

Philip shook his head. Naomi had given them a pep talk before heading back to her office to do whatever it was she needed to do. She had told them to be prepared for a few long days starting early the following morning. She had also told them to practice those skills they'd been taught and felt needed to be strengthened. And she'd advised them to get some rest because things weren't going to be easy for them going forward. It was what she hadn't said that had given him pause.

Philip sensed Naomi was on edge. She was desperate to hide it from everyone but there was no missing the nervous energy that laid heavy on her shoulders. He felt it in a way that surprised him, his empathy all encompassing. It took every ounce of his fortitude not to rush to her side, wanting to keep her safe.

"I don't know what everybody's all up in arms about," Brad said. "I don't know why we just can't have veal chops for dinner." He shrugged his shoulders dismissively, his expression blank.

A collective groan rang through the air.

"That was really bad, dude," Fred said.

"Too early?" Brad asked.

"Way too early," Grace responded. "You are such a…aargh!"

"What?" the man said, throwing up his hands.

"You're an ass," Philip interjected. "Try to show some compassion."

"You all are too sensitive. Just quit now so I can collect my winnings and get the hell out of here." He stood, storming off toward the barns.

"Where did they find that guy?" Malia questioned.

"He crawled out from under a rock," Grace said.

"And we all wish he'd crawl back to wherever he came from," Harold answered.

Nervous laughter eased the tension that had sprung up like spring flowers. Conversation continued for another few minutes, everyone questioning what had happened to the animals and how the event might impact the show or if it would have any effect at all. Philip listened, not offering a lot of information. Much like he'd witnessed Naomi do, he watched each of them closely, looking for a gesture, a facial expression, anything that might hint at wrongdoing. He also made a mental note to follow up on Brad's doings. His cavalier attitude was suspect, and Philip wondered if he might be causing the sabotage to distract from his own misdeeds. Thus far, he had only come across as a guy determined to win a game by any means necessary. "Any means" being the key phrase.

Grace eased her way to Philip's side. She pressed a manicured hand to his chest, fresh polish on each nail.

He tapped her fingers. "Someone's been busy."

"Those cameras are not going to catch me looking like death warmed over. I have an image to maintain!" She smiled. "And a man I hope to impress." Her expression was coy as her voice dropped to a whisper. She batted her eyelashes at him as she continued. "So, what are your plans for the rest of the day?"

"I think I'm going to go spend some time with my horse. Get some riding practice in."

"I'd offer to join you, but I can think of far better things to do with my time. When you're done, though, if you want some company, I'll be in my tent. Alone." She winked at him.

Philip tensed as she dragged those nails down his chest toward the waistband of his denim jeans. She tugged on his belt buckle, the provocative gesture meant to be an invitation of sorts. He smiled and nodded as he took a step back from her touch. "I'll keep that in mind," he replied firmly.

"Please do," Grace said, her voice dropping to a seductive tone.

As she walked away, Philip glanced toward the camera that had captured that entire moment. A million things went through his head but mostly he wished he could be there to explain it when Naomi would inevitably watch, not wanting her to get the wrong impression about him and the beauty queen. What Naomi thought was suddenly important to him, and he couldn't begin to explain why if his life depended on it.

THE DAY HAD been longer than Naomi had anticipated but it had also been productive. Despite the roadblocks, she felt as if things were still on track. They had a revised game plan, a new schedule, and were still on target to shave a few dollars off the budget. She was grateful for Jude and Janice, both of whom had come through in a big way. Their friendship meant the world to her, most especially since she knew she could never fully compensate them for their efforts.

She dialed Aubrey's cell phone number.

Aubrey answered on the third ring. "Hey, are you okay?"

"I could really use that cheap booze right about now," Naomi said.

"I can pour you a glass as soon as you're ready. And Luke made spaghetti!"

"I love him. I should be finished in about an hour, then I'll be on my way!"

"I'll call Rachel and see what she's doing. We'll make a night of it."

"A short night! I have to be up early in the morning."

"Don't we all?" Aubrey laughed.

"I love you, sis!"

"Love you, too! And please don't trip over any cows before you get here."

Naomi laughed as she disconnected the line, slipping her phone into her pants pocket.

Some sixty minutes later, Naomi stepped out of the makeshift office, closing and locking the door behind her. As she started toward Aubrey's home, her cell phone rang. She juggled her keys and a flashlight in one hand as she reached into the back pocket of her denim jeans to wrestle the phone back out. She cursed as she fumbled everything in her hands, her phone falling to the ground.

It took a quick minute to find the device and when she did, she sat down on the top step still feeling like something else could go wrong. She was surprised when she saw the caller ID, answering seconds before her brother hung up on his end.

"Naomi, I was just about to hang up."

"Oliver!" Naomi's excitement to hear her big brother's voice was palpable. Oliver was one of the Colton triplets. A venture capitalist, he was never in any one place for long, always searching out the next company with high growth potential. He hadn't been home since just after Caleb's wedding, and there was no telling when he would next step foot in the state of Colorado again. Most recently he'd been based in Malaysia but that could change on a dime. His visits were like passing storms coming as frequently as a leap year. He blew in on a breeze and blew back out as quickly as he'd arrived, years passing before he would blow in again.

"What took you so long?"

"Sorry, I had to find my phone. Where are you?"

"Paris. I think. Or maybe Madrid."

Naomi laughed. "How do you not know where you are?"

"I'm on my plane and we're in the air, headed to Morocco."

"I definitely feel special about you calling me then."

"You should!" Her brother laughed. "I hear you're filming that show you pitched. How's it going?"

"One or two bumps, but it's coming along." Naomi quickly changed the subject, not wanting to burden her brother with her problems. Determined not to burden any of her siblings unless she was forced to. It wasn't often that they caught up with each other and since he didn't often call to just say hello, she was curious to know what was on his mind. "What's going on with you? Everything's good, right?"

"Everything is good. Business is better and I'm as busy as always. I called because I have a question for you."

"Sure! What's up?"

"What do you know about Malcolm Beckworth?"

Naomi's eyes widened. "Child star Malcolm Beckworth?"

"The one and only. I know he's done a few projects recently, trying to parlay his *Kids' Room* fame into an adult career. I met him recently at the Cannes Film Festival and there's a potential investment opportunity that he would be the face of but there's something about him that's not clicking for me. Do you know him?"

"Not personally, no. And you went to Cannes and didn't invite me?"

"Stay focused, Naomi."

"I'm very focused. It's one of the biggest film festivals in the world. I could have hobnobbed with film royalty. You do remember that's the industry I work in, right?" A hint of annoyance tinged her words. Who knew what could have happened for her career had she

been able to rub elbows with other industry professionals? Professionals who were where she aspired to be one
day. How could her big brother not know and invite her?

Oliver laughed. "It's not that big a deal, Naomi. You
didn't miss much. It was actually a little boring."

"Says you."

"Fine. The next film festival I plan on going to I
promise to call and make sure you're invited to go with
me."

"Pinkie promise?"

Oliver chuckled warmly. "How old are you?"

"Pinkie promise, Oliver."

"Fine! Now, what do you know about Beckworth?"

"Like I said, I don't know him personally, but I have
yet to hear anyone who does know him say anything
favorable. He's got a wicked reputation. Personally, I
do know two women who've accused him of assault
and another who filed a civil suit against him that has
since been settled. They say he has problems keeping
his hands to himself and his pants zipped. Of course,
that's hearsay and I can't confirm it. But I can confirm
that Quentin Tarantino had pegged him for the lead role
in his last movie. Two weeks before filming started,
Beckworth was pulled and replaced after getting too
touchy-feely with his leading lady. Since then, no one
will touch him. His career is going nowhere fast."

"That's what I was afraid of. I appreciate the information. I'm glad I called you."

"And that's how you look out for your siblings. You
don't go to film festivals and *not* take the sister who's

in the business. I bet Ezra and Dominic would have made sure I was there."

"Ezra, maybe. If he can tear himself away from Theresa for ten minutes. I'm not so sure about Dom. He's in love now, too. And he gets dopey when he's in love!"

Naomi giggled. "You might be right. Sami would probably get my invitation from Dom."

"I miss you, kiddo. But I need to run. When are you going back to Los Angeles?"

"Two and a half, maybe three weeks? But it all depends," she muttered.

"Depends? On what?"

She briefly thought about Philip and if there could be something between them after the show was done and finished and their contractual obligations fulfilled. Would she go home, Naomi pondered? Would Philip want her to stay? She took a deep inhale of air before responding. "Just some loose ends I need to tie up before I return to the City of Angels."

"Well, I can't promise but hopefully I'll see you before you go back."

"Send me something good from Marrakesh. That should make up for going to Cannes without me."

Oliver laughed. "I love you, Naomi!"

"Yeah, yeah, yeah."

Laughter rang warmly between the phone lines as they disconnected the call.

Standing, Naomi slid her phone back into her back pocket. She slid the keys into the front pocket. The flashlight was the only thing in her hands. Easing down the short length of steps, she headed across the fields toward Aubrey's home, her heart happy and joy washing over her spirit.

AUBREY'S LOVE, LUKE BISHOP, greeted her at the door. His exuberance was infectious and instantly revived her weary spirit.

"How have you been?" he asked as he closed the door behind them.

"I can't complain, Luke. How about you?"

"Your sister takes excellent care of me. I am a very happy man."

Naomi pretended to gag on her index finger. "*Aaargh.* You two are so nauseating with your happy-happy joy-joy love fest!"

Luke laughed. "We'll have to find you a husband, so you'll know what this feels like."

She shook her head. "I'll pass. I'm good. Unless you've found you have a long-lost brother who is half as sweet as you are, I'm not interested."

"Your sister says there is a man working with you who's caught your eye. How is that going?"

"Aubrey has a big mouth! And it's not going at all. I don't even know why she told you about that man!"

Aubrey chimed in from the doorway. "I tell him everything. Well, almost everything! We don't have secrets. Do we, Luca?" she said, her gaze narrowed as if they shared a secret.

Luke winked at her. "No, *amore.*" he said, as he moved to kiss her cheek.

Naomi groaned. "Someone point me to the spaghetti, please, before I lose my appetite."

Aubrey laughed. "Head to the kitchen. There's a surprise there waiting for you."

Rolling her eyes at the two of them, Naomi turned and moved through the home to the kitchen in the rear. As she stepped into the room her twin sister called her name in greeting.

"Alexa!" Naomi jumped excitedly, rushing toward her twin.

"I didn't think you were ever going to get here," Alexa responded as the two women embraced.

"What are you doing here? Aubrey didn't say anything about you coming."

"I think that's why they call it a surprise."

"It must be a full moon because you suddenly have jokes," Naomi teased.

Alexa laughed. "Well, I wasn't sure I was going to make it. We figured we'd wait until I got here to tell you."

Naomi could feel a wealth of emotion rising in her midsection. How she had missed her family! It never dawned on her just how much she loved being with them until they were back together after an extended period. The way she was feeling, you would never know she had just been home a few weeks back for Caleb's wedding, the time between that visit and this one like a short holiday.

It might only take a day or two of all that togetherness before they were fighting like they were locked in a cage match, but they were everything in her small world. Since she'd been a little girl, she trusted her siblings would always be there for her. After losing her daddy, she didn't necessarily trust that anyone else would. "How long are you staying?" Naomi asked.

Alexa looked at the watch on her slim wrist. "I have to fly out in a few hours, but I couldn't pass up the opportunity when I heard you were here."

Naomi nodded. She didn't bother to ask where US Marshal Alexa was headed. Although her home was in Blue Larkspur, she traveled often for the job. Most of her assignments were top secret and dangerous as she worked hard to prove herself in another male-dominated profession. Since they'd been six years old, both had been determined to prove themselves capable of the impossible. To show strength during the most trying times so not to be a burden to their mother.

Naomi hugged her again. "I'm so glad you came."

"How's it been going?" Alexa asked as they took seats at the kitchen table.

Shaking her head, Naomi found herself suddenly fighting not to cry. Alexa pressed her palm to her twin's knee, understanding wafting between the two of them. Although they were like night and day personality-wise, there was no denying the connection between them. They were empathic with each other, which took their twin connection to a whole new level.

For ten straight minutes Naomi spewed annoyance and disappointment, dropping every ounce of her frustration into Alexa's lap. She told her sister about the television series and the drama that had ensued since they'd started filming. She told her about the contestants and her wishes for the show. Wishes that didn't look like they might come true. And she told her about Philip, the beautiful Black man who was wreaking havoc on her sensibilities.

Alexa listened, understanding that Naomi wasn't seeking her advice, just an ear to vent to and a shoulder to cry on.

"I have some friends at the police department. I can give them a call and ask them to come by and check things out. If someone is purposely trying to sabotage you, they might be able to help."

With a shake of her head, Naomi shut down that idea. "It's probably just my bad luck. Besides, I can't risk panicking the contestants and I don't want to give Jim any other complaints to take to my partners. They have the bigger purse strings, and I can't afford to lose them."

"You need to be careful," Alexa admonished. "It sounds like much more than bad luck. I'll leave a contact number with you before I leave. Promise me you'll call if anything else happens."

Naomi held up her pinkie. Alexa grinned as they each held tight to the other's appendage. "I promise," Naomi said.

They both giggled like they'd often done when they'd been younger. Naomi took a deep breath and held it briefly.

"So, do you plan to date this man named Philip or is he going to be a notch on that belt of yours?" Alexa asked.

Naomi rolled her eyes skyward. "He's not the notch-type. Something tells me he's one of those forever types."

"Are you ready for a happily ever after with one man? You've always sworn off long-term relationships."

"Men disappoint you," Naomi answered with a shrug. "They lie, steal your heart, then leave you to pick up the pieces all alone."

There was a moment of pause as the two women reflected on her comment.

Alexa reached for her sister's hand. "Not all men are like our father," she said softly. "You're going to have to trust some man at some point."

"I trust a few men. I trust our brothers."

"And Philip? Do you trust him?" Alexa locked gazes with Naomi, the two seeming to size each other up. The moment was telling, and Alexa smiled as tears pressed against Naomi's lashes. She nodded. "Give him a chance, Naomi. You have far more to gain than you have to lose."

Naomi swiped tears from her eyes, changing the subject. "So, what about you? Tell me something good, please."

Alexa sighed. "I wish I had something good to share. You know I've been trying to help Morgan and Caleb with the Ronald Spence case."

Naomi nodded. Spence had been the last person incarcerated by their father. He'd been sentenced to consecutive life sentences for operating a drug smuggling ring. After coming forward to say he'd been the fall guy, railroaded by the real leader of the operation, he claimed her father had been paid well to deny evidence that would have cleared him. Initially Caleb and the

Truth Foundation had been wary of taking on the case, but when another man came forward to confess to the crimes, they had worked to set Spence free. Soon after, the Coltons had learned they'd likely been conned, and had been working ever since to put Spence back behind bars where he belonged.

"That's not going well?" Naomi questioned.

"I've been trying to gather evidence to prove he's been behind some large drug smuggling cases we caught. But I haven't found anyone willing to talk to us. I keep hitting one brick wall after another and it's like pulling teeth to get information."

Their frustration was palpable, feeling heavy and murky as the two sisters waded through the thick of it. Being able to vent to each other was therapeutic and had been needed far more than either sister had realized, Naomi mused.

"I think you should send your résumé to the local news affiliate in Boulder. Stop wasting your time with reality entertainment, since that's not where you really want to be."

Naomi shrugged. "I don't know…"

"Look, you have nothing to lose and everything to gain. And if it works out, you and I will be in the same state again. It would be a win-win for both of us."

"You might be right," Naomi said, pondering the advice. "It would also allow me to work with the foundation more and maybe help with the Spence case."

She thought about the work her brothers and sisters did with the Truth Foundation to exonerate individuals who had been wrongly convicted. They were committed to reforming the criminal justice system to prevent future injustices from happening. Working with them had always been something she planned to do when the time was right. But she'd also found a multitude of excuses to keep her from it, the timing never seeming quite perfect enough. At some point she was going to have to figure out why it scared her so much. Now wasn't the time though. "I definitely have a lot to consider," she concluded.

"You do!" Alexa gave her a bright smile. "And since I'm always right, you just need to take my advice and get it done."

"Surprise!" Aubrey suddenly chimed, joining the two women. Their sister Rachel followed on her heels.

"It's a reunion," Naomi cried as she jumped from her seat to hug her older sister.

"I thought you could use some family," Aubrey said as she swiped a tear from Naomi's face.

"It's just good to see you all," Naomi responded.

"It's good to have you home," Rachel said.

"Where's my niece?" Naomi questioned. "Where's Iris?"

"You don't even have to ask that," Aubrey interjected. "You know exactly where that baby is."

Naomi laughed. "I bet Mom is spoiling her rotten!"

Rachel nodded "She is. I practically have to ask permission to hang out with my own child. And when she's not spoiling her, James is. That little girl has my man wrapped around those little chubby fingers of hers!"

Minutes later the women all sat around Aubrey's kitchen table, sipping blackberry wine and dining on baked pasta layered with marinara sauce and cheese. Laughter rang warmly between them. They reminisced, caught up with each other, and simply enjoyed the time they had together until Alexa had to leave to catch her flight and Rachel needed to pick up her infant daughter from her grandmother's house.

Naomi hugged Aubrey one last time. "Thank you," she said as she headed out the front door.

"Stay safe," Aubrey replied. "I'll check on you in the morning."

NAOMI BARELY MADE it halfway back when movement in the distance caught her eye. There was a full moon overhead, lighting the dark sky, so she knew she wasn't mistaken when she recognized Philip Rees sneaking off toward the woods. He stopped short, seeming to look around, and she ducked down swiftly, turning off the flashlight that had lit her way. When he continued on, ducking behind the tree line, she stood back up.

Something bristled anxiously in her midsection. Where was he going and what was he up to? And was he the reason things had gone south so abruptly? Had Philip been responsible for the accidents that had threatened to shut down production? Was his confession to her about her suspicions just a diversion? Clearly, if he was sneaking around, that meant he was up to no good, right? So, what was he doing and why?

Something between anger and rage at Philip's possible betrayal took hold of Naomi and pulled her toward the woods where he had disappeared. She didn't have a clue what she planned to do or say when she found him, but tracking him down was paramount.

She wanted answers and she damn well intended to get them.

Chapter Ten

Following Brad had not been on his list of things to do, but when Philip saw the man sneak out of his tent and disappear into the darkness once again, he took advantage of the opportunity. He had been on his way to the restroom when he'd seen Brad peek around the canvas flap to see if anyone was watching. His actions were dubious, and he looked guilty of something. Philip was determined to figure out what that something was, especially if it pertained to leaking tech secrets to the mob. Although he wasn't sure how Brad could manage that on the set of a reality show.

He was grateful for the full moon that lit his way. When Brad had disappeared into the line of trees that bordered the acreage of hay fields, Philip had hesitated. But only briefly, as he paused to check the weapon in his waistband and threw a look around to make sure no one else was following them. Now Philip concealed himself behind a massive pine tree, trying to eavesdrop on the other man's conversation. Brad stood in the middle of a small clearing, whispering loudly into his phone. Whoever Brad was speaking with apparently wasn't happy and Brad was doing his best to ease that person's concern. He seemed comfortable with his surroundings, not overly worried that someone might happen upon him and hear his conversation. The last thing Philip was able to hear was Brad saying they could make an exchange of cash and information before the week was out and promising to contact that person with a date and time. Brad assured them the data they wanted was secure and once he was paid, he would need to get out of the country.

Although Philip wished recording Brad was an option, he didn't have the proper resources to catch a conversation in the middle of the woods. He suddenly contemplated how he could put a tap on the phone Brad wasn't supposed to be in possession of.

Something moving in the woods on the other side gave them both reason to pause. Brad ended his conversation abruptly and took off back toward the camp. Philip paused, still listening for the snap of a branch or the crush of leaves and brush beneath a foot. He listened and when he was certain no one was there, he pulled his own cell phone from his pocket and dialed.

Chief Lawson answered on the second ring. "Hello?"

"Chief, it's Detective Rees."

"Rees! It's about time. I've been waiting to hear from you. What's going on?"

"Sorry. I would have checked in sooner, but this is the first opportunity I've had to get away."

"How's it going?"

Philip gave his superior officer an update, filling him

in on everything he'd accomplished since arriving. The chief was amused, his tone turning jovial.

"So, you're actually a contestant on the show?" Chief Lawson laughed.

"Yes, sir. Naomi wouldn't take no for an answer."

"She can definitely be persuasive."

"Is that what they call it?" Philip chuckled with him.

"Keep me posted, son. As soon as you find out more about Brad and his plans let us know. And keep your head down. I don't know about Brad, but Naomi has been known to hit hard and fast. You're one of the best and I can't afford for anything to happen to you. Your team in Boulder would have my head!"

"Yes sir," Philip said. "I will." He disconnected the call. There hadn't been much he could tell Lawson, but he felt comfortable about checking in and reasonably certain that continuing to keep a close eye on Brad would get them their bad guys.

Philip turned, took two steps and then stopped abruptly. Naomi stood at the edge of the clearing, staring at him. Her arms were crossed over her chest. He didn't need to be a rocket scientist to figure out she was mad as hell and every ounce of her ire was pointed in his direction.

He shook his head and swore.

Naomi snapped as she stomped toward him, moving into his personal space like a tidal wave. "Did I miss the memo that said you were authorized to use the phone while being a contestant on my show? Why do you even have your phone? Cell phones were confiscated when you signed your paperwork. Who are you calling?"

"It's not what you think," Philip said. "I wasn't…"

"You weren't what? You weren't cheating? You weren't breaking the rules for your own personal gain? Please enlighten me!" she quipped. "Tell me what you weren't doing on a cell phone, in the woods, in the middle of the night?"

For a split second Philip found himself distracted. Beneath the shadow of moonlight filtering through the trees, Naomi Colton was the most beautiful woman he'd ever seen. She'd lost the headband that usually held her hair out of her eyes and the lush strands billowed softly around her face. A hint of perspiration glistened against her skin and her eyes shimmered, despite the indignation that seeped past the pale irises.

"Did anyone ever tell you how beautiful you are when you're angry?" he said, the words slipping out of his mouth before he could catch them.

Naomi bristled. "Excuse me? Did you really just…"

He winced, shaking his head. "I didn't mean that the way it sounded," he said, interrupting the tongue-lashing he knew she was about to give him.

Naomi took a deep breath, drawing air into her lungs and holding onto it tightly. When she finally let it go, blowing it out slowly, some of the tension appeared to have eased away. She took another before she spoke. "I need answers, Mr. Rees. What you've done is grounds to remove you from the cast. Give me a good reason why I shouldn't do that. Please."

Philip hesitated, pondering his options. If he told her the truth, he risked his cover being blown. He had to decide whether he could trust her. Or not. Had there been an opportunity, he might have run it by the chief to get his opinion. But it was clear Naomi wasn't going to let it go until he told her what she wanted to hear. Her initial anger had dimmed, and there was something else gleaming from her eyes. Something pleading. Something that wanted to believe his explanation. To have it make sense so she wouldn't have to look upon him badly. She asked again. "Do you have anything to say, Philip? Why are you here using your cell phone?"

"I'm a cop." Philip said calmly. "I'm undercover working a case for the Blue Larkspur Police Department. Tailing one of your contestants."

"UNDERCOVER?" NAOMI'S EYES darted back and forth as she processed what he had just told her. It hadn't been at all what she'd expected. It only added to the questions she'd had previously.

Philip nodded his head. "Yes. We have reason to believe Brad Clifton is working with foreign nationals, selling them corporate tech information. We anticipate he will contact them while he's here on the ranch to make an exchange. And I need to catch them when that happens. Brad was out here on his phone. I followed him."

"Brad? But he's just a tech guy, a programmer or something. He doesn't come across as being savvy enough to commit espionage."

"Tech guys can be criminals, too," Philip said with a slight shrug of his shoulders.

"And who knows this?" Naomi asked. "Who knows you're here undercover?"

"Just my superiors in Boulder and the Blue Larkspur police chief," Philip answered.

Naomi shook her head in disbelief. Chief Lawson was a family friend. He and her mother were exceptionally close. Clearly, her mother's *He's-not-my-boyfriend* Lawson had lost his mind. Why he hadn't thought to tell her was an issue she would surely address the very next time she saw him.

Philip seemed to read her mind. "We didn't want anyone to know because we didn't want to risk our hand being exposed and Brad finding out. I'm telling you now because I trust you. Because I want you to trust me."

Naomi's eyes danced over his face. His umber complexion glistened in the darkness, and there was something decadent in his stare. Something that belonged to her if she were willing to claim it. She suddenly realized how close she was to him, the nearness of him radiating heat in every direction. She took a step back, needing just the faintest hint of cool air to waft between them. She bit down against her bottom lip, still trying to determine how complicated things had now become.

"Do you know about my family, Philip?" Naomi questioned.

"I only know what you tell me," he answered.

Naomi understood that at some point, everyone in the town of Blue Larkspur and the surrounding counties could have heard about the Coltons. Particularly about her father and the legacy of lies and deceit that had followed his children. But Naomi and her siblings had worked hard to be seen for their own accomplishments. Their reputations were their own and no one could take that from them.

She took a deep breath before speaking. "My brother Caleb and my sister Morgan have devoted their entire adult lives working to exonerate individuals falsely imprisoned, including those wrongly put in jail by our father. Over the years it's been a collaborative effort, with all of us pitching in to help whenever we can. I believe in fighting for justice and the tenets of right and wrong however I can.

"And I say all that to tell you I will help you however I can. If you need assistance taking down the criminals, you can rest assured I will do everything in my power to help. But you can't be running around the ranch in the middle of the night making telephone calls. That could get you hurt."

"I appreciate the warning."

The moment was suddenly awkward. They were eyeing each other and trying not to stare. Nervous energy flickered like fireflies dancing against a dark sky. It was bubbles waving out of a plastic wand and sparkling water gurgling out of a spring. Naomi giggled and he laughed, and just like that, the moment turned suddenly joyful.

PHILIP REACHED FOR her and before she changed her mind, she let him. He slid an arm around her waist, pulled her against him and captured her lips beneath his own. His kiss was eager and searching, his lips meeting hers sweetly. His mouth was satin-soft, like lush pillows gliding against silk. She had wondered about his kisses, how they would feel if his lips blessed hers. Seizing the opportunity to find out felt all kinds of right and she didn't give it a second thought.

NAOMI KISSED HIM BACK, and in that moment, she knew that no other man would ever be able to kiss her like that again. As her tongue eagerly searched out his, Philip claimed her, marking her with his fingers, which danced across her back and shoulders and down the length of her arms. She was all his, unable to explain the urgent need she suddenly felt for him. He continued to kiss her, and she clung to him, every square inch of her heart and head suddenly determined to never let him go. Naomi gasped when they finally parted. She struggled to catch her breath.

Philip pressed a large palm to her cheek, gently stroking her face with his fingers. He leaned his forehead against hers. "That was very nice," he whispered softly. He pressed his lips to hers one last time.

"You know we can't do this, right?" she whispered. She laid her hand atop his, lacing her fingers beneath his fingers. She thought about the consequences if they were to get caught. The ramifications if he did actually win the competition and people found out there was something between them. They were breaking the rules, and neither could afford to.

"We're not doing anything," Philip murmured beneath his breath. "Not yet anyway." He placed a damp kiss against the line of her profile, nuzzling his face into the curve of her neck.

Naomi closed her eyes, allowing herself a moment to

savor the delicious sensations sweeping through every nerve ending in her body. She inhaled swiftly, blowing warm breath out slowly. "We need to go back. You need to go back to your tent before someone else sees you out here." She took two steps, backing away from him.

Philip nodded. "Let me walk you back," he said.

Naomi shook her head. "No, I'll be fine. Besides, we can't risk anyone seeing us together."

"That's fine. One last kiss before we go?" he teased.

She laughed. "Hell, no!" And then she pressed her mouth to his, giggling softly.

They parted ways at the edge of the forest, Naomi crossing the fields in one direction and Philip walking off in the other. Thinking back to everything that had happened, Naomi was kicking herself. She'd broken cardinal rule number one, to never mix business and pleasure. Kissing Philip had broken that rule and at least a dozen others. It had also been the best kiss she'd ever had. It was inexplicable joy, the promise of things that could be. It had been ages since Naomi had held onto the possibility of anything with a man. Now here she was imagining things she and Philip could get into together and enjoy. Playing a game of what-ifs and maybes. Hoping against the odds that he truly was a good guy, and she too could have a happily ever after, just like her siblings. She was feeling like a teen with her first crush and kicking her backside for falling all over herself just to grab another moment and one more kiss. She was feeling slightly bewitched, and it didn't make an ounce of sense to her.

Climbing the steps to the cabin, she glanced one last

time in the direction where Philip had disappeared into the darkness. A part of her wanted to follow after him. Another part wished he'd sneak back to her. The rest of her felt slightly foolish because Naomi Colton had never chased after or yearned for any man before. She had never been willing to risk her heart being hurt. She hadn't wanted to endure pain like her mother had been made to endure. She'd always been determined to keep a protective wall between her and the men she welcomed into her life.

For the briefest moment she thought about calling her twin to bemoan her predicament. But she changed her mind, not wanting to pass her frustrations on to her sister. But she knew if anyone could understand, Alexa would. Instead, she stripped out of her clothes, crawled into her cot and danced a private two-step with Philip in her dreams.

His lips still tingled from the heat of that kiss. He had kissed Naomi Colton and that moment had been sheer perfection. But he found himself second-guessing that decision. He'd allowed a personal desire to intrude on his professional responsibilities and now he wondered if he'd made a mistake he wouldn't be able to come back from. Knowing that she had wanted him nearly as much as he had wanted her eased his concerns about what had happened, but only slightly.

Philip was grateful that no one was up when he arrived back at his tent. No one around to ask him questions he wouldn't be able to answer. Everyone was tucked away in their own enclosures. Even Brad seemed to have gone down for the night. He made his way into the enclosure and secured the flaps. Stripping down to his black boxer briefs, he lay back against the cot and thought about Naomi.

Women had always fallen into his path like leaves from a tree. They were sweet delicacies that he could savor, or not, as his mood dictated. He had rarely given any consideration to a long-term relationship, always choosing work before all else. There had never been a woman in his life who was willing to be second to his job. And because he'd often chosen style over substance, there'd been no woman he'd been willing to put first.

Now he was wondering how Naomi would feel. What Naomi would think. If Naomi would want what he wanted. Sleep came slowly as he tossed and turned from side to side, unable to clear his mind. When sleep finally pulled him into a deep slumber, Naomi had eased into his dreams.

Chapter Eleven

When Philip next saw Naomi the following morning, he was standing on his mark, the group readying themselves for competition. Jim and the director were coddling Monty, who was two sheets to the wind and irritated that he had to be there. Despite his late-night misadventure with Naomi, Philip had slept well, as he hoped she had.

Brad was up to his usual antics, his mouth writing checks the rest of him would never be able to cash. This particular morning Fred and Harold were the targets of his insults as he apparently hoped to throw them off their game before the contests began.

Naomi had avoided direct eye contact and so had he, neither wanting anyone to read anything into the two of them staring at each other. She was methodical, giving directions and ensuring all of them knew where to be when. All while personally plying Monty with cups of hot coffee to sober him up.

The film crew were in position and the day's rising temperatures hadn't yet become uncomfortable. She was determined that nothing would go wrong with the day's filming and her crew members were going above and beyond to make that happen. The only thing that could have made the moment more perfect, Philip thought, was if he could wrap his arms around the stunning woman and kiss her until she swooned.

THERE WAS ALMOST too much going on, Naomi thought as her focus shifted from one point to another. She had one camera catching the contest and another capturing individual confessionals and comments from the contestants. She could not have been happier that things were starting off well. Jasper had greeted her with good news and a glass of his favorite green juice. He'd been able to secure calves for the last leg of the competition so she could proceed as planned. And even drunk Monty was coming off well on camera.

For the briefest moment her eyes lingered on Philip. He was showing off his roping skills and doing an exceptional job. In fact, he was doing so well that Brad commented on camera that Philip was his only competition. He'd played it off like he was only joking but she sensed he really saw Philip as a threat that could keep him from winning the title. She rotated her index finger at the associate producer doing the interview, gesturing for her to get more from Brad. He liked to talk and she thought he might slip and say something either she or Philip could use.

Grace was primping for the camera, looking to be more concerned with how she looked than what might be coming. She had blinged her denim shirt with crystals and had pulled her hair into a high ponytail. Her makeup was pristine as she gave her interview. "I have no idea what we're in for today, so I'm super nervous and a little excited. I just hope it's a good challenge for me. There are so many little girls out there just like me who need to believe they can do anything they want to do. I just want them to see my confidence and hopefully find theirs." She had great one-liners, Naomi thought. How far she was able to make it in the competition would determine how many of them landed on the cutting room floor.

As the competition began, Naomi headed down to where the monitors had been set up to watch. She passed by Philip and Harold, who were both reflecting on their performances. She waved a hand in their direction. "Good morning. Good luck today, gentlemen!"

Philip tossed his own hand up. "Good morning!"

"And thank you," Harold added.

Naomi gave them both a bright smile, allowing her eyes to linger on him briefly. Philip gave her a nod and smiled back.

Minutes later, Monty had delivered his intro, detailing what each team would have to do and how they had to do it. He stammered once but did a surprising job getting his lines right the first time. After a coin flip, Melissa's team was going first. Grace and her team took seats under one of the tents so they could watch and wait for their turn.

Melissa's team huddled up to figure out who would be doing what. Brad pushed his way forward to suggest who he thought should do what. Watching him on-screen, Naomi still didn't see "criminal." It was hard to figure out how he was doing his dirt. He was good at hiding that personality trait. He came across as a major jerk but nothing more. For a brief moment Josiah and Stefan exchanged words, both wanting to fix the tire. After a quick back-and-forth Melissa settled the argument and put one on tire and the other on hay. The team was finally ready for the clock to start.

Naomi smiled, excited for the games to begin. She watched as Jim maneuvered the players into position. When the horn sounded Monty passed Melissa the baton and the timer started. Melissa was tasked with saddling her horse and riding it to the next station to pass the baton. Trouble started when she failed to secure her saddle tightly enough; it slid off as she tried to mount. The cameraman grinned, fighting not to laugh as Melissa struggled to get on the horse. She lost valuable time before she was headed across the field. At the gate she dismounted, looking panicked. Somewhere along the way she'd lost the baton. She ran a short distance back until she found it, then she ran back to her horse. Once she and the horse were on the other side of the fence, Melissa passed the baton to Josiah.

Josiah needed to throw twenty-five bales of hay up into the rafters, each weighing some fifty-plus pounds. Stefan was there to cheer him on as he handled the hay pile easily. In no time at all Josiah passed the baton to Stefan, who took off running to the tractor to change out the one flat tire. The team hit another bump when Stefan, who was slim-built and barely weighed a buck fifty, had a difficult time with the commercial-sized tire. It took him longer than anticipated to wrestle it into place.

Brad and Juan-Carlo were responsible for the last two legs of the relay. Juan-Carlo roped the calf on his first try. His success was a surprise even to him, and the young man laughed heartily.

When the calf was roped and tied, Brad raced to where the animal lay in the center of the field. A trailer had been backed up to the fence and he needed to heave the baby cow up, carry it and load it in the trailer. Because Juan-Carlo had laid the calf close to that end of the fence, the distance Brad had to cover was short and he was able to handle it easily. When the trailer gate was closed and secure, he tossed up his hands and Monty called time.

Naomi jumped excitedly. "Did you see that?" she exclaimed. "I can't wait to see this in postproduction."

Jude nodded and grinned. "We've got some great shots. Personally, I can't wait to see the drone footage."

"Me, too! That was such a brilliant idea," Naomi said to her friend.

Team Winning made their way back, taking the seats Team Beauties had vacated. One or two looked exhausted but they all gave encouraging interviews, believing they had done enough to beat the other team.

Grace was already giving her team a pep talk. She had gone back to her cheerleading days for inspiration. Amusement danced across Philip's face, and Naomi could tell he feigned interest in what they needed to do. When the clock started, things went swiftly. Grace had no problems saddling and riding her horse. She reached the fence and passed her baton to Philip.

"Get us some great body shots," Naomi said into the walkie-talkie she carried. Someone on the other end grunted and Naomi laughed. She knew viewers would get excited by his physique and getting that money shot was just good business. She didn't need to add that she too wanted those shots, most especially when he snatched off his shirt and stood bare-chested. Knowing she'd be saving that raw footage for her own personal enjoyment.

Philip made short work of the hay bales, bringing to mind the American folk hero John Henry. He was steel and muscle and he threw those hay bales like they were cotton Q-tips. Philip passed the baton to Harold and Harold had the tire changed in record time. Their one hiccup came when Malia needed to rope the calf. She missed on her first and then her second try. Once she got the animal down to the ground, its legs tied securely, Fred picked it up to his shoulders and tossed it into the trailer. Monty called time to a chorus of cheers and fist pumps.

"Great work, everyone!" Naomi high-fived Jude, who called out, "Cut," over the megaphone.

"Congratulations!" Janice said.

Jim came running over to her side. "That was so good."

"It was. You did a great job with the contestants," she told him warmly.

Jim smiled. "I appreciate that. What do you want to do now?"

"Let's give everyone a lunch break. We'll film the elimination ceremony right after. Until then I want plenty of reaction shots. Melissa was teary after her performance. Let's make sure we get that on camera."

Jim nodded. "Will do!"

Naomi stood with her hands on her hips as she took it all in. It was a moment she had dreamed of since forever and she felt immensely blessed to be standing in the midst of it.

She suddenly felt like she was being watched. She didn't have to look to know that Philip was staring at her. She wanted to turn, to meet his gaze, but she knew it would only lead to something that neither of them needed. What had happened between them had been questionable on many levels and they both knew it couldn't happen again. At least not while they were filming, and he was working his case. Maybe after, when they both had moved on to other things, but even that wasn't certain, no matter what they both might have wanted.

THE SENSE OF accomplishment spiraling through the afternoon air was palpable. Watching Naomi jump up and down with excitement pulled Philip's entire face into a deep smile. She was happy and he was happy for her. He only wished he could openly wrap his arms around her and join in her celebration. Suddenly realizing he was staring at her, he tore his eyes away, shifting his focus to Brad.

Brad stood off to the side, his expression blank. Philip sensed that he was plotting, making plans that no one else was supposed to know about. But he knew. Something deep in his gut was readying him for whatever was coming. And his new friend Brad didn't have a clue.

"Good job out there," Philip said.

"I told you I'm in it to win it!" The two men slapped palms. "You headed to lunch?" Brad asked.

Philip nodded. "Yeah. I'll walk with you."

As they began to saunter slowly toward the commissary, Philip stole a quick glance in Naomi's direction. He sensed she was watching him while pretending not to notice. He shifted his focus back to the man walking beside him.

"One of the guys was saying you owned your own company. What's that like?" Philip asked, trying to make conversation.

Brad shrugged. "It's cool, but I'm trying to make twice the money with half the work. And my partner is an asshole. It's not much fun anymore."

"That's not good."

"Nope! Which is why I'm putting some things in place to change my life. As soon as I win this prize money, I'm headed to Cancun."

Philip laughed. "You're gonna need more than my prize money to get to Cancun."

Brad laughed with him. "*My* prize money is for tips. I've got some opportunities on the line that will net me some *big* bucks." He emphasized the word *big*, drawing it out and letting it hang in the air longer than necessary.

"That sounds like something you should let a friend

in on," Philip said as he cut an eye in the man's direction, his eyebrows raised curiously.

Brad grinned. "Maybe I would," he said, "if I had a friend."

"Ouch! And here I thought we were getting along so well," Philip teased.

"You're cool, dude. A little moody, maybe, and for the life of me I don't understand what's up with you and Miss America. The way she's all over you and you keep ignoring her? I don't know any guy who turns down free kitty when it's thrown at him like that. I bet she'd even wear her crown to bed if you asked her to!" He smacked his lips.

Philip could see Brad envisioning Grace naked, wearing only her tiara and stiletto heels. He cringed as he shook the image from his own head. Naomi was the only woman who occupied his fantasies these days, especially after their red-hot kiss last night. "Why don't you shoot your shot? She might want someone to warm her pillow at night. Kind of like what happens on the ranch stays on the ranch!"

"I might have to offer my services," Brad said, grabbing at his crotch for emphasis.

Philip shook his head a second time, feeling his lip curl in disgust. The sooner he could bring down Brad, the better.

NAOMI WAS GRATEFUL. After everyone was fed, the sets broken down and cleaned up, they were ready for the elimination ceremony. Only she, Jim, Monty and necessary crew members knew the results of the competition. She had personally gone over each and every line with Monty and was confident he'd be able to deliver them without a hitch.

The barn had been transformed and the cast all stood in their respective spots, looking anxious and nervous for the results. The two teams were separated by bales of hay that were being used as a prop and the horses in the stalls behind them made for a great visual shot on the screen. Naomi stood behind the cameraman and Jude, watching it all unfold on the monitor.

Monty made his dramatic entrance. Naomi knew it would have great impact once the sound engineer and Foley artist worked their magic in the production studio. He moved to his mark and allowed the scene to unfold. His baritone voice sounded deep and throaty, and appropriately ominous. "There are ten competitors here and two of you are going home," he said, pausing as they reacted to the news. "I'm taking the advice of your mentors here on the ranch, but in the end, the decision on who stays and who doesn't is up to me."

Monty continued. "I want to hear from the team leaders." He nodded at Grace first, gesturing for her to take a step forward. "Miss Grace, how are you this evening?"

Grace gave him her best beauty pageant smile. "I'm well. Thank you for asking."

"How do you think your team performed?"

"I was very happy with my team. Everyone stepped up to pull their weight and get their job done. I believe our performances have given us the win." She tossed a look over both shoulders, applauding her team.

Monty winked his eye at her as she took a step backward. He waved Melissa forward. "Good evening, Miss Melissa, tell me about your team."

Melissa clapped her hands. "I have the best team in the world, sir! They really came through. I had some personal bumps in the beginning and made some mistakes, but everyone stepped up to help and get us back on track. I think our teamwork and sportsmanship was outstanding."

Her team clapped and cheered as she stepped back on her mark.

Philip was caught off guard when Monty called him out by name. His eyes widened as he stepped forward.

"How do you think you and your team did, Philip?" Monty questioned.

"I think we won," Philip answered. "And I was happy with my contribution to our efforts."

"So were your mentors. The way you threw those hay bales was impressive. So impressive that you've won immunity in our next competition. Congratulations!"

Grace reached to give him a hug and the other men tapped him on the back. Philip looked stunned, the announcement unexpected. "Thank you," he muttered.

Monty gestured for him to take a step back. "And congratulations to Team Beauties. You all won, and it wasn't even close. You all clocked in at fifteen minutes and Team Winning clocked in at twenty-eight minutes. Congratulations!"

Naomi nodded as the cameraman panned everyone's face, capturing Melissa's unhappy expression and

Brad's annoyance with all of it. It was going to be great TV when it finally aired.

Monty pointed the winning team to the fence to take a seat. There was a momentary break to get the losing team in place for the elimination and then they continued filming.

Monty looked at each one of them, his gaze pausing on everyone's face. "There are five of you left on Team Winning," he started, "and two of you are going home." He took a deep breath, blowing it back out slowly. "This is the part I hate. Where I think you suffered was your allocation of manpower. Going forward I think it's important you draw on everyone's strengths when making decisions about who will do what."

Melissa nodded, tears beginning to mist her eyes. Naomi gestured for a close-up of her face, the camera focusing in until she filled the frame.

"This was my biggest worry right here. I let my team down," Melissa was saying. "I fumbled a little bit, then I lost my baton, which ate up our time. It's definitely not the result I wanted."

Monty took another breath. "I appreciated that even with those hiccups, no one quit. You all continued to pull through. Unfortunately, Melissa and Stefan, your time here is done. You can't stay…in the saddle. You need to pack up your stuff and leave. Thank you and good luck to you."

Quiet descended over the group. Stefan stepped forward first to shake Monty's hand. Melissa's tears were rolling over her full cheeks as Monty hugged her. They said their goodbyes to the other players, then followed an associate producer to go make their exit statements, gather their belongings and wait for their rides home.

Monty made his final speech, then wished the remaining players good-night. When Jude yelled, "Cut," Naomi wanted to hug and kiss them all. She applauded all their efforts.

"Thank you, everyone. It's been a good day. Everyone get some rest and be ready to do it all again tomorrow! Craft services is throwing a barbecue tonight, so make sure you all come out and eat well."

Chapter Twelve

There was a camaraderie of sorts growing between the cast and the crew. After a really great day they were all piled into the barn enjoying a good meal of barbecued chicken, ribs, corn on the cob, baked beans and yeast rolls. Icy lemonade flowed freely and frosty bottles of beer were available to those who wanted one.

Naomi worked the room, starting at one corner and moving counterclockwise to the next. For most of the day she had focused her full attention on the work that needed to be done, avoiding Philip at every opportunity. Avoiding him because she knew if she looked in his direction for longer than a split second, everyone would be able to see every decadent thought she'd been having about the man. And her thoughts had been pure, unadulterated debauchery!

Philip looked scrumptious and she would have sworn off her favorite pistachio ice cream for just a few minutes with his body pressed against hers. She wanted his hands to travel the length of her back, until he cupped her buttocks beneath his large palms. If his fingers slipped between the parting of her feminine spirit, even better. She was damn near desperate for his touch and just the thought of him had her craving more. A quiver of electricity raced up her spine and down again. Naomi shook the sensation away, refocusing on the task at hand as she continued to move around the room.

She took time to speak to each and every one of them, calling them by name and expressing her appreciation for their contribution. Laughs were abundant and the chatter was loud. From what she could tell they were all having a great time.

Across the room, Philip sat with Marvin and two of the boom operators. Grace sat on his other side, practically in his lap. Once or twice he shifted in his seat, putting an inch of space between them, but Grace was right back, her lean growing closer and closer. He looked uncomfortable about the whole situation and Naomi found it all amusing.

She laughed at Harold's joke, or maybe it was Josiah's, even though she hadn't heard the punch line. Everyone else was laughing, so she laughed, too! She kept moving, eventually landing at Philip's side. He had risen from his seat, leaving Grace in conversation with Malia and the set designer. When she joined him, he stood against the wall in conversation with Marvin and Brad.

"How's everyone doing over here?" she asked as she stood beside him, her arms folded in front of her.

Marvin tipped his bottle at her. "Life is good, boss lady. How are you doing?"

"No complaints," she said. "I just wanted to check in with everyone and make sure you all are doing okay."

She looked from one, to the other, side-eyeing Philip beside her. They stood shoulder to shoulder, just barely touching each other. But the heat that had risen between them was combustible. Naomi felt moisture dampening her panties and perspiration pooling between her breasts. She allowed herself to brush up against him for a split second and when she did, she felt him quiver in response. His brow raised and he bit down against his bottom lip. Naomi shifted her body from his and they both took a deep breath.

"If every day was as good as this one, I might stay longer," Brad said.

Naomi gave him a smile. Despite everything she knew, she was still finding it hard to believe he was a criminal up to no good. "Are you planning to leave us soon?" she asked. Curiosity flooded her expression.

Brad shrugged. "I think it all depends on my friend right here. He's gunning for my prize money!" He gave Philip a light punch in the shoulder.

Philip chuckled. "I'm just playing the game," he said, his tone jovial.

"Well, the two of you are playing it well. The camera loves you both and I'm sure the viewers will, too. Just keep doing what you're doing."

"Thank you!" Philip said. "Appreciate that!"

She smiled. "Looks like they're bringing out the desserts. Is that chocolate cake I see?"

Marvin's head snapped as he looked toward the food services table. "I don't know if that's cake, but I do see me some coconut pie. You all need to excuse me."

"I'm right behind you," Brad said. "I haven't had

good coconut pie since my granny used to make it." He tossed Philip a look. "You want something?"

Philip shook his head. "I'm good but thank you for offering." Marvin and Brad were across the room before he finished his comment. He laughed.

Naomi turned to face him, hoping their conversation looked as casual as her talk with all the others. "So, how are you really doing?" she asked, her voice dropping an octave.

Philip shook his head. "I hurt. I think you people are trying to kill me!"

"We're just making you earn that prize money. Seriously, though, don't hesitate to go see the medic if you need to. They're getting paid to make sure you don't hurt from any injuries."

"I'd prefer to come see you so you can kiss my boo-boos."

Naomi laughed, feeling the blood rush to her face and color her cheeks. Blushing was not what she had planned.

She changed the subject. "It's good to see you making friends," she said, her eyes shifting toward Grace. The woman was deep in conversation with one of the associate producers.

"I hope you know there is nothing going on with me and that woman."

"I know that you are a very attractive man and women can't help but be drawn to you."

"Well, she's aggressive. It's like fighting off flies at a family reunion."

Naomi laughed. "It's not that bad."

Philip smiled. "I miss kissing you," he said. He shifted his weight from one leg to the other, crossing them at the ankles.

"You should," Naomi quipped. "I'm pretty good at it."

"I might have to get caught walking around the ranch tonight."

"And that would not be a good idea."

"So that's a no? I shouldn't do it?"

"It's definitely a no."

"You could sneak into my tent after everyone goes to bed so you can tuck me in."

Naomi laughed again.

"No, huh?"

"I don't think so, Mr. Rees."

"Mr. Rees!" Philip pressed his palm to his heart and threw his head back. "The pain!"

She shook her head fighting not to giggle. "You should stop."

"Last night I got to second base and today you've gone formal on me. I'm crushed. I thought we'd moved our relationship to the next level. I was expecting *honey* or *baby* but you gave me *Mr. Rees*!"

"I'm walking away now, Philip."

"Before I know it, you'll be breaking up with me by text message"

Naomi's laugh was gut-deep, filling the room with joy. Others turned to stare at the two of them, curious to know what was being said. She wished a quiet prayer that none of them could see how much she wanted to lose herself in his arms and taste the laughter on his lips. She shook her head, then waved a hand for Jim to come join them.

"Now I know you hate me," Philip muttered under his breath. He smiled as Jim joined their little circle.

"Jim, Philip was curious to know more about the security protocols that we have in place for each of the competitions. Since that was your expertise, I told him you'd be delighted to brief him. We want to make sure all the contestants feel safe."

"Definitely!" Jim answered. "Whatever you want to know, I'll be delighted to ease your mind."

"Thank you," Philip said politely. "I really appreciate that."

HOURS LATER, NAOMI was still giggling. Jim had held Philip hostage for almost an hour. She knew that once her second-in-command had an audience, he wouldn't want to let go. Jim needed attention and was desperate for people to think well of him. Philip would think twice the next time he wanted to give her a hard time. She also hoped it would convince him that walking around late at night was not a good idea, no matter what the circumstances were.

After reviewing her checklist of things to do she was more than happy with where they stood. She was well within the budget, the crew and cast were happy, and the production company hadn't called to give her a hard time. There wasn't much more she could ask for.

She opened the front door and stepped outside on the porch. The waning gibbous moon was obscured by thick clouds and there wasn't much to see off in the distance.

For a brief moment she considered going to her sister's house to sleep but changed her mind. Aubrey and Luke didn't need a third wheel in their space. Being alone had never been an issue for Naomi, but for reasons she couldn't begin to explain, she was wishing for someone to be there with her. That previous evening in Philip's arms, pressed against Philip, kissing Philip's lips, had left her wanting more of Philip Rees. That wanting was a deep, all-consuming desire, the likes of which she'd never known before.

She wrapped her arms around her torso as she stared out over the landscape. For the briefest moment she thought she saw movement in the distance, but just like that, all became still. She chalked it up to wishful thinking as she moved back inside the cabin and secured the door.

"You really should keep that back window locked," Philip said softly. "Anyone can sneak into your room if they wanted to and I can't spend all my time worrying about you being here all by your lonesome. It's a good thing I'm the only one who thought crawling through your window was a good idea."

Seeing him sitting in the leather executive's chair had her discombobulated and she nearly jumped out of her skin. She turned back to make sure the door was locked and pulled the blinds on the window. "What are you doing here?"

"I missed you."

"Philip, you can't just…"

Philip stood. "Well, I did," he said cutting her off. "I needed to taste you."

He moved around the desk to stand before her. His eyes danced over her face and then he nudged her chin up with his index finger and lifted her lips to his. The kiss was a slow drag in a blue-light basement party. Skin teased skin, their mouths gliding easily together.

Naomi felt herself falling fast. She was dizzy, her knees weak and shaky, and her body throbbed with wanting. It was almost too much for her to handle. She slid her arms around his neck, pulling him closer. The intensity of that kiss went from a low simmer to a volcanic eruption. He teased her sensibilities, playing her like a musician playing a classical instrument. He had her humming and purring and praying for release and she still had her clothes on. She suddenly pulled herself from him, panting heavily. She raced to the other side of the desk to put some necessary distance between them. She pointed her finger at him, her whole hand shaking. A lecture about why they shouldn't be doing this bubbled in her head, but she had no words. She dropped into the seat and tried to collect herself.

She cursed once. And then again.

Philip chuckled softly. "I think you'll agree that we both needed that."

"I'm not agreeing to anything," Naomi replied. She shook her finger again. "I knew you were going to be trouble. What was I thinking?"

"Hopefully, you were thinking you wanted me as much as I want you."

"Have you thought about what will happen if anyone finds out about us? We'll both lose our jobs!"

He shrugged. "Then we'll go get new ones. Or you

could stay home, have my babies, and let me take care of you."

She giggled, his teasing causing butterflies to flutter with excitement in her midsection. She teased back. "I could have those babies and you stay home."

"Exactly! We have options. We can do whatever we need to do and, more importantly, we can do what we want to do."

"Well, I don't want to get fired. I've worked too hard for this."

"Then we keep things a secret while you finish the show and come out in a few weeks. But don't expect me not to want you, Naomi. And don't think that I won't make an effort to spend time alone with you when I can."

"We barely know each other!" she exclaimed. Although she appreciated his directness and found his self-assurance sexy as hell, there was still much they didn't know about each other. One of them had to be practical, even if practicality felt overrated as he stared at her, his gaze like warm honey raining over her.

"Just think how much fun we will have changing that. Because I really want to know you better. I want to know what excites you. What scares you. What you read for fun. How you like your coffee and eggs in the morning. If you shiver when I put my tongue…"

Naomi held up her hand to stall his words. She shook her head. "What if someone comes looking for you?"

"No one's coming to look for me. But if they do, we'll lie."

Her mouth lifted in the slightest smile. "I am not

making love to you tonight, Philip Rees, and I don't care how much you tease."

Despite the assertion, Naomi knew it wouldn't take much for him to change her mind. She had no qualms about having a physical encounter with him, but gut instinct told her that once they crossed that line there would be no going back. No resisting his ministrations or acting like they were strangers. Making love with Philip would be the start of a relationship she had only imagined, and she hadn't yet figured out how she could have it and all the other dreams she imagined for herself. And she still didn't know with any certainty if he wanted it for himself.

"That's fair," Philip responded. "This can go as slow or as fast as you want. I will take all my cues from you. I just wanted to be near you. I wanted to hold you even if it was only for a few minutes." He held out his arms, his brows lifted as he stared at her.

"I can't think straight when you touch me."

"I would promise to keep my hands to myself, but I know I couldn't keep that promise."

Naomi was still shaking her head, still trying to calm her frayed nerves. She wasn't sure how to respond, her mouth opening and closing like a fish out of water.

"Do you want me to leave?" Philip asked. He took two steps toward her, closing the distance between them.

A moment passed between them, neither saying a word. Finally, Naomi shook her head. "No," she said. "No, I don't want you to leave." She closed that distance, pressing her body back against his as she eased her arms round his back and hugged him. "We're going to get in so much trouble," she concluded.

"I promise it'll be good trouble!"

PHILIP AND NAOMI talked until the wee hours of the morning. When the temperatures cooled they moved from the front office to the back room and lay side by side on that narrow cot, his body curled around hers, his arms wrapped tightly around her torso. Their conversations drifted from the serious to the nonsensical, and back.

He discovered her affinity for K-Pop boy bands and Japanese anime. She collected owls and Christmas nutcrackers and was obsessed with horror movies. She had the most engaging laugh and smiled with her whole body; her quirky sense of humor kept him laughing. She learned that he was an avid hiker, was well-traveled, and collected menus from every restaurant he'd dined at. He hoarded containers of Pringles plain potato chips, detested cottage cheese and considered himself a master chef on the grill. He wanted a dog but was never home long enough to spend time with one; and he imagined himself married with a half-dozen kids before his thirty-fifth birthday.

"You realize that even if you started having kids right now, that those six babies would all be in diapers at the same time."

"We could handle it."

"We? Who said anything about *we*? I don't plan to do diapers."

"Okay, that might be a problem."

He gently palmed her tummy, his fingers lightly grazing her breasts, teasing the length of her arms and resting gently against her upper thigh. He planted kisses against bare skin and nibbled her bottom lip like it was a sweet treat.

Naomi dozed off first, falling into a deep sleep. As she lay cradled against him, Philip watched her. She was dreaming, he thought, her eyes flickering back and forth behind her closed lids. She also snored. Loudly, the air blowing a low whistle past her lips.

Although she had assumed he was teasing, Philip had been serious about taking care of her and them having children. Before Naomi there hadn't been a woman who gave him reason to think such a thing was possible. Naomi had him wishing for a future with her. He knew it sounded clichéd, but he'd fallen in love with her the moment he first laid eyes on her. The more time he spent with her, the more he believed it. She had a lock on his heartstrings, and he wasn't willing to have her let go.

He hadn't been able to tell her that he was also there because he was worried for her. He didn't know if she were truly safe. During his brief conversation with Jim, the man had said something unsettling. As Jim had grown comfortable talking about Naomi, there had been a hint of attitude in his tone. He was not a fan of hers and it had become increasingly obvious with each word he spoke.

Philip trailed a finger along the line of her profile, gently caressing her face. He pressed a damp kiss to her cheek. Thinking back to his conversation with the other man he knew there would be no way that he could trust him.

There are no such things as accidents, Jim had intoned. *What you call accidents, I call lessons. Things happen when people need to be taught a lesson.*

When mistakes are made, you do whatever is necessary to make sure they get corrected.

Jim had a warped sense of morality and Philip's entire conversation with him, had given him pause. So much so that before arriving on Naomi's doorstep, he had placed a call to request a background check. Until something came through that eased his mind, Philip planned to stay close to the beautiful woman.

WHEN NAOMI WOKE, Philip was gone. He had snuck out as quietly as he had snuck in. She rolled onto her back, pulling an arm up and over her head. Everything about their night together had been sheer perfection. He'd been sweet and attentive. He had allowed her moments of vulnerability and had answered hard questions without hesitation. He continued to make quite an impression on her and, again, left her wanting more of him.

It was the wanting that had her emotions twisted in a tight knot. Because what was happening between them had taken on a life of its own. It was racing toward a finish line at a pace that didn't seem possible to keep up with. She thought of the autobahns in Germany, where road traffic traveled at unlimited speeds. That was them, and the rising emotion sweeping like a tsunami between them. Naomi knew she'd be heartbroken if they crashed and burned.

She sat upright and as she did, she noticed the Post-it stuck to the mirror above the dresser. Philip had left her a note that read, *I miss you already!* ♥

Naomi smiled. If the previous day was an indication of how great her days could be, then she wished that for herself every day of the week. She was excited about what might come and looking forward to seeing just where she and Philip could take their new relationship. He had declared them officially a couple, no hesitation in his heart. She found his determination to build a solid foundation for them both endearing.

She slid out of the bed and moved toward the bathroom to wash up and change. It was still early, but the cabin would soon be TV series central, people in and out until the day was finished. She didn't have much time before she'd have to give orders and answer questions, and she wanted just a few more minutes to reminisce about her night in Philip's arms, his large hands easing every ounce of tension from her.

Chapter Thirteen

Philip wasn't hating his situation as a reality TV show contestant as much as he thought he would. It had been a busy morning and he'd actually placed first in the immunity challenge. Once again he proved himself safe from elimination. He had drawn on his Boy Scout experiences to achieve the win, grateful for those badges others had once told him would never amount to anything.

He sat in the commissary enjoying a bed of salad topped with grilled chicken. Naomi faced him at a table across the way. She sat in conversation with members of her production team. Grace sat across from him, chattering about the condition of her hair being stuck out in the high summer heat. He feigned interest in the beauty queen's dilemma, but his focus was on the beautiful woman on the other side of the room.

Everything about their night together had further cemented his commitment to her. A commitment he had never before considered. She had stolen a solid chunk of his heart and he wanted her to have it. He cherished the conversation they'd had, knowing there was so much about her that he was anxious to discover. He imagined them sharing a lifetime together, being a blessing to each other. And he felt completely out of his element, unsure where those feelings had come from or how he was supposed to process them. For the moment though, he knew he would let time and fate guide them, and things would inevitably be as they were intended.

Grace snapped her fingers in front of his face, pulling for his attention. "You there?"

Philip waved his head from side to side. "I'm sorry. What were you saying?"

Grace sat back in her chair, her eyes holding tightly to his. She took a slow sip of her beverage, swallowing before she responded. "Why aren't you interested in me?" she finally asked. "And it's okay if you aren't, but I just need to know."

Philip shifted in his own seat, leaning forward. He propped both elbows on the table and laced his fingers together. "Why are you asking?"

"Short of stripping naked and crawling into your bed, I've done everything I can to show you I'm interested in you. So, what is it?"

Philip took a deep breath. "You're a beautiful woman, Grace. And I'm flattered by your interest. But I'm involved with someone, and I would never disrespect her that way."

"I wasn't interested in a love connection, Philip. I just wanted good sex!"

He laughed. "It wouldn't have been good if my heart wasn't in it."

"Trust me," she said, rising from her seat. "You

would have enjoyed every minute of the ride and no one would have ever had to know."

"I would have known. And probably everybody here!"

She giggled. "You're probably right. This is one nosy lot! You can't fault a girl for trying, though."

He smiled. "You're going to make someone very happy one day, Grace."

"Just not today, right?"

"Not if it's me you're looking to entertain. Sorry!"

Grace leaned over the table and kissed his cheek. "Whoever she is, she's very lucky. You're one of the good ones, Philip Rees!"

"Thank you. I appreciate that. I hope we can still be friends."

She laughed. "Maybe in another lifetime. Right now, you'll always be the one that got away. And I don't like to lose!"

Philip chuckled as she strode away. He didn't miss the look that Naomi gave the two of them, her own curiosity spilling out of her bright eyes. He nodded his head in her direction as they exchanged a look.

THEIR HORSES HAD been staked the length of a football field away. Between where the contestants stood and where the horses were, there were several stations set up and spaced evenly out, with activities that would have to be completed at each. Naomi watched from the monitors as Monty gave them their instructions. Their illustrious host had really picked up his game.

"On go," Monty said, his voice deep and commanding, "you will carry two buckets of water to the next station. At the next station you will need to split a log into four pieces. From there, you will carry those four pieces of wood to the firepit. A length of rope has been stretched across the top of each pit. You need to make a fire and when it burns through that length of rope, you can race to the next station, where your horse will be waiting for you. Saddle up your horse and ride to the finish line to ring your bell. Everyone understand?" Monty's eyes shifted over each one.

Heads nodded as contestants glanced around at one another. It was clear that some got it, and some didn't.

Monty held up his arm, paused, then dropped it in a dramatic gesture. "And, go!" he shouted.

There was a chorus of whoops and cheers from the contestants as they all took off running. Even though he had immunity, Philip was gunning for the win. He had a competitive spirit and Naomi found that intriguing. He didn't like to be bested by anyone or anything. But what she found even more entertaining was that Brad Clifton didn't want to be bested by Philip, turning it into a personal one-on-one competition between them.

The two men were neck and neck at the start, both carrying their water buckets easily to the first station. The wood-chopping proved to be more problematic for Brad than for Philip. Philip slammed his ax easily in the center of the stump, splitting the lumber. Brad missed the center of his stump multiple times and then broke his ax. He lost time waiting for another. Fortunately for Brad, he was able to catch up at the firepit.

Both managed to get their fires started easily, Brad's

burning as swiftly as Philip's. But Philip had done a better job of stacking kindling to get the flames high enough to reach the rope and turn it to ash. His rope burned first. As he jetted across the field toward his horse everyone assumed it would be an easy win for him. But no one was watching Grace or Fred, and both were closer on Philip and Brad's heels than they realized.

Watching the action Naomi was grinning from ear to ear. Seeing Philip in action, she was silently cheering him on in her head, wanting him to win. So much for not showing favoritism, she thought. She felt her canyon-wide smile suddenly sag and she raised her brows as she suddenly spied Grace.

Fred beat Grace in the foot race, but she held her own, reaching her horse as the three men were still struggling to get their saddles secure. With the ease of a professional and the elegance of a gazelle, Grace was atop her horse and saddle in no time.

"I need a photo finish," Naomi breathed excitedly as she and her team watched it unfold.

Behind her, Janice was muttering under her breath. "Go, Grace. Go, go, go! You got it! Go!"

Jude laughed at his wife. "No picking favorites!" he quipped.

Grace did have it, beating Philip by a hair to reach her bell and ring it first. Brad and Fred tied for third place although Brad proclaimed himself the winner between the two of them.

Grace leaned forward to hug her horse's neck. Her

excited words rang like a sweet melody through the afternoon air.

"Congratulations!" Philip exclaimed. "That was a good race."

"We got beat by a woman," Brad sniped, he and his horse dancing about.

"Yes, you did!" Grace responded. "But don't be upset. It won't be the last time," she said smugly.

Philip laughed. Brad was not at all amused.

They all moved toward the associate producer gesturing for their attention.

"Interview time!" Grace exclaimed. "You boys make sure to say something nice about me to the cameras."

"Or not," Brad quipped.

Fred shook his head. "That's not a good look, dude. She got us fair and square."

"I don't know about fair," Brad said. "I got saddled with the slow horse. There's nothing fair about that."

Philip eyed the man smugly. He hadn't forgotten that Brad was still the target of an investigation and he'd been keeping a close eye on him, even when it didn't look like it. There hadn't been any more attempts on Brad's part to sneak away and use his phone. For the most part he'd been keeping a low profile, seemingly focused on the show and winning. Since Naomi had caught him, she'd had members of her team doing random checks on all of them when it was least expected.

Philip was still trying to connect Jim to the previous accidents, but then mused he just might have been wrong since nothing else had gone awry and the past few days had been problem free. Maybe the accidents had been just that. He slid his attention back to his surroundings and their conversation.

"I've heard it said that all is fair in love and war!" Philip slid from the top of his horse and headed toward the cameraman waiting to film his reaction.

THE WEATHER WAS picture-perfect. Even with the dry heat, they could not have asked for better. The fresh air was rejuvenating. The sun was shining down between the occasional cumulus clouds. The backdrop of tufted cotton candy clouds dotting the bright blue sky complemented the loveliness of the landscape. Everything about the ranch could have been a Bob Ross painting. But storms were predicted for the following day, threatening to spoil the tranquility of the show's backdrop. Because of that, Naomi sat with Jim and Jude assessing the schedule and reevaluating their plans.

"Them corralling the cattle in bad weather is not an option," Naomi said emphatically. "That's not a risk I'm willing to take. Too many things could go wrong and right now everything is going perfectly. Let's not jinx it."

They were down to their final six contestants. After Grace's win, Malia and Juan-Carlo had been eliminated, the two coming in last place. Malia had crossed the finish line, but Juan-Carlo had thrown in the towel at the wood-chopping station. Naomi wasn't willing to purposely put the remaining players in harm's way.

"We can move up the bull competition and film in the arena. It's covered, so the rain won't be a factor," Jim suggested.

Naomi nodded. "That's a good idea. Let me double-check with Jasper. If the bull I want is ready, then that's what we'll do."

"I also think we need to put a little more focus on the other players and less on your boyfriend," Jim suddenly interjected.

Naomi bristled. "Excuse me?" she said. "My boyfriend?"

Jim shrugged his shoulders. "Well, you did handpick him. Some people think you actually threw in a ringer, hoping to help his career. He does seem to be winning immunity more than anyone else and a few of the guys think he may have pulled up in that run yesterday to give Grace the win. You know, to throw everyone off."

Suddenly pissed, Naomi found her good mood tossed into the wind. "And who are *some people*?" she demanded, thrown off by his comment. Jim always had a way of sucking the joy out of a moment. Even if he was right.

"People talk," Jim said. "But you've been around long enough to know that."

She shook her head, fighting not to spew venom through the room. "What I know is that no one here has done anything to influence any of the competitions in favor of one player over another. And if anyone says that, then they damn well better have proof." Naomi couldn't help but wonder why he'd chosen now to challenge her, feeling like Jim was up to no good. Philip's theory about someone sabotaging her suddenly rang loudly in her thoughts.

Jim held up his hands, his expression condescending. "I'm not saying anything, so don't get upset with me. I'm just the messenger. Everyone can see he's your favorite and they think you're giving him a leg-up in the competition."

Naomi stood, annoyance blanketing her expression. Frustration was holding hands with a sense of betrayal. Jim clearly didn't have her back and wasn't there to support her efforts. There was also an internal battle pulling at her spirit, knowing her feelings for Philip had gotten in the way of her job. If Jim wanted to hurt her, outing them even if he didn't have proof would be enough to tarnish her reputation and cast a shadow of doubt on her abilities. She sighed heavily as she went on the offensive.

"If someone did say anything of the sort to you, then you should have shut it down. Because this reflects as much on you as it does on me. And for the record, Mr. Rees is not my boyfriend. I don't date boys!"

Jude stood with her. "On that note, I will catch up with Janice and update the call schedule. Is there anything else I can help with?" he asked.

"No. Thank you," she said, as she glared in Jim's direction. "Everyone knows what to do. I'm headed to the main house to talk to Jasper."

Jude shook his head at Jim as he eased past him toward the exit. "That was not cool, dude."

"So now this travesty is all my fault!" Jim threw up his hands in frustration.

"What is your problem?" Naomi snapped. "You've been gunning for me since day one. This is supposed to be a team effort and you've been everything except a team player."

"Everyone knows you didn't deserve this job. Who did you cuddle up to?" Jim had stepped toward her, standing toe to toe as he spit malice in her face.

Naomi spat back, "I've got three more years of experience over you and a more impressive résumé. I started in the trenches, and I earned this spot. My *daddy* didn't give it to me," she sniped, thoughts of Ben Colton piercing her stomach. "The better question is, who did *you* cuddle up to? *Rumor* has it you have a thing for kneepads."

Jim's face turned a brilliant shade of beet red. He looked like he was about to implode. For a brief second Naomi thought he might actually throw a punch at her. His fists were clenched tightly together at his sides and his left eye began to twitch. She took a step back, her stance defensive, but she had no intention of backing down.

"You stupid..." Jim began to scream in her face, his voice cracking with rage.

The moment was interrupted when Felicia stepped into the room, Philip, Fred and Brad following after her. The tension in the room was corporeal, sitting in the air like flames atop a log. Their laughter came to an abrupt halt as they looked from Naomi to Jim and back.

"I'm sorry," Felicia said, "I didn't mean to interrupt. We were looking for you, Jim. You're supposed to do their confessional interviews down by the pond. They've been waiting." The young woman looked nervous, as if fearful that Jim might turn his ire on her.

"Y'all look mad," Brad said, an amused smirk pulling at his lips. "Not having a lover's quarrel, are you? 'Cause I had an ex-girlfriend who looked at me just like that when she was mad and I was screaming at her."

"Jim was just leaving," Naomi said, tension still lingering in her tone as she grew annoyed with Brad. "I apologize for holding him past his appointment time."

Jim turned, hurrying toward the door. "Let's do this," he muttered.

Felicia gave Naomi a questioning look before turning to follow the man. Fred and Brad scurried after her. Philip lingered, his body language tense.

"Are you okay?" he asked when the others had disappeared out the door.

She nodded. "No. He just infuriates me. I probably said some things I will have to apologize for and that makes me even madder."

"What can I do?" Philip asked, concern washing over his expression.

Naomi shook her head. "I'll be fine. You need to catch up with them. He's already accused me of playing favorites and rigging the games in your favor."

Philip grunted. "Really?"

"Please, don't make an issue of his ignorance. I know better. And anyone who has ever worked with me knows my integrity. He doesn't bother me."

"Well, he bothers me. And him screaming in your face like that isn't going to happen again. But, no worries. I'll set him straight and I'll do it very nicely. I promise."

Her voice dropped. "I wish I could kiss you."

Philip stepped forward and wrapped his arms around her shoulders. "Will a hug suffice?"

Naomi leaned into his chest. Her arms hung down to her sides and she pressed her face against the front of his shirt. Taking a deep inhale, she savored the scent of him, his cologne scented with bergamot and cedarwood wrapped in subtle citrus tones. He smelled divine and Naomi felt her tattered nerves beginning to calm. Philip held her tightly until she finally took a step back.

"You should go do your interview," she said. "I'll be fine."

Philip nodded, and then he leaned to press his lips to hers, leaving her with the gentlest kiss ever.

THE POND WAS a beautiful expanse of water situated behind the main lodge and a fence of perfectly manicured American elm trees. Many weddings had been photographed by the waterside.

Jim's bad mood followed him to the interviews. His disinterest was acute and his questions were dry. Felicia had twice prodded him to stay on script. The third time he snapped at her, bringing the girl to tears. She excused herself, rushing back toward the makeshift office space.

"Women!" Jim spat, a string of expletives following his opinion of women.

"Sounds like someone's still mad," Fred said jokingly.

"Women need to know their place and stay in it," Jim continued.

"And where might that be?" Philip asked.

Jim didn't bother to answer. "It's your turn," he said

instead, gesturing for Philip to take the seat Brad and Fred had held before him.

Brad stood, brushing his hands down the front of his slacks. "I think I'll head down to get me something to eat. I'm starved," he said. "I'll catch up with you later."

Fred nodded. "That's sounds like a plan to me. I hope they still have some of those chocolate chip cookies left."

"You should try the peanut butter ones," Brad said. "Those are my favorite!"

"I'll see you both later," Philip called after them as they headed off toward the commissary.

He sat down and waited as the cameraman adjusted his equipment. When they were ready, Jim fired questions at him about his experiences thus far, his loss to Grace, his immunity win, and how he was feeling about the show's progress in general.

The production team had schooled Philip on how to answer most of his questions to gain fans. He was also mindful not to insult anyone. The cameraman nodded his approval as he watched him give his best performance yet.

Jim suddenly slid his clipboard under his arm, clasping his hands together in front of himself. "Do you feel like you have an unfair advantage in this game?" he asked.

The look Philip gave him underlined his skepticism, knowing Jim was up to something. Maybe, he thought, he hadn't been wrong at all, and Jim was behind the sabotage. He was curious to see where the man was going with his interrogation. "I don't understand your question. What advantage would I have that would be seen as unfair?"

Jim shrugged. "Well, you were cherry-picked for the spot."

"I was asked to replace someone who couldn't participate. I don't see that as being cherry-picked," Philip answered.

"Are you sleeping with the producer?"

"Are *you*?" Emotion flooded Philip's face. He wasn't about to let anyone, least of all Jim, be disparaging toward Naomi. The insinuation that anything that existed between him and her was wrong didn't sit well with him at all.

"Don't get smart with me," Jim snapped, his tone curt.

Philip stood up. "I think we're done here. You are way out of order."

Jim held up both hands, the gesture meant to be apologetic. "Look, I'm sorry. I was out of line."

"Yes, you were!" Philip turned, disconnecting the audio equipment strapped to his torso.

"You don't understand," Jim started. "That woman…"

Philip shook his head, interrupting him. "Let it go," he said.

"You're right," Jim said shaking. "I'm sorry." He extended his hand as an olive branch.

It happened before Philip could even consider stopping himself. As he shook hands with Jim, he suddenly snatched the man off his feet, sending him crashing into the pond as he stumbled. "Oh, Jim fell!" Philip called out.

Jim floundered, unable to get his footing and pick himself up. He sputtered water as he tried to speak. Philip reached out his hand, grabbing Jim's arm. Just as Jim tried to pull himself up and out of the brackish water Philip shoved him back under, holding him there until he began to struggle.

"I got you, Jim!" he yelled over his shoulder. "Hang on, buddy!"

Philip pulled him and then pushed him back down; once, twice and then a third time. He was angry and trying hard to harness his rage. "You're a slippery sucker, Jim!"

The last time he pulled the man up out of the water, he tugged him close, leaning to whisper into his ear. Philip's voice was low, his tone even. There was no missing the intent behind the words that followed. "If you ever speak to Naomi like that again, if you even look in her direction sideways, I will hurt you. In fact, if I see or hear of you disrespecting any woman, you will regret it. Do we understand each other?"

Jim nodded, still unable to speak, a faint hint of fear clouding his eyes.

Philip pulled him forward until he was standing on solid ground. He brushed at the water dripping off the man's shoulders. Jim's whole-body shook, and Philip wasn't certain, but he thought he might be crying. "Now," he said, his words coming quietly, "we can be good friends or bad enemies. It's your choice. But you do not want to be on my bad side."

He smiled, then waved a hand. "He's good! I fished him out. Jim's okay," he shouted.

THE DOOR SLAMMING vibrated throughout the entire lower level of the lodge. Jasper rounded the corner, coming from the office to see what was going on.

"Have you lost your mind slamming doors like that?" he asked when he spied Naomi in the large great room.

Tears suddenly rained down her cheeks. "I hate this job," she said.

Her brother stood staring at her, suddenly at a loss for words. Before he could respond, Aubrey pushed past him, her brow furrowed with concern.

"What's wrong, Naomi?" she questioned as she rushed to her baby sister's side and sat down beside her.

Naomi leaned her head on Aubrey's shoulder as her sister wrapped her arms around her torso. She sobbed softly.

"Okay, then," Jasper said, looking nervous. "I'll just leave you two girls…"

"Go away, Jasper," Aubrey snapped at her twin. "Don't you see she's upset?"

"I'm going, Aubrey," he snapped back. "But you are not the boss of me!"

Naomi suddenly laughed, reminded of when they'd been little kids and her brother would always profess Aubrey was not his boss. The memory was like a sweet treat against her heart.

"Well, he made you laugh. That's a good sign," Aubrey said, giving Naomi a smile. "Do you want to talk about it?"

"Jim is infuriating!"

"Jim is one of those men who don't like women. He's a nice-looking guy, but he has zero personality with women," Aubrey remarked. "Because he's been turned down so much, he blames all of us for his lot in life. His disdain is almost pathological."

"You psychoanalyzed all that from him?" Jasper raised a brow.

"I've just known one too many men like him."

"What did he do?" Jasper asked, still standing across the room.

Naomi shifted her gaze to where her brother stood, curiosity seeping from his eyes. "He's accused me of playing favorites with the contestants. Then he insinuated I slept my way into this position. He's called my integrity into question. Then he had the audacity to get in my face and scream at me like he'd lost his mind. I honestly thought we were going to come to blows."

"Oh, hell, no!" Jasper quipped, his eyes widening. "Sounds like he needs to be reminded where he is and who he's dealing with." He spun on his heels and tore out the door.

Naomi called after him, but her brother never looked back, intent on defending her honor. She shook her head. "He's going to make it worse if he does something stupid."

"Let him go be your big brother. He really does like thinking he's our defender and protector. It's a Colton male thing!" Aubrey shrugged.

"I didn't mean to drop this in your lap. I really didn't."

"You needed a shoulder and I had one."

"Well, I need it for a little longer," Naomi said. She took a deep breath, gathering her thoughts. Her eyes shifted from side to side as she pondered her sister's reaction to her next words. There was a sense of relief when she finally said them. "I think I'm falling in love."

Aubrey's expression lifted in surprise as Naomi continued.

"I know we barely know each other. But there's something about him that's pure joy. When we're together…"

"You've been together?" Aubrey interrupted. "And I'm assuming we're talking about tall, dark and delicious?"

Naomi nodded. "He snuck into my cabin…"

"I told Jasper he needed to check the windows and doors on all the cabins!"

"…and we spent the night together…"

"You tramp! I'm telling Mommy!"

"If you do, I'm going to tell Mommy I saw you kissing that Lancaster boy behind the school dumpster when you were in the sixth grade."

"Ewww! Billy Lancaster with the lazy eye! And he kissed me. I did *not* kiss him. But for the record, Billy has blossomed in his old age. I stalk him on TikTok!"

"Seriously, though, I didn't have sex with him, Aubrey. We just talked and held each other. Philip has me feeling things I've never felt before." Naomi spent the next few minutes updating her sister on everything that had happened between her and Philip. "I've never wanted any man this much, and it scares me. With other men it was always about the physical connection. Our connection is so very different. I find myself sharing things with him I would never tell any man. When we're together I feel comfortable and confident. He makes me feel complete and I've never before felt as if I were lacking. The energy between us is magical, and I don't want to ever see that end."

"Tell him that."

"We are not supposed to be fraternizing with each other. My credibility with the production company and my crew would be ruined. I could lose my job if this gets out."

"Then either don't fraternize or don't tell. But this show isn't a guarantee of anything in your future. You're proceeding with hopes the production company can sell it to a network when it's finished. If they don't, then what? I'm thinking Philip might be a better risk if he's feeling the same way about you. Another perfect show will come, Naomi. I can't say the same thing about another perfect love."

Naomi sat in silence for a good few minutes pondering her sister's comments. What was she willing to sacrifice for the future she wanted? Was the fight for the show and her producer title worth the possibility of a happily-ever-after with Philip? Would being with Philip mean giving up her long-held dream of career success? Could she possibly have both or potentially lose everything trying? It felt as if it were too much for her to consider and come up with an answer for in such a short period of time.

Her whole body seemed to cave, her shoulders rolling forward in defeat. For a brief moment she gave herself permission to not be okay. To be angry and hurt and frustrated that nothing ever seemed to be easy. When that moment was over, she pulled herself upright, straightened her shoulders and looked her sister in the eye.

Aubrey kissed her cheek, then stood up. "I need to get back to paying the bills on this joint. Are you going to be okay?"

Naomi nodded. "I'll be fine. I really just needed to vent. I appreciate you always being here for me."

"That's what family is for."

PHILIP WAS STILL standing with Jim when Jasper stomped toward them. It didn't take rocket science to figure out Naomi's brother had heard what Jim had done, and he had something to say about it.

Jim looked like a wet cat. He was soaked through, and his feelings were apparently bruised. The camera man was still filming, not wanting to miss a minute of anything else that might happen.

"What happened here?" Jasper asked as he moved into the mix, sensing the tension in the air.

"Jim had a little accident. He fell into the pond."

"You...you...drowned...me..." Jim sputtered.

"You're still very much alive, Jim."

"You pushed..."

Philip laughed. "It's going to be okay, Jim." He turned to Jasper. "Jim and I had to come to an understanding. Jim promises to behave going forward."

Jasper looked from one man to the other. He nodded. "Naomi was upset."

"She doesn't have to worry." Philip slapped Jim on the back, the man pitching forward and needing to stop himself from falling. "Isn't that right, Jim?"

Not bothering to answer, Jim stormed off. The other men stood and watched him as he stomped away like a petulant child. Jasper and Philip exchanged a look.

"What'd you do?" Jasper asked.

Philip shrugged, a wry smirk on his face. "I had to remind him how to treat a lady."

"It was dope!" the cameraman exclaimed. He shook Philip's hand. "Remind me to never mess with you!"

"Thanks," Jasper said. "My sister's important to me. She doesn't deserve to be mistreated by someone who's supposed to be working toward the same goals and supporting her efforts."

"I agree. Your sister's a very special woman. She means a lot to me," Philip answered. "And no one is ever going to treat her badly on my watch."

PHILIP RETREATED TO his tent, reflecting on what he had done and why. Jim's blatant disrespect toward Naomi had infuriated him, and to see him screaming in her face when they'd walked into the office had sent him right over the edge. Jim had been lucky that Philip had had some time to cool off before he responded. Had he reacted in the moment, it might have ended differently.

He sighed. He wasn't sure what would happen next. Jim might insist he be removed from the set. That moment had jeopardized his assignment and he was beginning to feel some kind of way. Naomi had become his priority when his priority should have been Brad.

He could have kicked himself for making that mistake but he didn't have one regret about putting Jim in his place. Coming to Naomi's defense would always supersede all else and knowing that had him considering what their future might look like. Because he was determined to have a future with Naomi Colton. He'd fallen hard, his whole heart caught up with emotion. He loved her, the simplicity of that statement feeling monumental.

He enjoyed every moment they spent together. Falling asleep by her side ranked high on his list of favorite things to do. He only wished they didn't have to keep things hidden, and he was excited for the day when he could make love to her. Having to settle for her kisses was thrilling, but every time he held her he wanted more. And so did she. But more couldn't happen until they were both done with the show and didn't have to be the dirty little secret they couldn't share. And he couldn't be done with the show until he figured out Brad's end game and he took him down.

He sensed, though, that something was about to change. Something he wouldn't be able to control. And that feeling unnerved him. He wasn't certain how to prepare, and that bothered him, too.

Chapter Fourteen

Naomi had watched the footage of Philip and Jim a dozen times, rewinding and watching it over and over. The cameraman had slipped it into the dailies, the film not labeled or included in the log sheets. Philip stood over her shoulder watching with her, his nonchalant expression showing his disinterest.

She shook her head. "You should not have done that." She smiled, grateful that he had. No man had ever defended her like that before, and it moved her spirit to know he'd been willing to risk everything for her.

"I didn't do anything. I think the footage shows I was trying to help him get on his feet. He was having a hard time standing upright."

They both laughed.

"Have we seen Jim this morning?" Naomi asked Felicia, who was also in the room.

The young woman shook her head. "No. He hasn't reported in."

"He probably flew to LA to tattle in person. He's really good at that." Naomi pulled her hands over her face and through her hair. "Well, we can't worry about him right now. I need to start filming on schedule and that doesn't give us a whole lot of time. We need to…"

The telephone rang, stalling her comment. Naomi shot Philip a look as Felicia moved to answer it.

"*In the Saddle!* You've reached the production office. This is Felicia."

Shaking her head, Naomi knew who was on the other line before Felicia told her. Cupping her hand over the receiver, Felicia whispered, "It's Mr. Wallace. He wants to speak with you."

Philip gave Naomi a questioning look.

"Allan Wallace is the production company's president." She held out her hand for the handset as Felicia passed it to her. She took a deep breath before she spoke. "Allan, good morning. I'm surprised to hear from you this early."

Philip crossed her arms over his chest as she paused, listening to the man on the other end.

"Is that what you were told?" Naomi chuckled. "Well, I can assure you that no such thing happened. It's my understanding that Jim slipped and accidentally fell into the pond. Mr. Rees, one of the contestants, helped Jim out. Apparently, that was not easy because of the slope of the landscape and Jim fighting against his help. We have it all on videotape. Personally, I think Jim may be under too much stress and I'm not sure how we can best help him. The schedule is tight, and I'm committed to keeping us well within the budget. We're all pulling more than our own weight to see that happens."

There was another lengthy pause as Naomi listened. She rolled her eyes skyward before she spoke again. "I can appreciate that, Allan, but you also have to look at it from my perspective. I'm determined to give you a good product and I can't do that if he continually tries to undermine me. I respect his connections as well, but his connections aren't going to help either of us get this job done. Hard work, determination and grit will. You entrusted me to accomplish this job and I hope you will continue to support me in doing just that."

Philip dropped his hand against her shoulder and give it a light squeeze. Her body was tense and she appreciated him comforting her without even having to ask.

She finally concluded the call. "Thank you, sir. I appreciate your support… I'm glad you liked that. We've got some great shots. I'm willing to risk everything to prove this can be a number one reality show." She paused. "You have a good day!"

As Naomi disconnected the call, she shook her head from side to side. "I told you. Apparently, he's been making calls since yesterday afternoon, trying to get production shut down. I just don't get him."

"Don't you worry about Jim," Philip said. "You just do what you need to do. We will all support you."

Naomi pressed her hand atop his. "I appreciate that." Heat simmered on low between them, and the flutter in her midsection felt like millions of little dancing feet performing a recital in her tummy.

There was a moment between them. Neither spoke; no words were needed. It felt natural and right as they inhaled the breath the other exhaled, sharing space that was comforting and safe. He squeezed her shoulder a second time. "I should go," he said softly. "Will I see you later?"

Naomi nodded. "I'll see you at the next event. Good luck!"

Philip smiled. "Thanks. Something tells me I'm going to need it." He winked his eye at her.

Naomi smiled back, biting down against her bottom lip as that flutter in her belly began to beat like a drumline.

THE REMAINING CONTESTANTS didn't look overly confident as Jim explained the next challenge to them. The contest was an adult version of one Naomi remembered doing at a local rodeo when she'd been a little girl. It had involved a flag and a baby bull. The goal had been to snatch the flag off the calf who raced like lightning from one end of the field to the other. It had been exhausting as she'd sped after it, and a good time was had by all.

For this game there would be a flag but no calf. The bull, a young stud, was sizeable but not as massive as others. Naomi had chosen him specifically for his size and temperament. Since it was usually kept with the female cows it tended to be less aggressive than those sometimes kept alone. Her brother had named it Charles, and Charles Bull had personality galore. He would give the remaining players a run for their money, and she anticipated the entire experience would be entertaining to watch.

Naomi didn't bother to comment on Jim's return. He acted as if nothing had happened, or had been said, and so she followed his lead. They were polite to each other, but it was clear they weren't going to be the best of friends.

Grace was the only woman remaining, and when Brad prodded her to just drop out of the competition she declined. "I may not be able to get the flag," she said, "but I will give it my best shot."

"I plan to win," Fred said. "I'll even take the hit if I have to."

Philip was less inclined to put himself in the line of fire, slightly intimidated by the animal's size. They all laughed when he said so.

"He's young," Naomi said as he stood with Harold and Fred, the trio debating the best way to go about winning the challenge. "He's only three years old and he's not oversize. I think he's still weighing in under a thousand pounds. They do come bigger!"

"I'm sure it's big enough," Grace said.

Minutes later Monty made his entrance, riding in on a white horse. He wore white denim jeans, a white dress shirt and the slickest pair of white cowboy boots. He dismounted the horse and stepped with ease into his frame. A smoke machine provided a hint of special effects around him and the contestants. His monologue was short and sweet as he wished the final six good luck.

Behind him, the bull, locked in the chute, was not happy, bucking before he was even released. From where she stood watching, Naomi instinctively knew something was off and then Monty lowered his arm signaling them to release Charles. But it wasn't Charles that suddenly shot out of the chute. The yellow Char-bray bull standing in the center of the arena was three times the size of Charles. It was muscle upon muscle with thick bones, larger feet, a massive neck, and a large, bony head with protective ridges over its eyes.

Naomi suddenly thought of Bodacious, a bucking bull infamously known throughout the rodeo sport of bull riding as "the world's most dangerous bull." Bodacious had a reputation for injuring riders. He was not an animal to play with, and neither was his cousin standing there in the arena, snorting at the contestants. She instantly recognized that anyone close to the animal with no experience in how to handle him was in danger, someone wanting them to get hurt.

Naomi leaped from her seat, rushing to the metal fencing that bordered the enclosure. The bull was tossing his head from side to side. He widened his stance, then lowered his front end as he began to paw at the dirt. She knew the beast was ready to charge and saw Fred standing directly in his path, preparing to grab the red flag threaded through the harness around the bull's neck.

She screamed, waving her arms for attention. "Everyone get out! Now! Get out!"

Confusion reigned in the moments it took for Naomi's cries to register. Philip pulled Grace toward the fencing and Harold tripped running toward the other end of the arena. The bull charged at Fred, who hadn't moved fast enough. The moment was surreal, playing out in slow motion. Everyone heard the sound of the bull slamming its massive head into Fred's side. They heard bone snap, crackle and then pop, as the large man went down like a rag doll, hitting the ground with a loud grunt. He screamed out, the level of hurt unfathomable to the others.

It was Jasper who jumped in the arena with them all, he and his team waving their arms and prodding the bull back toward the exit. As Jasper slammed the gate closed, the team of paramedics rushed forward to assist Fred, who lay writhing in pain on the ground.

Naomi climbed the fence and jumped down inside. She ran to Fred's side, kneeling down to take his hand. As they lifted him onto a gurney she whispered into his ear. "It's going to be okay, Fred. You're going to be just fine. I'm right here and I'm not going anywhere." As they loaded the man into the back of an ambulance, Naomi climbed in with him, headed to the hospital.

"What just happened?" Grace questioned.

Philip shook his head. "I think they sent in the wrong bull. The one we were supposed to use is smaller."

"That one looked like a killer!" the woman exclaimed.

"It sure wasn't looking to be friends," Philip said.

"I think I need a drink," Grace responded. "This is too much!"

Philip watched as she turned from him, searching out the exit. He turned his attention to Jasper, moving in the man's direction. Jasper met him midway of the arena's center.

"What went wrong?" he asked.

Jasper shook his head. "I'm not sure. My ranch hand

says that was the bull Jim requested. He thought it was too much, but Jim insisted. And Jim said Naomi approved the change."

"She would never do that," said Philip.

"I know." Jasper took a deep breath. "There's something else, too."

"What?" Philip eyed him with a raised brow, his expression questioning.

"The vet just called. Those calves didn't eat mushrooms. They were poisoned with cyanide. We found the bottle in Jim's cabin. One of our cleaning staff found it under the bed. She didn't know if she should touch it and asked Aubrey to come take a look. We had just gotten off the phone with the vet and knew immediately. I locked down the room to preserve any evidence and called the police. They're on their way to arrest him."

Philip's eyes darted back and forth as the news registered. He hadn't been wrong. Jim had been responsible for the sabotage. He hated that it had taken another act of harm for the truth to come to light. "Does Naomi know?" Philip asked.

Her brother shook his head. "No. That wasn't something I thought I should tell her over the phone while she's at the hospital. Naomi pretends to be tough but she's extremely sensitive, and I imagine this is going to hit her hard."

Both men knew Naomi was going to be devastated when she heard the news. Philip was grateful Jasper had prioritized his sister's feelings. "Good call," he said with a nod of his head.

"Have you seen Jim?" Jasper questioned.

Philip shook his head as he headed toward the exit. "No, but I'm going to find him."

Naomi was pacing the hospital waiting room. She'd been there for a good hour waiting to hear how Fred was doing. She'd fielded telephone calls from Felicia and Aubrey, everyone waiting for news. Philip was the only one she wished she could have a conversation with. Everything had happened so quickly that she hadn't had an opportunity to ask if he were all right. She'd seen him running off behind the bull and then Fred had gone flying into the air, landing so harshly that *she* still hurt from the impact. She could only begin to imagine what was going on back at the ranch and how the others might be feeling. Because she was broken. And scared. And worried for the gentle giant who had only wanted to make his wife and family proud.

They had canceled production for the rest of the day and Naomi felt horrible that in the back of her mind she was trying to figure out how to get things back on track by morning. She also had a lengthy list of questions about the animal that had derailed the day.

When the emergency room physician finally came out to speak with her, she was ready to pull out her hair. It had felt as if an eternity had passed, the waiting putting her in a foul mood.

The doctor shook her hand. "My name is Dr. Patterson, and you must be Ms. Colton?"

"That's correct. How is he doing?" Naomi asked.

"Mr. Harmon suffered some serious injuries. He has broken his leg in multiple places and has fractured his hip. It's my understanding he was headbutted by a bull?"

Naomi nodded. "Yes, sir, he's been competing in a Wild West competition and the bull got the best of him."

The doctor gave her a nod. "Unfortunately, he's going to be of commission for the next six weeks at a minimum. We have called his wife and she is on her way. That's really all I can tell you until she arrives."

Naomi extended her hand to shake his. "Thank you, Dr. Patterson. We appreciate everything you're doing."

As the doctor walked away, Naomi texted a message to Felicia, and then a second to Aubrey, giving them a quick update. Heading back to the ranch, she wanted nothing but to see Philip and throw herself into his arms. Then she had questions that someone needed to answer, starting with how Charlie Bull had been replaced by that mammoth creature who'd been ready to decimate everything in its way.

JIM WASN'T IN his cabin when Philip went looking for him. One of the ranch hands was standing guard over his personal property, waiting for the police to arrive. He was polite but firm about Philip not getting inside.

Philip stared out over the landscape, his eyes shifting back and forth as he considered where the man might have disappeared to. He was headed back toward the production office when he spied Jim speed-walking toward the barn. His pace was rushed, and Philip reasoned Jim probably knew it was over.

He hurried in that direction, breaking out into a sprint after him. As he entered through the barn doors,

Jim was pulling a saddle from the rack. The horse he was preparing to mount was the one Grace rode and had often claimed.

"Headed somewhere?" Philip asked.

Jim jumped, his expression stunned. "Don't touch me!"

Philip chuckled, lifting his hands as if he planned to surrender. "I just want to talk to you."

"You think I don't know what's going on with you and that woman," Jim spat, his tone bitter. "And she thinks I'm stupid."

Philip shook his head. "You shouldn't have done what you did, Jim."

"They will never be able to prove I did anything. I'm not stupid and no one will be able to tie me to any of the accidents."

Philip shrugged. "That's not true."

"They don't know a damn thing!" Jim snapped. "They don't know what I've had to put up with since I got here!"

"So why don't you tell me." Philip's tone was even and controlled. He took two steps back and leaned against a stall door. He could tell Jim had begun to unravel. He was emotionally fragile, and Philip sensed it wouldn't take much for him to snap. He had to keep Jim talking for as long as he could. He slid his hands into his pockets, not wanting to appear threatening. Jim began to ramble, perspiration beading across his brow.

"I was there when they took that first meeting with her, and she pitched her show. From the start the production company was going to roll with her idea and let me run production. Then just like that I got down-graded to her second in charge and she's pulling all the strings." Jim snarled. "Batting her eyelashes at every Tom, Dick and Harry for attention! Just like you those guys were falling over their own feet for her."

"But you didn't fall for it," Philip interjected.

"Hell no! I knew she didn't have the experience. And she brought a lot of baggage to the table. Everyone's heard about her father being shysty. They say the apple doesn't fall far from the tree. She couldn't be trusted! Anyone could see that!"

Philip shook his head. "So what did you do?"

"I had to prove she wasn't competent for the job."

"Even if it meant torpedoing the season?"

"By any means necessary!" Jim shouted. "Once she was out the door, I would have turned it all around."

"What went wrong? What did you try to do?"

"I wanted her to be out of compliance with the con-tract. If she started the show short a player, they'd have no choice but to put me in charge."

"So you were responsible for that player falling?"

Jim shrugged his shoulders. "It's not like I actu-ally pushed him. So what if his saddle…" Jim paused, seeming to think about what he'd done. He suddenly continued, not finishing his thought about that saddle. He threw up his hands in frustration. "Then what hap-pens…she puts you on the roster!" Jim tossed him a look, his face flushed, looking like he might implode.

Philip's head bobbed up and down as if he agreed with the man. "That wasn't cool. I can see how that would piss you off."

"It did. I had a great lineup ready to compete and she undermined my work. Frat boys…" he muttered, recalling what Naomi had said to him.

"She needed to pay." Philip nodded. "I would have made her pay, too. What did you do next?" Philip questioned as he pulled his hands from his pockets and folded his arms over his chest.

"What didn't I do!" Jim was suddenly gleeful, excited to detail his antics. Then just like that he turned, hostility seeping from his eyes.

"I know what you're trying to do. I know she's got you wrapped around her finger. You can't trick me."

"That's not what I was doing, Jim. I just wanted to talk."

Jim finished saddling the horse and pulled himself atop the animal. He shook his head. "I should have taken care of you when I had the chance," he said. "You should have never walked away from that fire!"

JIM BAUER HAD purposely sabotaged the show. Philip was still missing pieces to the puzzle, but he would have bet everything he cherished on Jim's guilt. After comparing his suspicions with Jasper, he was certain Jim's actions had critically injured two men and killed small animals, and now he was about to ride off into the sunset as if he hadn't done anything wrong. Seeing him trotting off on horseback had Philip ready to spit nails. Jim was a threat to himself and to others and he needed to be stopped. Philip needed to make sure he was never able to hurt Naomi ever again. He reached into his pocket and turned off the recorder hidden inside. He had hoped for a full confession but that didn't happen. He also wasn't willing to let it, or Jim, go.

Philip had saddled Bubbles, and he and the horse were galloping across the fields after Jim. Jasper had called in the law, and Philip knew it was only a matter of minutes before the place would be crawling with police officers. By then, he needed to have Jim detained and hopefully a full confession on tape.

"Where is Philip going?" Naomi asked. She'd seen him headed into the woods as her Uber driver had pulled in. Jasper had met her in front of the main lodge, his hands clutching his hips and his expression grim.

"I think he's gone after Jim," her brother answered.

"I don't understand."

"Jim was responsible for all your mishaps. Philip even thinks he caused your first guy to fall off his horse. Apparently my 4-H students told him Jim had been checking the saddles before those first contestants went down to ride. And we know he's the one who poisoned my calves."

Naomi's eyes widened. "Oh my gosh!"

Jasper nodded. "The police are on their way."

Naomi suddenly turned and bolted toward the barn.

Her brother called after her. "Naomi, where are you going?"

Naomi didn't bother to answer. She knew she didn't have the words or the time to explain that something deep in her gut was telling her to go find Philip. And that meant riding a horse into the woods after the man she loved.

PHILIP FOUND HIMSELF questioning his choices. The brush was substantial beneath the thick trees, and they seemed to be headed far from Gemini Ranch. He wasn't sure what Jim's end game was or why he'd chosen horseback as the means to flee the scene. If making an escape was what he was striving for, Jim was riding too casually, not seeming to be in any hurry to get wherever he was going. So casually that Philip had caught up to him in no time at all. Now he followed behind him and his horse as if they were both out for a casual stroll.

They suddenly moved out of the woods into a clearing. The open fields went as far as the eye could see, a landscape of green, lush grass and the occasional sunflower in full bloom. Above them the sky was a brilliant shade of blue and the sun was just beginning its afternoon descent toward evening.

Philip called his name, pulling up on his horse to slow him down. "Jim! You need to stop!"

"I don't need you to tell me what I should be doing!" Jim shouted back. He and his horse turned to face off with Philip. "Why are you here?"

"I want to help. I think you need support right now!"

Jim tilted his head ever so slightly. It was almost as if he were listening to someone no one else could see.

Philip pressed him. "Why, Jim? Why did you do it?"

"I didn't do anything!"

"Why did you lie about the bull?" he questioned, still fishing for a full confession from the man.

Jim laughed. "He was a beauty, wasn't he? Naomi wasn't willing to push the limits and the show needed a push."

"A man was injured, Jim. We don't know his condition yet, but it was bad."

"His stupidity. No one told him to stand in the bull's way."

"Why lie and say Naomi approved it when you know she didn't? If you thought it was necessary for the show, then why not stand by your decision?"

"You ask too many questions, Rees!"

"I need answers, Jim. The students from the 4-H program claim they saw you the morning of the first accident. That you had gone to the barn to check the saddles. Is that true?"

Jim laughed. "You should always check your own saddle. He claimed he was an expert rider. He should have known that. What if someone had cut one of the straps?"

"Did you cut the straps?"

Jim laughed again. His horse danced from side to side, the two suddenly looking like they were practicing for a rodeo sideshow.

"Why did you poison the calves?" Philip asked. "They found the cyanide."

Jim suddenly stopped, his expression dropping. "I did what I had to," he snapped. "Had I been the producer none of this would have been necessary. None of it. This was supposed to be my project." He slapped the palm of his hand against his forehead. His frustration was palpable as he seemed to fight demons that had turned on him.

Philip took a deep breath, holding it tightly as he assessed his options. Clearly, Jim wasn't acting rationally, and he didn't want to do anything to further aggravate the situation. Jim needed help and Philip was obligated to help him get that aid. "Come back to the main lodge with me," he said, his tone calm and even. "We can talk about it. Figure out what we need to do. I'll even help explain it to everyone so they understand."

Jim's gaze narrowed as he lowered his head. At the same time Philip heard his name ringing through the air and he turned to see who was behind him. His breath caught deep in his chest as his eyes widened. Naomi was galloping toward them, she and her horse moving out of the shadows of the tall elm trees.

Later, he wouldn't be able to explain what happened first, just that everything seemed to happen all at once. He was looking toward Naomi when his horse suddenly reared back, nearly throwing him from his saddle. A familiar rattle startled the horse just as Philip caught sight of it out of the corner of his eye. The timber rattlesnake was vibrating its tail to announce its annoyance.

As he turned back, he heard Jim's awkward laugh as the man shook multiple snakes to the ground from a canvas sack, throwing them in his direction. Bubbles bucked a second time, throwing himself back again as he shied away from the reptiles. Philip was thrown off balance a second time, but again, he caught himself. Bubbles suddenly pitched forward, breaking out into a full gallop. It happened quickly, too many parts at play as Philip struggled to get the horse to stop. Panic spread through him as control slipped even further through his fingers. He was lost.

Bubbles was careening forward, evidently ignoring

Philip's cues despite his efforts to safely bring the animal to a halt. Naomi gave chase, tightening her legs around her own mount, to move him to a full run. As she caught up to Bubbles, she shouted, the wind carrying her voice through the warm air.

"Shorten both reins!" she yelled, "and hold them tightly! Then brace one hand on your horse's neck and grab his mane!" She nodded as Philip did what he was told, galloping alongside. "Raise the other rein up and pull it back toward your shoulder!"

Philip tossed her a confused look.

"Pull it back toward your shoulder!" she yelled again. "Your shoulder!"

As Philip mimicked what Naomi was trying to demonstrate, it clicked for him. The rein he'd braced against the horse's mane kept the horse from bending his neck. The other exerted just enough leveraged pressure to get the animal's attention. Bubbles came to an abrupt halt, stopping so swiftly that Philip was thrown forward, almost falling headfirst to the ground. Placing his feet firmly, he took a deep breath as he wrapped his arms around Bubbles's neck and hugged him.

Naomi jumped from her horse, racing to his side. She threw herself into his arms, wrapping herself around him and Philip realized she was shaking as much as, or even more than, he was.

"Are you okay?" she gushed, still clutching tightly to him as she whispered into his ear.

He nodded, his arms wrapped around her torso. He couldn't begin to express how grateful he was to see her.

He hugged her closer. "I'm good. Now! Thank you. I wasn't sure I was going to make it for a moment there."

"Neither was I. You had me scared to death."

"I'm sorry," Philip said as he nuzzled his face into her hair. "I never want to make you worry about me."

"Something tells me that worrying about you will come with your profession."

"Maybe so," he said softly. He gave her another squeeze before he changed the subject. "Did you see which direction Jim headed?"

She shook her head. "No. I saw him shaking that canvas bag and then all those snakes and then I was trying to catch up to you."

Naomi finally loosened her arms from around his neck. She pulled back and pressed her mouth to his. The kiss was intense, and he felt as if she'd found her way home. She kissed him as if it were the first time. And the last time. And every time in between. Her lips lingered sweetly against his and in that moment, he couldn't begin to imagine his life without her.

A police helicopter suddenly appeared in the sky, hovering above them. Philip shaded his eyes with one hand as he waved his other arm above his head.

"Do you have your cell phone?" he asked.

Naomi nodded, pulling the device from her back pocket. "Where's yours?"

"Wrapped in a pair of dirty underwear, hidden in my dirty clothes bag in my tent."

Naomi laughed as she handed him her phone.

He dialed, pausing as it finally rang. On the other end, the chief answered promptly.

"Where are you?"

Philip filled his superior in on everything that had happened. "And I have most of it on audio tape," he concluded, sliding his hand back into his pocket to retrieve the recorder he'd hidden inside.

"Is your cover blown?" Chief Lawson asked.

"No, I don't think so. I think I'm still good," he said. "But I've lost sight of the perp I was chasing."

"No worries! We have your perp in custody and air patrol has you in sight. Do you need rescue and assistance, or can you find your way back?"

"I think I can figure it out."

"Humph…" Lawson grunted, a hint of amusement in his tone. "I'm sure you can."

"Yes, sir!"

"Well, you tell Naomi I said hello, please. I'm sure she'll be of help if you need it."

Philip cringed, his cheeks warming with color. "Yes, sir."

The chief was laughing as he disconnected the call. And then Philip remembered the caller ID and the visual identification the helicopter had probably made to his superior as they had kissed.

"I think we've been made," he said. "Lawson knows we're together."

Naomi shook her head. "Which means I need to take you to meet my mother because she'll probably know about us before the day is done. Will you be free in a few weeks?"

"In a few weeks?" Philip looked confused.

"We still have a show to finish, and you're stuck here until that's done!" Naomi laughed and the sound of it billowed through the air on the sweetest summer breeze.

Chapter Fifteen

"Dude! Where have you been? Things have gotten real around here!"

Brad accosted Philip the minute he made it back to the campsite. The whole cast was sitting around the empty firepit, worried expressions staring in his direction.

"I was trying to help. They arrested the guy who's been causing all the accidents. Turns out it was Jim, trying to get the show shut down."

"I knew that guy was bad news," Josiah said. "He had beady eyes!"

"Have you heard anything about poor Fred?" Grace questioned.

Philip nodded. "Fred is resting comfortably. He has a broken leg and a fractured pelvis. They say it's going to be at least six to eight weeks before he'll be back to it again."

"Poor thing! No one would tell us what was going on." Grace bemoaned their old friend's situation.

"I think they plan to film Monty giving us all the

news later on this evening to explain him leaving the show," Philip said. "At least that's what Felicia told me."

"So will there still be an elimination ceremony?" Brad asked.

"There was no competition," Harold said. "How can they do an elimination ceremony?"

"You're correct." A familiar voice sounded behind them.

They all turned to see Naomi sauntering in their direction. She smiled as she took a seat beside Josiah, closing ranks. "There's no ceremony this evening since Fred can no longer participate. We regret he has had to leave us the way he did. But his wife is with him, and we wish him a speedy recovery. Now, instead of a ceremony this evening, we do want to explain Fred's accident and let the audience know he's on the mend. We would also like to film that in the next hour, before supper, if that works for you all."

There was a quick exchange of looks, head nods and a chorus of affirmations. "Sure!"

"No problem!"

"Whatever."

"Of course!"

"So, are you going to tell us about Jim? We saw him being taken away in handcuffs." Brad asked the question the others had been thinking.

Naomi took a deep breath. "Because of the ongoing investigation, I really can't tell you much other than Jim is no longer affiliated with the production company. We also regret if any of Jim's actions impacted any of you negatively. We wanted this to be a very positive, fun experience, and are disappointed that it has been marred by mishaps and injuries." She nodded, contrition painting her face.

"It's all good, pretty lady," Brad said. "Although I think we're all tired and ready for this to be over so that I can go home with my money!"

Philip shook his head and laughed. "I really don't know why you keep trying to claim *my* money," he said teasingly.

Grace waved a dismissive hand at the two of them. "Please, all of you know I plan to take the entire prize."

Laughter rang abundantly around the circle.

Naomi stood, pushing both hands into the back pocket of her jeans. "I really want to say thank-you to all of you. Each of you has been a champ!"

Grace stood to give her a hug and Josiah shook her hand. As she passed, she gave Harold a gentle slap on the back and she squeezed Philip's shoulder. Winking an eye at Brad, she made her exit.

"That's one classy lady," Brad gushed, eyeing her as she walked away. "Is she single?"

Grace threw up her hands, annoyance pulling her mouth into a deep frown. "Do you ever stop?"

Brad feigned innocence. "What? I didn't do anything. Why are you mad at me?"

FOOD SERVICES HAD gone the extra mile, setting up a dinner buffet for the cast and crew that put their barbecue night to shame. Naomi was grateful for it, the partylike atmosphere holding everyone's attention so that no one was thinking about anything bad that might have happened during the day.

Someone had organized a talent show. When she entered the space, Grace and Brad stood on a makeshift stage singing a classic Tammy Wynette and George Jones tune. Neither could sing but their enthusiasm and effort made up for their lack of talent.

Naomi took a seat beside Marvin. Felicia kindly fixed her a plate of lasagna and a bowl of garden salad. She was grateful as the young woman gave her a bright smile. Naomi ate well and clapped her hands along with the karaoke player.

Across the room Philip sat alone. He sat with his back against the wall, his legs stretched out in front of him. His eyes were closed and there was a smile on his face as he sat listening to the music. He looked comfortable and at peace, and that made Naomi's heart sing. She had truly been afraid for him earlier. Scared that Jim's antics had put him in harm's way, and something might take him from her. She'd been scared in a way that was foreign to her, the wealth of it gut-deep and numbing. So scared that she didn't have the words to begin to explain it, an entire vocabulary lost in the darkness of it.

Seeing Philip now, nothing at all about him feeling out of sync, brought her immense joy. Now she had to figure out where to put all that happy.

On the stage, her sister was whispering into the karaoke guy's ear. Aubrey and Jasper were being the perfect hosts, working the room with apt precision. They were still very much about their customer service. They had taken keeping a client and gaining a new one to a whole other level. It suddenly surprised her when Aubrey called her name over the microphone.

"And next up we have your series producer, Naomi Colton, and rising TV star Philip Rees singing 'You are the Reason'! Come on up, you two!"

Naomi felt like a deer caught in the headlights. Her eyes went wide, and her mouth dropped open. Philip on the other hand was already up and out of his seat, sauntering up to the stage. He grinned in her direction and held out his hand.

She shook her head. Being on a stage or in front of a camera had never been high on her list of favorite things. There was a reason she worked behind the scenes, catching other people's actions. She had no desire to be the center of attention. People staring made her nervous. Her father had made them the center of attention when he'd been arrested, and it hadn't ended well for any of them.

The room was suddenly chanting her name and Marvin had risen from his seat to help her from hers. Aubrey moved to her side. "Go sing, little sister!"

"I'm going to kill you!"

"Kill *him*. He planned this!"

Philip was still grinning broadly, chanting her name with everyone else. She shook her head as she slowly moved to the front of the room. When she reached his side, he hugged her as he handed her a microphone.

"This was your idea?" she questioned, her expression less than amused.

He shrugged. "I thought it would be fun."

"I don't sing."

"It's karaoke! No one sings! Now you be Leona Lewis and I'll be Calum Scott. Let's kill this." He began to bob his head as he gestured for them to start the audio. When he sang the first line, every ounce of joy inside her exploded through the room.

PHILIP DIDN'T BOTHER to sneak in through her back window later that night. He came through the front door. The invitation in the song lyrics had been open and direct, both knowing what they wanted and why, especially after the intensity of that day's experience. Delaying the inevitable was not an option either was willing to consider.

He had waited until the only sounds he heard outside of his tent was Brad snoring loudly and the whistle of wind rustling through the late-night air. As he exited his tent, he had tossed one last look around the campsite to make sure none of the other players were watching him. Now he stood in the middle of her office with his arms wrapped around her torso and his lips capturing hers.

Kissing Naomi would forever be his most favorite thing in the world to do, Philip thought. She always tasted of chocolate and mint and her tongue danced a curious two-step against his own. They left a trail of clothes from the front room to the cot in the back room, snatching at the garments fervently. Eventually, he stood in nothing but his briefs and a smile.

Naomi took a step from him, pulling at the straps of her bra. She had slowed her striptease, her hips shimmying slowly from side to side. The black silk and lace undergarments contrasted nicely against her pale skin. She exposed one round breast and then the other, the protrusion of nipple rock-candy-hard. She sat back against the cot and gestured for him to join her.

The air caught in Philip's chest, anticipation flooding through him like lighter fluid. He leaned to kiss her again, their connection an exploration of magnanimous proportions. He dipped past her lips, slid across each tooth and tap-danced over her tongue. He trailed damp kisses across her nose, down the length of her profile and then he nuzzled his lips against that sweet spot under her chin.

Naomi wrapped her arms tightly around him, pulling him to her. The hard lines of his torso fit against her soft curves like the perfect missing piece of a puzzle. She dragged her nails gently down the length of his back as he slowly lowered himself against her. She teased him with her fingers, her hands gliding against his skin. Where they led, her mouth followed, a trail of wet kisses teasing his nerve endings.

A condom appeared and she sheathed him swiftly. Their coming together was like two perfect storms colliding on one pathway. She moaned his name over and over again as she met him stroke for stroke. They were perfection together, two halves of one coin, mint chocolate chip ice cream and a sugar cone, peanut butter and marshmallow fluff.

She wrapped her legs around his waist and held on. Waves of pleasure washed between them, sweeping cataclysmic explosions that had them both gasping to catch their breaths. He panted, gulping deep, nourishing inhalations of air, like water. Her breathing was static, and tears pressed hot against her lengthy lashes. It was love, and love had never been so sweet.

THEY LAY TOGETHER wrapped comfortably around each other. Naomi rested her head on Philip's chest, his arms cradling her torso and their legs tangled. Heat simmered on low, a hint of perspiration against warm skin. She'd lost count of how many times he'd brought her to orgasm. It had been a tidal wave of bliss that seemed never-ending. There was little she didn't know about his body, or he hers. She'd traced a finger along the line of his scars, and he'd teased that spot behind her knee that left her weak and shaking. It was the beginning of something beautiful that she knew they both looked forward to exploring further.

Trading easy caresses, they talked about everything and about nothing. Casual conversation followed them into the early morning hours. Sleep proved elusive, neither wanting to close their eyes and lose sight of the other, and so they talked and held each other tightly.

"What's going to happen when you go back to Los Angeles?" Philip asked. "Have you thought about that?"

"I don't know if I'm going back. I mean, I'm thinking that I may stay here. I've actually submitted an application to the Boulder TV studio to work with their news team."

Philip trailed his fingers down the length of her arm. "Have you considered what a long-distance relationship will look like if you decide not to stay?"

"I haven't. Typically, in the past I haven't done well with long-distance relationships. And not that I've had many. But the one long-distance relationship I did have crashed and burned quickly."

"You want to tell me about him?" Philip asked.

Naomi dropped into reflection for a brief moment. His name had been Taylor. Taylor had been a theater student moonlighting as an extra on an independent film she'd worked on for a friend. Taylor had been funny, spontaneous and not interested in anything long-term. After the film was done, Taylor headed to London to perfect his English accent. When her astronomical phone bill became ridiculous and Taylor was no longer interested in sharing his mileage points, they'd called it quits, nothing motivating either of them to keep their relationship going.

She lifted her eyes to Philip's and shook her head. "There's nothing to tell. It just didn't work and neither of us cared enough to want to work on it. But I'm committed to making this thing between us work."

"This *thing* isn't going to *settle* for long distance."

Naomi laughed. "Would you consider moving to LA?"

"I will consider whatever will work for both of us. But I'm not going to settle for telephone conversations and the occasional back-and-forth trips. I want to wake up to you every morning and fall asleep with you every night. I want to know that if I want to touch you then all I have to do is reach out for you. I'm selfish and I want what I want when I want it. And I don't want to miss you!" He kissed her forehead.

"I don't want to miss you, either. It's not a good feeling. I miss my family every single day, and I miss being party to the things they're doing."

"Do you think you'd consider working here at the ranch, or maybe for your family's foundation?"

"I would definitely volunteer. I believe in what my siblings are doing."

"They've done an impressive job. You should be very proud."

"The case they're working on now is giving them a run for their money."

"Someone they're trying to vindicate?"

"Someone they vindicated and need to put back behind bars!" Naomi shifted against him as she told him the story. "His name is Ronald Spence. My father was the judge on his first trial. He was convicted of operating a drug smuggling ring and sentenced to multiple life sentences. A few months ago, he reached out to the foundation to say he was railroaded and was falsely convicted. Someone else actually came forward to say that it was him, not Spence, who'd been guilty. Spence was freed. But it turns out that was all a ruse. Not only was he guilty, but he's now back at it and the challenge is finding the evidence to prove it."

"Interesting. Maybe once we're finished here, I can help out, too. I'm told I can be very persuasive."

Naomi lifted her lips to his and kissed him gently. "Do you think you can persuade me to make love to you one more time?"

Philip chuckled. "Maybe even two or three!"

Hours later, when Philip headed back to his tent, the sun was just beginning to peek over the horizon. The

night had been more than he could have ever anticipated. Naomi had fallen off to sleep and he'd left her
snoring softly, pressing the slightest kiss to her bare
shoulder before taking his leave. Every moment of their
time together was burned into his memory like a fresh
tattoo. He smiled, wishing it never had to end.

Easing his way past the line of tents, he stepped into
his, the flap falling down behind him. He had enough
time to grab a quick nap, he thought as he reflected on
what he hoped to accomplish that day. He wanted to
make sure he was ready for anything that was thrown
at him. But what he wasn't prepared for was Brad Clifton stretched out on his cot, eyeing him with a smug
expression.

"It's a bit past your curfew, isn't it?" Brad's loud
whisper startled him and he turned abruptly, feeling
as if he'd just jumped out of his skin.

"Brad. What's up? What are you doing here?" Philip's gaze narrowed.

"I think the bigger question is where did you sleep
last night? Because I slept here."

Philip pondered the lie he could tell, but Brad spoke
again before he could comment.

"So, I need a favor. A big one. And if you do me a
solid and keep my secret, I *might* be willing to keep
yours!"

HEADING DOWN TO the barn for the first competition of
the day, Brad appeared to be in a joyful mood, humming and joking with his fellow contestants. His good
mood belied the intensity of his earlier conversation;

him trying to coerce Philip and Philip pretending to be intimidated. Bringing up the rear, Philip thought back to that conversation and Brad's true colors.

"No wonder you weren't interested in sticking it to the beauty queen. You were already sticking it to the producer woman!"

"Watch your mouth!" Philip had snapped.

Brad had stood, meeting him toe to toe. His gaze was narrowed, and he'd snarled. "You and I both know that if word gets out that she put her boyfriend on the show and has been playing favorites against the rest of us, she's done. And so are you!"

"What do you want from me?"

"I have a business deal I need to run point on. Things around here have gotten too hot with the police all over the place. I'm going to need you and your little girlfriend to run interference for me."

"What kind of deal?"

"Now, that would be none of your business. I just need you two to make sure I can conduct a trade of sorts without being interrupted. It'll be easy-peasy and then you two can go right back to playing footsie with each other. I'll forget everything I know, and you'll forget anything you see. It'll be a win-win for us all!"

"And if I say no?"

"You won't. Because if you do, I'll be forced to tell what I know and corroborate Jim's story that you two were in cahoots and this whole show was rigged from the start. That might kill your girlfriend's career and I know you would hate to be responsible for that happening."

"You're an asshole, Brad."

Brad pretended to clutch imaginary pearls. "Ohhh, my feelings are hurt!"

"Whatever. Get the hell out of my tent."

His voice dropped an octave, his tone malicious. "It'll be my pleasure. I'll let you know when it needs to happen. Until then, you and Naomi try not to get pregnant! Wouldn't that be a scandal!"

Brad had crawled back to his rock, leaving Philip with a lot to think about. Now, as they headed toward their next contest, he was still trying to figure out how to play the new hand dealt to him. Brad had literally dropped a windfall in his lap, and he didn't have a clue. But Philip still had to make sure none of this blew back on Naomi or jeopardized what she was working so hard to accomplish.

Chapter Sixteen

Philip stood off to the side, leaning against a pile of commercial tires piled high near the fence. There was a flurry of activity around him as the production crew prepared for the next contest. He stood debating his options with Brad, who was strutting around like a peacock on steroids. The man's arrogance would make slapping the handcuffs on him even sweeter.

Naomi had joined the ranks, she and her assistant Felicia moving among them to double-check that everyone was well. He sensed that she was fearful of something going wrong, her nerves on high alert. He hated to be the bearer of bad news, but she needed to know what they were up against.

At one point he looked up, feeling like all eyes were on him. Brad stood across the way staring, his expression smug. Had he been able, Philip would have wiped that smirk off his face, but he knew that would have to wait. He looked forward, though, to the moment when he could watch that smile fade into oblivion.

His eyes still on Brad, he strolled to where Naomi was standing with the cameraman. The conversation looked intense, and he hated to interrupt it, but there was really no point in waiting.

"Excuse me, Ms. Colton. May I have a quick word with you, please?" He looked at the other man and apologized. "I'm sorry for interrupting, but it's important."

"I think that was all I had," the cameraman said. "Unless there's something we missed?" His eyes were focused on Naomi, who was jotting notes onto her clipboard.

"No," she said. "That was everything. I'm good. Just make sure everyone else is on the same page," she concluded. She waited until the man was out of earshot before turning her attention to Philip.

"What's wrong?" she questioned, concern furrowing her brow.

Philip got straight to the point. "Brad knows about us. He was in my room when I got back this morning. He says if we don't help him, he's going to out us publicly and take his grievance to the production company."

Naomi shifted her gaze to where Brad stood, still staring at the two of them. He tipped his brown leather cowboy hat at her, his grin widening. Rolling her eyes, she turned her attention back to Philip. "Un...believable..." she muttered. "Is this streak of bad luck ever going to end?"

"I'm sorry, baby. On a positive note, he's exactly where I want him. He's going to give me the information I need without realizing I need it and then we're going to take him."

"Either way, we both know it means the end of my show and maybe even my career. If we don't do what he wants and he tells, I'm done. If we do it, and he's arrested, it will probably still come out with all the publicity and attention. I'm damned if I do and damned if I don't."

"I don't know how to make this right for you, Naomi. I just know he needs to be taken down. Falling in love with you is the best thing that has happened to me, but I still have to do my job."

Naomi's head snapped as she turned to stare at him. Her eyes were wide with surprise.

As if reading her mind, Philip said, "Yes, I love you, and if it takes the rest of our lives for me to make this up to you, I will do whatever I have to do." A slow smile pulled at his lips, his gaze dancing with hers.

She tossed up her hands in frustration. "How can you tell me you love me when you know I can't hug and kiss you right now?"

He laughed. "I'll let you make it up to me later."

Naomi tossed Brad another look, her disdain for the man thick and abundant. She turned back to Philip. "I really haven't enjoyed this job anyway. Let's destroy him!"

Philip reached out a warm hand to squeeze her forearm. "That's my girl!" He winked an eye at her.

"I still have to finish this show," she said. "It may never see the light of day, but no one will ever be able to say I didn't give it my best shot."

"How can I help?" Philip questioned.

She smiled. "Just go have some fun! And make sure you beat that clown over there!"

Philip nodded. "I can do that."

Naomi turned, heading in Brad's direction. Watching her stroll off, Philip braced himself. She suddenly hesitated, turning back to face him. Philip took three steps toward her, curiosity pulling him to her.

"Everything okay?" he asked.

Naomi smiled. "It's perfect," she said. "I just wanted you to know that I love you, too."

PHILIP, BRAD, GRACE, Harold and Josiah stood in a single line as Monty greeted them warmly.

"Good morning, cowboys! You all are the top five players still in the competition. Congratulations!" Monty saluted them with his hat.

They applauded, giving themselves accolades for having gotten as far as they had. Monty continued. "Way back when you first started this process, we had you work with five young horses. In today's competition we want to see the fruits of your labor. You're each going to take one horse through an obstacle course. First, you'll have to guide your mount over some logs. After that you'll cross a deep creek, walk over a tarp, then push a steer into the arena. You'll each have thirty minutes to complete your tasks. Now it won't be about how fast you finish, but also how well you handle your colt."

They filmed more of Monty before the director called, "Cut," and sent them off to the barn to be paired with one of the young horses. Jasper and Kayla met them all inside.

"Is everything okay?" Grace asked, easing her way to Philip's side.

He nodded. "Fine. Why do you ask?"

"You look so serious, is all."

Philip shrugged. He gestured toward Brad, who was making a spectacle of himself, in need of attention. The man had been egging him on since they started filming, his snide comments beginning to wear on Philip's nerves. "He's being a real idiot today."

"Yeah, something's going on with him but I'm just ignoring him. It must be a full moon."

Philip chuckled.

Minutes later he stood in front of the last stall, a colt named Souza eyeing him warily. He stroked the horse's muzzle and whispered into his ear. "It's you and me, kid. I'm good with it if you are."

The horse leaned into his hand.

"He likes you," Kayla said, moving behind him.

Philip tossed a look over his shoulder. "I like him."

"You'll both do well together. Just remember, you're an extension of each other. Just relax and trust him so he can trust you."

"I can do that. Anything else I need to know?"

"Yeah," Kayla said, her voice dropping to a loud whisper. "The tarp will probably be the most challenging because a colt doesn't understand the look or the feel of the tarp. Just take it easy with him and he'll be okay."

"I appreciate the advice," Philip said. He nuzzled the horse a second time, wondering if Naomi might one day enjoy ranch life with him, the kids and a dog.

"There's always plenty of that to go around," Kayla said with a smile.

In the distance someone called the woman's name.

"Find me if there's anything else I can do to help," she said as she turned, heading in the other direction.

At the other end of the barn, Naomi stood in conversation with Grace and Harold. Brad interjected himself when he could and although she was polite, anyone who knew her well could sense her disinterest in anything he had to say. For the briefest moment she and Philip locked eyes and held the gaze. Something affirming passed between them; something that promised all would be well as long as they had each other. Emboldened, Philip began to saddle his horse. He had a game to win.

ONE BY ONE the remaining five put their horses through their paces. Going first, Grace gave an impressive show, laying the groundwork for a battle with the men. Harold followed but his horse worked against him, and he lost valuable time. Josiah did better than Harold, but everyone sensed Grace still had him beat. But they wouldn't know how they did until the elimination ceremony.

Philip wasn't interested in besting Grace, but he was determined to set a better time than Brad. He and his horse moved forward to go next when Brad suddenly appeared at his side, pushing his way in line. Neither horse was happy about the move and Souza reared up, suddenly skittish.

"Whoa, baby! Whoa!" Philip crooned, adjusting his stance to calm the large animal. "That's a boy, whoa!"

Jasper rushed forward and grabbed Brad's horse by the bridle, easing some space between the two animals. "Don't ever do that again!" he scolded, his eyes narrowed on Brad. "You don't get in front of another cowboy like that."

Brad held up a hand. "Sorry about that!" He smirked at Philip, lifting his eyebrows as he gave him a look.

NAOMI SHOOK HER HEAD, watching it play out on the monitor. She let go of the breath she'd been holding as it all unfolded. Brad was taking risks that could easily get others hurt, and she wasn't in the mood for his antics. Annoyance crossed her face and seeped from her eyes. "Let Clifton go next," she said into the walkie-talkie to the assistant who sat atop his own horse with Monty and his horse at the start line.

Monty suddenly went into a rant about proper conduct and courtesy, throwing in a diatribe about the code of the cowboy and respect to his fellow man. It was a thing of unscripted beauty and Naomi couldn't wait to splice it into the show.

BRAD MOVED FORWARD and when Monty gave him the go, he pushed his horse to a full gallop. They took the logs easily, but his mount balked at the edge of the water. It took longer than Brad had anticipated, the animal not willing to oblige.

Jasper was talking to himself as they all watched. "Slow him down. Ease him in," he whispered loudly. "Idiot! Slow him down!"

Jasper and Philip exchanged a look and Philip gave him the slightest nod, not needing words to express they were both thinking the same thing.

It took some maneuvering, but Brad eventually made

it across, then barreled at full speed along the edge of the tarp.

"Okay, Philip, your turn. You ready?" Monty asked Philip after Brad's time was logged.

Philip took a deep breath. In all honesty, he wasn't. The previous day had left him wary of riding. Although he knew it hadn't been the horse's fault, he still wasn't comfortable but he couldn't say so aloud. "Let's do this," he said confidently.

He gave the horse a gentle tap and shifted him smoothly into a slow trot. They approached the logs, and he didn't give the animal a chance to hesitate, continuing to move him forward easily. The second set of logs went even smoother. The two reached the creek and Souza seemed to test the water with one hoof, hesitating briefly. Philip stayed steady, continuing to coax him forward and Souza crossed easily. As they approached the tarp, Philip understood that the horse saw danger, not quite sure of his footing. He knew he had to stay confident for his horse to trust that all would be well. He took a deep breath to calm his nerves.

"Easy, Souza. Easy!" Philip said softly, trying to find a sense of balance with the horse.

Souza took a step forward putting two feet on the tarp but backing himself up. Philip continued to talk to him and eased him across as if the two had been doing it together forever.

The steer was next, and Philip showed real control as he guided the steer and horse into the corral. He was happy with his performance but not prepared for what came next.

Monty was there to greet him. "Philip, we need you to take this breakaway rope and show us what you and your horse can do. You have five minutes to impress us."

Although Philip had been practicing his rope work, he hadn't practiced it with Souza and had no idea how the animal would respond. Taking the rope from Monty's hands, he took another deep breath and guided the horse to where the steer was pacing along the fence. He used everything he could remember to keep control of the steer and the colt. The whir of the rope was off-putting to Souza, but Philip held the line. He missed on his first throw but kept both animals on target for his second. Even he was surprised when he lassoed the steer successfully.

"Nice job," Monty said.

"Thank you, sir!"

"Go rest up and we will see you at the elimination ceremony later this evening."

Moving back to the barn, Philip was happy with his run. Souza had served him well and he leaned forward to hug the horse's neck. "Good job, kid!" he said. "Really good job!" Now all he had left to do was lasso two criminals: Brad *and* Jim. Once both were incarcerated with lengthy sentences, Philip could claim the win.

ALTHOUGH THEY'D GOTTEN great shots of the players strolling toward the elimination stage, the elimination ceremony was somber at best. Grace looked like she wanted to cry. Josiah was fidgeting like he had to use the restroom. Harold was trying not to doze off to sleep.

Philip and Brad were giving each other the evil eye. As it played on the monitor, Naomi knew exactly how to edit the tape to make it look like their doom and gloom was excitement and anxiousness. Clearly, she thought, the film editor was about to be her new best friend.

Monty had insisted on smoke and mirrors for his arrival. He rode in on his black horse, dressed from head to toe in black, looking like death come calling. Maybe editing wouldn't help, Naomi suddenly thought, her head waving from side to side. Jude whispered in Monty's ear, put the contestants in place and called, "Action." The camera zoomed in on Monty's face as he studied each player one by one.

"Good evening, players!" Monty cheered.

A chorus of good evenings greeted him back.

"Five of you left, and tonight, two of you are going home. Tonight is a *double* elimination." The emphasis on his last statement left the players wide-eyed, gazes darting back and forth in surprise.

Monty continued. "We're not going to judge you on your performances today. I thought about it and how you worked with those colts earlier was very much a representation of how you've approached this whole thing."

He looked at Philip. "Philip, you were impressive today. You handled that colt masterfully. And as I look back to how you started, you were a little reluctant and very apprehensive. I have to question you coming on strong now, if it's just a little too late."

Philip nodded. "I respect that, sir, and I agree, I was apprehensive in the beginning but only because this was all so new to me. It took me a moment to build up my confidence. But I've gained new respect for the cowboy lifestyle, and I actually enjoy it. But I also respect that for the men and women that do this daily to feed their families, it isn't a game. In the beginning I had to honor that by not thinking I could just jump in and do it and do it well."

Monty nodded. "Who do you think should go home tonight?"

Without a moment of hesitation, Philip answered. "Brad."

Naomi hadn't expected that, and she fought not to let it show on her face. The camera shifted to Brad's face and clearly, he was not happy.

"Why?" Monty asked, oblivious to the tension between the two men.

"Because he has no respect for this process or for the rest of us out here doing our very best. He's arrogant and he believes he should win without putting in the same level of effort."

"I have something to say about that!" Brad interjected.

Monty held up his hand. "You'll get your chance." He turned his attention to Josiah. "Josiah, you've been exceptionally cautious this whole game. I feel like you've been trying to fly under the radar. Was that intentional?"

"No, not at all. In fact, I'd have to disagree. I haven't been flying under the radar. I think I've done a good job putting myself front and center in the challenges and taking on some leadership roles. I just wasn't boisterous about it." Josiah shot Brad a quick look.

"And who do you think should go home?" Monty asked.

"Brad!"

Monty turned to Brad. "And why do you think everyone sees you as being the weakest link?"

"There's nothing weak about me. They see me as a threat because I'm their biggest competition. Getting rid of me makes it easier for them to win."

Monty critiqued Harold and Grace next, asking them the same question. Everyone was surprised when she said Philip should be sent home. Still watching, Naomi laughed.

"Why do you think Philip should be sent home?" Monty asked, amusement dancing across his face.

Grace pulled a hand through the length of her hair, playing to the camera as she spoke. "I don't think Philip is here for the right reasons. His heart truly isn't in this. Yes, he's good, but then that's how he is in life. With things he loves, he's better than good. He's excellent. He just doesn't need or want this as much as the rest of us."

Monty shifted his eyes toward Philip. "Would you like to respond to that?"

"She's entitled to her opinion. But I want this just as badly as anyone else. If not more. Just to prove that I do belong here, and I am here for the right reasons."

Monty nodded again. "I think I see things clearly. And Philip, I do think you're here for the right reasons. Welcome to the top three!"

Philip grinned. "Thank you."

Monty pointed him to the fence to take a seat before he continued. "Grace, last couple of challenges you disappointed me. You've come in last on a few challenges now. Anything you'd like to say about that?"

Grace gave him her best beauty queen smile. "Yes, I may have come in last, but I still deserve to be here because I got the job done. Yes, it may have taken me longer but as you can see, I don't have the same muscle mass or weight as these guys. But like them, I'm working just as hard, if not harder."

"Like I said, I've had to take a look at everything overall that you did. You started out strong, showed us your leadership skills, and have done a great job overall. It's been a pleasure watching you." Monty hesitated, as if he needed to think some more. Then he looked her in the eye and smiled. "And I'd like to see more! Congratulations, you're in the top three. You can join Philip over there on the fence."

Brad, Harold and Josiah closed ranks, side-eyeing each other as they waited to see who'd be chosen to fill that third and final spot.

Monty hung his head as he considered what he would say next. When he finally spoke, he had paused long enough to make Naomi nervous, and she knew who'd made it to the finale.

"Harold, Josiah, pack your bags and say your goodbyes. Your time here has come to an end. Congratulations, Brad! You're still…in the saddle!"

MARVIN AND HIS crew had broken down the stage, returning the barn to its original condition. All of the horses had been fed and bedded and the cast and crew were all headed to grab something to eat. Food services had promised them something special and they were excited to see what that might be.

Naomi had crossed the last *t* on her to-do list for the following day. She and the production team had reviewed their notes, revisited the budget and put a contingency plan in place in case the next day's challenges went awry. They were in a good place and the only thing that would have made her happier was if Brad Clifton disappeared, never to intrude on their lives ever again.

Thinking about Brad and the situation she found herself in put her on edge. She knew helping Philip was the right thing to do, but she also knew it would come back to bite her and bite her good. She also worried for his safety. What if things went left and he was hurt? She understood the hazards that came with his job, but she wasn't ready to have something happen to him.

Brad suddenly called her name and as she turned to see him walking toward her, she cussed under her breath. Thinking about that devil had manifested him and she was not in the mood for whatever it was he wanted. She took a deep breath.

"Mr. Clifton, how can I help you?" she said as he moved to her side, walking with her as she headed toward the office.

"It's how I can help you," he said. "I'm sure you'd like this to be over and for me to be out of your hair."

Naomi didn't bother to respond, gesturing for him to continue.

"There's a helicopter scheduled to land here in the

morning. You need to make sure your people stay out of the way."

"And how am I going to do that? A helicopter is going to draw attention. Someone is going to want to check it out."

"Then you might have a problem. But if you don't want to see anyone get hurt, then you'll make sure I have at least thirty minutes of privacy when it lands."

Naomi shook her head. "What time is this supposed to happen?"

"Don't you worry about the time. You just do what I tell you and we won't have any problems," he snapped.

Naomi shook her head, annoyance tying a knot in the pit of her stomach. She took a deep inhale of air, filling her lungs with oxygen. "I have work to do," she said, picking up her pace.

Brad suddenly grabbed her arm, spinning her around. His gaze was narrowed, and he looked like he wanted to spew. Naomi snatched her arm back, her own expression challenging.

"We don't want to have any problems," Brad said harshly.

"And we won't," Naomi snapped back. "But put your hands on me again, and I will blow this whole thing up in your face. I don't care what you're trying to do but piss me off and you won't be doing it here. And I'm not scared of you. You want to go tattle about me having a relationship with a cast member. Go right ahead. I've flipped burgers and waited tables before. I can do it again, and I'll rebuild again."

Before Naomi could blink Brad was pointing a pistol in her face. "It's hard to rebuild from your grave."

Naomi's expression remained blank as ire seeped from his eyes. She began to laugh, her gaze still locked tightly with his.

"What's so damn funny?"

"Because if you shoot me, this place will be crawling with police and your helicopter won't land anywhere near this property. And you will become a very wanted man. While I'm sipping piña coladas up in heaven, the wraths of hell will be here on earth raining down on you. So, pull the trigger and give me a front-row seat watching as you make new friends in prison when you drop the soap."

"Everything okay over there?"

Brad dropped his hands to his sides, both of them recognizing Kayla's voice as she moved in their direction. By the time she reached them, he'd placed his weapon back into the waistband of his jeans.

"Everything's good, pretty lady! How are you?" he said casually.

Kayla looked from him to Naomi. "Is everything okay? They're looking for you."

Naomi nodded. "I'm good. Have you seen Jasper?"

"He was headed back to the main house the last time I saw him. Is anything wrong?" Kayla shot another look in Brad's direction.

Naomi shook her head, preparing a bold-faced lie to roll off her tongue. "No, I forgot to tell him the production bigwigs might be flying in tomorrow. I wanted to make sure he didn't mind if they landed a helicopter on the back fields."

"A helicopter? They must be really big bigwigs."

"Not really. Just a bunch of men with small penises, big egos and arrogance the size of bull balls." She shifted her focus to Brad, who didn't look amused.

Naomi said, "I appreciate that information, Mr. Clifton. You should probably hurry along and go get something to eat before food services shuts down for the night."

He forced a smile to his face. "Sleep well, ladies," he said as he moved off toward the commissary.

When he was out of hearing distance, Kayla gave Naomi a questioning look. "That didn't look kosher. Are you sure everything's okay?"

"Just another man being a jerk."

"That one is the king of jerks! Where did you guys find him?"

"Good question," Naomi answered. "I just got stuck with him. He wasn't on my top ten list. He wasn't even on my top one hundred list."

"As long as you're okay."

Naomi changed the subject. "Are things with you and my brother any better?"

The young woman shrugged her narrow shoulders. "He's a man...and most men are jerks," Kayla concluded.

"Thank goodness for the one or two who aren't!" Naomi said.

"HE PULLED A gun on you?" Philip bolted out of the bed. He stood in all his naked glory, sweat glistening against his dark skin. He snatched his pants off the floor, stepping into them swiftly.

Naomi rose up onto her knees and reached for him. "Stop. Come back to bed."

"You really don't think I'm going to let that pass, do you?"

"That's why I didn't tell you earlier. Brad was just being a blowhard. Trying to exert the power he thinks he has. It was no big deal." She wrapped her arms around his waist and pulled Philip to her.

"No, it's a very big deal. I should never have gotten you mixed up in this. I should have known it would be too dangerous. Now you're caught right in the middle of this mess! Brad needs to be taught a lesson."

"This is all going to be over tomorrow. You just need to keep your cool, catch him doing whatever illegal thing he's planning to do and put handcuffs on him. There is no reason to blow your case trying to teach him a lesson. Besides, what's that saying, you can't teach poetry to someone who doesn't understand what words are?"

"I've never heard that saying before."

Naomi pressed a kiss to his belly button. "Okay, maybe I made it up. Either way, just don't mess this up. You're too close to achieving your goal. Come back to bed, make love to me, and forget about that fool. You can deal with him tomorrow when you take him down."

Philip wrapped his arms around her torso and hugged her tightly. "Weren't you scared? I know you're tough as nails, baby, but he pointed a gun at you!"

She sighed, a low gust of wind blowing past her thin

lips. "I was, but I learned early in life that even when your opponent has the upper hand you never let them know it. So, yeah, I was scared, but I didn't give him a chance to use that fear against me."

Philip shook his head. "I still plan to bust him in the mouth the first chance I get."

Naomi smiled. "You can even hit him twice," she said. "Once for me and once for you."

"Then he's getting punched three times. Because I plan to nail him twice for what he did to you!"

She gave him the slightest smile. "Everything's going to be okay, right?" she asked, a hint of concern rising in her voice.

Philip kissed her forehead. "I'm going to make sure of it."

Chapter Seventeen

The weather was near perfect. The morning sun rose early, eagerly searching for its place in what promised to be a bright blue sky. Philip hadn't slept well, only dozing off and on, once or twice. He was too focused on everything happening to let himself rest. It didn't sit well with him that Brad had pulled a weapon on Naomi. Brad had come off as an opportunist or grifter, and not at all violent. He could be temperamental and surly but that had always made him look spoiled, not vindictive. His actions proved Philip didn't know him at all, and Brad definitely could be dangerous.

Philip was making his second lap around the perimeter of the property and considering his third when he saw Naomi heading to the main lodge. She wore her signature Levi jeans, a Gap Band T-shirt and heavy hiking boots. He had left her sleeping soundly, sneaking quietly out of her cot to keep from waking her.

Thinking about Naomi made him smile. He looked forward to the day when they could sleep in and not worry about who might see him leaving her place in the wee hours of the morning. He realized that there were things he and Naomi needed to discuss. What did a future together look like? Would she consider moving back to Colorado or was she married to her life in Los Angeles? Would they have to do long-distance, or would she want him to move to be with her? He still didn't know how she felt about marriage or children. Was the possibility of family and forever in their future? He had more questions than answers, but what he didn't have was any doubt about his feelings for this woman.

Thinking about her, Philip realized he'd fallen hard and fast for Naomi Colton. He was head over heels in love, and the prospect of her not being in his life was something he wasn't willing to even consider. He loved her and the ease of that was as natural for him as breathing.

He would do one more lap, he thought as he rounded the pasture by the barns. One more to clear his head and gather his thoughts. He was ready for anything Brad had planned. He also had a plan B and plan C in case he misread any aspect of what Brad intended to do. Local police and agents from the cybersecurity unit would be close, ready to rush in on his command. There would be no mistakes as far as he was concerned. And definitely nothing to put Naomi, her family, or any of her crew and cast in harm's way. If Philip had anything to say about it, taking down Brad Clifton would be a sweet walk in the prettiest park.

JASPER STARED AT Naomi like she'd completely lost her mind. Confusion painted his expression, and his frown was pulling tightly against his facial muscles. "A helicopter?"

"What part didn't you understand?"

"The part where you plan to let a helicopter land in my fields."

"It'll land on the back part of the property, away from the animals and the outbuildings. You'll barely know it's there. And I promise it won't damage any of your crops."

"And why is the helicopter landing?"

"The powers from the production company want to see how things are going firsthand."

"And they can't fly into the local airport and take a limo like everyone else?"

"Why are you being difficult? It really isn't a big deal!" Naomi threw up her hands.

"Why are you being so defensive?" Aubrey asked, eyeing Naomi suspiciously.

The sisters traded evil eyes. "I'm not being defensive. I've just got a dozen things to do and I'm not understanding why Jasper needs to make a big deal out of this. You've never had a helicopter land here before?"

"No!" Jasper snapped. "And I'm not sure how the noise will affect the horses and cattle. I have reason to be concerned."

Naomi took another deep breath. Her mind raced as she quickly thought of her budget. "Would an extra thousand dollars for the inconvenience help?"

"It's not about the money, Naomi," her brother said.

"Although the money would be a nice incentive," Aubrey interjected.

The twins exchanged a look, Jasper not amused by

his sister's position. He shook his head. "You already owe me for the calves your guy euthanized."

"And we have every intention of making that right. I just haven't had an opportunity to talk with you about it. We would never expect you to eat that loss."

"I'm not going to eat it. You can trust that!"

An uncomfortable silence descended over the room. The siblings seemed to be gearing up for a second round, eyeing each other cautiously.

"I'm sorry," Naomi finally said, her voice dropping an octave. "I'm not trying to be disrespectful. And I'm not trying to take advantage of you and your generosity. I would never do anything to put your property or the animals at risk. But this is important to me and it really needs to happen. So, if you can please tell me what you need from me in order to make it work, I'd appreciate it."

Jasper blew a heavy sigh. He looked from one sister to the other and back, then shook his head slowly. "The cattle are on the south side of the ranch. We'll keep the horses corralled by the barn. Your helicopter can land on the north side. There's a large stretch of land near the stream that should work. There's a drivable path that leads in to pick your guests up. You can take one of the trucks if you need it. Will that work?"

Naomi threw her arms around her brother's neck and hugged him tightly. "Thank you!" she exclaimed.

"Thank God. Pay me," Jasper quipped. "That'll cost you one thousand dollars. Aubrey will add it to your final bill."

Naomi laughed.

"What time is this supposed to happen?" Aubrey asked.

Naomi shook her head. "Sometime before lunch, I think. I'll update you as soon as I know more."

Jasper muttered under his breath as he headed toward the exit.

Aubrey crossed her arms over her chest as they watched him walk out. "Something's going on with him, but I haven't been able to figure out what it is."

For the briefest moment Naomi thought about Philip and what he'd said about her brother and his feelings for Kayla. She dismissed the thought, since sharing the idea with any of her siblings would probably be more trouble than it was worth. Jasper had done her a big favor and she owed him. Minding her own business was a great place to start.

"I'm sure he'll tell you when he's ready," she said in response. "You know how Jasper is."

Aubrey shrugged. "You're right. I'll wait him out. How are things going with you?"

Naomi paused, reflecting on all she could tell her sister if given the opportunity. But now was not the right time and she was sworn to keep Philip's secret, and keeping his secrets meant not saying a thing about Brad or the uncertain status of her show's future.

She smiled. "I'm good," she said. "But I need to go get ready. It's going to be another long day."

"Let's talk later," Aubrey called out as Naomi exited the room and headed for the front door. She mumbled under her breath. "Like I wouldn't know a lie when I hear one."

Naomi laughed as she stepped out onto the front

porch. If only her sister knew, she thought. Heading back to the office, she considered what needed to happen with the show. Then she thought about what could possibly happen with Brad and his damn helicopter. There was no denying her frustration and she knew her sister had picked up on it.

Thoughts of Philip crossed her mind and she wished she could find him and throw herself into his arms. He had asked her if she'd been scared and she had downplayed it, not wanting to anger him more than he already was. She'd almost regretted telling him what had happened with Brad, but she knew he needed to know the man was armed. Now she worried what might happen when that helicopter landed. What was Brad planning? More importantly, how did Philip plan to respond? She had wanted to ask, but he'd made it clear that he didn't want her anywhere near the transaction when it happened. She didn't, however, make him any promises and she wasn't willing to sit idly by while he threw himself into the midst of trouble.

She loved Philip Rees. She loved him with every fiber of her being. She had never known love like what she was feeling for him. If she were honest, that scared her more than Brad pointing a gun at her did. What if she messed things up? Or worse, he did? Naomi wasn't willing to have her heart broken and something told her Philip had probably broken a lot of hearts. There was still so much she didn't know about him. What had ended his past relationships? Why had he fallen for her? What did he see for them in the future? Did he see *her* in his future? It was far more than she'd been willing to admit, a new question coming every time he crossed her mind.

Philip had been as forthcoming as one could be in their situation. There had yet to be a question she asked, that he wouldn't answer. He was an open book and she was still turning pages, never wanting to get to the end of his story. The prospect of what they might share in the future excited her. She found herself fantasizing about beautiful babies, that storybook home with a picket fence and the dog and station wagon. Well, maybe not the station wagon, but a really cool SUV. Philip had her wanting forever, and forever had always been a dirty word in her vocabulary.

As she thought of everything that could go wrong, Naomi knew she couldn't stand by and do nothing if Philip put himself in the line of fire. She wasn't willing to lose him.

"Good morning!" Naomi greeted the final three contestants. "I hope everyone had a good night's sleep."

Grace, Brad and Philip echoed the sentiment.

"What do you have planned for us today?" Grace questioned.

"We've actually revised the schedule today," Naomi answered. "But you'll be busy. Right after breakfast, each of you will be partnered with one of the ranch hands. You'll be shadowing that person today and tomorrow. They'll be readying you for the final challenge, an overnight cattle drive."

"A cattle drive?" Brad feigned surprise, acutely aware there was a camera still on him.

Naomi nodded and smiled, pretending as well. "It's going to be a great experience and will challenge each of you. Later this afternoon, Monty will fill you in on what he will be looking for. We anticipate that all three of you will excel. But whoever excels the most will win *In the Saddle*!"

"So, there's no filming today?" Philip asked.

"We're always filming," Naomi responded, smiling a second time. "Today will be no different. One of our camera people will pop up every now and again to get some candid shots of you. There will also be a few confessionals and random questions from one of our associate producers. Just the usual stuff you've become accustomed to."

"Is there anything we need to be aware of?" Grace asked.

"Be prepared for a challenging day. You'll probably be on a horse for at least six hours today."

"I'm going to need to change," Grace said, her hands trailing across her thighs. She wore a pair of skinny jeans that looked like they might have been painted on her.

"Definitely wear something comfortable," Naomi said. "Grab some breakfast, definitely get yourselves a cup of coffee, and your ranch hands will come to get you at nine o'clock." She stood, that smile of hers like a neon sign shining brightly. "And good luck to you!"

GRACE WAS FOLLOWING KAYLA, the two women headed toward the barn and their horses. Grace was excited, already plotting how she could maneuver to beat the two men she was up against. "You boys have a good time today. Don't get into any trouble," she'd said before sashaying away.

Philip and Brad sat opposite each other, neither man saying a word. The atmosphere was tense, static energy pinging through the air.

"Your girl did a good job making sure everyone is out of my way," Brad said smugly.

Philip leaned back in his seat. "You want to explain the gun in her face last night?"

Brad waved a dismissive hand. "That was just a minor misunderstanding."

"A minor misunderstanding?"

Brad shrugged. "She didn't come across as the whining type. I guess I was wrong. Did she cry, too, when she told you?"

Philip cracked the knuckles on both hands. His expression hardened and his muscles tensed. He was just a split second from throwing a punch when Brad suddenly rose from his seat.

"Look, things got out of hand. And I'm sorry for that," Brad said, contrition washing over his face. "But we're good. This will all be over soon. I'll have my money. Your girl will have her show. And we both get to ride off into the sunset with beautiful women. I know what you think about me, but I'm really not a bad guy. I just can't blow this. It's a once-in-a-lifetime opportunity. Because this deal will set me up for the rest of my life with everything I could have ever dreamed of."

Philip blew his anger past his full lips, allowing the

rise of ire to slowly dissipate. He gave Brad a nod, pretending to understand his position.

Brad extended his hand for a fist bump.

Philip nodded, but his own hands never left his lap. They weren't friends and they weren't going to be. He didn't want to seem too eager to let things between them go. After all, Brad still thought he was blackmailing them to do what he needed him and Naomi to do.

"Whatever," Brad muttered as he turned to make his exit. "But holding grudges isn't good for your heart, dude."

Philip's expression was still blank as he studied Brad intently. He shrugged, turning his attention back to the muffin he'd been eating. He still didn't bother to respond.

"I need a nap before my ride gets here," Brad finally said, and then just like that he was headed back down toward the tents.

Philip watched him walk away, each step of his cocky stride filled with arrogance. Clearly, Brad was feeling confident, believing he'd gotten away with his crime. He didn't have a clue what was coming. Leaning back in his seat, his hands clasped behind his head, Philip smirked.

Chapter Eighteen

Philip had been sitting there a good thirty minutes watching for Brad to leave the tents when Naomi entered the room. She gave him a look before moving to the counter for a cup of hot coffee and a bagel. He laid the binoculars he'd been holding on the table and saw her stop to speak to the food services staff, his eyes following as she finally moved to the seat Brad had vacated earlier.

"Do we know what's going on?" she asked, her voice dropping to a subtle whisper.

Philip shook his head. "We're in wait mode. But something doesn't feel right. I just can't put my finger on it."

"Should I be concerned?" Naomi asked.

"No, not at all. You've done everything you needed to do. I'll handle it from here. I can't risk anything happening to you."

Naomi reached for his hand and squeezed his fingers against her palm. She wanted to hold on and not let go, but she didn't want to risk anyone reading more into the gesture and running wild with the rumors. Not after all the secrecy and hiding they'd done, trying not to get caught. She pulled her hand from his, resting it in her lap.

"What's going to happen when this is all done, Philip? What's next for you?"

Philip shrugged. "I hadn't thought about it, but I'm sure there'll be another assignment. What about you? What's next after this?"

Naomi hesitated, falling into thought. She lifted her eyes to his, hot tears pressing against her thick lashes. Philip felt his heart jump in his chest, a knot tightening in his stomach. He understood her tears before she spoke the words. Seeing her hurting shredded his heartstrings suddenly.

He shook his head. "I am so sorry, Naomi. I wasn't thinking."

Naomi swiped at her tears with the back of her hand. "It's not your fault."

"It is, and I don't know how to begin to make it up to you." Philip had been so singularly focused that he hadn't considered the consequences of telling Naomi the truth and pulling her into the middle of this mess. Once they arrested Brad, he would no longer be a contestant. Philip, too, would have to forfeit his standing in the competition. That would just leave Grace with no one to compete against. Naomi's show was essentially done and over. Everything she'd worked for was going up in smoke.

"This show was my dream come true," she said softly. "I was going to make this series the next big thing! The producer credit would have done volumes for my career. Now I'm not sure that can happen."

"Have you thought about how you might be able to save the show? Is that possible?"

She shook her head. "I doubt it. Too much has happened. First, Jim purposely sabotaging the show is not a good look. Now one of my top three contestants is a criminal. I don't think the production company is going to be overly eager to air the show after this."

"You'll be able to get other producing jobs, I'm sure. You're good at what you do."

"I'm not so sure about that. I'm starting to think it might be time to move on. Reality television has served its purpose, but I'm ready to sink my teeth into something more substantial. I have an interview next week with that local news affiliate I'd applied to. If I get it, I think I'm coming back home to Blue Larkspur to live."

"How do you feel about that?"

"In all honesty, I'm scared. Suddenly my entire life plan has been turned upside down. I'm having to regroup and consider other options. If you knew how long it took me to get to the first plan, you'd understand why I'm concerned!" A frown clouded her brow.

"I believe everything happens for a reason. I think fate had a hand in bringing us together. And I'm glad there's a possibility you'll be staying, because I don't do long distance well."

She tossed up her hand, feigning disbelief. "Now you tell me! What if I had planned to go back to Los Angeles?"

"I would have done everything in my power to convince you to stay." Philip stated, the faintest hint of a smile pulling at his mouth. Beneath the table he slid his leg against hers. "Everything," he repeated.

Naomi giggled softly. "I love you."

"I love you, too! And we really have a lot to figure out."

She shook her head. "What's to figure out?"

"Where we plan to live, for starters. You could always move into my condo at first. I have two bedrooms, but I'm sure eventually we'll really need to find a larger space."

Before the conversation could continue, the humming sound of a jet engine rippled through the late morning air. An airplane was flying lower than necessary and Naomi and Philip both jumped from their seats. Both were surprised to see a jet circling the ranch, before it dipped down past the tree line in the distance.

Naomi was suddenly firing a dozen questions into the air. "What happened to the helicopter? That's not where he's supposed to be," she said. "He's on the wrong side of the ranch! And why is he so low? He's going to spook the animals. What is he doing?"

"He's avoiding the global flight tracker, trying to stay under the radar," Philip answered. His eyes shifted down to the tents, not missing Brad as he suddenly hurried toward the tree line. Without giving it a second thought, Philip bolted after him, leaving Naomi staring anxiously as the two men disappeared, one after the other, into the thick summer brush.

NAOMI'S MIND RACED as she considered her options. Beside her, one of the cameramen had lifted his Canon to his shoulder, beginning to film. Jasper suddenly pulled up on his all-terrain utility vehicle, practically jumping from his seat. He yelled, his frustration thick, "What the hell, Naomi! Are you trying to cause my herd to stampede? I told you to keep that airplane on the other side of the ranch! And what happened to the helicopter?"

"I need your four-wheeler," Naomi responded as she pushed past him. "It's an emergency!"

The cameraman was on her heels, throwing himself into the passenger seat as Jasper stood staring, his jaw slack as shock registered on his face. "What are you..." he started. "Naomi!"

She gunned the engine, the vehicle picking up speed quickly. Out of the corner of her eye she spied Grace and Kayla racing to the edge of the corral, staring in her direction. She realized she was going to have to do a lot of explaining when this was finally over.

"Don't stop filming," she said to the man beside her as she shifted into another gear. "No matter what happens, do not stop!"

"No worries there," he answered, still cradling his camera on his shoulder. "Just don't get us killed." He grabbed the roll bar with his free hand, not wanting to fall out.

For a split second, Naomi questioned if following after them had been a good idea. The forest was thick with vegetation, and she had to do some serious maneuvering to get past larger limbs that had fallen to the ground. At one point, the ATV tipped up on one side, dropping down harshly, but she kept pushing it forward, determined to get to Philip as quickly as she could. If he needed help, she was determined to be there for him.

Chapter Nineteen

Philip had a good idea where the jet was planning to land. His morning runs around the ranch had given him a good sense of the landscape. It also made sense when he considered where he'd found Brad on his cell phone and where he often disappeared to on his morning jaunts. As he made his way through the thicket, he realized he'd forgotten his cell phone. He only hoped whoever the chief had close would realize there'd been a change in the game plan. He had lost sight of Brad minutes earlier, but he continued to push forward toward the sound of the plane's engine. He guesstimated the aircraft would land on the other side of the small stream that ran parallel to the tree line. There was sufficient clearing on the other side of that stream for the pilot to land and potentially take off with no problems. It could continue to fly low to land and never be detected as it headed back to where it had come from.

As he reached the creek, stepping out of the trees, he could see the jet plane in the distance. He ducked down low and lifted his binoculars for a better view. The jet had come to a standstill. The logo Pilatus was scripted in dark ink on the side. Brad was running toward the aircraft, meeting it as the cabin door opened and the airstair was lowered down. A tall man stepped through the entrance. His gaze swept over the landscape as he pulled himself upright. His blond hair was wispy and beginning to thin, and his complexion appeared ruddy behind dark sunshades. He wore a dark suit and a white dress shirt. The man took the steps easily and moved forward toward Brad. He cast glances from side to side, appearing nervous to be where he was.

Lost in conversation, neither man noticed the ATV coming out of the woods. Overhead, a second helicopter suddenly appeared, and in the distance, armed law enforcement was moving in swiftly. Brad's buyer suddenly pulled a gun, slamming it against Brad's head before backing up and racing back toward his ride. Brad shook off the lethargy from the blow as he moved onto his feet and took off running back in Philip's direction. Racing toward him, Philip closed the distance between them and tackled Brad to the ground. That was when he heard a round of gunfire ringing through the air. The first shot came from the opposite direction, and when the second shot whizzed by his ear, he realized someone was shooting at him.

NAOMI CROSSED THE shallow stream and drove up the slightest incline, to come out onto a grassy pasture that was occasionally used to graze the cattle. A man was screaming in Russian as he raced back to the aircraft. Above their heads a second helicopter was circling, and uniformed officers were barreling down from her left side.

Movement out of the corner of her eye pulled at her attention and she turned in time to see Philip barreling toward Brad. Then she heard the first gunshot and instinctively turned the vehicle, heading in Philips's direction.

Naomi saw the other woman before Philip did, recognition knocking the wind from her lungs. Her eyes widened with surprise as shock washed over her.

The shooter had come in on horseback, straddling the massive animal as she pointed a Glock in his direction. She was charging toward him, firing her weapon randomly, as he worked to handcuff Brad. Naomi turned the ATV between the two men and the woman on the horse, making herself a barrier between them.

She screamed Philip's name as she and the cameraman jumped from their seats, using the utility vehicle to shield themselves. Her heart raced and she felt herself begin to panic, feeling like something was curdling in her stomach. She was desperate to get to Philip, frightened that he might be hurt, or worse.

From somewhere behind them a single shot was fired from a sharpshooter's rifle, hitting its target with ease. The horse reared, whinnying loudly as its rider fell to the ground. The animal came to an abrupt stop, turned and ran off in the opposite direction.

The moment was surreal. Naomi stood, searching for Philip as he was looking for her. Brad sat on the ground, tears raining out of his eyes as he saw his perfect plan implode around him. Philip had stopped short, his head waving slowly from side to side in disbelief. Officers rushed past to clear the shooter. Naomi moved to Philip's side, easing her arms around him. He was still stunned as they both turned to watch an EMS officer check on the one and only casualty that would be reported. When they pronounced Grace the Beauty Queen gone, Brad screamed at the top of his lungs, sobbing like a baby.

CHIEF LAWSON SAT in Naomi's desk chair, witnessing her signature across her official statement. The cybersecurity team was ransacking the office, confiscating all the video tape from her reality series. Philip stood at the window staring out over the landscape. His hands were pushed deep into his pockets, his pensive expression speaking volumes.

Most of the crew had been interviewed and were now headed home. Naomi had been able to thank them for their service and wish them well. She'd hugged Felicia and Marvin, tears misting her eyes as she had said goodbye. *In the Saddle* was officially done and finished, no other contestants left to complete the show. Naomi suddenly found herself battling an inner demon that wanted to proclaim her a failure. She swiped at a tear that threatened to fall from her eyes.

"I really am sorry that this happened to you, Naomi," the police chief said. "Although the mission was a success, this wasn't how we hoped things would play out."

"It's not your fault, sir. We can't control how other people respond or react to things we do."

The older man nodded. He turned toward Philip. "You gonna be okay, son?"

Philip nodded. "Yes, sir. I'll be fine."

The chief eyed him with a hint of skepticism. "You couldn't have known all the players, Detective. You did well with the intel you did have."

Philip tried to smile. Although Grace had flown so far under the radar that it would have been next to impossible to find her, he still felt a level of guilt about her death. If only he could have prevented it, he thought. If only he'd seen the clues, he would have put two and two together. But he had missed the connection between her and Brad. It had gone right over his head. He'd had no idea that the two had history, a relationship that was years long. They'd been best friends and lovers, and from what they were learning, Grace would have followed Brad to the ends of the earth. Their dream had been to disappear after Brad made the exchange, riding into a sunset of their own making. Now Brad sat in a jail cell and Grace rested in the morgue.

"Take some time off. I believe you're owed a vacation," Lawson said.

Philip started to argue. "I really need to get back…"

"Your boss said he doesn't want to see you for at least two weeks. And that was an order, Detective Rees."

Philip nodded. "Yes, sir, Chief."

The police chief rose from his seat. "This was good work, son. We accomplished what we needed to do and despite the loss, you should be proud of yourself."

"What's going to happen to Brad?" Naomi questioned.

"He's being indicted on a lengthy list of charges including espionage. We're fairly certain a conviction is guaranteed, so he'll more than likely serve at least twenty years in a federal prison."

"It's so sad," Naomi said softly.

The chief moved toward the door. "Naomi, I am headed to your mother's house to check on her. Would you like a ride?" he asked. "I'm sure she'd like to lay eyes on you to make sure you're okay."

"Thank you, but I still have some things I need to clear up here, and I need to speak with Jasper and Aubrey before I can leave."

"I understand. Detective, do you need a ride home?"

Philip and Naomi shared a look. Philip shook his head no. "I'm going to stay and help Naomi. I don't want her to be alone."

The chief nodded. "I believe cybersecurity is done debriefing you but if they have any other questions, I will give you a call." He looked from one to the other and shook his head, chuckling softly. "Please tell your mother soon, Naomi. You really don't want her to hear it from me."

Naomi smiled. "Yes, sir!"

Philip moved against her as the police chief made his exit. He wrapped his arms around her torso as she leaned against him, the two staring out over the horizon. The sun was just beginning to set, the sky in shades of purple and orange, looking like liquid glass. It was one of the prettiest sunsets either had ever seen and they allowed themselves to be mesmerized by it. As darkness settled around them, dropping like a warm blanket on a winter's night, they leaned on each other, settling into a level of comfort neither could have imagined.

"Do you think he really loved her?" Naomi whispered, still thinking about Grace and Brad.

Philip shrugged and tightened the hold he had on her as she melted into his chest. They were still learning the truth about the duo but thus far it looked like the relationship Brad shared with Grace had started well before their arrival at the ranch. Both Naomi and Philip had questioned how the two had managed to be selected for the competition together, only to discover that Jim had sabotaged more than they had initially believed. He'd been paid handsomely to put the couple in place on the ranch.

Philip struggled with how blatantly she'd thrown herself at him, wondering what would have happened had he taken her up on what she'd offered. Had seducing him been a part of their plan and if so, what had been their end game? He wanted to believe that Grace trying to kill him had been more about Grace trying to free Brad, but they would never know. He leaned his face into Naomi's hair, inhaling the sweet aroma of passionfruit and mango that scented the strands.

She turned in his arms and lifted her lips to his, kissing him sweetly. It was the barest touch of skin against skin, feeling needy in a way that only they could understand. It had been a long, gut-wrenching day, and in all honesty, they were past ready for it to be over.

The phone on the desk suddenly rang, pulling them from the reverie that they had fallen into. Not wanting to let go, Naomi pulled herself from him with a heavy sigh. She moved to the desk and answered the call on the fifth ring.

"*In the Saddle* production office. This is Naomi."

There was a lengthy pause as she listened, a loud voice on the other end resonating through the phone line.

Philip frowned. He caught her eye and mouthed a question. "Is someone yelling at you?"

She shook her head, mouthing back. "No."

When she spoke again, he could hear the frustration in her tone. "I can appreciate your position, Allan, but what you clearly fail to understand is that I and my crew were as completely thrown off guard as you. We had no control over what happened but have worked diligently to try and recover each time Jim Bauer sabotaged us. I also think you fail to own that you selected him for the job. He is not who I asked for or was wanting on this production and I said so when I was first informed he'd been added to the team. So, I think you need to take responsibility for your choice."

Naomi paused again, the voice on the other end getting louder. She leaned into Philip's side as he came to stand beside her, sensing she needed some support.

"Unfortunately, all the film is now being held as evidence and there is nothing that I, personally, can do about that. You are free, however, to have your legal team contact the local police chief for additional information."

It got quiet. Even the voice on the other end of the phone line was no longer talking loudly. Philip could feel Naomi bristle, her entire body tensing.

"That won't be necessary, Allan. I have no problems resigning. I quit." Naomi slammed the phone down and cursed, sounding like a sailor on shore leave.

Philip eyed her with a raised brow, amusement lifting his expression. "That didn't sound good."

"To hear him talk, you would think I was single-handedly responsible for everything that happened. I don't have time for that."

Philip slid her hand into his and held it. "Would you like to go to dinner?"

"On a date?"

"On a *real* date!"

"That would be very nice. I have to go talk to Jasper and Aubrey first."

"Whatever you need to do. Then I will wine and dine you."

She hesitated, then giggled softly. "Maybe we could just dine in? I think I'd rather just watch a movie and chill. I don't think I'm ready for public appearances just yet."

Philip hugged her again. "It's going to be okay," he said.

"Says the man who still has his job!"

"You will find another gig and until you do, I've got you."

"So, when do you disappear?" she asked, shaking her head.

Philip looked confused. "Disappear?"

"You're too good to be true, Philip Rees. You can't be real."

He laughed, leaning to capture her lips in a quick kiss. "I am very real. And I am all yours!"

THEY SAT AROUND the dining room table in the main lodge. Aubrey had put on a pot of coffee and there was just enough leftover spice cake to make them very happy. Naomi was waiting for the interrogation she knew was coming. Her brother was furious, and her sister had questions she wanted answered. But recognizing that Naomi was unsettled after everything that had happened, they were handling her gently.

Jasper finally spoke, annoyed by the silence. "So, how long did you know the police suspected this guy of being a criminal?"

Naomi shook her head. "Not long."

"How'd you find out?" Aubrey asked.

"Philip told me."

"Philip?" Jasper shot the man a look. "And just how did Philip know?"

"I was working undercover, assigned to catch him in the act of selling secrets. Unfortunately, I had to tell your sister to keep my cover from being compromised."

Jasper looked shaken. He shifted his gaze toward Naomi. "And you didn't think that was important enough to tell me?"

"If I had told you, you would have told Aubrey. She would have told Rachel. Rachel would have told Mom. Mom would have said something to Chief Lawson and that would have been the end of Philip's assignment."

"You should have trusted us."

"It wasn't about trust. I made a promise and I honored it."

"And where do you get off putting my sister in harm's way?" Jasper threw his question at Philip, his tone harsh.

"Your sister's safety was my first priority. I would never have purposely done anything that would have hurt Naomi." Philip reached for her hand. He kissed the back of her fingers and held it, locking their fingers tightly together.

Jasper's eyes skipped back and forth like a tennis match gone awry. "Is something going on with you two?"

Aubrey laughed. "I swear, you are so slow!" She dropped her face into the palms of her hands and shook her head.

Naomi giggled. "He loves me!"

Her brother balked. "He barely knows you!"

"What's that supposed to mean?"

"It means you haven't known each other a whole month and now you're in love. That's ridiculous, Naomi!"

Philip smiled. "You don't believe in love at first sight?"

"No! I believe in grifters hoping to take advantage of our family."

"I can't believe you said that!" Naomi snapped.

"Wait until Mom hears this! I should call her right now," Jasper shot back.

Aubrey pushed the speed dial on her cell phone and put it on speaker, laying it in the center of the table.

Naomi's eyes widened. "You're helping him now?"

Her sister laughed. "I figured we might as well get this settled once and for all."

"I didn't realize my love life was up for debate."

"Hey, I'm fine with it. He's cute, but it helps to have the whole family on board with you."

Naomi tossed up her hands.

Philip caressed her back, his large hands easing the tension across her fingers. "It doesn't bother me," he said.

Isa answered after five rings. "Hello?"

"Hey, Mom!"

"What's wrong, Jasper?"

"I'm here with Aubrey, Naomi and Naomi's new boy-friend." There was a hint of venom wrapped around that last word.

"Philip, hello! It's a pleasure to meet you although I'm sure my son's intentions weren't kind."

"Ma!"

"Don't you 'ma' me! What's the problem?"

"Naomi says she's in love and this Philip guy loves her and I'm calling foul! He's obviously after her money!"

Isa laughed. "Jasper, Naomi has no money, son!"

Naomi's eyes rolled skyward, and her sister laughed.

"It's pleasure to meet you, Mrs. Colton," Philip interjected. "I look forward to doing that in person very soon."

"The pleasure is mine! Theo has spoken very fondly of you. I've heard wonderful things and I look forward to getting to know you better."

"Thank you, Mrs. Colton," Philip said with a wide grin pulling across his face.

Jasper whined again. "Ma… Really?"

"Get some sleep, son. And leave your sisters alone. They know what they want, and personally, I would like more grandbabies. What are you doing to accommodate me?"

Jasper ignored the question. "Good night, Mother!"

Isa's warm laugh continued to echo through the room even after she'd disconnected the call.

The two men were like bulls, large and bumbling as they squared up. The sisters shook their heads.

"Are we done with this yet?" Naomi questioned.

Jasper pointed toward his eyes with a backward vee, then turned his hand and pointed it at Philip. The two men laughed.

"She's in good hands. I promise," Philip said.

"Don't say I didn't warn you if you find those hands full!"

Laughter rang around the table. Naomi hadn't realized how much she missed the comfort of family until she wasn't ready to leave, wanting to stay a few minutes longer to keep laughing with her siblings. Her brother and Philip talked sports and politics, discovering they had more in common with each other than they didn't.

When Naomi suddenly yawned, Aubrey shut their little party down for the night. "I put clean sheets on the bed in that back bedroom upstairs. Get some rest and we will see you two in the morning. I'm going home to my husband! Jasper's just going home."

"I need to go check on Kayla and the horses first,"

Naomi's brother said as he moved onto his feet. He extended his hand and Philip shook it. "Tomorrow I'll tell
you what you need to be afraid of," he said to Philip
with a nod.

Naomi flipped her middle finger at her brother
cheekily.

PHILIP WAS STARTLED out of a deep sleep. For the first few
minutes he didn't know where he was or why and then
he remembered, everything flooding back like a movie
played on fast-forward. Outside, it had begun to rain,
a storm blowing through with a vengeance. Rain tap-
danced against the windows and the wind blew loudly.
The room was comfortably warm, only a light blanket
tossed atop the bed. Naomi snored softly beside him,
her body curled into a tight ball.

They were both fully dressed, still wearing the
clothes they'd fallen asleep in. After saying goodnight
to her siblings, they had climbed the flight of stairs to
the upper level and had made their way to the back bedroom. The space was pretty. Lace curtains adorned the
windows and a hand-stitched comforter decorated the
bed with a simple patchwork design.

After weeks on that cot, Naomi was grateful for the
plush mattress. She had thrown herself across the bed
and was sleeping soundly before he could blink an eye.
He'd lain down beside her, watching her sleep. He knew
the day had been a challenge for her and it eased his
mind to see that she could finally rest and rest well.

He thought back to her brother's concerns, understanding that Jasper only had his sister's best interests

at heart. If he'd had a sister, he too would have questioned his intentions. He looked forward to meeting the other family members. The Coltons were a formidable force, and he appreciated their commitment to each other. It was enviable.

Naomi suddenly rolled against him, her eyes opening to meet his. She smiled ever so slightly as recognition settled in. "Can't you sleep?" she muttered as she yawned.

He smiled back. "The rain woke me up."

She snuggled closer against him, pressing her face to his chest. "I hope my brother didn't offend you earlier."

"Your brother loves you. He only wants what's best for you."

"He's a good guy. All my brothers are. I can't wait for you to meet them."

"You understand why he's worried about you, right?"

She shrugged. "I think if things don't bother me, it shouldn't bother them."

"But even you have questioned how quickly our feelings for each other grew."

"Yeah. I have. But I trust that if I can feel the way I do, then you can, too. I don't understand why we work, but I know without a doubt that we are perfect together."

Philip nodded. "I'm excited to take this journey with you, Naomi Colton. I look forward to discovering all there is to know about you." He leaned forward and kissed her lips. He felt Naomi shiver beneath his touch.

Making love to the beautiful woman was as easy as breathing. They were out of their clothes and naked in the blink of an eye. Naomi rolled above him, pushing against his chest with her palms until he lay back against the mattress. He pulled both arms up and over his head, clasping his hands together. He gave Naomi full control, following where she led. She teased every nerve ending, taunting him as she rode him slowly. She licked the line of his ear, nuzzled his neck, nibbled his bottom lip and made him forget his own name.

Hours later, as the sun began to rise and warm slivers of light seeped into the room, they were still wrapped tightly around each other. Naomi mumbled under her breath as she drifted back to sleep. "Congratulations," she murmured, "you won the grand prize!"

Philip chuckled. "Thank you," he whispered softly, knowing that what she'd said was true. He had won the best prize of all: he'd won her and he was sitting pretty in that saddle.

* * * * *

COMING SOON!

We really hope you enjoyed reading this book.
If you're looking for more romance, be sure to
head to the shops when new books are
available on

Thursday 4th
August

To see which titles are coming soon, please visit
millsandboon.co.uk/nextmonth

MILLS & BOON

THE HEART OF ROMANCE

A ROMANCE FOR EVERY READER

MODERN

Prepare to be swept off your feet by sophisticated, sexy and seductive heroes, in some of the world's most glamourous and romantic locations, where power and passion collide.

HISTORICAL

Escape with historical heroes from time gone by. Whether your passion i for wicked Regency Rakes, muscled Vikings or rugged Highlanders, awa the romance of the past.

MEDICAL

Set your pulse racing with dedicated, delectable doctors in the high-pressure world of medicine, where emotions run high and passion, comfort a love are the best medicine.

True Love

Celebrate true love with tender stories of heartfelt romance, from the rush of falling in love to the joy a new baby can bring, and a focus on th emotional heart of a relationship.

Desire

Indulge in secrets and scandal, intense drama and plenty of sizzling hot action with powerful and passionate heroes who have it all: wealth, status good looks…everything but the right woman.

HEROES

Experience all the excitement of a gripping thriller, with an intense romance at its heart. Resourceful, true-to-life women and strong, fearless m face danger and desire - a killer combination!

To see which titles are coming soon, please visit

millsandboon.co.uk/nextmonth

LET'S TALK
Romance

For exclusive extracts, competitions
and special offers, find us online:

- facebook.com/millsandboon
- @MillsandBoon
- @MillsandBoonUK

Get in touch on 01413 063232

For all the latest titles coming soon, visit
millsandboon.co.uk/nextmonth

JOIN THE
MILLS & BOON
BOOKCLUB

- ✱ **FREE** delivery direct to your door

- ✱ **EXCLUSIVE** offers every month

- ✱ **EXCITING** rewards programme

50% OFF
YOUR FIRST
PARCEL

Join today at
Millsandboon.co.uk/Bookclub

JOIN US ON SOCIAL MEDIA!

Stay up to date with our latest releases, author news and gossip, special offers and discounts, and all the behind-the-scenes action from Mills & Boon...

 @millsandboon

 @millsandboonuk

 facebook.com/millsandboon

 @millsandboonuk

It might just be true love...

GET YOUR ROMANCE FIX.

Get the latest romance news, exclusive author interviews, story extracts and much more!

MILLS & BOON
Desire

Indulge in secrets and scandal, intense drama and plenty of sizzling hot action with powerful and passionate heroes who have it all: wealth, status, good looks…everything but the right woman.

MILLS & BOON
MEDICAL
Pulse-Racing Passion

Set your pulse racing with dedicated, delectable doctors in the high-pressure world of medicine, where emotions run high and passion, comfort and love are the best medicine.

MILLS & BOON
True Love
Romance from the Heart

Celebrate true love with tender stories of heartfelt romance, from the rush of falling in love to the joy a new baby can bring, and a focus on the emotional heart of a relationship.